# Nothing To B

'In the case of his novel, Eaves has nothing to be afraid of.
He is to be read, relished and watched very closely'
*Independent*

'Polished . . . A work of considerable comic vitality . . .
[Will Eaves] is a fleet and funny writer'
*Daily Telegraph*

'Luminous . . . The novel gracefully peels away masks to
reveal its characters' vaulting ambitions, crippling
insecurities and submerged traumas'
*Time Out*

'Clever and intricate'
*Sunday Times*

'*Nothing To Be Afraid Of* exceeds its precursor
in terms of both ambition and emotional range.
Eaves juggles his narrators and time periods
with seemingly effortless control'
*Guardian*

'[Eaves's] prose is a joy'
*Metro*

'Eaves boasts a style of extraordinary delicacy and acuity:
the sentences are perfectly cadenced, the various
narrative voices eerily convincing'
*Independent on Sunday*

ALSO BY WILL EAVES

*The Oversight*

WILL EAVES

# Nothing To Be Afraid Of

PICADOR

First published 2005 by Picador

First published in paperback 2006 by Picador
an imprint of Pan Macmillan Ltd
Pan Macmillan, 20 New Wharf Road, London N1 9RR
Basingstoke and Oxford
Associated companies throughout the world
www.panmacmillan.com

ISBN-13: 978-0-330-41875-1
ISBN-10: 0-330-41875-0

1 3 5 7 9 8 6 4 2

A CIP catalogue record for this book is available from
the British Library.

Typeset by Intype Libra Ltd
Printed and bound in Great Britain by
Mackays of Chatham plc, Chatham, Kent

All Pan Macmillan titles are available from
www.panmacmillan.com
or from Bookpost by telephoning +44 (0)1624 677237

*in memoriam*

SUSAN BUTTERFIELD

Donalbain: What is amiss?
Macbeth:                         You are and do not know it.

*Shakespeare*


Round the corner is – sooner or later – the sea.

*Louis MacNeice*

# One

THE WHITE SHED of the Theatre was separated from the fishermen's huts at the west end of the beach by a squalid alley of shingle and tarmac. Scummy water sluiced down the alley, bubbling over shreds of discarded bunting, and a picture of the Queen on one torn triangular tooth stared up through the accumulating froth. The Hutchings family waited for ten minutes beneath an illuminated sign with letters missing that read 'age d or'. It took four knocks before the door was finally thrust open by a thin man in his forties with cold cream on his face.

'Yes?' he said, not even looking at his visitors.

Ray Hutchings chuckled nervously, and jiggled the car keys in his pocket. He still saw Tony Glass every two years or so – usually when Tony had been without work for a while – but their rapport was never easy or instant. It had to be re-cued each time they met, and always, Ray felt, to the actor's advantage. There were certain rules of engagement. Typically, for instance, Tony would be unable to recognize Ray in public until Ray had been forced to identify himself.

'My God, *Ray*.' Tony snapped his fingers and closed his eyes. 'Ray, Ray. Christ. Forgive me – I was away with the birdies. Fairies.' He laughed. 'Well, hey. You got here. It's good to see you. Look at *you*.'

Ray looked in the dressing-room mirror opposite and didn't much like what he saw; wondered, briefly, who the tubby grinner with the eczema and the double chin might be. Next to him in the doorway stood a handsome, younger brunette with slightly hooded eyes, her arms around the shoulders of two girls.

'And this is Lilian. How could I forget.'

'And the girls.'

'Of course. We've met. You won't remember me, though. You were both very little.' Tony paused, kindly. 'I didn't stay long – Lilian, wow. *You* always look fantastic. I say "look", but what do I know? We only speak on the phone.'

Well, they would have done, Ray decided. Tony never asked to be put through to the workshop. He rang off quickly, a step ahead. If you rang back, he could be cross; sometimes you got someone else. Lilian smiled blankly. Her grip on the two girls tightened unconsciously as the thin man squatted in front of them.

'And how old are you now, Princess?' he asked the smaller, blonde one.

The little girl squirmed, smiling. Her lips moved, but the sound that escaped them was unintelligible, no more than the lisp of the sea inside a shell. Tony laughed indulgently, and at once she stopped smiling; backed a half-step to rest her head against her mother's thigh.

'You're frightening her,' said the taller girl.

'Who, me?' Tony looked shocked and put his hand to his chest. His frilly white shirt was still unbuttoned, almost to the waist, and up close you could see how grimy it was, stained orange-brown around the buttons and on the inside of the wide sequinned collar. Sweat-oiled hair covered his chest like a pair of sticky black wings.

'Yes, you,' the girl confirmed. Tony laughed again, and Ray laughed with him.

'Don't be rude, Alice,' said her father. To the youngest, Tony probably did look alarming, his face smeared white and red, but that didn't excuse Alice, whose grasp of situations, though she was only nine years old herself, exceeded the usual reflex candour of infancy.

'They're just a bit shy,' Ray explained. 'It's the first time they've met a real actor, isn't it, girls?'

'Second,' Lilian murmured.

'As good as the first, then.'

Alice breathed in deeply before replying.

'I liked it when you pulled the ribbons out of your hand,' she ventured at last.

'Ah, that's magic. I can't tell you how I did that.'

Alice frowned. 'They're in a special glove on your finger. Everyone knows.' Her little sister looked at her in awe. 'But you did it very well.'

'Thank you,' said Tony Glass, inclining his head. 'Perhaps I'd better not ask you what you thought of my singing.'

Alice sighed, remembering the news that day and the pictures of a sad, fat man dressed a bit like Tony, who'd made lots of women cry.

'It was a tragedy,' she said. 'Wasn't it? The man you were being at the end. I heard it on the radio this morning. He was only forty-two and they found him on the toilet. I suppose *that's* why – ' she paused for effect ' – they had to ask you instead.'

Ray chortled with confused pride, and Tony made a witty remark about the fearless logic of childhood. His son was just the same! Lilian's grip loosened and all three adults talked for a while as though the children were not there. Soon they were saying goodbye. Alice heard the chords of conversational farewell move faster as she led little Martha out of the dressing room into the briny August night.

'So, where are you staying?'

'The Anchor.'

'Porlock, the Anchor.'

'The Anchor in Porlock?'

'That's Porlock Weir we're in, Lil, remember, not Porlock.'

'I think I knew that.'

'Porlock Weir? Just down the road . . .'

By the time they'd reached the car, Tony Glass had invited himself to lunch the next day on the beach, and Alice's parents were exhausted without quite knowing why. As the children clambered over the seats, the stars that filled the top half of the windscreen bounced up and down. Ray watched them with distant professional interest. It was like sitting inside a huge pianola and looking through the holes in the music roll. Lilian snatched a length of orange peel off the dashboard, wound down the window an inch and poked it out.

'Shush, Martha,' she said. 'It won't harm. It's not plastic.'

Two things stuck in Alice's mind while the white Mini spluttered along the coast road. The first was that people who believed her no matter what she said were themselves a bit unbelievable.

The second was that Tony Glass had a voice like a duck.

*

'Let me *buy* you lunch. How about that?'

The next day, the Hutchings stood in the hotel's Artexed lobby, their way blocked by a figure in a leather blouson, cinched at the waist. Lilian put down a bag of picnic food and looked at Ray, whose legs had flushed pink.

'That's very—' Ray jerked his head and swallowed

4

' – thoughtful. The thing *is*, we've got some sandwiches, so while it's fine we thought . . .'

'Tell you what,' said Tony. 'You go round to the Ship and get a table. I'll put these' – he picked up the bag of sandwiches – 'in the kitchen fridge, here. They won't spoil. Go on. It'll be my treat.'

But the tiny Ship Inn Restaurant, when they got there, was fully booked, and Ray had to order bar snacks instead. There was cod, plaice, haddock or fish pâté – and, for the kids, less of the same.

From a sunlit corner of the smoky saloon, Lilian and the children stared reproachfully at the head of the household. Ray realized that he should have insisted on the picnic, and felt a watery resentment of life percolate through his side-burns. What if they just ran for it? What kept them inside on a day when other families were busy clambering over the harbour's hot stones and slippery breakwaters? At the Ship, they couldn't even sit under a parasol. The beer gardens, fore and aft, were closed for 'works', a sign said, and in joyless confirmation of the fact, above the thrum of old salts complaining about the tourists, there skirled the wide vibrato of a builder's whistle.

'Hey,' said Tony, when he entered the room ten minutes later. 'This is all right, isn't it? Can't have too many horse brasses.'

He made his way to the corner table, took off his jacket and looked for somewhere to put it. The Hutchings were comfortably accommodated by a pair of high-backed pews at right angles to each other, with room for at least one more adult next to Martha and Alice.

'I'm so sorry,' said an old man in a yellow cardigan, as Tony drew up a stool. 'My wife was sitting on that. She'll be back in a minute – she just went to the toilet. Do you mind?'

'God.' Tony sprang up. 'Of course. Are you OK?'

'Yes, perfectly, thanks,' said the man, a little thrown.

Tony turned to look over the rest of the pub, still holding his jacket. There were two empty chairs by the door.

'It's always busy at lunchtimes,' he said, and then, rubbing his chin, 'Well – I don't know – maybe if – Ray, if you move round – if you go next to the girls – I can budge in here on the end, next to . . . ? How's that? *That's* it. There we go.'

The meals arrived in tantalizing relay, one full plate replacing another empty one, with Tony's last of all because he'd forgotten to order at the bar when he came in. The others ate quickly, but Tony took his time.

He seemed different today; even his hair was lighter. Listening to him reminded Alice of the feeling she had when a stranger tried to tell a favourite story. An overeager woman on *Jackanory*, say. Or Lilian, trying to do Aslan. None of it was right to begin with, and then you forgot to be upset.

Tony asked the barmaid if she had any mayonnaise, and she said yes, if he meant salad cream. That got a laugh – the chortle of experience – though he was unsure, when it came, of how to tackle the fish itself: a golden scabbard so glisteningly entire all he could do for a while was prod it, smiling.

Alice's mother stuffed a crisp packet into a glass.

'You wouldn't believe it,' said Tony, pointing at the dimpled window with his knife. 'What this place used to look like. Remember, Ray?'

He spoke in a resonant whisper.

'There was nobody here. See those cottages, on the other side of the quay? They were the only buildings on the *actual* shoreline between Culbone Wood and Hurlstone Point. Hardly any boats. The place was absolutely unspoiled – if you can call deserted unspoiled.'

Alice glanced out of the window while Tony paused to

swallow his last mouthful. Yachts leaving with the tide filled the harbour channel. On their decks, fleshy blondes held ropes at arm's length.

'And it was still like that when I used to come here after the war, which was a *very* long time ago.' Tony winked at Martha.

It was only when they were outside the pub that Alice remembered she'd left her crab-lines and towel on her seat. She was met in the passageway by the man in the yellow cardigan, who handed her things over. He had beer foam on his upper lip and sharp, soap-shiny knuckles.

'Here you are, my dear,' he said brightly, and tapped the glass of one of the photos on the panelled wall. 'This is the Weir when *I* was a baby.'

Alice nodded.

'Thank you,' she said, and turned to see how far the others had got. They were a few yards along the quay, just past the pink scumbled facing of the Anchor Hotel, ambling towards the wharf. Tony was chatting away amiably. Lilian was listening. Then Lilian said something in reply, and Tony leant nearer to her, as though her words were not quite audible. Every few steps, Alice's father looked back to see where she might be.

Alice paused before bolting out of the dark. With a satisfying shiver, she realized that from where she stood, just shy of the triangle of light on the doorstep, she could see how the world went on without her.

'Is that your daddy?' asked the old man.

'Yes,' Alice replied. 'Can't you tell?'

\*

The resemblance was clear enough. Like her father, Alice ran to fat (her best velour top had split under her armpits). Like him, she avoided eye contact when ordering chips, and enjoyed a healthy appetite, not least for self-deception. So that if lace-limbed Martha decided to vault the bollard on the wharf, Alice could well imagine doing likewise.

The ancient bollard was of course too wide and tall for a six-year-old to clear, but in Martha's case it didn't seem to matter. A row of pensioners on benches chuckled broodily as she pinged into the pillar and picked herself up, laughing. It was the charm of her failure they admired. Strange, then, that they seemed so much less taken with – even irritated by – Alice, who charged along on flat feet, her tongue sticking out. 'Careful, dear,' said one, as the big girl body-checked the bollard's pitted head. Sliding off it, winded, Alice made an effort to smile.

'Nearly,' said Ray.

At the wharf's end, father and daughter climbed down to the sloping harbour beach, where Alice felt her confidence return. The ore-streaked rubble and grey boulders favoured a ruminative approach which ill suited the lightweights in the family. She saw Lilian and Martha, yards behind, making their way towards her in the lee of the breakwater, turning their ankles on the stones, crying out. Alice shook her head and worked a finger beneath two slimy pebbles, where for a moment she thought she'd glimpsed a pair of feelers.

'Dad,' said Alice, as she got changed. 'Where do all the bits of coloured rope on the beach come from?'

Ray faced the breakwater to put on his purple trunks.

'Now that,' he said, fiddling with the drawstring, 'is a good question. To which I do not have a good answer. There are nets and fish-traps all along the beaches here, I suppose, or there used to be.' He turned round and palped his chest. 'But they're hanks, not bits. A bit of rope is a hank.'

Alice had only asked the question to distract attention

from a towel that refused to stay on. Wrapping the thing around her was the easy part. It was the fold-and-tuck of the loose corner she couldn't master.

'What *are* you doing?'

Lilian stood over her.

'I'm getting changed into my—'

'Like that?' She snorted. 'You don't need to do it like that, not at your age. Take it off. Come on, no one's looking at you.'

Alice sat down and drew in her knees. The holiday had gone sour. Her crab-lines were tangled.

Martha nestled between her mother's tawny legs, while Lilian rubbed Ambre Solaire into her back. From the other side of the breakwater came the sound of children crunching across shingle and scrambling over the slumped stone hut – the pillbox – Alice had sheltered in last year. Last year, there had been a drought. People had collapsed from heat exhaustion on the beach. Roads had melted. Along the coast, the salt-grasses turned brown and burst into flame. This year, it was cooler. You could sit out all day, except when it rained. Or then especially; in rain, the wooded cliffs towards the headland steamed, like a row of quenched irons.

'Lil,' said Ray, after a bit.

'What?'

Lilian shifted as Ray leant down, still patting his chest, to make a suggestion. 'What, Alice? . . . She's fine. No . . . no, I won't . . . I've told her before . . .' She flicked the pages of a magazine horoscope.

'Bitch,' whispered Alice, staring at the ground. The pages stopped turning, and the world's longest car crash, or something like it, began playing on a nearby radio.

*

Tony arrived carrying four ice creams topped with clotted cream and chocolate flakes. Alice refused hers.

'That's not like you,' said her mother. 'Are you feeling well?'

'I'm afraid it's too soon after lunch for me,' Alice deadpanned. 'And besides, he's only got four.'

'That's because I didn't buy them for me. I bought them for you.'

They were all eating their ice creams now, except Alice – and Tony, still dressed, still acting, who held his out as a kind of peace offering.

'Well, if she doesn't want it, she doesn't want it,' Lilian said, licking around the rim of her cone. 'There won't be another this afternoon.'

Lilian turned her attention back to Tony and his career. He was considering becoming a full-time agent – a good friend needed help in that department, and since he had a flair for running things, he'd thought, why not? 'The trick is support. You need someone good behind you in this game.'

'Come on, Ally,' Ray said, whose drive to get in the water had lost its momentum. 'You can share mine.'

Fairness, not sarcasm, brought the tears to Alice's eyes, and she was on the point of yielding – the ice creams from the sweetshop were one of the best things about Porlock Weir – when Lilian spoke up.

'It's very generous of you, Tony,' she said, picking invisible crumbs off her swimsuit. 'You bought us lunch, too, remember.'

Alice waited for Tony to correct her, or for Lilian to realize her mistake. But Ray said nothing, and Martha lay down, giggling, as Tony teased her, slowly won the little girl's trust. He put his hand over Martha's eyes, to shield her from the sun; then took it away. Put it back, took it away.

The radio flared up.

'No he *didn't*,' Alice shouted above the noise. 'He *said* he was going to, but he didn't because he was late, so Dad paid for it. And we were going to have a picnic *anyway*.'

No one moved.

'And he's a liar. He makes everything up. Porlock has *never* been deserted. The Vikings were here. And one of their ships ran aground on a petrified forest, but it didn't put them off. We did a project *all about it* at *school*.'

Alice beat an unsteady retreat to the open beach, where at low tide the exposed rocks stayed black. She was bewildered and ashamed. The truth seemed less vigorous for having been so vigorously expressed, and Tony's offence less offensive. A little way behind her, she could hear her parents apologizing, arguing. Their exclamations faded in and out of all the other sounds: the gulls, the radio, the constant (now she listened for it) clink-clink of boats at anchor.

As she approached her daughter, Lilian, stumbling a little in flip-flops, adjusting her sunglasses, seemed almost to be smiling. It was the same expression she wore when she met other women in the street.

'Not one word,' she said, hoisting Alice by the arm.

When Alice got back to her towel, Tony Glass came over and started talking to her. He was interested, he said, in the project she'd mentioned. Was it the best in her class? No false modesty, now. (He explained the term.) It was, wasn't it? She didn't know. He thought it was, and asked her – in the same soothing, implacable tone – what she wanted to be when she grew up.

Alice, crying, told him.

\* \* \*

When the tide is in at Porlock Weir, the thin tree at the entrance to the harbour channel is as far as most people dare to swim. Families cling to it, a wizened sapling, an alder, which has never in living memory put forth leaves or borne fruit, but which, because it is a tree, evokes landfall. When the tide is out, the same tree becomes upended driftwood, and swimmers ignore it, wading through a ticklish slick of sewer crabs and engine oil to the free waters beyond. These are inviting; the sea stays warm most days, and if you swim straight out into the bay, towards South Wales, it will be a while before you are out of your depth.

Only, think carefully before you enter the water. For the Bristol Channel is estuarial and its currents pull everything around and out. In their grip, even a strong swimmer, swimming in the sun's path with the harbour entrance at his back, may turn a hundred and eighty degrees to hail his family, and find them gone. The shore, he soon realizes, has moved to the right; the pillbox is unfeasibly distant. There is no sign of the tree.

*

Water floods Ray's ears, gulping and trickling digestively. He takes a breath and ducks under, thinking to hasten his return by avoiding surface wind resistance. But the salt blinds him, and it is a measure of the slippery nature of calm – a mood you cannot reinforce – that he chooses to head straight for the beach, cutting across the longshore drift. He knows that if he gave in to the drift, he would come ashore a little further down. Still, the nearest way is so near, it is surely worth the effort.

He swims with his eyes shut and surfaces, blinking, in the middle of a swell. Because eye-level is only a few inches above the water, the gentle incline seems severe. The water is black with shadow, its surface strewn with weed and open-sea litter. Things other than the dross of lazy picnics, the lolly-sticks and pots and peel, float past: dead kelp and worse, in gouts and ribbons which bear down on you, the melted aggregate of a mudslide. The swell passes, moves through Ray, or he through it, blindly. Its seaward slope reveals more sea, another swell boatless and sheer.

The land is behind him, and Ray, turning again, must fight a clockwise countercurrent, cranked up by shelves of sub-merged rocks, to keep the shore in view. (Where is he now? What are these cliffs and thundering coves?) Spray pimples the water, and underneath his pedalling feet an icy fume, the breath of depth, rises.

He is further out than before. Changing his stroke to crawl itself seems like defeat, the officer's misgivings after the order's given. To rest, he hangs in the water, holding his knees.

Ray's body swings in the current, rolls with a surge. Hair lifts on his belly.

A rush of private thoughts experienced as cold: numb feet and cramp in both his calves, a lumbar ache, iron on lungs and chest.

Helen struggling. The man gulping. Unrelated punish-ments.

For an instant, the rip slackens. Our swimmer hesitates – looks down and sees, not far below the cysts of his toes, a mass of spikes. They cover the sea-floor, less than a fathom down, their forms treelike, with nests of sand and white untenanted shells filling the thicker forks. Are they alive, like coral, or do they merely recall life? There is wreckage, too, beyond. Rust, glass, netting.

Out of the eye of panic, Ray comes to in the surf. There are toys moving on the shore. One has a hand over her mouth. A round shape, with straight brown hair, in a green bathing suit, shouts and points. Another, thinner figurine sits dazed, her legs straight out, beside an overturned, abandoned rowing boat.

*

'He had to go,' Lilian explained, later, as they sat in the cafe-lounge of the Anchor. 'He had a show to do.'

'I'm hungry,' Ray said, with a Bunterish shiver. The lifeboat men had given him tea, but now he craved bread and cheese.

Alice returned from the hotel kitchen, shaking her head. 'They're gone,' she told her father. 'Elvis ate them.'

# Two

MUDLARKS TOOK some explaining. A few people in most groups knew what they were. Others looked at the pub sign behind them in Montague Close and put two and two together, while Dickens fans of course remembered the opening to *Our Mutual Friend*. But this afternoon's party were kiddishly vague, unwilling to make an effort. They'd struggled with the concept of Christopher Wren as an amateur; chewed their lips beside Nancy's Steps.

Alice asked the question anyway, and waited.

The tiny American woman in corduroy carried on scribbling while her beefy husband, chin up, scanned his surroundings. His name was Robert McCallister. He had introduced himself when Alice arrived five minutes late at Monument and been appalled to learn that the Great Fire began in a bakery. He was dismayed, too, by her suggestion that the vegetables left on the ground in Borough Market represented a bounty for enterprising scavengers. She said they had come out of the ground to begin with, so what difference did an hour on the tarmac make? He said he ran a food-distribution company in Vegas, that's what.

'Gaffer Hexam got his living along-shore. What does that mean? What did people like that do?' Alice asked again. 'Anybody?'

She glanced meaningfully over her shoulder at the river. Mrs McCallister scratched at her pages.

'I guess they were beachcombers,' said the distributor, hands behind his back. 'Gettin' down there by the river-side . . .'

He chortled.

'On the right lines, Robert,' Alice said, and pointed towards the Southwark shingle, which today showed mud glistening like receding gums. 'Although' – her face fell – 'they weren't quite that innocent.' Mrs McCallister's pen stopped moving. 'Because apart from the pots and pans and bottles and hanks of rope, mudlarks used to fish dead *bodies* out of the Thames and strip them of their valuables. Coins, rings, bracelets . . .'

Alice thought the list dull.

'. . . teeth,' she added, with feeling.

Mr McCallister's moustache twitched as he slid his shades further up his nose. At the end of the tour, in front of Cardinal Cap Alley, he gave Alice a £10 tip and shook her hand. He was sorry he'd been so terse.

The walk finished on time at six o'clock and there was a good hour before curtain-up, which Alice spent in the Festival Hall's basement cafe. Unlike the chic franchises of the upper-level concourse, the basement cafe served a menu unembarrassed by choice. It boasted tea, coffee, tumblers of irradiated orange and slices of pork pie in dew-spotted clingfilm. Encore! was often empty. No one ate there much, except perhaps the staff when they were desperate, and Alice, who had nothing against pork pie. She counted her takings: ten walkers at £5 each, less 25 per cent to the Board, equalled £37.50. She had another two walks at the weekend and there'd be this evening and tomorrow night on top of that.

With half an hour to go, Alice made an effort to relax. If

she got too tense, she might start 'grinding'. At night, she ground involuntarily and had to wear a mouthguard. It was, her dentist explained, a psychological condition with its roots in 'repressed inferiority'.

She'd asked him to say that again, and astonishingly he'd obliged.

Alice separated the American's tip from the rest of the day's cash. Robert McCallister had dry fingers that chafed. It was a while since anyone had held her hand and she resented the gesture. In the absence of love, she thought, let there be affection. In the absence of affection, professional regard. But anxious civility? What kind of substitute – what inadmissible revulsion – was that?

* * *

To give a performance had once been reward enough. At university, Alice discovered the ability to make an audience laugh and played comic roles, often *en travestie* – 'The best Dogberry I've seen in years,' said a woman with a glass eye from the *Stage*. She could do any accent – a prerequisite for the convincing performer – and found, so she thought, the art of pretence easy and satisfying. Other students agonized about their 'craft', but Alice had no time for them. They talked endlessly about truth and the removal of excess theatricality, when it was clearly theatricality their vanity craved. 'Actors hide,' said a genial Australian polymath on TV. 'They wear masks.' Rubbish, thought Alice. Real people wore the masks: the serial-killing car mechanics and pin-striped child-molesters. Whereas you only had to spot an actor shoplifting to see how constitutionally useless they were at hiding things.

Alice spent her three years at Sussex unhidden. In the

space of one term, she was a sleepwalking Charlotte Corday in *Marat/Sade*, a corseted Doll Tearsheet, and a spoof Lady Macbeth ('For I have given suck and know how pleasant 'tis'). She gave her Dogberry all summer at the 1989 Edinburgh Fringe, said hello to Eddie Izzard (who said hello back) and got a Pick-of-the-Fringe mention in the *Scotsman*. Her friends roared and clapped; encouraged her to think seriously about training. So Alice applied to the Central School, to Bristol Old Vic and to the Royal Academy of Dramatic Art, and was rejected by all three. The friends were puzzled.

No sympathy is without its portion of condescension, however, and for the first time Alice began to suspect that she was being indulged. On closer inspection, even the praise struck a false note. An unmasked, 'instinctual artlessness' (the woman from the *Stage*) returned to haunt her. After every performance of *Much Ado*, surely it was not the pretence – the distance between the illusory and the real person – that impressed her admirers, but rather the contemptible proximity? She was funny, she now saw, because she was fat.

RADA and Central rejected her straightforwardly: in corridors of marbled green linoleum, others were named and anointed. Bristol Old Vic, by contrast, made her work and wait.

Upstairs in a Soho pub, a minor cad from *Poldark* listened while Alice did Lady Macduff ('Whither should I fly?') and a page of *Happy Days*, for the contrast in mobility. The greying cad smiled graciously at the end and told Alice that Billie would have been impressed.

'Billie Whitelaw?' asked Alice.

'Yes,' said the actor, sleepily. 'Do you know her?'

'No.'

'An extraordinary person,' he whispered.

'Oh,' said Alice, her neck prickling. 'Is – has—'

The actor cleared his throat. 'I want you to go to week-end school,' he said. 'It's very relaxed and non-competitive.'

When Alice walked into the common room of the Bristol Old Vic Theatre School, the lie was exposed. Her fellow applicants were already working, most of them – model-ling, dancing, tennis-coaching. A number had Equity cards. They'd chosen the same speeches: Henry V, Hamlet or Portia. And they were beautiful: tall, muscular, slender, with pore-less complexions and the slow gait of the infinitely eligible. When they spoke, laughed, scratched or lifted the flap of the drinks dispenser, there was silent applause. If you said any-thing, they smiled before answering.

Candidates were divided into three groups of ten and sent away. The audition consisted of three different 'modules': workout/gym, voice/singing and text/performance.

Two of the three classes held no fear for Alice, who sang well and had her extended metaphors on a leash, but the third she dreaded. To a certain kind of child, the gym remains a scene of primal distress in which it is discovered that no wit or human kindliness can break a fall. One look at the dance-studio brought it all back: the high louvred windows behind wooden bars, the ropes hanging from the ceiling, the chewed mats, the lopped horror of the horse.

'Acting,' croaked the martinet in charge, 'is what you *do* to become who you *are*. It starts with your *body*.'

To illustrate the point, she punched herself in the stomach.

'Acting,' she confirmed, in a subtly different register, 'is *the* most physical discipline.'

Lisa Lee – Ms Lee – stopped to light a cigarette. She was small and ill with fitness, sun-dried almost. Her calves gleamed, but the bronzed skin was slack at the elbows. Her back was so supple, it was bent. Her yellow hair, teased into a spray, looked sore.

'You've heard about staying power? Yeah? Well, it's not just a figure of speech. It's about physical stamina. Excuse me.'

The instructress coughed something up and nodded to herself.

'*Stamina*. OK. Let's get loose.'

She hit a boom-box and the gonging chimes of the Jacksons' 'Can You Feel It?' sundered the air. Where Ms Lee had been, there was soon only a whirling vortex.

'You gotta be able to breathe,' said the vortex. 'And *breathe*. And *kick*. And *stretch*. And a-*round*.'

After five minutes, the music stopped and Ms Lee rematerialized. Nine out of the ten hopefuls adjusted their bandanas, did a quick shake-out. The other one simply shook. Her legs had gone into spasm, jerking backwards and forwards. Breath came in pants and squeaks, with cries intermingled. The T-shirt in which she did the housework clung to her like a collapsed umbrella. She gagged and swayed, cheeks aflame, gripping the perished hem of the Turkish slacks she'd put on, just that morning, for luck.

A girl in spandex brought Alice a chair. Lisa Lee took it away again.

'She needs a rest,' the girl remonstrated.

'Don't.' Ms Lee held up a warning finger. '*Not* on my time.'

Stomach acids blurted into Alice's throat. She swallowed quickly.

'I can't—'

'What did you say?'

'—can't – too fast . . .'

Ms Lee slung the stack-chair into a corner.

'OK. Up and downs. Ceiling, toes. Fifty times. And *one*. And *two*.'

At the end of the line of jack-knifing athletes, Alice retched and quaked. She'd put her back out with the first stretch, but carried on feebly splaying her arms, trying to reach over herself for fear of what might happen if once she stopped. An anaesthetic surge of terror bore her along. It was only when her torturer stopped the music for a second time and lit another cigarette that Alice realized she had been crying out in pain.

Lisa Lee slouched towards her.

'What are these?' she said, pointing at Alice's slacks.

'It said – it – the list said – casual clo—'

'Do you *do* any exercise?'

'Yes – no—'

'Do you have any kit?'

'—my back – I just need – to sit—'

'You do realize that this is an *aesthetic* profession?'

Ms Lee's eyes were grey and dim, as though in principle unexercised by any sight, however dazzling or piteous. Pain, pleasure: they couldn't feel either. Only the pupils, like balled ticks, rocked with spite.

*

Alice moved to London when she was twenty-five and still a virgin. In a moment of involved weakness, she suggested to her sister, Martha, that they move in together. Alice was temping by day and finishing a post-graduate Acting Diploma at the Rudner–Beck Studio by night.

Martha, newly graduated from Bristol University, hadn't thought of living as far out as Putney, but in days was forced to admit that the area exceeded her expectations. It had all the right shops, and the boathouses were a walkable distance.

On her early morning run, Landor Consulting's blithest trainee waved hello to the oarsmen and breathed in the odour of damp tarpaulin and linseed oil. The basement flat Alice had found was small, so Martha bought a mirror to make it look bigger.

Two weeks into her job, Martha confided in her elder sister that she'd had an audition at RADA and been given a recall. This was a surprise to Alice: Martha had shown no prior interest in the stage, with the possible exception of exotic cameos at student toga parties. In any case, the second audition was a disaster and Martha got a letter the next day.

Alice sympathized – told her not to be in too much of a hurry – but Martha said she wasn't giving up that easily, and wrote back to the panel informing them they'd made a serious mistake. For her next recall, she cut her hair short, gelled it flat, wore a sleeveless black tunic with breast-cup seams and serenaded someone she dimly recognized from an Eighties cop show – *Bergerac*? – with 'Everything Happens To Me'. She also did Hedda Gabler, and bustled about hitting herself on the forehead.

There was another letter in the post the day after. The panel had been impressed. In view of the breadth and vigour of her re-audition, it read, the directors of the Royal Academy of Dramatic Art were pleased to offer Martha Hutchings late entry to the present nine-term Acting Course, or a deferred place for the academic year 1995–6.

'But, how?' was all Alice could say, when she got home. Her pulse bucked like the drum of a top-loader.

Martha sprinkled salt on half a beef tomato. She ate it with three fingers raised and fanned her other hand in front of her mouth.

'Mmmm,' she explained. 'One of the girls in this year's

rep got kicked in the head last week. I don't know. I don't *think* she's coming back.'

Lilian sent Martha flowers, and Ray mentioned the workshop's Breitkopf & Hartel – the one with the white box veneer – which he could always sell . . . At the same time, he wondered if Martha mightn't be able to squeeze fees out of the Academy itself? But she couldn't, so away went the piano to Kennards, where it was bought by an actor.

'That's a good sign,' Martha remarked.

\*

Desire is an inference, badly drawn. It obeys a defective but inescapable logic. If one person wants a thing, Alice discovered, it means another must already have it. In order to *have* that thing, one must not want it; or at least not want it too badly.

Because Martha had never laid claim to the stage – to the carnival camaraderie of Leichner Nos 3 and 5, to the Drama Club's clattering tea-urn, to a signed copy of *Year of the King* – it followed that her entitlement to it could not be in dispute. What she did not lack, by definition she had. As much might have been said of Alice, as Dogberry, though here the logic grew wonderfully twisted. The shy elder sister did not *want* to be a lumpen absurdity, after all – but by God that's what she was.

At night in the bath, which seemed always to be overflowing, Alice sighed and played Wise Owl, the discreet enabler of youth, while Martha thrashed about next door with Jez or Jem or Jake. Alice pretended to remember what it was like and found that 'it' was unimaginable. She looked down at her breasts, slack in the water, with a vein or two already visible. She could easily have worn a bra in bed, like (yet how unlike) Jayne Mansfield. Once, she'd opened the bathroom door to find a teenager on the other side, waiting to use the loo. Alice was wearing a robe, loosely. The boy coloured, muttered, 'Cheers,' and dived past. His shoulders were buried fishhooks, his nipples two shells in the sand. She heard him scamper-spring back into bed and soon the noises started again, her sister's smooth vowels ragged by lust into a scat of consonants.

A few weeks later, a third letter came – this time for Alice. It was from the assistant to the producer of a new early afternoon programme for toddlers, and read in full:

Re: Higgledy-Piggledy Pop!

Dear Alice Hutchinson,

Thank you for coming to audition.

As you know, we are looking for a very special person to be Peggy Patch's friend, and the competition has been exceptionally strong. However I regret to inform you that on this occasion you have been unsuccessful and so will not be pursuing with your application.

With all good wishes for your future career.

Penny Hills

pp Carol Kreisler, Producer.

Neither the rejection nor its pre-school grammar shocked Alice – she'd grinned like a death's head all through the casting – but it came at a bad time. Size and isolation were beginning to tell against her; she'd lost two waitressing jobs (no reason given) and been sacked from a nursing home for getting into bed with a ninety-year-old. (He'd asked her to hold him. She'd given him a hug. Then he'd died.)

Finally, she gave in and, on her dentist's advice, went to see a counsellor. Fees were charged on a sliding scale, Mr Donnelly told her, and Alice was amazed to hear herself say, 'Oh, good,' as if the hint that she had nowhere left to slide might be considered a reassurance.

Mr Donnelly's consulting room was a converted privy in a holistic practice off the Kilburn High Road. It had a desk, two chairs and a wall-mounted electric fire. There were not enough curtain rings for the orange drapes, which sagged to one side of the streaky window. The counsellor sat in one corner of the room and Alice slumped opposite him, talking. Why, she wanted to know, would someone so under-confident even *want* to be an actor – to be in a profession which judges you constantly?

Mr Donnelly cocked his head.

'Now, Alice, I don't know if I follow you there.'

Alice ignored him.

'Well, I suppose I *know* why – you know, rejection forming part of a confirmatory pattern and so on – but . . . but it's incredible, isn't it? It's madness, and I'm still doing it. I still want to gamble—'

'Ah.' Mr Donnelly raised both eyebrows without opening his eyes.

'It's the appeal of the bet,' Alice went on, quickly. 'You *can't* earn your living, but everything human and responsible in you wants to believe that you *can*. Persistence, you think, must surely narrow the odds, when experience shows quite clearly that it doesn't. Because—'

Mr Donnelly coughed and looked at his watch.

'—the dice have no memory.'

It was eight o'clock in the evening.

'Dice *and theatrical agents* have no memory.'

'Now there again, Alice, you see – you've lost me.'

Alice felt her jaws stiffen.

'All right. I'm not saying that we should deduce a universal principle from my personal experience. Obviously not.'

'No, indeed.'

'But perhaps we can agree that in acting, and in auditions especially – insofar as they enter the field of observable human relationships – the laws of chance are not, in fact, *laws* at all. We just treat them as though they are. And that is a delusion. Because they're not just, or even – or even mathematically describable. D'you see?'

Valleys formed in the high plains of Mr Donnelly's forehead.

'What's that grinding noise?' he said.

*

Sex with Brian Donnelly was a mistake, and Alice explained it to herself as she explained her weight – by treating it as an inconvenience. This sleight-of-mind covered the unignorable aspect of the affair (the fact that she had decided to have one) while minimizing what Brian might have called her agency, had he been a real therapist.

For six weeks Alice yielded, with some grace, to his hushed shuntings and whispered inanities. (There was a flotation tank on the floor below, so they had to be careful.) She was curious, of course, and duly unimpressed. The sticky filament Mr Donnelly teased to rigidity looked as if it should have ants on the end of it. Put it down to experience, Alice reasoned, and in this forgiving frame of mind found that it cost her nothing to listen to Brian as he wept, afterwards, into his pint of sweet cider. 'Maybe you're not ready for this,' she said, 'It's difficult when work's involved'; even 'I think it's me, *I'm* making you feel guilty.' She was relieved to have lost her virginity – wondered if he had noticed – and slightly smug about her emotional detachment. It did not occur to her that such detachment was itself a marker of the rawest innocence. Or that its theft was imminent.

On Valentine's Day, at last, Brian Donnelly came up with some advice.

'Theatre is your passion, Alice. And you must find a way of being rewarded, not punished, for it.'

Exhausted by this insight, Brian spent the rest of the session in tears, crying even before the removal of his farmer's shirt and trousers. But the next week, perhaps in guilty compensation, he cancelled therapy and presented Alice with a pair of tickets.

'We're hitting the town, you and me.'

He slid them towards her across the desk. She gave a quick snort, delighted by the suppleness of the gesture: surprised that it could be so tender and so shocking. She'd mentioned Cheek by Jowl only last week . . . Maybe it was something new at the Royal Court? *Burned*, was it, or *Destroyed*? Or the gay-evangelical thing everyone had been talking up, *A Sceptic in Texas*? Where was that on? In her excitement, Alice had that inkling of personal indelicacy which is the fat child's hated familiar. Smiling, she lifted the dark hair that cupped one ear; let it fall back.

'Go on,' said Brian, grinning. 'See what they are.'

Before she turned the tickets over, Alice said to herself, 'Remember this feeling,' lifted the Ticketmaster slips like a pair of aces, held them first to her chest and then set them down, face up.

'Oh . . .'

She put her hand behind her neck.

'There. What do you think?'

'*Oh*. Yes.'

'You've not seen it?'

27

'Yes, of course. I mean, *no*. But I've heard. I've heard it's really – they're really quite amazing. Amazing, er, formations and . . . lines . . .'

'Michael Flatley is a genius.'

'Is he the—'

'The genius of hard-shoe?'

Brian clenched his fists. He stood up and walked to the window. A draught whistling through the rotten frame flicked his long and thinning hair. He held himself strangely, one plimsolled foot pointing forwards and ahead of his belly, arms stiff at his sides.

'It's as if, watching him – watching Michael – it's like you're seeing this deep energy in the culture breaking surface. But not, you know, culture as some insular tradition. It's not just a poky jig in Willesden. It's more like . . . it's like all the old ideas – the community, togetherness, rituals – reborn, revitalized. Am I making sense?'

' "O body swayed to music",' said Alice, who recognized enthusiasm even when it seemed to exclude her. ' "O brightening glance! How can we know the dancer fr—" '

'Sure, you don't have to *know* anything. *Riverdance* is the language of action and being, Alice. Urgent, all-embracing.'

Brian turned and smiled. There was perspiration on his forehead.

They made love quickly but keenly, and for the first time Alice moved without thinking about moving. Her counsellor's soap-white body – the body she had mocked privately – was not so unlike her own, she found, and its embrace made her feel – what? – unselfconsciously awake? Seriously calm. The memory of grief, unattributable to any one event, evaporated.

There were many pleasant surprises that week. Of them all, Alice treasured most her awakened sense of a lover's dues: that shy confidence in the prospect of intimacy which forgives each subterfuge, every blunder. The day after the 'cancelled' session, Brian came to dinner in Putney and Alice suggested that he save himself the ordeal of a night bus home. At first unwilling to impose, Brian agreed when the lateness of the hour – eleven o'clock – had made imposition inevitable. He rang his flatmate (a worrier) to say he wouldn't be back, and took out his contact lenses. Alice offered him a lens case but was impressed, even a little scared, to see that Brian had his own. At 2 a.m., she awoke to unconcealed whispers and liquid kisses in the hallway. They stopped, briefly, when Martha, back from another first-night party with the latest new friend in tow, saw the unfamiliar man's coat, the unwashed plates, the empty bottle. In the double-bodied well of her bed, Alice savoured her sister's silence and the pert evasions that succeeded it:

'. . . don't know . . . must be someone's . . . get off . . .'

For once, Alice slept without her mouthguard, and soundly.

*

On the day of the concert, she arranged to meet Brian in the lobby of the Hammersmith Apollo. She spotted him, rubbing and chafing his hands, long before he saw her. He was wearing a suede bomber jacket and a green shirt. She wore – bravely, she thought – a buttoned dress of fawn crêpe.

'Someone needs a haircut,' Alice said, sparkily.

Brian laughed, hands pocketed. 'Why's that?'

'Because you look like a – like a drummer.'

'Ha.'

Even as he brushed the comment aside, Alice felt her smile slip; smelt her own make-up. How could she have been so rude? The defeated parental refrain hung in the air. Her jaw locked. 'Wait! You don't understand!' she wanted to cry, as Brian merged with the crowd. 'I'm sorry.'

She shut her eyes against the whickering pain in her cheeks, and opened them again to see Brian, above and beyond the melee, on the steps leading to the circle. In his hands he held the contents of a small sweetshop. Alice followed, avoiding the waving poster-tubes, trying to make allowances for the poor spatial awareness of the thin and hyperactive.

As she climbed the staircase, the din inside the hall acquired mass and definition. The stamping and shrieking reverberated through the walls, weighed on the gum-dotted floor. Nearby, you could hear the individual shrieks of children as they caught their first glimpse of the auditorium; further off, the braying of the stalls implied the Apollo's chasmal depth and height. Ushers with long-dead eyes, dressed in over-large and vaguely runic T-shirts, greeted them at the double doors for rows A to F, and Brian, all slights forgotten, pulled Alice down the shaking aisle. Emerald lasers, launched from a swivelling nipple in the roof, fanned out over the audience, swiping it like an enormous barcode.

Alice was unsure how excited she was supposed to be. Everyone else in her row – everyone else in the theatre – was open-mouthed and either screaming or staring, in a stupor of anticipation, at the empty stage, onto which dry ice jetted periodically. A cyclorama of gold and green throbbed in place of a backdrop, and a wash of augmented tambours and uillean pipes inspired pockets of applause at the end of each drubbing cadence. When the live band answered the looped music with a louder, faster drubbing of their own, the audience seemed cowed by its actuality and perplexed by the fact that, after a relatively short while, it stopped. The renewed cheering, to Alice's ears, had a dazed quality.

Of course, Alice wasn't immune to the occasion, and enjoyed a lot of the dancing, especially the solos – which had as much flamenco in them as anything else. A while back, she'd seen the Christina Hoyos troupe at Sadler's Wells, and thought she recognized some of the spin-kicks in *Riverdance* from the Andalusians. Like most of her generation, she was vague about Irish history, though in the fug of textbook memory she could still recall the Ulster lords offering Philip of Spain 'the crown of Ireland', and something about Spanish involvement at Kinsale.

And what was it Brian had said about all-embracing gestures? At its best, *Riverdance* was truly synthetic, a hoedown of European traditions and Broadway know-how; but at its worst, the show's Irishry – its appeal to Celtic pride – seemed bullyingly kitsch. All those harps. The torcs! That spirit-of-the-glade choir, wafting you beyond history and dissonance.

Alice worried, suddenly, that she was being unfair. It's OK, she thought, as Michael Flatley returned to the stage, hair freshly bouffed; in fact, it's perfectly good of its kind. I'm having a *good* time.

Far away, the star of the evening described another circle, arms outstretched, billowy black shirt open to the waist. He stomped about like a pirate chasing rats. Women screamed. Even Brian, pitching back and forth in a slew of sweet wrappers, responded with honks and bellows. What is wrong with me? Alice wondered, as the corps rejoined Flatley and the audience erupted. What gland am I missing? What gift for joy?

She worked another Murray Mint around her aching mouth.

A sentence began to form in her head: 'With a fairy-tale décolleté not seen since . . .' Since what? (Try again.) 'His décolleté would make . . .' What? Someone blush? Perhaps. (Who, though, and why?)

Before Alice could resolve the matter, applause broke in on her like sea through a window, and she rose to her feet. Moistness to one side of her breasts, where sweat had darkened the crêpe of her dress, confirmed the sense of deluge. Her own almost plaintive cries were swept away.

A sparsely toothed woman in the next seat screamed something at her, but the words buzzed unintelligibly in Alice's ear.

'It's all bollocks!' Alice yelled back, and the mad woman roared her approval. She was waving a home-made banner. The banner read 'Be mine, Michael'. Her eyes shone.

\*

'No, well, you just don't get it,' Brian agreed, later. 'I mean, you either get it, or you don't. And you don't. It's all right. It's a shame, but there you go. Don't worry about it.'

'I'm sorry.'

Brian sipped his pint, played with a lock of his hair.

'Sorry? What is there to be sorry about? *I* don't get Blur or Oasis. Britpop, is that it? Just a lot of noise. *I'm* not sorry.'

'Actually, I can't stand Oasis,' Alice said, more to herself than to Brian, who refused to meet her gaze. 'I'm still on Al Green.'

'"Let's Stay Together?"'

'That'll do.' Alice smiled pleasantly. 'Or "Take Me To The River".'

It seemed like a good note on which to end the evening. Brian had a clinic the next morning, so they said goodbye at the tube station and Alice trundled home with her head in her hands.

When she next visited the West Hampstead Homeopathic Institute, there was a new woman at reception, greying black hair, late thirties, tired-looking. Alice gave her name and the woman made a very soft clucking sound with her tongue. She squinted at Alice as if trying to place a face.

'No,' said the woman. 'I don't think Mr Donnelly can see you today.'

Alice sighed. 'Look, I'm a regular. I have a Tuesday appoint—'

'I know.' The woman placed both her hands on the diary. 'But I'm afraid Mr Donnelly doesn't think he can see you on Tuesdays any more, Ms Hutchings.' She folded her hands just as an unfamiliar man, with shortish hair, opened Brian's door at the top of the stairs. The door shut quickly.

'And neither does his wife.'

\* \* \*

Alice left Encore! and made her way through Waterloo Station to York Road and the Cut. In bars along the way she looked at the couples holding hands, the hip young blades strolling towards dinner and sex, the women with legs like tweezers; none of them looking at her.

This is not a random sample, she told herself. These people are not all better-looking, more successful and more talented than me. Bad things happen to them, too. They suffer; they fail; they pick themselves up and carry on. The probability of any one person possessing all the most desirable qualities of the group would have to be very small.

She stopped just short of the entrance to the Young Vic,

where critics from the dailies milled about, audibly tolerating the white wine.

And the probability of that person being your sister?

Alice collected her ticket from the press desk, went into the theatre and sat down. The two-minute bell sounded, then the one.

# Three

AT SEVEN THIRTY, the day ended. A last image of the street, of traffic reflected in glass, of open-mouthed, heat-dilated faces peering in, dissolved, and it was night. To the generality outside, the evening stayed warm and sunny, with a little of that burnt flavour of cities awaiting rainfall, but in the theatre at least, the light had gone.

Inspiration arrived with the blackout, and Alice sat, hunched over, with her pen-top in her mouth. 'Magic defines a community . . .' she scribbled, as the auditorium filled with the voices of distress. These were remote, at first, dispersed by wind and spray, until the crack of timbers and what sounded like the toppling of a mast gave a near shape to the void.

'. . . *fall to't yarely, or we run ourselves aground: bestir* . . .'

In the flashes of stage lightning, all that could be seen of the set was a wide, coffered ceiling, like the inside of a dome or the interior swirl of a cyclone. Shapes appeared beneath it – some stooped, others erect – but whether they were props or figures Alice found it hard to tell. They weren't moving. The idea was presumably to play the squall offstage, in order to emphasize its unreality. Whatever the reason, Alice had a good mental picture of the wings, where members of the cast would now be standing arms folded, rolling their eyes, laughing silently, gesturing at principals behind their backs, doing everything actors do in their contained world to conjure a sense of risk.

In that world, the din of the external is usually muffled; audiences will make allowances for sirens, car alarms, tube trains and crazies at the door. Or the noise may be dramatically absorbed by the imagination, so that, for example, a peal of thunder over Southwark intrudes only as part of an interior argument: the thud of footsteps on the ceiling, doors being slammed and plates hurled to the floor.

Occasionally, it is just too loud to be ignored.

Outside, where you could have looked up and read the signs, the thunderclap was unexpected enough. People warped and swayed and fell into doorways with their arms and evening papers over their heads. But in the resonant concavity of the theatre, there was, absurdly, nowhere to hide. The thunder wasn't like thunder: it was more like cannon-fire in a metal hut. For five seconds, the exit doors buzzed in their frames. Alice's pen-top fell from her lips and rolled away.

The wings were quiet until the rattling stopped. Seconds after came the sound of footsteps slapping in from the street and stopping in front of the box office. The mariners resumed shouting and members of the audience turned to each other with wry relief. Laughter was heard; hands squeezed, passed through a varying quantity of hair. But Alice's pulse thrilled on: to her mind, the coincidence of elements gave an invocatory edge to Ariel's smoke-and-mirrors fire. It was an exemplary confusion of worlds, where the real could be at once so near and far. And, as with everything not strictly present, it jarred the memory, echoed the past—

'*Mercy on us! We split!*'

36

Alice lifted another page of her reporter's notebook and the man sitting next to her hissed, 'Do you mind? That is *most* distracting.'

She wasn't sure if she recognized him.

On stage, the lights came up to half as Alice whispered an apology; shrank back into her seat. She glanced at the pad on her lap and saw that in the darkness her writing had become impossibly small. Lines crossed and overwrote each other: it was the sort of annotation you found in charismatics' Bibles. Well-intentioned. Mad.

Her eagerness to have something on paper before the main action had even begun was, of course, a sign of insecurity. In 250 words, Alice wanted to review the show *and* describe the play, though she appreciated the fact that *The Tempest* wasn't a play you could describe, because its net of real and imaginary experience wasn't something you could ever be beyond. It was her favourite Shakespeare for precisely this reason, because it seemed to her to grapple with mysteries which did not bear too close an inspection – like the deep glimmerings of a lake.

*The wills above be done! but I would fain die a dry death* . . .

Late sunshine returned to the street. The storm trails fled the Cut as quickly as they had arrived, and for a moment, in the bracing light, the whole of dull, grey London – roads, rails, cardboard boxes, fire escapes and slimy overflows – oozed quicksilver.

*

It was an evocative set. A patio tiled in green and lapis blue, closed on three sides by arcades and anchored in the middle by a dry fountain, suggested Moorish influence. The columnar arches were checked with brick and pitted stone, and clustered upstage like date palms. Beneath them ran a broken line of privet with, here and there, a pile or two of, possibly, carrots. To reinforce this correspondence of the mineral and vegetable, a real palm fanned out, upstage-left, from some higher, balcony horseshoe lost to shadow. The eye was raised, irresistibly, as to a towering canopy, but what it might have seen there the designer left to the imagination – and, as the upper reaches of his set withdrew into the night, so Alice had the sensation that she might be falling, or sinking, and that the stars sifted across the roof were not stars at all but coralline motes in tidal suspension.

The light changed slowly, in washes. The pillars turned to porphyry or jasper, then back again to white marble. In the keystone of the farthest archway, an outstretched hand had lost the tips of its fingers.

Music, the essence of which was rhythm not melody, performed a summons: the low notes were the groans of a seawrack reshaped into a booming figure of drums and bells, repeated at odd intervals, like waves striking the back of a cave. Three octaves higher, the screams of the sailors trickled ashore, much closer to the audience in the sound picture, above their heads almost, and sinisterly charmed into a piercing descant of piccolos and gulls. The fountain sprang to life.

Alice breathed out.

Her neighbour twitched at this, though not in anger. Rather, Alice had sensed his head flicking towards her like a bird's, when she responded to the bells, as though he would know what she heard in them.

Spell-stopped, Alice watched Prospero rise from under the keystone, his face a mask of clown-white with black eyes and purple lips. She saw him enter much as a person talking on the telephone sees someone else enter the same room – in a sort of daze.

The sorcerer raised his right hand to silence the invisible orchestra, and pattered forward on bare feet to the fountain, at the base of which lay his daughter, in a dream-coiled heap. As he came downstage, one or two members of the audience gave a satisfied murmur of recognition and Alice smiled to herself. On *Desert Island Discs* that morning, the adventurously cast Bob Ladd had sprinkled his chat about preparing for 'the K2 – dare I say the Everest?' of Shakespearean roles with repeated references to Japanese Noh theatre and ritual masks. Certainly his posture now, as he leaned in towards the sleeping Miranda, had a stylized quality to it – head bowed, half-kneeling, with one leg and an arm stretched out behind. On top of a cobwebbed dinner jacket he wore a mantle of spidery grey rags, echoed in the ferns and fronds of the set, and the whole effect was commendably subtropical, if only arguably Japanese. The world of hospital situation comedy seemed unthinkably remote.

'Hard to believe it's him,' said a woman in front of Alice to her companion. 'In all that clobber.'

The actor fluttered his chalky fingers, not quite brushing them against Miranda's eyelids, and she stirred, fighting her way back to consciousness. A cry escaped her as she opened her eyes. Then it dissolved into a groan of painful recognition, her raised hands grabbed at ghosts and she plunged again beneath the surface of her waking dream.

She delivered her first speech – the plea for calm – in fitful bursts. Prospero stayed bowed, fingers twitching, while his daughter bewailed the horrors of the night and hauled herself upright. The things she saw – the ship, the sky, the blazing deck – became real when she spoke of them, and hinted at a kind of visionary authority.

*O, I have suffered with those that I saw suffer!*

Alice's skin prickled. There would always be the mingled

pang and thrill of watching someone you knew take to the stage; she expected that. But here was something else besides – something more than infected pride.

In four years of reviewing, Alice had seen plenty of *Tempest*s: *Tempest*s in space, on building sites, or scrap heaps; *Tempest*s radically reworked for small-scale tours without a Prospero. Hardly one with a Miranda you felt anxious for, or even liked. None, certainly, with the present interpreter's emotional range, on fire with indignation one moment ('Had *I* been any god of power . . .'), bruised by adolescent longing ('a brave vessel . . .') the next. Off the stage, Alice knew to her social cost how listlessly unengaged and unengaging her sister could be, when faced with situations and people beyond her immediate control. About real-life crises – their parents' recent separation, for instance – Martha Challen, as she now styled herself, was phlegmatic to the point of paralysis; and her scattered TV appearances to date, including one as a nurse with Dr Perfect himself (aka Bob Ladd), had only sounded the same nerveless note. Agents and casting directors said they admired Martha's 'reserve', which Alice had always taken to mean 'high cheek-bones'. In fact, she was certain that this was exactly what they'd meant – but were they right? Was that all she had to offer?

Here, in a difficult and usually thankless role, a different person – admittedly with the same cheekbones – seemed to have emerged: one who made you suspect that, until now, Martha had not been trying; one who knew what she was saying; who spoke verse well, without showing off or putting on a silly voice (why did so many actors still do that?); who could immerse herself in a part and yet remain attentive to the audience, plying them with a glance here, a dropped eyelid there; who understood, and made you ache for, her character's charm and mischief – her disingenuousness. Her youth.

When, later in the scene, Miranda took off a grubby white shift and washed in the fountain, the action seemed unforced, and, to Alice's eyes, imbued with an autobiographical truth which she found touching. Martha, a topless sunbather since puberty, had always been laughably frank about her body. The audience laughed, too, as Prospero, midway through the story of his bitter exile, sighed and produced a clean dress from a deep pocket. A metaphor about screens and conceal-ment gained a jokey appropriateness, and Alice acknow-ledged how deftly the director had rooted the play's magic in the common mysteries of growing – and waking – up.

Martha looked down before putting on the dress, and brushed a speck of dirt off her chest. Prospero seemed a little cowed by his maturing daughter. The sense that she might already be, in some way, out of reach lent pathos to his hauteur and disdain; and behind all the talk of Art and Power, on which Ladd had decided to elaborate with a reper-toire of mimed gestures that reminded Alice of Joel Grey in *Cabaret*, you could see a parent made anxious by his diminishing influence.

The spectre of power lost, or transferred, grew paradox-ically more powerful as the play went on. It showed itself at first as forgetfulness on the sorcerer's part ('In Argier, / O was she so?'), then, increasingly, in a kind of magical mischief which was beyond any one person's control; belonging to the island, perhaps, and not its inhabitants. The music for Ariel's songs – sung by a battered-looking woman in bandages – had a habit of returning unexpectedly, almost mockingly, in the middle of other people's speeches. The dark arches of the set whispered to life whenever the mage laid down his mantle. And as soon as Caliban – played as an older, tragical parody of Prospero himself – spoke of an isle 'full of noises, sounds and sweet airs', tended by a 'thousand twangling instruments', the instruments appeared among the fronds of the date palm – an orchestra of oboes, clarinets, horns and flutes turning on moonlit silver threads like notes on a stave. There was even a white piano set at an angle on top of the second, shadowy tier of arcades. Its lid had been removed and there were keys missing.

The different worlds of the production, its sounds and moods, were so alive to Alice that her pen lay idle in her lap for most of the first half. When the house lights came up, her neighbour turned and smiled.

'That big bang was rather unexpected,' he said, with superb understatement. 'I'm sorry if I snapped.'

It was an apology conscious of its dignity, and Alice would have laughed if, just then, she had been able to open her mouth. The man, now easy to identify, tilted his head. His green eyes floated in pools of white.

'I'm sorry,' he said again, this time almost shyly. 'Do I know you?'

Alice had to wait for her jaw to unlock before she could reassure him that he did, then all was confusion. The chorus master of the South London Sinfonia clapped his hands over red ears and moaned.

'Wait a minute.'

'Last year,' Alice prompted.

'You were in the choir.' He held a half-breath.

'You even put me in the semichoir, Neville – well, once or twice, for the part-songs.'

'Warlock at Blackheath? Armstrong? Year before – no you're right, it was last year. What did we do? "She Is Not Fair"?'

They reminisced briefly. The concert had not been a great

success, and besides, Neville Clute worked with several different choirs in London – he could hardly be expected to recall individual faces.

'First alts!' he reaffirmed, the high dome of his head beginning to glisten. 'I *do* remember.' He stroked an earlobe, patted the monkish band of mousey-grey hair that sprouted from the back of his neck.

'It's Alice,' said Alice.

Recognition scudded across Neville's face; his eyebrows lifted and then dropped almost immediately. Finally he blinked, looked down, and when Alice suggested a drink, let out a long, meaningful 'Ahh'.

The theatre was quiet now, but from the bar on the far side of the foyer came the sound of a full room – laughter and exclamation batted to and fro by swinging doors.

Neville rose, adjusted a plum-coloured woollen tie, and glid towards the noise, his right hand dancing on the seats in front.

\*

At the Young Vic, interval drinks for the critics are usually served from a table inside the adjoining cafe. Tonight, there are no such drinks (there was wine beforehand) and the table, which has been moved out into the foyer, has been given over to books – four piles and a wobbly carousel of the same title, *Don't Mind Me*, by Bob Ladd, an affectionate memoir of early days on a penniless No. 2 tour of *French Without Tears*. An apologetic publicist stands guard, explaining, pointing journalists in the direction of the bar proper. Dapper little Alex Grew, of the *Telegraph*, smiles pityingly, but Michael Leaming of the *Standard* and the *Times*'s Charlie Devereux are fish-lipped and thirsty. They cannot help noticing that the woman from *What's On* – the one in the pink velveteen shirt with the lank hair and footballer's shoulders – has just been given a bottle of red to share with her friend . . .

'That was quick,' said Alice, as the young barman handed them the wine, winked and disappeared through the swing doors.

Neville flushed. 'Perks of the job.' He nodded in the direction of the theatre. 'Bach was paid in booze, too.'

When this had sunk in, Alice gave an excited squeak.

'You mean, you did—'

Neville's free hand flapped modestly.

'I had no idea. I mean, no idea you wrote music. What else—' Alice's voice cracked. 'Of course, when I say "no idea", I suppose it's just that I've not seen your name, or been to the right concerts. Obviously, there are all sorts of venues . . .'

'I dare say,' Neville said, faintly, 'but I've never been what you'd call a proper composer, so there's no need to apologize. I'm more of an arranger. Sessions, settings. I believe the technical term is "charlatan". Anyway' – again he indicated the theatre – 'this is what I'm doing now. Edgard Varèse put through the blender, poor love. What about you?'

After babbling something about the performance aspect of being a London Walks guide ('Edward Petherbridge does them, too'), Alice fell back on 'actually, Martha Challen is my sister.'

'Mmm.' Neville pursed his lips. 'And you're an actress as well.'

The 'and' was kindly meant.

'Well, yes, I act. I would act, only I don't have an agent and there hasn't been much, you know, demand. Lately.' She managed a smile. 'The last thing I did was on radio, two – oh, a while back.'

'Radio Two?'

Alice let it go. 'It was a science-fiction pilot,' she explained, reluctantly. 'I had a few lines. "The sequence will grow exponentially, Marek" – that was one.'

Neville poured more wine.

'But Diana crashed and we were dropped for the funeral, so it didn't.' She paused. 'Which is fine.' Another pause. 'I like what I'm doing and Martha is the real thing, I think. Don't you? She has such presence. I've never seen – I can't recall her ever having been this good. Before.'

'It's certainly a confident performance,' Neville allowed. 'I'm not sure it's in keeping with the rest of the production, though. It seems too realistic and lifelike.'

'I think that's the point.' Alice looked away to gather her thoughts. 'It's sad, isn't it? The magic must seem so routine to Miranda. Not fake – just routine, right down to the business of being awestruck and terrified, which is for her father's benefit anyway. I expect she thinks romance and men are cutting edge. And the sad part' – Alice could see herself chasing after shadows – 'is that it's a universal blind spot. You know, the idea we all have that *our* needs are real, but everyone else is a bit deluded.'

Neville smiled with the corners of his mouth turned down. There was a spark in his eyes as he admitted, with a grunt and a shrug, the plausibility of this report. Then he did something unctuous with his tongue and lip and tapped the side of his nose.

'Though – if it's an agent you want, I may be able to help.'

It was usually other actors, Alice reflected, who liked to read between the lines of a conversation; who interpreted before they listened. (And you always covered for them; agreed and said, 'That's very perceptive.')

For an instant, staring over Neville's shoulder into the whirring street, Alice had a vision of someone wry and superior, an observer of persons and foibles, being mauled by a truck.

'Of course,' Neville spluttered, 'what you say is perfectly true. I just couldn't help thinking – while you were speaking – of someone I know who might be . . .' He stopped. 'Are you OK?'

'Yes, perfectly. Fine,' Alice said shortly, refocusing on the table and bookstand to the other side of her flushed companion. He was right, of course; she *did* want an agent.

The prominent display was attracting attention. Quite a few people – Alex Grew and Charlie Devereux among them – had bought, or acquired, copies and were milling around the foyer with a drink in one hand and a glossy picture of Bob Ladd, beaming cheek-on-fist, a little chest hair sprouting from his open collar, in the other. There were some RSC-endorsed plays available, too, but no one seemed interested in those, apart from the thickset, powdery creature with the torn bald wig and red-lake tramlines who'd crept through a door marked 'private' behind the press desk a few moments earlier.

Beneath lively blonde curls, the publicist's face had gone a lumpy grey-blue, like a packet of half-thawed giblets.

'Although in *fact* I first met Bobby,' the white creature was saying to the women from the row in front of Alice, 'at Windsor, where we doing *Lear* and *The Circle* back to back, which was perfectly normal in those days. I was Arnold and he was the juve, though in *fact*, I was only one year older than him. He was thirty-four already, which is getting on for a juve I'd say, and I was thirty-five. Just the year, you see.'

'Oooh. Yes.'

'Then, in *Lear*, well' – he thumped the top of the pile in front of him – '*I* was Gloucester, and he was the most incredible Kent.'

'We'd like to have seen him do that.'

'I'm sure you would have.' Caliban smiled and nodded, puffing talc over the books. 'What a Kent. But it's too late now.' His mood seemed to change suddenly. He coughed and waved at the perfumed cloud with an empty mug. 'Far too late for all of that.'

This, surely, required some explanation.

'What's he doing?' Alice whispered to Neville, whose face was almost as white as Caliban's. The lobby hummed now with people attracted by the pungency of vowels and talc; critics tittered by the racks of flyers or tried to lounge and look as if they'd seen it all before; the publicist stared hard at an earnest young man in a smart leather jacket, who approached from the bar, put a hand on Caliban's shoulders and whispered in his ear.

Caliban shook him off and turned back to his original audience.

'*Whyee?*' he shrieked, the syllable ripped and quivering like something flung from a cage. 'Because he's a fucking star, madam, that's why.'

The young man tried again.

'Equity minimum and commitment to ensemble, my arse. Adrian, *stop* pawing. Bob Ladd – madam, hello? Over here. No, it was only the director. Bob Ladd will be on three thousand a week *at least* when we transfer to the Shaftesbury in five weeks' time. And he will have right of veto over the recasting. Which means that I will be back on my knees. On my *knees*, ladies, where I've been most of my life. Professionally.'

'Oh, no, Leslie,' said Neville, softly.

The two women exchanged looks and tried to move away from the table. Caliban came out of his momentary fugue. 'Nunnery,' he bellowed at the publicist, and pushed her to one side so that he could command the desk.

'Well, it was nice to meet you,' said one of the other women.

Caliban's face flinched. The white make-up gave it the appearance of a sodden canvas beneath which something small and mammalian moved in search of warmth. The eyes danced, but dispiritedly.

'Where are you off to?'

'We're, er, well – we're going in for the second half. Janice, after you.'

'Without me? I am the second half.'

'Yes. Ha, ha. The show must go on. Break a leg.'

'I *am* the second half. I'm in the cast, woman. You're going into the theatre to see me, and I'm not there. I'm here. They can't start without me. Can they? Can you, Adrian? Adrian? Where are you?'

The director, who'd been standing apart whispering to the publicist, now squeezed past the drunken actor and through the door that led backstage.

'Oh, that's right. Off you go. Don't mind me,' Caliban mumbled into his cup, withdrew his nose and swallowed, wincing. 'Don't mind . . .' he repeated, his voice rising to an incredulous, constipated squeak, '*ME*. What kind of a fucking title is that?'

A brave soul in the breathlessly silent lobby audience attempted a defence of the show's star. Without listening, Caliban waved an arm and knocked two piles of the memoir onto the floor.

'Just wait till I tell my side of the story . . . wait till you read the truth. If you're going to read about a – a mediocrity, at least read about one who's not afraid to say it. To stand up and say: "I have known grief and heartache and *betrayal* and I have caved in. I come from Bewdley. This is my shit life." ' Caliban belched. ' "Read all about it." '

He picked up a copy of Bob's book, as one might a dead animal, and shook it by its dust jacket until the contents fell out.

'"Actor, painter, writer, mountaineer",' he read from the back flap. 'Funny. They forgot "grasping little tit on the make".'

Neville made a hurried excuse to Alice and edged his way forward. There was a muffled exchange – 'Leslie' and 'Leave me alone, Errol' – followed by a creak and a crash. Caliban leant heavily on the desk, grabbed at Neville's arm, lost his balance and sat down on nothing. From the floor, the actor's vituperations, now cracked with pain and frustration, rose above the murmuring of the onlookers.

'If they – if you – if you lot only knew,' Caliban called out, his cup now in pieces, his hands trembling. 'If you only knew.'

As the door marked 'private' closed on three stagehands and the director struggling with a fourteen-stone pensioner, the shaken publicist apologized for what she described as an unfortunate episode.

'Episode,' wailed a voice in retreat. 'Telly. Dorothy Squires.'

The door opened again a minute later, and at the far end of a white breeze-blocked corridor Alice saw her sister talking animatedly to Neville and the director. Then they were beckoning her, motioning urgently. She manoeuvred past the desk and paused on the threshold.

A girl with a black rugby shirt and plait led Alice towards the soft blue-yellow working light and the three debating figures. It was the light of a new day glimpsed above a curtain rail. To her surprise, Alice felt perfectly calm. As a child, she'd been given sugar to help her sleep; the sweetness helped to melt away tension and dissolve bad dreams.

The director explained the situation. The first cover was already on for a sick Sebastian. He told her there'd be an announcement and shook his head.

'I can't believe we're doing this,' he said.

'Perhaps it's not—' began Neville, but got no further.

'Well, we are,' Martha insisted, and took Alice by the arm. On their way to make-up, they passed the rest of the cast, hanging around a wall of lockers, eyes down, arms folded, stubbing out cigarettes. In a blue dressing room that smelled of spirits and coffee, Alice was handed a filthily familiar costume – still warm, like a skin – and a copy of the play.

Her sister sat her down and ploughed gel into her hair. A moment later, Prospero appeared, dead-eyed, in the mirror and said no. No. Alice stared at a wall-mounted fire extinguisher, the sweet floating sensation already diluted by cold flushes. Her eyes wandered. A tartan thermos inched its way across the bitten carpet.

'It's one scene,' Martha was saying, 'and she's the same size.'

*Evening Standard*, September 3, 1999

# MY CITY: MARTHA CHALLEN

Urban sprawl and overcrowding aren't really me, but I've been in Putney now for nearly five years and couldn't imagine living anywhere else. My flat is close to the tube and the river, and – most important of all – the bric-a-brac shops on Upper Richmond Road, where I enjoy a good rummage when I'm not working. The flat is stuffed full of junk, especially old tiles and bottles – and clothes, of course, my weakness.

I don't drink much. I've seen what it can do to people, especially in my profession. In any case, if I feel in the mood, Young's Brewery is just down the road, and John Young, the 76-year-old owner, is a friend. He gives me a half of bitter (I'm a Triple A girl) whenever I drop in to see the shire horses, or if I'm on my way to my sister's. She lives in Battersea, and it's nice to know that she's around the corner, even if we don't see as much of each other as we'd both like.

Life is busy at the moment. I'm playing Miranda [in *The Tempest*] at the Young Vic in the evening and filming another series of *Practice Makes Perfect* during the day. It's a gruelling schedule, which means I have to get the eating right: orange juice, cereal, toast and honey in the morning, a sandwich at lunchtime and something else before the show. Miranda can easily come across as a milksop, but I'm trying to be more hardline about her, so it's lots of hearty food and fresh air. The riverside walk from the Design Museum to Hungerford Bridge is one of my favourites, and you can grab a crab salad and some Orvieto along the way.

For inspiration, I go to the greenhouses in Kew, and Dulwich Picture Gallery. For relaxation, I get right out into the country, or take myself off to the ballet. I love Balanchine for his purity, and Irish dance for the discipline and tradition. I used to play at being a ballerina as a little girl, but gave it up when I turned into a gawky adolescent.

It makes me laugh when people say 'how exciting, to be an actress', because I've never thought of it like that. It's something that happened one day, and that's how I approach life. I'm a reserved person, not an extrovert at all, and I don't go out much. I'm nominally a member of Soho House and the Green Room, though I can't remember the last time I went to either. Kwame [Dankwah], my boyfriend, is an actor, too, so he understands. My idea of heaven is a summer night in with the window open, a good book on my lap (Stephen King, Barbara Pym – anything with a proper story), just listening to people on the towpath, having fun. Then it's bathtime, whisky and bed.

*Interview by Ann Hemp*

# Four

'YOU'VE SEEN HOW Leslie does it,' said Martha, talking over Alice's shoulder into the mirror. 'It's shouting and cringing, mostly. And when he turns round or steps back, he uses Bob's physicalization – the sweep of the arm.'

'The *Psycho* thing with the hands in front of the face,' said the beanpole actor playing Trinculo, who looked kind and relaxed, even a little stoned.

'I thought that was the Noh bit,' said Stephano, his smaller sidekick. If they were as concerned as the other actors, it didn't show.

'Nah.' Trinculo blew smoke and span on a swivel chair. 'It's your actual Tony Perkins Grand Kabuki, innit? In the motel, with the stuffed bird. Leigh walks in wearing the full uplift. Clocks the bird. Perk backs off, hands up. Magic.'

Martha gripped the sides of Alice's chair.

'Do you want to go through the lines again?'

Alice shook her head.

'Are you sure?'

'It's the moves I'm worried about, not the lines. I'm on this side, leading, and then it's over past the fountain and piano, centre right, and off right.'

'Right.' Martha gave her sister a thin smile. 'I have to go now,' she said, put her fingers to her lips and placed a kiss on Alice's bald wig. 'These two will take you up. Remember to breathe.'

'Go, go, go.' Trinculo waved her away and revolved slowly into a clothes rail. Martha gestured as she left.

'*Pray you, tread softly,*' said Alice, '*that the blind mole may not hear a foot fall: we now are near his cell.*'

The two actors looked at each other in silence, then at her.

'That was when I knew she'd be a star.'

Trinculo whistled softly and got to his feet.

'A bloody star,' Stephano echoed, perched on the sink dresser nearest the door in an attitude of exquisite appreciation, eyes closed, hands clasped between his knees. 'She was so naked and raw . . . risking every syllable . . .'

'Are you ready,' said Trinculo, 'for how *famous* you're going to be?'

'No,' said Alice, who was running over the last scene in her head. On the closed-circuit monitor, Prospero invoked the masque and a son-et-lumière effect turned the patio's arcades into impromptu shrines.

'Well, join the club,' said the beanpole in his normal voice. 'And don't stand under the piano whatever you do, because it drops ten feet at the end and plays organ music to frighten us off. Tentacles and vines and shit come out of the arcades. Give yourself a few seconds of comedy – grapple, grapple – and then leg it. Don't get trapped – head for the blue light.'

'I'll do my best.'

'Have fun with it,' said Stephano, who was wearing tight leather trousers that made him waddle. 'Someone has to.'

Trinculo flicked ash as they climbed the stairs.

'Remember, use Bob's *physicalization,*' he whispered, and led the way up into darkness, laughing.

*

In the wings, Alice farted, and the burns-victim Ariel, who had just come off, trailing bandages, and was about to re-appear via a ladder somewhere in the second tier of arches, hissed, 'Where's Les?'

The cast-change announcement had been forgotten.

Alice stared into the chalk-scored hardboard of the back of the set. The trick to staying calm before an entrance, she knew, is to avoid being too aware of any one thing. The lines should be on a mental gel, rolled up and tucked away in your forehead. Unnecessary eye contact should be avoided, as should the temptation to notice things for the first time – the size of the counterweights in the flies, the coincidence of the numbers scrawled on the nearest flat with your actual weight, the striking resemblance between a grumbling stomach and the vowel sounds of Kenneth Williams. Best to look straight down at your feet. The cue is what counts: that, and nothing else.

It came quickly, Prospero's *I will plague them all, even to roaring*.

'Water,' Ariel almost screamed behind a flat. 'They've come out of a bog. They're supposed to be wet.'

How interesting, thought Alice. Ariel has an Australian accent.

The lights changed. Music played – a sort of minimalist gamelan confection, louder backstage than Alice had antici-pated – and the assistant stage manager, the girl in the rugby shirt, threw a pint of water in her face.

'Wait,' said Alice, coughing.

'Now,' said Trinculo. 'Go. NOW.'

Alice Hutchings fell through the archway, stage left, still coughing.

But for the water, it was like being pushed out of doors into the dry buzz of noon, where small sounds clustered. She had forgotten how, though your own sounds lacked an echo on stage, the shifts and whispers of the audience – the rustler five rows back, especially – provided the perfect acoustic map of the theatre. Forgotten, too, how unlike anything resembling art the whole business was of standing up and shouting things out. How sweaty and makeshift the illusion seemed from the inside. Porphyry and jasper? The arcade's pillars were MDF, wrapped in sheets of marbled vinyl. The fountain's granitic stone casing was styrofoam. Glue, sawdust and fabric conditioner flavoured the air.

*Come*, Prospero boomed from somewhere upstage, somewhere Alice wasn't going to look, *hang them on this line*.

This was the cue for the appearance of Ariel's 'glistering apparel' – the seductively shimmering garb which Caliban alone recognizes as a trap. Another lighting change revealed the slow descent of polythene gauzes from the flies. They floated down, a few already attached to the real palm (which had shed a frond during the interval), others catching on the box-tree borders of the patio, one settling on Alice's head. She shuddered, groped at the gauze as it stuck to her face, opened her mouth – and dried.

*Pray you*. The line began, she knew, with 'pray you' – but that was all she knew. Her debut snagged on a single phrase. Soon, in the thudding vacuum of concentration, even that was gone.

Alice had never dried before, or fluffed her words. It was a point of pride with her: not the kind of thing she would have bragged about, but a matter of simple fact which she had come to regard as a proof of her vocation – the one thing that entitled her to be called an actress. After all, if you couldn't learn lines or hold a short scene in your head, what were you doing on stage in the first place? To begin with, she could almost hear herself saying, 'So, *this* is what it's like.'

The sensation was partly familiar: the orange swoon, the wadded ears and mouth; the humiliating frustration of knowing that she knew the answers, deep down, only she wasn't telling – couldn't tell. Less familiar – more distressing – was the serenity of the moment, as though she had all the time in the world to consider her plight, and all the time in the world would make no difference. A voice in her head asked what, if anything, she remembered. Alice cast around. She remembered that she hadn't used powder to fix the clown white on her face; then realized that it didn't matter, because she was wet anyway.

She heard a 'tsk' in the audience. The thought that she could bear failure if there were no one else to witness it impressed her with a fleeting brilliance, before she noticed that she was shaking and about to fall over.

Feeling sick, Alice tried a random move, leaning forward as if to touch her toes. The shaking got worse as she bent over, one hand picking at her face. No, said the voice. That's no good either. Say something. Speak the speech.

'Pray you, I pray. You pray—' she mumbled, but the gauze clung to her lips. She sucked it in with a sob. Stephano covered for her.

*Monster, your fairy, which you say is a harmless fairy, has done little better than played the Jack with us.*

Alice jerked upright and wiped away the gauze. Cries rent the air.

There was accusation in Stephano's voice, and a more rational Alice would have wept with frustration, if she had not, just then – with no warning, only the liquid consciousness that she had to *do* something, and that no one could blame or stop her, whatever she did – struck out with her fists.

The punch missed Trinculo's ear, but it missed on the

audience's blind side, and the bathos was masked by Alice's noisy, animal grief. Trinculo, the innocent bystander, went down with his strings cut. Stephano scratched his chin. Alice stopped roaring, and the audience took over.

She turned to look. Only the first two rows were visible from the stage, but the people in them had their heads thrown back or hunched into their chests. Some sat with hands shielding their eyes, shoulders moving. A woman who squeaked and honked got her own laugh. A few pointed.

The urine, too sudden to be absorbed by Alice's tattered parody of a dinner suit, spattered through one of the many vents in her costume onto the floor, where Trinculo lay face down. He lifted his head and shook it like a dog.

*Monster*, he said after a calculated pause, *I do smell all horse-piss . . .*

Stephano had to shout to keep the scene moving: *Do you hear, monster?*, he bellowed twice. And the second time, Alice heard.

*

After that it was plain sailing; Act Five went without a hitch. Prospero banished Caliban and his fools into an archway stage-right, where they froze for the epilogue. Ladd delivered this downstage, and from where she was standing Alice could see his tracer-fire spittle spraying the dark. As the mage prayed for applause, the goddesses of the masque descended once more, and the opening tintinnabulation of shrieks and cries and booming waves greeted a final fade.

'Come on, Adrian,' whispered Trinculo, as the stage blacked out and Neville's music died away. 'Get them going.'

An authoritative clap broke the spell and in two beats was absorbed by applause. There were supposed to be just three full company bows, but with each pulse of the lights the noise seemed to increase, and on the last bow Bob Ladd held on to Miranda and Ferdinand, who held on to everyone else. There were whistles and cheers; Stephano gave Alice's hand a squeeze; and Alice looked out into the theatre with a kind of blank astonishment, half delighted to have perpetrated, with apparent success, such a fraud, and half ashamed of it. Not everyone was clapping, she noticed. The critics, who never clapped anyway, were scurrying out, and a number of professional young men with sleepy women in tow simply tapped an arm rest while groping under their seats for bags and coats. The cheerers and whistlers were a bit further back – less visible from the stage but eager to make an audible impression. Those who stood were lonelier still, Alice reflected: older women, mostly; or theatre buffs with plastic bags, check coats and hair-grafts.

In the wings, the cast crowded round to pay their compliments. Not all the actors were clear about what had happened in Alice's first scene, so Ariel told them and there was concentrated, impish hilarity. The ASM swore, perhaps a shade too revealingly, that she couldn't have filled in off book herself; Kwame Dankwah, the production's Ferdinand, whom Alice knew vaguely because he was going out with Martha, said something about talent running in the family; and Bob Ladd signalled the inadequacy of words with three thumps to the chest and a shake of the head. The director, Adrian, held on to Alice's shoulders, saying they'd talk. Martha took her sister back downstairs.

'I'm sorry,' was all Alice could think to say in the clowns' dressing room a few minutes later. It seemed indelicate of her to specify what for.

Trinculo lifted his head out of the sink and reached for a towel.

'Don't be,' he said, rubbing hard. 'Call it an inspired

moment, and we can all settle for being grateful.' He threw down the towel and inspected his chin in the mirror. 'Nothing wrong with the house white, that's what I say.'

'I just went blank. I couldn't breathe – I don't know. I knew the line was there, but it was as if I'd left it down here. I could remember saying it, *here*.'

'There you go – you were over-rehearsed. Anyway, we thought it was deliberate. We thought you were doing a Horrocks, didn't we, Huw?'

Alice realized that they hadn't been introduced by name.

'We did,' agreed the tubbier friend. 'The lovely Jane. Trapped in that pony of a *Macbeth* at Greenwich. Been widdling away for weeks, she has. Longest bout of cystitis in theatrical history.'

'But the line – the—'

'No one missed it,' said Trinculo, sniffing his armpits. 'You should have seen Leslie in previews. Whatever play he was in, it wasn't the sodding *Tempest*. We were lucky to get three acts out of him.' He paused. 'Poor bugger.'

Without make-up, the still nameless actor appeared unexpectedly well-proportioned: rangy rather than thin, with tense but solid shoulders and long muscles that slid up and down his arms as he got dressed. His eyes were perhaps too deep-set and bruised-looking to convey the full carelessness of youth, but the skin on his back and shoulders was flawlessly boyish. The room's light pooled in it, like the sun behind smoked glass; two clipped wings of chest-hair seemed hardly to belong to the same person.

Alice coloured and turned back to her mirror. The former Caliban's make-up box had been removed along with the rest of his effects, although someone had left a few cotton-wool balls and a jar of cold cream. One of three drawers beneath the work surface was wedged open with an exercise book and the tartan thermos that had been rolling around on the floor.

'Right, then,' said Trinculo, hoisting his bag, with a nod. 'See you in the bar.'

'Yes. See—' Alice began, but he had gone, idly singing to himself a golden oldie Alice knew and couldn't quite place.

She found Stephano – Huw – with a reflected glance, and frowned.

'He's angry.'

'No,' laughed Huw, who had changed from one pair of tight leather trousers into another and was pink with the effort. 'He's impressed. That's all.' The laugh coughed to a halt. 'I can tell.'

'Oh.'

Alice brooded. Out of the corner of her eye, she watched Huw swab the boil on his neck with neat Dettol. The fetor of the room, its off-cut carpets, dead joints and old coffee-mugs, acquired an institutional note.

'See that terrible picture?' he said brightly, pointing to a naive landscape of cloudy lambs and a smiley sun painted directly onto the wall.

'Yes,' said Alice, not looking.

'Judi Dench did that.' Huw sighed. 'But it isn't signed.'

'Very nice.'

'It's a funny thing, though,' the dumpy actor went on. 'What people notice. Or,' he sneezed and excused himself, 'don't notice.'

He winced.

'Are you all right?'

'Mm.' Huw screwed the top on the bottle of disinfectant. 'For example,' he continued, smiling, 'speaking personally, I thought you were *un*believable, stepping in like that. I mean, you hear about it in concerts all the time, don't you, when the conductor faints and some bloke who knows the score takes over, but not in the theatre. You knew it off pat. Fair play.'

'Thank you.'

'Just don't be put off, if – if they're all a bit done-and-dusted about it.'

'Who?'

'The others.'

'Oh, I won't. I—'

"'Cus it'll be, like, "Oh, thanks, you were really great, life-saver," and then it'll be, "Can't stop, love, have to see my agent," and "Guess who was in tonight? Tom Hanks and Sue Pollard." ' Huw was silent while he tugged on a top embla-zoned with the word 'Army'. When he next spoke his voice was almost a whisper. 'We're a shifty lot, us pros, let's be honest. We don't like surprises.' Another pause. 'We want it lifelike, but not too much, see. We don't like the idea that just anybody can do it without weeks of rehearsal, because that'd make us less special.' He curled his lip at his reflection. 'It's a contradiction, like. You *say* you want everyone involved, but *do* you? Really? 'Cus we can't all be putting the slap on, or who'd be left out front to say hello afterwards?'

'I suppose so.'

Huw sniffed. 'Though from your point of view, I wouldn't worry.' He pulled back from the glass and swivelled to face Alice directly, who had let her head hang, a hair brush in her lap. 'You might get a nice mention.'

Alice shrugged, but said nothing, aware of a double reti-cence on her part: the actor's nervous desire to hoard a compliment compounded by guilt. 'I might,' was all that she let fall from her lips, when Huw had left the room and she could at last undress. 'I might.'

*

61

The name of the golden oldie came to her as she stood outside Bar Konditor, the theatre cafe. It was 'Love Letters', an Elvis cover with a distinctive sprinkling of top notes in the accompaniment that stood out in all the wrong ways if the piano was out of tune. Her father often played it, but it wasn't his voice Alice recalled now. Nor could she remember the words, apart from the bit Trinculo had been singing, 'I me-mor-ize every line / And kiss the name that you sign,' which was either a joke or an irritable dig. The latter, probably.

Through the port-hole windows, she could see a first-night party beginning to bubble and seethe. The public had been weeded out and the conversations and anecdotes of the remaining actors seemed at once confidential and exclamatory. They shared an obvious subtext: relief. A holiday spirit – the euphoria of exam candidates as yet untroubled by their results – reigned in tilted glasses, open mouths and eyes screwed shut with mirth. Alice withdrew her hand from the door and watched her palmprint evaporate. This was merely the preliminary. Later there would be drinking and eating at Maison Bertaux in Soho, and Martha had invited her along. Excitement at the prospect shaded into resentment, however, and a part of Alice felt curiously diminished by the invitation, almost as if it offended an unspoken vow of exclusion.

Her reverie was interrupted when Bob Ladd, looking smaller than he appeared on stage, dressed in a black silk shirt with the top three buttons undone, opened the door and laid a hand on her shoulder. The crest of shiny brown hair didn't belong on a man in his sixties. His arm, stretched across the doorway while he spoke to someone else inside, effectively prevented Alice from entering, but its restraining weight also carried with it a next-in-line reassurance. His first words to her were, 'I want you to know,' and Alice's vanity quickened, though what it was he wanted her to know remained mysterious, for it soon became clear that Bob Ladd, off-stage, had the schoolmaster's knack of speaking softly in order to focus his listener's attention. The din of celebration rushed to greet them, and all Alice could grasp of Ladd's meaning was the emphatically repeated monosyllable 'most'.

With a double-handed clasp, the demobbed mage brought Alice into the room, pointing out the various groups of people she might care to join. It was a dubious gesture of welcome, announcing principally Ladd's own intention to depart, and Alice was soon on her own again.

Before long, Martha was at her side and introducing her ('properly this time') to Nick – to Trinculo – who had, she said, a family connection to divulge. Martha made some very flattering comments in Nick's favour, including the observation that it was he, and not Kwame, who should have played Ferdinand. Alice had nothing to add to this. It was candour rather than truth, delivered with heartless confidence, a way of handing on the baton of conversation, but it made her smile: Nick, too, whose air of understanding and suppressed amusement appeared to her a subtler, more compelling form of flattery.

As Martha turned away, Nick apologized for his stand-offishness in the dressing room, brought on he claimed by 'nervous surprise'. When the director first told him they'd got another cover, a 'double' who knew the words, he hadn't believed him, hadn't thought they'd get away with it; and then, when they had, found that he couldn't face the post-mortem backstage. It wasn't superstition, exactly – just, strange experiences made him reticent.

Alice understood exactly what he meant. She nodded, without knowing what to say herself. He nodded back, and when he put out his cigarette Alice assumed the 'introduction' to be at an end. She waited for his polite excuses.

But there weren't any. Instead, he stayed where he was and carried on chatting amiably. For the moment, the consciousness of being in agreement with someone was itself so agreeable Alice could barely attend to what else was being said. She didn't mind; he didn't seem to mind either. It couldn't matter much. And then there was a gap of several seconds, before Alice realized that she was being asked what she'd like to drink. Nick disappeared to the bar, and in the middle of the long refectory-style room with tables and benches on either side of her, Alice found herself looking at her shoes, which had tassels.

When he returned and handed her a glass, she felt hot, said, 'Thanks,' rather briskly, and then, 'Sorry.' The feeling that it wouldn't matter if she tripped over herself a few times was dimly comforting.

He nodded again.

She said, 'Mmm,' and decided not to enquire about the family connection. Perhaps he'd forgotten about it, or thought it irrelevant. Perhaps. At any rate, Alice liked the way this Nick, whoever he was, apparently took for granted the part she'd played in events, without feeling obliged to praise her performance. His approach suggested a sensitivity to the unexpected which made room for strangers by reserving judgement.

She also liked the funny habit he had of looking straight into your eyes and tapping the knuckle of one finger against his chin as though you'd made him see something in a new light.

'Shall we sit down?'

It seemed the thing to do. They found a corner of a table nearby, and Nick asked her if this was her 'first' at the Young

Vic. Alice flushed. His as well, it turned out. He'd just finished the two new Ayckbourns in Scarborough, *Moving Target* and *Sitting Duck* – OK plays, he thought, but *Scarborough*! It wasn't what it used to be. Or maybe, scarily, it was: the only place you could still find the Black and White Minstrels on the seafront. (No kidding, every Monday night.) Before that? Well, not much. He'd not been acting long. Last year a Joe Penhall at the Bush, and two commercials for a Spanish department store, El Corte Inglès. He spoke Spanish, yes: lived there for a while. In Spain. Taught tennis and TEFL after college with the guy who wrote *A Sceptic in Texas*, the Waco thing at the Royal Court; came back to London, got a part in it. That was, oh, what, three, four years ago?

He smiled at her. The hint of time passing was pleasantly off-hand, implying that three years might easily be spent like *that*, without planning, without regret. As an actor, he could scarcely have put them to better use, Alice reflected, but being young (or younger, as she told herself), perhaps he wasn't aware of his good luck. There were worse crimes. To an observer, it might also have appeared that the young man with dark hair – and, when you looked closely, scar tissue on his neck – preferred to speak rather than listen; Alice noted with little leaps of sympathetic amusement her partner's tendency to ask questions and then answer them himself. But that was part of the emerging charm: he understood that she'd rather not talk about herself. She wasn't offended.

They sat, and 'talked'. To begin with, Alice could feel eyes watching them, or glancing over from the bar with an ironical glint; on the other side of their table, a smoker disguised his grin as the effort to exhale. It struck her with the slow force and logic of a dream that she was the subject of debate.

The nondescript chat she was having, about Wandsworth and Battersea (where Nick lived, too), had a claim on others' attention. She quailed. It would be dreadful if they got the wrong idea or read too much into a couple of drinks.

About the other members of the cast, he was skilfully droll. Each had a flaw or trait, a personal history to keep you amused; though the ease of reference and parody were never harsh and only confirmed Nick's sympathy. He came across as witty, impish, essentially sincere. The thumbnails were complete – all lives are comic and cruel, they seemed to say – like little plots: 'Ariel? Cressida Dunn? She's a disinherited jam heiress. Down to her last three hundred grand. Huw? Huw I love. He's very bright. He was a Pentecostalist at uni, even managed to convert his folks. Then he came out and dropped God, but his parents didn't. And now they think he's been possessed. That's your actual irony, that is.'

'It's a whole play. You ought to write it,' Alice remarked, loosely.

'Maybe I will,' Nick said. He sipped his beer and frowned. 'I'd like to leave a body of work behind.'

Alice began to laugh, sensed this was the wrong thing to do and coughed it away. The combination of insecurity and ambition in his remark was surprising, but also – looked at another way – impressive in its unguardedness. It dared you to be as true yourself.

Across the room, Martha was gesturing, beckoning; beside her sat Huw, looking wan, his T-shirt riding up over a superficial paunch. Martha approached, three fingers pointed diva-style to make her destination known, and told Nick that he had to sit with Huw to stop him pining.

'I need the loo first,' Nick said, turning to Alice. 'Party later?'

'If that's all right with you.'

'What d'you think, Mart? Is that cool?'

He grinned and left.

'Tsk,' said Martha, after he'd gone. 'Huw's sat there all alone.'

Alice breathed out.

'I'm sure he'll cope.'

'Oh, I know that.' It was almost a whine. 'It's just' – Martha spoke through a yawn – 'he's *so* in love, it hurts.'

'Who is, Huw?'

'Huw's, yes. Bless.'

'We shouldn't be staring. It makes things worse.'

'They can't be, not for him.'

'That's not the point. It's voyeuristic and – unkind. And anyway – Nick's straight.' Alice tried not to sound hopeful.

'Yes,' Martha said, leaning her head thoughtfully against her sister's arm. 'Mind, so's a piece of spaghetti until you boil it.' She sighed. 'But no, you're right. You're right. He's definitely his father's son.'

Alice expressed her bafflement.

Martha raised her head an inch. 'You *were* engrossed. He didn't tell you? Tony Glass. The one Dad trekked around with years ago. In Porlock. Well, his son. He's – Nick's – *Ni-cho-las*, crikey. Is Tony's son.'

'The Anchor man.'

'I don't know if they're close,' said Martha, oddly. 'But I don't suppose it can be too much of a hindrance, having your dad as your agent. I mean, it wouldn't be like working with him, would it? And Glass House is respectably big. There'd always be room for manoeuvre.' She looked around vaguely. 'Four from here, in this show. Bob and Leslie. *Leslie*, Christ. Neville you know. He's with them, now. They do music. Obviously. And Nick, of course.'

She stopped. 'I can't say any more. I'm pissed.'

Alice propped her sister up and went to get some air. She took her bag and cardigan because she had it half in mind to slip away, but in the lobby saw Nick on the street threshold. He kicked the door away from him with one foot, let it fall back, idly kicked it again. His right hand supported his head as if he were asleep; he murmured rather than spoke; the tone was wry, affectionate, not too solicitous. He said, 'Perhaps you should. Maybe. We'll see,' and Alice moved back, unobserved, into the bar. It pleased her to have heard his voice in a different circumstance. He could be plain; she valued that.

*

Neville was unattended at a small corner table, eating peanuts singly but in strict rhythm. On anyone else, a dark vest worn beneath a white shirt and tie would have looked strange; on him, it argued the richness of an inner life to which the key had possibly been mislaid. A second glance, as Alice descended the entrance steps, revealed the composer to be inattentive rather than unattended, for beside him sat a smoking pile of coats, topped off with a beret.

As the pile smouldered, Neville's eyebrows rose and fell in a manner which more or less failed to convey surprise.

'I've had that flask since 1966,' a voice said tragically. 'They've swept that up, of course – I went back to look. And my book. The mere lees are all that's left this vault to brag of. Erased from history, that's me.'

'Forgotten, but not gone,' agreed Neville, rising to greet Alice. 'Leslie, allow me to introduce your understudy.'

The pile of coats looked round and gave a little cry.

'How did you do?' it said.

Alice fished the thermos and exercise book out of her bag, and told him.

# Five: *Leslie*

I TRIED IT ON while my mother was up at the house cleaning, and got an erection. She came back early, found me
tugging away in front of the wardrobe mirror and said,
'What are you doing?' Her face was congested. 'Get out of
that at once.' Later – not much later, either – she came back
up the stairs and laughed, with her hand over her mouth,
then held to her forehead, her cheeks. 'Oh, Les, you did give
me a turn. And all dressed up for it, too, like you was in
a bank.' I got confused and started to cry. 'Now, Leslie,
don't take on.' My mother sat me on the edge of my bed
and stroked my hair, still laughing, forcing it out as if she
were practising. I couldn't look at her because I knew what
I'd see if I did. All evening she was the same: breaking out
into giggles over the potatoes, ho-hoing to the chickens in
the coop, puffing her cheeks when I came into the room.
She didn't think it was funny, though, and when I finally
made some remark, the empty giggling stopped. I suppose
I must have looked like him.

That's my clearest memory of adolescence: a posh wank,
as my friend Neville would later call it. Why that memory
and not some other? I don't know. Perhaps it was the first
time I'd been taken seriously.

I was a docile child. A show-off when occasion called for

it, which it didn't often (once a year at church, at Christmas, or whenever poor liver-spotted Mrs Medlock tried putting on a Variety Bill in the Bewdley Scout hut), but otherwise reserved. Difficult to rouse. Some grown-ups were amused by this. 'He does everything in a slightly bemused daze – a very charming trait,' wrote my English teacher. It drove others mad. Mr Markley threw chairs at me and Ms Crune sent me home with a note because she said I smelled. 'Well,' my mother wrote back in her neat copperplate, 'Les has the sam smel what my late husband had and we slep together for twenty year so all I can think is you must be sum kind of old made what cannot get a man.'

The suit, by Montagu Burton, was bewitching. It smelled, as adult clothes always seemed to, of preparations: hair oil and Imperial Leather soap, starch and nicotine – the last Senior Service on the way to work. It was my father's smell, of course, and so the smell of the past. But the past was gone; the cool, lined sleeves were empty, and I suppose I fancied myself as a sort of fairy-tale youngest son – ready to fill those abandoned sleeves; to venture out into the bright new world of chain-link fences and nationalized utilities and win his pot of gold. Responsibility and necessity were pressed and stitched into the collars and pockets. The boy who put on his father's trousers would be *required*.

The next time I wore it was to an interview for, as it happened, a job in the Kidderminster branch of Lloyds Bank. The Campaign had started the day before, so the whole town reeked of beet and I made a little joke about smelling like a brewery. I didn't get the job. A few weeks later, I was similarly passed over by a subsection of menswear at Samuel and Proud's in Birmingham. The bank found me insufficiently serious. The Dept of Half-Mourning ('Mitigated Affliction') settled for 'youthful' (I was an old-looking nineteen). In the end, I had to make do with a menial post at the *Kidder-minster Bugle*, where I spent two years running between the newsroom and the printers in the basement with hot copy, proofs and a variety of empty editorial threats. I was also deputed to look after Gerald, the *Bugle*'s sciatical court reporter, who had to be escorted from the pub back to the magistrates in the afternoon lest he remain at the Dog and Trumpet all day. I liked Gerald. About the third time we went to court, he asked me if I really wanted to be a journalist, and I said no, I wanted to act. I'd not been asked before. 'Good for you,' was Gerald's quick and expressionless reply, at which point the man who'd interviewed me at the bank was brought in on a charge of loitering. 'Just don't get caught.'

There was something sad in that, of course, but I was amazed that he should whisper anything so unguarded – amazed and delighted. The combination of tolerance and prejudice in the remark didn't strike me as forcibly then as it does now. And now that it does, what of it? One way is as good as another; the fear of exposure (the art of conceal-ment) is universal – that's what Gerald meant, and lived to prove I'm glad to say. Until my fourth season in rep I assumed he was still a repressed, alcoholic bachelor living on the fringes of Blakedown with his mother. Then one day in Windsor, halfway through Act Four of *The Circle* and just before my elopement, I heard a voice from the stalls cry out: 'Get on with it, Les,' and it was Gerald with his new wife, Chris. Short for Christabel, although you'd never have thought it with the hair on her hands. 'My eye,' said Gerald afterwards, 'but you made us laugh.' I bridled a bit and pointed out that *The Circle* was regarded by many as Maugham's most serious play. 'True enough,' said Gerald, who saw no contradiction. He died outside the Victoria

Palace in 1978, waiting for Jimmy Tarbuck's autograph. Better than inside, that's what I told Chris, and I should know.

*

I suppose the urge to act must have been lying dormant. Probably it wasn't pinpointed because so much of my life, growing up, was a private performance anyway. I lived in my head, reading and rereading Conan Doyle and *Precious Bane*, my favourite book. Mary Webb was Shropshire borders rather than Worcestershire, but that didn't matter; as far as I was concerned, she was Tolstoy and Hardy and weepy Wednesday matinees at the Rolfe Street Gaumont all rolled into one. My loyalties were evenly divided between the 'hare-shotten' heroine and the strapping weaver Kester Woodseaves, though it was Prue's yearning I took with me on walks through the Wyre; Prue, who taught me to see beauty in nature. I was sixteen before I noticed that cherry leaves in frost were the same colour as the forest on the horizon or the local brick chimneys, that kind of thing. And it was Prue, the secret scholar, who wrote letters in which she made the touching discovery that 'labour brings a thing near the heart's core'.

To a diligent dreamer like me, that was the perfect encouragement. The other side of it – the way docility can be made to conceal a romantic ambition – I didn't see at the time. I was trapped in Bewdley, and it was the world's fault.

So when I told my mother I wanted to be an actor, she frowned and said, 'What's brought this on? *Variety Bandbox*?'

*Variety Bandbox*, or its northern cousin, *Variety Fanfare*. There were some good turns on those shows, and we used to listen in every Saturday at seven over the washing-up.

Mum indulged a fantasy of being a concert-party soubrette by singing along to Joan Turner, who did wobbly versions of 'hits' from revues called things like *We're So Inclined* or *Grab Me a Gondola*, or whatever had gone down well in the *Fol-de-rol*s that year. They were pretty terrible. Naturally, the songs I wanted to hear were from the flashy new musicals – *Carousel* and *South Pacific*. The comedians were a better bet: Sid Field; Sandy Powell ('Can you 'ear me, mother?'); the young Jack Tripp; Frankie Howerd; Peter Sellers, Spike Milligan and Harry Secombe before they became the Goons; a lot of Windmill regulars (doing, so I gathered from Gerald, *very* watered-down versions of their club acts); and Tony Hancock. Best of all was a man called Rex Jameson, who did a spot as a tipsy vicar ('This is the House Beautiful, madam, and I am the Church Broad'), until he was sacked.

But they weren't the reason I got interested in acting.

*

'I've met a girl,' I confessed, one evening. 'At work.'

'Have you, then,' my mother said, who was darning a pair of my socks. 'First I've heard of it.'

'Yes I have, and she's – she's bright. Sparky.'

'Oh, ho. You noticed that, did you? There's hope, then.'

It was shock, you see. Ours was a self-sufficient household. A good deal of pride was invested in the skill with which Mum managed to eke out a widow's pension with money from cleaning at the Rose and Crown and other odd jobs, including mine at the *Bugle*. And it was a self-sufficiency of its time, based on the understanding that it took two people to make it work; a third was a threat, and without a husband to fall back on (not that he'd been much use when he was around) I could already see Mum wondering what she'd do if – when – I upped and left. That obviously concerned her. For a woman in her mid-forties, she was still pretty herself, as long as you didn't object to false teeth.

Prettier, truth to tell, than Beatrice Sadler, who was sturdy before she was buxom, solid before she was voluptuous.

Let's face it, she was built like a central tunnel support.

There *was* a personal physical attraction, I think, but it seemed inseparable from a general delight in her presence. You just wanted to be near Bea, because she was charismatic and loud and liberating in a way I had not thought it possible for a woman to be. Like everyone else, I laughed at the big pleated skirts and knee-high socks, the mannish shirts and raucous cackle, the incongruously delicate silver necklace with its tiny pendant bell. And then she'd make her morning entrance, swatting the other mousy secretaries away from her desk in the Deputy Ed's office, calling out, 'Heighho, and *off* to work you go,' and there'd be a different kind of laughter – the laughter of an expectant audience – because we knew the curtain on the day had just gone up.

Bea joined the paper soon after I was taken on in '51. She was supposed to be a copy-taker with 'secretarial duties', but her typing was execrable and it turned out that she didn't know any shorthand, 'only Latin'. We knew something was up when the Editor called her in to dictate a filler, based on a notice he'd read in the *Sunday Times*, and we heard Bea remark, 'You can't just repeat Harold Hobson verbatim, Michael. You have to have your own opinion and back it up.' There was an outraged squeal, followed by a whimper of defeat. 'No,' said Bea, 'that won't do either. Let me have a go. There's a decent-sized feature, here. Start with *The Ghost Train*, and then expand. How about . . .'

The result of that teatime coup was a stridently literate article, quite out of place in a local rag and signed under the unlikely name Ronald De Souza, about the future of British theatre: how it was all doomed unless Tennent Productions, Gielgud, Thorndike et al. had the nerve to do what American playwrights were doing, and put on high-profile plays about the here and now. Beatrice had cruel things to say about Rattigan and people like N. C. Hunter; she was horrible about Christopher Fry, too. She used words like 'society' and 'pusillanimous'. And, as her hook, she savaged the nearest rep company, a beleaguered troupe at the Cradley Civic, for an 'amateurism almost magical in its fumbling consistency'.

'Almost magical,' repeated Gerald all through court sessions the next day, his face purple with compressed glee.

It caused a minor scandal, that piece. Someone – it was Bea, I'm sure – sent a copy to Barry Jackson to ask for his response. Sir Barry, late of Birmingham Rep and the Shakespeare Memorial Theatre, sent back a lordly rebuttal, accusing the writer of a 'wanton and defamatory insolence at the expense of a struggling art form'. But the high moral tone was soon undermined by another letter from Jackson, addressed to R. De Souza and marked Private and Confidential, in which the great man revealed that he, too, had suffered performances of 'rare and wonderful putridity' at the Civic, and, furthermore, that it was run by a sinister little mesmerist – the 'Smethwick Svengali' – who had a reputation for harbouring grudges and liked to play tricks on his actors. This creepy little story was corroborated by none other than J. B. Priestley, to whom the article had evidently been passed by Jackson, who wrote in (again, confidentially) to say that he remembered a 1927 Civic performance of *The Ghost Train*, by his friend Mr Arnold Ridley, in which, by some awful and inexplicable quirk of nominal aphasia, the entire cast of twelve appeared unable to remember the word 'train' for the duration of the evening, with imaginably chaotic results.

Beatrice was gratified by these responses to her work, and at the same time disturbed, I think, by her pseudonym's growing taste for mockery and assault. The irony was that Mr De Souza's severe critical distaste for bad plays, ham performances and cheap tricks concealed a great affection in Miss B. Sadler for all these things. We loved going to the Civic together, which was a surprisingly grand building with a broad gabled red-brick front on Bank Street in Cradley Heath. I don't know how I afforded it on £3 a week, less than a cub reporter's wage, but we were devoted regulars, and the glamorous front-of-house transvestite in the toque turban took a shine to us, which meant that we got the best five-shilling seats for one-and-six. Naturally, no one knew the identity of the mysterious Ronald De Souza – there were sometimes jokes about his latest pronouncements in the interval cabaret – or we'd have been thrown out.

These were the days when actors at small, busy reps gave eight performances, twice nightly from Wednesday to Saturday, and then went home to learn an act of the following week's production for rehearsals the next morning. Productions at the Civic were frankly not of the first rank, or even, perhaps, of the fifth. They were rushed and incoherent, nowhere near the standard of the major regional companies, like Birmingham Rep, and there was no design to speak of. Everything you saw on stage was borrowed from shop owners or besotted theatrical landladies. (Or from Cradley Print Works, which had lots of signs and hoardings and bits of scrap that looked impressively sinister when lit with a gel, or covered in talc to suggest antiquity.) But that the plays happened at all was a miracle, and the point. Nightly exposure to mishap and memory loss on the part of the overtired cast bred a strange discernment in the audience, who toiled in from Smethwick and Lye, Langley Green, Old Hill and Blakedown, and from Kiddie, of course, to be told a story. They didn't care if the old retainer forgot his lines, or the leading lady gave her Rosalind in plaster; we could laugh at that out loud, and see beyond it to the shape of the evening. In *The Ghost Train*, the play which launched Mr De Souza's brief, vituperative career, there is a moment when the elderly Miss Bourne has to respond to the stationmaster's superstitious scare-mongering with the words 'What a horrible story.' The stage direction reads 'quick on cues here to avoid laugh', but scatty Win Hunter, who played Miss Bourne, was one of those actresses who have an allergy to being instructed in anything. She took for ever to respond, and eventually came out with 'What a pretty tale.' The next line is the stationmaster's: 'I warned you it weren't no pretty tale you was making me tell.' Winnie's face was a blank; then she had an idea, held up a finger and shouted, 'Oh, no you didn't!' at the top of her voice. She'd done panto and summer season with the stationmaster and they had ten minutes of patter up their sleeves, which they performed to loud acclaim before carrying on with the rest of Act One.

I looked at Bea as we sang along to 'A Bit of a Ruin that Cromwell Knocked About a Bit' and saw, in profile, the face every actor wants to see, sees once at an early age and spends his life trying to find again. The face of an ordinary sceptic, a person with worries and secrets and bills to pay, giving way. Others around us were singing louder and laughing harder at the unprompted anarchy of Win and Bert Rich, the stationmaster; but Beatrice was wide-eyed, unblinking and pink with exhilaration, sitting upright, her hands clasped in her lap.

Notices in local papers are hardly ever more than press

releases – favours done to the management of the relevant theatre or cinema. Five three-line paragraphs about what's on, who's in it, the story and set, the audience, and a final word of encouragement to Mr Leslie Barrington in his first professional role. Bea's reviews, by contrast, were 400-word essays of imperial impudence. The rest of the *Bugle* was a plod through births, deaths and industrial accident (bodies in the copper hopper, again) at a time of privation and local depression. Banners unfurled for the Festival of Britain in London, but not in Kiddie. Celebration in Kiddie was a cup of Horlicks at the Golden Egg and a new lipstick from Boots.

So there was a kind of quixotry about 'De Souza at the Theatre'. On the bus back to Bewdley, you'd hear an old boy clicking his pipe at the 'Day by Day' diary, where the notices appeared, and turning over with a shake of his head, his left thumb still on the previous spread, to which he would flick back with a tut and more shaking of the head. It probably gave semi-literate readers a weird thrill to see words and opinions which conveyed no real meaning except that they were biliously out of the ordinary, hugely affected, and – this was the clincher – home-grown. That is a very English trait, I think, the entertainment of suspicion by a simultaneous and deep-seated pride. Ronald De Souza would have been beaten up in any pub in Worcestershire; he was a right little fookin' Oscar Wilde, he was. But he was *our* Oscar, say what you like, no one else's.

It suited Beatrice to have this largely imaginary influence over a small audience. She was a cabaret performer, and, like a lot of vaudevillians, her ambition scared her; on a bigger scale – not even that much bigger – it assumed a different aspect. I remember the *Birmingham Evening Post* sent her to cover Gielgud as Leontes at the Phoenix Theatre in London, and I went with her. It was a Peter Brook production, and everyone – Ivor Brown, Hobson especially – raved about it. Like most (though not all) of Gielgud's performances, it was a triumph of vocal gesture over felt emotion. 'O, she's warm!' says Leontes, when he touches Hermione in Act Five. 'She's hot,' Beatrice whispered aloud. There was a tremulous titter. Still, we both left the Phoenix agreeing that we'd witnessed a great performance of a great play. We missed a connection on the train home, and Bea wrote her review in the waiting room at Coventry. I read it the next day. It was rancidly contemptuous, and the more shocking for the intimate cruelty of its exaggerations. 'The extent to which Mr Gielgud seems unaware of his own insincerity as an actor is itself moving,' she concluded, and I told her I thought that would hurt anyone. The production seemed brilliant in retrospect.

There's no way now of telling whether or not Gielgud ever read her review. Why, with all the national acclaim, should he, or his publicity people, care what the *Brum Evening Post* had to say? But if by chance he did, I'd like to know how long he spent afterwards with his head under a pillow, or sitting at a table with his hands over his ears, watching ants in the sugar.

Because, in the end, all you have as a performer is your confidence. Talent, ambition and the rest may be developed or cultivated; but your inner confidence is an unthought, unnegotiable thing, not an aptitude or a taste. It can be found, it can be lost, and it can be taken away.

\* \* \*

It was an unusual feature of our friendship, mine and Bea's, that I didn't feel the need to conceal the content of our private conversations, mostly about books and films and plays, from my mother, who listened sceptically for a year or so to Bea-said-this and Bea-did-that before finally remarking, 'Well, let's have a look at her, then. Invite Bea to tea, you great wosberd.'

I had misgivings about this. Mum meanwhile chuckled to the chickens, tee-heed over the wringer, and I sensed the scalp-prickling, potentially irreversible effects of an error of interpretation – though on whose part I couldn't usefully say. I hadn't prevaricated over an introduction because I was shy, or worried, particularly. I simply felt Mum wouldn't understand if she saw us together. It would be so much easier to tell, offhandedly, as a story.

Class came into it, and also, less clearly, 'ways', which youth made me think untranslatable, it being an ironic property of the younger generation to regret the innocence of the older. I had been, often, to the end-house on the Habberley Road, where Beatrice lived with her Uncle Mitchell – a greyly handsome former flight lieutenant who pronounced 'alas' to rhyme with 'arse' – and it was my idea of eccentric heaven. Downstairs was the newsagent's and local shop which Maurice Mitchell worked hard to make a success. It sold every periodical and paper and American comic you could think of – *Crime Patrol* and *Flash 92* hung up on a washing line in the window to attract the schoolkids; *Photoplay* and *Flirt*, teasingly, on the end of the same line. Upstairs was another world again. The sitting room was book-lined – historical romances, military travelogues, Dickens and Twain – and the furniture, which included a chaise longue and footstool, covered in dusty plush. The real transformation, though, was in Uncle Mitchell, who shut up shop about the time Bea and I came home from the *Bugle*, and would make rather a show of unbuttoning his waistcoat while saying, 'I will discase me, and myself present as I was sometime Milan.' Then he'd put on a silk robe and a George Shearing '78, get out the damson wine and gossip filthily about his customers. 'Maurice!' Bea would say, in mock horror, and that always threw me. Her calling him by his other name.

Gerald told me that Beatrice had been accepted for Girton after the war, which I knew meant the University of Cambridge, but that she'd turned down their offer when Uncle Mitchell said he couldn't cope on his own. I was touched – and mystified. What was there to keep her at home?

*

The story was that Uncle Mitchell had the shakes and couldn't drive, so Beatrice learned instead. She suggested that we make a night of it: have tea at ours, and drive to the Civic for the Tuesday music hall.

'Mum'll be pleased,' I said, while we parked.

'Good,' said Bea and checked her face in the mirror, the first time I'd seen her do anything like that. She was wearing a dark green skirt and a white silk blouse with the pendant bell, and looked impressive. She had a slide in her hair, which startled me, too, not because I liked the victory-curl look in particular, but because the parting helped me see how thick her hair was at the roots, how far forward it grew, how much there was to keep back. A loose crop would have been more stylish, though perhaps ahead of its time.

'What do you see in me?' I said.

'You?' Beatrice asked, smiling, and got out of the car. It was cold. The air was like a knife pulled out of the ground. She locked up and threw her coat around her shoulders. Our creaky front gate seemed to banish my question, until we got to the front door, and Bea said: 'You make me laugh, Les. You even look a bit like Danny Kaye, in that suit.'

Uncle Mitchell had taken her to see the great man at the Palladium in '49, so this was praise indeed.

'And you smell nice.'

Mum had the door open before I could find my key, or hide my blushes.

'I'd just sat down. What's the matter with you?'

'Mum, this is Beatrice. Beatrice—'

'Good evening, Mrs Barrington. It's very kind of—'

'I'd just sat down. I was in the other room.'

Mum squinted at us with her mouth ajar, as though we were figures in the distance. The pretence that she'd been surprised in some way was touchingly belied by her appearance – she'd put on her best cream cotton dress, with a floral lilac panel – and by the laid table behind her.

'In with you, then,' she said, at last.

The new houses on Cleobury Road had rudimentary hallways. You came in the front and faced a flight of stairs, to the side of which ran a strip of carpet leading to the kitchen and sitting room. Our house was a much smaller farmer's cottage, attached to the grounds of the big coaching Inn, the Rose and Crown. There was no straight, landscaped concrete path; the front door was really at the side, and opened straight into the kitchen, with closed-off stairs on your left. The first objects you saw were the range and the wringer.

Mum stepped back from the door and into an enamel bucket.

'You can go through, if you like.'

I'm quite tall, I suppose, about five-ten, and Beatrice was an inch taller. On our own, of course, I never noticed; but together, we towered over my poor mother, in whose nervous movements a mixture of obstinacy and birdlike flutteriness now struggled for supremacy.

She retreated to the stove, and began rattling saucepans around.

'You go through,' she repeated. 'I'll put the eggs on.'

'I'm cosy, here,' said Bea, and went to sit down at the table.

'Go through,' Mum commanded. 'Leslie, take her through. I won't be long. I'll bring the tea in.'

'But, Mum, you've laid the table here.'

'I said I'll bring it in. I always lay the table. Tsk. Anyone would think we never had visitors.' Mum's face was grey. 'I expect you're hungry.'

Bea smiled pleasantly. 'Is there anything I can do to help?'

'I can manage, thank you. Just you go and make yourself – in there, that's right. Where you like. Les, here a minute. Try this for me.'

It was a pot of blackcurrant jam. Mum made jam herself, from the blackberry bushes at the back and down Hop-Pole Lane, but this was bought blackcurrant. There was something about the first pots coming in towards the end of rationing that made them desirable. I think it was the bright reds and yellows on the labels.

I went purple trying to get the lid off.

'Blessed nuisance,' said Mum. 'Try it with a tea towel.'

Beatrice turned at the living-room door.

'I don't want you to go to any trouble.'

'Oh, no, no, no.' Mum shrilled, pointing vaguely at me. 'It's just this blessed jam-jar we can't, um.' She paused, looked up at Beatrice and gestured again at the jar between my legs. 'Open. They put them on that tight, see.'

I felt a hand on my back. Mum took a step back.

'I know a trick, Leslie,' said Bea, her hand still on my shoulder blades. I handed her the jar, and she banged the top of it with her balled fist. Then she breathed out, gave a sharp twist and the lid wobbled free.

Mum squeaked. 'Oo! What did you do?'

'It's just a trick. Sometimes it works.'

Mum looked wonderingly at her, and nudged me. 'Oo. We could do with one like you,' she said to Bea, her voice awed with approval. 'I said, Les, did you hear? We could do with that.' Her lips pushed out to express satisfaction.

'How do you like your eggs, dear?'

Something in my mother yielded with the opening of that jam-jar. The need for words to be said, points to be proved – gone, with a tiny gasp.

'I said, Les.' Mum tugged at my elbow when Bea had gone back into the front room. 'Isn't she a strapper? You never told. I hope there's enough.'

'Of course there's enough.'

'No, but it's *nice*.' Mum took my hand and smacked it. 'She's a lovely lass. Twice the size of me, not that I was ever much to get hold of.'

We had poached eggs and toast and jam, followed by figs in syrup, which Bea, playing Mum like an instrument, said she 'adored'.

'So do I, Beatrice. Don't you, Les? Les doesn't mind either, do you, Leslie?

' "*I don't mean to be rude / But I'm not in the mood / For food.*" '

'Am't you? Oh, well, suit yourself. We'll live!'

'It's Danny Kaye, Mum.'

'I've always abhorred figs,' Mum said, ignoring me. 'Down Market Street, there used to be Mr Hendricks, the confectioner's. Lovely trays of fig toffee he used to have, first thing. And you could get such a big bag for a penny. Whole figs in great pieces, like this. Mind, I had a sweet tooth. Mr Hendricks said so. I had a bet with the girls at work – I said, come the time, I'd have all my teeth out in one go and be at work that afternoon, and they said, "You never will." But I did. All of them out with cocaine, and went back to the machines with a red bandage round my – right round. Painful? You try it! (That's my fun, Beatrice. Don't you think of it. You'm got lovely teeth, both of you.) But I won my bet!'

*

We got there at eight twenty, comfortably in time.

The Theatres Trust *Guide to British Theatres* describes Cradley Civic as a 'modest and unpromising survival', which would have done for most of its variety acts: especially in early autumn, when the new season hadn't got going and the better turns were still in Cromer, or Minehead, or wherever. Somehow, though, the leery old soak who owned it got a bill together every Tuesday, and the place was always full. A spotty national-service quartet on the apron hacked its way into 'Danny Boy' or 'Pale Hands I Loved' while you got your pints in (mild and bitters for the wife), and the audience sized each other up.

Most of the members of the ex-forces and working-men's clubs in the area shuffled along, because there was always a fair chance of seeing an act from ENSA, or, failing that, a stripper. Not an all-the-way Windmill Theatre affair; just something a bit saucy, trailing a tune. Then there were the variety diehards, who turned the bar at the back of the stalls into a smoking ruin of British Oak Shag and bored the bar-maid in cancerous whispers about the time they saw Jimmy Jewell top the Manchester Palace. You could always spot the experts. They told each other jokes from the week before (the ones it had taken them a week to get), traded punches to the ribs and wore cardigans with big chestnut buttons.

The rest of us were – well, whoever you please: play-goers, punters, print workers coming off shift, skinners from the tannery next door, husbands and wives (more husbands than wives, perhaps); the remnants of soldiery;

sons, mothers, girlfriends. In the street, we were a rabble of resentments and looks askance, a war of bad smells: tar, coke, fog and sulphur; perfume (bootleg Lentheric) and grey mince. But once through the Civic's heavy wooden doors, with their arching yellow-etched glass panels, we were aromatically united by the scent of beer and cigars on seventeen rows of lumpy seats, their braided edges dangling or torn away.

I don't recall the names of the first-half turns that night, which is probably a blessing. I do remember the creepy MC, coming on to boos and catcalls and making announcements, giving some poor soul with a unicycle, or a dog, a big build-up, but you could tell his heart wasn't in it. When he didn't like an act, he began to froth at the mouth. A horrible sight – like watching a slug fizz to death. There you are, though, it couldn't be helped: variety was a mixed bag, true to its name. For every Reg Dixon or Sandy Powell, there were scores of rotten singers, acrobats, plate-spinners and novelty acts, like Val Vette and his 'amazing quick-fire rag paintings'. (I'm looking at Val now, fifth on a Worcester bill I've got hanging on the wall, but my mind's gone blank. What did he do?) Or the Curtseying Dwarf, a halls routine dating back to the days of a tiny camp comic called Little Tich, which consisted of a small man in drag getting lost in the bunches and frills of an exploding black crinoline.

Tich's legacy was a cert, to be fair: an intrinsically funny sight gag. Mime always went down well, because it didn't have to compete with the yakking of the audience, and grabbed your attention without requesting it. The rot set in as soon as you felt someone was pleading with you. In fact, all the bad acts had this in common: they couldn't be heard; they sounded desperate. And all the good ones were instantly audible, their whole presentation a kind of nuanced scream. Which, come to think of it, partly explains the popularity of drag, where the one thing you couldn't forget or get away from was the voice.

The look of the thing, in those days, was often – and deliberately – unremarkable; the aim for the men was to be recognizable, both as drably respectable women, and as themselves beneath the wig and hat. You weren't meant to be confused by what you saw, but you were meant to draw a breath, laugh and gasp at the same time. A drag act with authority got everyone going. The old-timers at the Civic used to speak of George Robey – aka the Widow of Colonel de Tracey – in an almost longing whisper. It wasn't just sex comedy; it was economics, you see. You can always find some pinched little puritan to tell you that drag is awful, and the only reason it exists is because men hate women, but that isn't true. It's subtler than that, more self-aware.

What was a club, or a palace variety, after all? It was a retreat from home life, where men were powerless. That's the truth. Until the end of the 50s, I'd say, the majority of working-class family nests were still built by women – women like my mother – and it was their job to grab the pay-packet on a Friday, or as much of it as they could, before his eminence disappeared down the pub. What was the defining characteristic of their stage-life counterparts? They aspired to be better than their situation would ever allow them to be. The original drag act is a man pretending to be a woman who wants to be a lady. Sidney Fairbrother, a great Edwardian star of the halls, had a crowning insult for her drag partner, Fred Emney: 'You're a *woman*,' she used to shriek, 'not a lady!' The gag survived that famous pairing: I've heard versions of it across the country. And if the men always laughed, you should have heard the women, screeching and hugging their bags, heads up, teeth bared. They knew what Sid meant.

I'm not denying that sex was part of it. Obviously it was

– the jokes, the winks, the clothes, the strange obsession with fey men in uniform (usually in Hyde Park after dark) and second wives; the attitudes, the batting of eyelids. It's a baffling misconception that the British never mentioned sex in public before the trial of *Lady Chatterley*, because the halls barely talked about anything else, and Cradley Civic was far from being an exception.

But – and this is my point, my excuse – escapism has to have somewhere to escape from. You leave home to find out why it was home in the first place. And for the performer as much as for the audience, sex, like the accident of talent – or inner confidence – is a reminder of things you can't change about yourself, or the changes you can't avoid. One moment you're a boy with a boy's voice, playing with yourself in front of a mirror, the next you're what nature intended.

\* \* \*

He came on without fanfare or a word of introduction, while the house lights were up and that bloody terrible quartet were still playing 'Love Is Here To Stay'. At the time, it looked like a mistake – a rookie's bungled entrance, born of nerves and eagerness – but it wasn't a mistake at all. He wanted you to know, as the light faded and the tablet of the proscenium swelled, engulfing ceiling, boxes and balcony, that he was there already, in the darkness, waiting.

'Good evening,' said the darkness, and voices at the bar gulped down silence. 'I want you to imagine – a lemon.'

We looked round. Everyone was checking the row behind, laughing, being caught out, apologizing and turning back. Beatrice, I noticed, nearly jumped out of her skin, and Mum went rigid. It was a throbbing voice, the voice of conscience, disembodied, placeless, yet somehow gently physical, like a finger brushing the top of your ear. It was the voice of a dream-guide, sleep's hidden observer, telling you what will happen next.

'Says here,' Bea whispered, peering at the bill, 'amazing. "The Amazing Ant. Mind-binding. Unique act." '

'Bending?' I suggested.

'No, *binding*. Distinctly says – unless it's a misprint.'

'Concentrate, please.' The voice wheedled briefly into a higher, peevish stage-register, and dropped again. 'A lemon. Such a sour and juicy lemon. Hold it to your nose and breathe in deep. Smell it, ladies and gentlemen. The zest and the pith, the whiff of acid. Feel your nostrils flinch – like baby oysters!'

I doubt if anyone in that audience had ever seen an oyster – it was a line for the end-of-the-pier crowds – but it didn't seem to matter. Beatrice giggled and found my hand. I heard her swallow and say, 'My God.'

'Now, take a knife.'

The figure on stage appeared to glint. His voice dropped further, and, as it fell, the coaxing grew more intimate, as though that finger touching your ear had drifted down along the rim to find a lobe.

'I want you to cut the lemon. Cut it now, and taste it.'

Mum squeaked and dribbled a barley sugar from her mouth. I noticed other people around us doing the same.

'Hold it to your lips. Open your lips, wide. Squeeze the lemon – and drink!'

My mouth filled – exactly as though I'd been about to suck on a half-lemon or an orange – and a murmur of surprise rippled, back to front, through the stalls. Glasses were dropped. The lights came up, and a sensitive-looking young man, about my age, perhaps a little younger, with an enormous bulb of brilliantined dark hair and purple-rimmed eyes, took an awkward bow. He smiled, but the smile had a clenched quality about it. The mouth curved downwards; the skin over his cheeks looked as if it had been grabbed from behind and pulled back over a wire frame. The hair shone like bakelite.

On came the MC in a flurry of little steps, arms open to the audience, his horse's grin champing with self-congratulation – 'Marvellous! Isn't that marvellous? Ladies and gentlemen? What d'you think?'

The MC and Ant were dressed alike, in tatty blue jackets with wide black facings and a single, loose gold button each.

I felt I knew what was coming next, and sure enough we got a high-speed family history. The MC's travelling stock, his *gitano* blood. Parents who fled Madrid in '36 and came to work at Tate and Lyle's. Life in the song-halls of Southwark. Later, on the circuit, doing the fairs. Putting down roots in Brum. And now, at last, the first of the new batch, making his way. Proud to present: young Antony, his nephew. Ant, the talented. A man of influence. A turn with testimonials – 'Yes, madam, what every woman's a right to expect!' Trained with Hilgard and Weitzhoffer, no less. A hit in Sheppey and Hove, two seasons down in Weston and Lynmouth (terrible business about the flood). His first time here in Cradley. Bound to make a splash—

'Give him a hand!'

We applauded, but I felt sorry for the lad. Like every unnatural performer, the MC managed to make even the truth sound phoney, and Ant, who was the talent after all, didn't need support.

The older man led the applause and backed towards the wings while the lights dimmed. Behind him glowed a forest scene, a house drop depicting a shepherd and shepherdess asleep and various cherubs circling them, some plump and cupid-like with arrows, others skinny and fire-eyed.

At a signal from young Antony, the drop rose to reveal a dark stage, bare save for a crate in the middle labelled 'Property'. The single top-lit object in all that hollow darkness drew one's attention. Was it my imagination or did something blink and sparkle between the slats of the crate? We laughed, in the belly of the theatre. Only the MC, off-stage, still clapped.

Ant took a step forward onto the apron and whispered behind his hand, 'I think he likes me.' His natural speaking-voice was cracked, like an adolescent's. The clapping continued. He frowned at it, shrugged (more laughs), and spoke again – this time throwing his words to the back of the auditorium, where they buzzed off the pillars and panelling.

'He likes me,' the boy repeated, in the voice that wasn't his, and made an impish face as he snapped his fingers.

The clapping stopped. From the wings we heard a muffled curse. Ant craned his neck back and around, returned to face us, dusted off his hands, folded his arms, and caught someone's eye in the front.

'He likes me not.'

It was his ordinary voice again this time, but modified for direction – aimed at the front row.

'I don't know. Some men. Hot and cold, aren't they? Does he like me? Do you think he likes me, madam? Do you? You do?'

Ant flashed his teeth, and bowed quickly to the giggling woman. Almost hidden in the move was a lightning gesture – a finger targeting the woman, beckoning her closer, as if he intended to have a confidential chat with her.

'Give yourself a big round.'

*Snap.*

The wings fell silent for good, but the woman in the front row yelped. Her arms lifted as if she'd been grabbed, and she began clapping. There was a lot of scattered, disconcerted laughter now, and Ant played to it.

His other persona pretended to object. 'It'll go to his head,' rumbled the thrown voice, like an amplified heckler.

Ant looked surprised and held out his hands in appeal.

'Oh, don't *you* start, sir,' said the voice, mysteriously. 'Yes, *you*, sir. You with the yellow cuffs and high colour. Don't *encourage* him.'

A man not far from us in one of the middle rows, grey-haired, red-faced, genially apoplectic, started to applaud, and Bea glanced at me, her breath half-stopped. When people look at each other in the audience, it means one of two things: either you've lost them or they've got it, they're in. Well, we were in.

Ant undid his jacket and produced a pair of frilly gussets from his pocket. There was a roar as he passed them to the woman in the front.

'You left these behind, love.'

He shook his head, walked over stage-left and started gossiping, in and out of earshot, to other members of the audience.

This is an old panto-gag, but Ant's voice-throwing gave it a twist. The idea is to rattle on, as though what you're saying is really important, while missing out words and phrases – like someone moving about behind a microphone – so that nothing makes any sense, and what does come over sounds rude. The way Ant did it, there were snippets of suggestive rubbish interspersed with wireless crackle and feedback.

'. . . her first husband, the fakir . . . lovely carpets . . . stiff as a board . . . I don't mind if I do . . . couldn't find the pulse . . . fell about laughing . . . twice with the King of Jordan . . . in a hot wash and hope for the best . . .'

Ant let the laughter build, bending, darting forward here and there with a needle-thrust of the finger to snare another victim, stopping now and again to brush aside the 'heckler's' misgivings (reduced to a reverberant 'tsk, tsk'), making his way slowly back to the pink lady holding the pants.

Beatrice sat on her hands and bit her lip. Mum stared, clutching her bag.

Ant posed rather camply right on the edge of the apron, arms folded, shaking his head at the lady in mock disbelief. There was something funny about so young a performer aping the exasperation of his elders.

'Are you sure you want to put those knickers on?' he said at last.

'No!'

'You're not sure?'

The woman almost screamed: 'No!'

'I see.' Ant smiled. 'So, really, you're sure.'

'Yes!'

Out came the hooked finger. Ant's eyes opened wide and white.

'Sure you want to put them on your head?'

'YES!!'

About thirty people were clapping dementedly by now.

'Madam, be my guest.'

She put them on, the place erupted and I thought: Christ, he's good. No material (or no material that sounded like material, which is the best kind), not much of a plan, just a faintly ruthless combination of innocence and appetite, like an eaglet or baby god.

His routine was essentially flattering. Unlike his uncle, he wasn't a *Ghost Train* prankster; he had no wish to make people look foolish. And yet at the same time you felt that if such a thing were to occur, amazing Ant would find it hard to be amazed. I had an inkling even then, as I watched and laughed, that his becoming air of modesty, which took no credit for the possession of talent, also took less than full responsibility for it. When he leaned over the footlights towards the audience, a groping shadow appeared above the proscenium.

'Let's clap together now, that's it.' Ant clapped along. 'In rhythm, please, softly, with me, so you can hear my hands.' The shadow bulged and pulsed. 'Softly, and softer still. The knickers, madam, take them off. Shhh, everyone. Softer and softer. Slower, softer, till you – stop!'

We sat in humbled silence. Ant stood for a moment with his eyes shut. Then he stepped back from the edge of the stage, unclasped his hands and blew on each palm. Now there was real applause. Feet drummed the carpet so that a dusty mist like incense appeared and floated down the aisles.

'I want some volunteers,' he cried, above the tumult.

I raised my hand without thinking.

'A couple to assist in an experiment.' His eyes found me. 'You, sir, are you a pair? The lady, sir, is she willing?'

Beatrice was torn. Her hands were in her lap again. She looked sadly at me, tried to say something, seemed confused. I reached out to her. Our row bawled its encouragement, but Mum held on to me as I got up. She mouthed, 'Don't go.' And so, of course, we went.

*

When Beatrice and I reached the stage, the first thing Ant said to us as we climbed the three steps at the side to shake his hand was 'Got you.' Bea faltered, half turning back, and whispered something I couldn't quite hear. I gripped her other hand tighter, kissed her on the cheek and let the audience have its way with this unexpected piece of gallantry. I'd not yet dared to do the same thing offstage. It was a gesture born of courage in exceptional, perhaps unreal, circumstances – yet its effect was real enough. She took a decisive breath. It pleased me that I could be strong for her, and that she trusted me.

As if he knew the source of her anxiety, Ant raised Bea's hand and showed her to the crowd. We walked in a chain to the centre of the stage. He positioned us either side of the property box and turned his back on the audience.

'Remember,' he said gently, 'all I can do is suggest. I can't make you do things you don't want to do. Do you trust me?'

It sounded like reassurance to me; but then I was practically swooning with a sense of opportunity and the desire to prove myself. I simply didn't notice, as Bea must have, that with his first suggestion Ant had made the whole idea of noncompliance look irrational, even shameful. Were we willing? Or were we willing to disappoint? And what had wanting to do with that? Many acts are willed without being desired. I hardly want to finish another bottle of Bell's before I turn in, but, Lord, put me out with the empties if I do not.

*

Antony Glass carried on talking as if the audience didn't exist. Occasionally, he'd turn round and say something witty or placatory, to show he hadn't forgotten them, or make a sudden movement in Bea's direction, a sort of outstretched wiping motion with his left hand, as though he were trying to reach a high windowpane. Mostly, he talked.

I could feel the lights and the darkness beyond.

He asked me about Beatrice and how long we'd been friends, what we liked about each other, where we lived, what we did. I said straight away that I hoped he wasn't fishing for anything mucky because it wasn't like that, yet. Everybody laughed, Ant seemed genuinely amused – smiled a smile of professional sympathy – and said, of course not. The laughter was comforting. The truth was that I'd begun to concentrate hard on controlling the flow of information about Bea, well aware that the less I said about the *Bugle* or, God forbid, Ronald De Souza, the better. So what I took to be Ant's intuitive grasp of the situation put me completely at my ease. I said I'd better watch myself and Ant agreed that we could all learn from that: nothing wrong with a bit of self-awareness, doing as you would be done by, and so on.

Again, this was all said in a reassuring tone of voice. Except that, this time, I felt trapped by my better instincts, the way you do when someone offers you a treat and you say no, because in the back of your mind is the old fear of ruin and the feeling that life is rations not portions. Even as I nodded and agreed – what room was there for disagreement? – my timidity rose up against me; I realized I was cross. The thought of being so continuously watchful and circumspect, lest one iota of the truth offend, had not previously occurred to me, and now that it did, it had, naturally, the force of a revelation. I was shocked to find myself saying one thing and, bitterly, thinking another. It seemed as though I had sacrificed to a charade of self-restraint not minutes, seconds or hours, but years – the best of my young life.

On the other side of the property box, which had by this point mysteriously opened itself, Beatrice was in full spate. Impossible to believe that it was her! So lately trammelled by misgivings, and now released! From the box, she'd selected a diseased-looking bit of fox fur, with shrivelled head and claws, slung it round her neck, and was in the process of telling the audience how she came by it, advancing propositions and explanations along the way that would have made Nero blush. At least a hundred men seemed to have been involved; they'd made donations of a pound each and the whole generous ritual of acquisition ended in a gin-soaked odyssey to Stockport with a busful of naked constables.

The interesting part was that Bea glid around the insinuations and baited obscenities with an Uncle Mitchell-style gentility to which it was impossible to object; there was no foul language. It was exactly as I'd have done it – the words, the pop-eyes, the perpetual air of affront; the kind of thing I'd *dreamed* of doing on *Variety Bandbox* or at the Palladium, only – naturally – in a suit.

End it with a song, I thought. And she did. The firstlings of my mind were, lo, the firstlings of her hand. Before I knew it, we were all singing the chorus to 'The First Wife' by Marie Kendall, one of Mum's favourites.

'*Do you worry* (Bea sang), *if your hubby says to you*
*All the won-der-ful things his first wife used to do?*
*Don't start crying! If you do, you are a flat.*
*Grab 'im by the whiskers, swing 'im round and say –*
*Did your first wife ever do that?*'

Bea curtseyed and made a great show of staggering drunkenly into the wings and back again for an encore, waving her fox. The thought obsessed me that these were tactics borrowed from me, from our dawdling walks along the Severn and through the Wyre, our leg-kicking Sundays in the Kiddie chippie, our chats over coffee and damson wine in Habberley Road. Then it was my turn. I was asked if I had anything I'd like to say in reply, and I was stumped.

A voice that sounded sufficiently like my own to take me by surprise began singing 'If I loved you', and words I didn't think I knew hung in the air:

'*Kinda scrawny and pale, pickin' at my food*

*And lovesick like any other guy*
*I'd throw away my sweater and dress up like a dude*
*In a dickey and collar and tie . . .'*

The Civic was quiet when I'd finished. It wasn't a hostile silence, but it was faintly uncomprehending and anxious.

Ant appeared by my side. 'That was lovely,' he said. The theatre murmured in corroboration. He asked me to close my eyes, and a hand strayed to the pendant bell that had been fastened around my neck. Darkness beat out a brief tattoo.

I made my way with haste through a maze of high-ceilinged rooms. The last of these had wings and a presence. I ran across it to feel the comfort of a wall, as I used to run to the oil pipes in school on a winter's morning and think how different they were to the frozen railings outside.

But the wall vanished as I drew near.

When I lifted my head, I found myself on the apron, lathered in sweat. Faces smiled their recognition and surprise. I had my father's jacket and tie in one hand, and an evil-smelling fur in the other. Danny Kaye I was not.

# Six

AT MAISON BERTAUX, the mood on the third floor was one of peculiar disappointment. There had been laughter and congratulations enough, but no excitements. Leslie had not been sacked (his silence on receiving the news was deemed to be a symptom of emotion), and Alice had not been plucked from obscurity by any agents or scouts. Nick had been 'seen', it was alleged, by a woman from Working Title; Michael Nyman had sent a note of congratulation to Neville (who made a face when he saw the name) and one of Tom Hanks's people had put her head round the door to say how much Tom had enjoyed *Mamma Mia*. A dinner at Bob Ladd's swank riverside apartment in Limehouse accounted for the absence of top-notch theatrical celebrities, although during a brief how-do-you-do downstairs Leslie claimed to have made eye contact with the man who'd had a hand in Basil Brush.

According to the director, the reviews would be balanced. From what he could gather, most of the praise from Charlie Devereux and Alex Grew seemed likely to be reserved for the set and for Ms Challen, the rising star.

'It could be worse,' said Neville, stoically. 'Remember *Bernadette*? "What a nice backdrop." One quote and that was a lie.'

Alice tried to be more optimistic. 'I shouldn't be surprised if you were to get very complimentary notices, all of you.'

The actors refused to be comforted, however – even Martha, who quashed the rumour of her mention with convincing despondency. Kwame described his own perform-ance as a 'cartoon'. Leslie took swigs from his thermos and, wisely perhaps, would not be drawn on the prospects for a Wyndham's transfer, except to say that it was a first-rate show once you cut the rind off.

For all their professed gloominess, Alice felt that they were remarkably composed: lounging about, smoking, gos-siping. A certain kind of artist regards a party, particularly if it's a lock-in, as a sacred obligation, a ritual extension of the moment, and it was in such company, full of the collective unwillingness to pack up and leave, that Alice now found herself.

The night was still, but on the way to Soho, over Water-loo Bridge, looking up through the windows of the taxi, she'd seen long clouds racing across the sky. Everywhere, stillness belied the possibility of things opening up. A glass of wine or coffee cup refilled seemed like a toast, and when Nick saw the time, whistled and said, drily, 'Last tube's gone. Looks like it's the N19 for us, Alice,' her heart, briefly, flooded. There could be nothing meant by it, of course – by words so casually uttered – but to Alice's ears, unattuned and open as they were, 'for us' had an echo which carried forward far into the future.

\*

'I have no intention of telling you,' Leslie said, with the clarity of purpose that occasionally inspires the drunk. 'One's life is not a parlour game. *My* diaries, unlike some people's, are personal.'

'Lordy, that's the whole effing point,' sighed Martha. She was sitting forward on Kwame's lap while he dozed with his head thrown back. Alice was glad no one had a camera. 'It has to be something of value. Like, oh, I don't know, the worst thing you've ever done.' Leslie groaned. 'All right, all right. OK. Or a bad thing, anything, you've had to do, or know of, that's been done. But – no, wait – it has to be a thing you'd never dream of telling anyone, that's why it's called "Withhold". You say it, I withhold it. It's about trust.'

'No, it isn't,' said Neville, from a three-legged chair in the corner. 'It's a forum for sadists. The people who like these games are the people who like to see others betraying their own trust—'

'Bollocks.'

'—because then no one will be able to expect any better of *them*.'

'I do so *not* fucking get that.'

'Martha, dear,' Leslie purred. 'Have you ever considered a job speaking English as a foreign language?'

Alice decided to intervene. 'It's not betrayal, though, is it? It's showing off.' Martha rolled her eyes and collapsed back onto Kwame's chest. 'I don't mean you, Martha. But the aim of these games isn't shared knowledge, let's face it. It's self-promotion – disguised as honesty.'

Leslie rumbled into life. 'Like that silky cunt, Mr Ladd.' The corner of the sofa into which Alice and Nick were also uncomfortably squeezed twanged as he spoke. 'It's a shabby trick, as my understudy, Miss—'

Kwame laughed in his sleep.

'—well, what *else* do you want me to call her?' Leslie shouted. 'As I was saying, it's a shabby showbiz trick. Look at that book of his. "I have another side. I was unforgivably cruel to my first wife." As if we won't think he's so shallow if he says something horrible about himself. Whereas—'

'The floor, Leslie,' said Kwame. 'You are making it move.'

'—whereas, in fact, the only reasonable conclusion one can draw is that the said silky cunt is both shallow *and* horrible.' Leslie paused. 'I'm sorry, that's an unfortunate, er, combination of . . .'

Martha took a drag on a dead cigarette.

'Of course,' she said, 'there is a simpler way of looking at it.'

Leslie sneered.

'Which is that clever clogs like you and Alice are only being spoilsports because you know you've got something to hide.'

The noise of late-night kitchens being emptied, bins clattered and dumped in back yards filtered through the half-open window.

'What's wrong with that, Mart?'

Nick had been quiet for a while, and Alice, feeling his voice in her shoulder, was at once aware of her hands on her thighs.

'Nothing,' Martha said, opening her eyes. 'But then I'm not the one trying to be moral.' Her narrowing gaze swung from Leslie to Alice and back to Nicholas, between them, who smiled.

Alice tried to appear unconcerned. The worst thing that had happened to the Hutchings family – the death of the youngest child, Helen – was never discussed, and Alice had no fear of its being offered for inspection now. This left, well, everything else: the limitless vista of her sister's spite.

It was Martha's custom, when piqued, to find a way of making those who had displeased her feel left out, and a telling silence or pointed look often did the trick. She was an economist by instinct and training (though like her father she had repudiated science) and retained a value for the shortest way to a desired effect. But Martha was also highly sensitive to the matter of her sister's intelligence, which took the long way round everything, and at a deeper, more impenetrably vexed level, could not bring herself to treat it realistically – 'She won't get far in this profession, if that's how she goes on' was her private judgement. So the intelligence became a matter of flip legend ('Alice is so clever!'), or a useless luxury, like a cloak of invisibility. The social implication was that her bigger, slower sister dwelt on situations and opportunities instead of grasping them. At the same time, the ruminatory approach was not without a sense of threat, and Martha often felt as though she was being watched.

\*

For Alice, more obviously, the accusation of hypocrisy stung because she acknowledged it to be true. Her review of *The Tempest* was half-written and in her bag. She hoped it wouldn't offend.

She knew it couldn't, in at least one respect, because it would be untraceable. She wrote under a pseudonym – as did all the unestablished actors and directors unwilling to compromise their careers on the right side of the curtain. She'd even, once, interviewed Martha over the phone for a 'My City' column in the *Standard*'s free magazine, and put on a high-pitched secretarial accent to cover her own light drawl. Martha had suspected nothing and Alice congratulated herself on a plausible performance. But it was a guilty pleasure, this kind of manipulation, with a coolness about it which gave her little delight. It worried her that her review would not be as optimistic as she'd meant it to be; then again, who read *What's On*? And could so tiny and benign a deception be said to matter? (She needed the fifty quid.) Alice tried to ignore the suspicion that, in other circumstances, such a useful sense of proportion might blunt the edge of one's moral delicacy and be used to excuse, well, anything.

'OK,' said Martha. 'I've got one. Try this. I mean, it's not *bad*, but it gives you an idea. Something that happened to me.'

She paused and glared at Alice.

'Now you know what I've been saying about Allie, what a dark horse she is.' Alice knew, or could guess. 'Well, there's "another side" to it. Because when I was little, right – this is a true story—'

Alice froze.

'—I wanted to be on *Jim'll Fix It*. I was really little, 'kay, and I wanted one of those badges saying "Jim Fixed It For Me".'

'As for so many,' remarked Neville.

'And I'd been going to ballet lessons and Dad had taken us both to see *The Nutcracker* in Bristol and I wanted to be the Sugar-Plum Fairy, of course. That or the Bionic Woman, either'd do. And in one episode, Lindsay Wagner, that's the Bionic Woman, had to eat this awful brown stodge in a foil wrapper to become superstrong. So one day, Alice finds out that Lindsay Wagner is going to be on *Jim'll Fix It*, and asks me would I like to meet her and be the Sugar-Plum Fairy at the same time, and I'm over the moon. But what I don't realize, see—'

Martha swallowed and looked up at the ceiling.

'—this sounds stupid – what I don't fully *appreciate* is that being on *Jim'll Fix It* involves writing a letter, being selected, filmed and invited to the studio. Plus, Alice has told me to keep my appearance a secret from Mum and Dad, or the "magic" won't work.'

The room fell silent. Brakes squealed in Greek Street, there was a solid crunch and a burst of shouting. Nick eased his shoulder away from Alice's and leaned forward to put his glass down on the carpet.

'Anyway, you can probably guess the rest.'

Nick nestled back into the sofa.

'I'm there at six thirty in my little tutu in front of the box, wondering when it's going to be my turn. And there's a silly housewife who wants to be rescued by firemen, and a milk-man who wants to go waterskiing on Coniston, and we have to sit through that, and then a little girl comes on who wants to bend steel bars like the Bionic Woman. And she's just like me, only she's *not* me and I'm not her and I *can't* understand it. And Alice has given me this wodge of cold gravy and trifle sponge to eat beforehand – in a foil parcel – and then it's the end of the show and I'm sick all over my tutu.'

Alice sensed that Nick had been watching her.

'She didn't give you a badge, then?' Leslie crooned.

Martha couldn't speak. Beneath her, Kwame wheezed with laughter. The windows rattled their applause.

'I'm afraid you'll think me rather literal,' Neville began, and stopped. He was in a peculiar posture, forced to favour one side of the chair so as not to fall into the fireplace. With eyes raised to the ceiling and one hand stroking his chin, he looked like a British Home Stores mannequin cast in the mould of the prophet Elijah. 'But I thought the point of the game was that you told a story against yourself, not someone else. Not that I think you should do either—'

'It *is* against myself. I looked ridiculous. We had to throw the dress away.'

'—but you don't bear any of the responsibility for that. It wasn't your fault. The story tells against Alice, not you.'

'Oh, come on. You know that's not what I meant.'

'Yes, but that's the way it *sounds*.'

'I'm not blaming her.' Martha pointed angrily. 'I'm saying it's me. *Me*.'

'And very shocking it is too, my dear,' Leslie twanged, rubbing his hands with glee, 'very shocking, to assume that we'll be so appalled by your sister's censure of vanity – a bionic Sugar-Plum indeed! – that *we* shall forgive *you* for trying to corrupt our good opinion of *her*. You minx.'

'You're warped, Les.'

'From the start,' sighed Kwame, tickling Martha's hair, 'you wanted to be an important somebody.' He lifted his head briefly from the sofa, grinned into Martha's ear and fell back.

'As I said,' Neville murmured, 'it's a horrid game.'

'And what do we do now?' asked Nick. 'We just agree not to say anything more about it, is that it?'

Martha pushed Kwame's finger away and yawned. 'Yeah.'

'I don't understand.'

'How pointless,' agreed Leslie.

'Completely,' Alice said, 'but the funny part is that Martha's left out – or maybe you've forgotten, I don't know – the best bit.'

'Which is?'

'Which is,' and Alice waited before she went on, 'that Lilian – that's our mother – was so cross with us both, but particularly with me, that she wrote to Radio One about it, substituting my name for Martha's, and Dave Lee Travis told ten million schoolkids the whole story two days later over the breakfast table.'

Leslie and Neville made disgusted noises.

'Leslie,' Kwame butted in. 'You are going backwards and forwards and the room is going backwards and forwards with you. Sit still.'

'I *am* still,' the old trouper said, hiding a belch inside a hiccup. 'Christ, though. What some people do to take the gloss off their kids.'

A low keening, as of green wood in a fire, came from the grate.

Neville jumped up. They looked; it was nothing.

*

The still busy streets sounded a fanfare of car alarms, sirens, woofers and tweeters of which Alice barely took any notice. She was in a state of anxiety: mortified by Martha's tale, which she felt made her look cruel, and ashamed of her response to it. Lilian Hutchings had had her faults as a parent; discipline and resentment had not always been distinguishable in the care of her first child, and she had said unpleasant things. (The one that stuck, when they were out in town weekend-shopping, was: 'Walk in front of me.') But these things were Lilian's misfortune, too, as it turned out, and Alice did not care to speak of them in self-extenuation. Her coda to Martha's story was something else: a credible lie, the sort of thing Lilian might easily have done, though borrowed, in fact, from the vague memory of a school friend's prank in the hope that Nick would see she'd been served right and taught a lesson in kind. Because it was his opinion of her, now, that mattered.

What did he really think of her? What was he doing with a person who could only be – she bit back the word while it was a thought – grateful?

Try as she might, Alice could not rid herself of the idea that she was bait: the means by which a more attractive, subtler man could find his way to her sister. The smiles between them – between Nick and Martha – were evidence of a more understandable rapport: the fruit of rehearsal, talent and physical favour. One look from Martha must surely weigh heavier in the balance of probability than all of Alice's panicked attentiveness.

Together, they sped along Piccadilly towards Green Park and the N19. Nick was talking fast, in the vein of comic confession, apparently unperturbed by what had been said about Alice, or by what she'd said herself. He took her arm when they had to negotiate drunken oncomers and somehow managed to maintain shoulder contact after the lads in large blue-and-brown rugby shirts had swum past. The constant, shy nudging deprived Alice of her powers of concentration. It was a sign of his interest; and yet Alice dared not acknowledge it. She was too aware of its implausibility, and of the air of stifled amusement among the others which all evening it had seemed to excite. In Neville's case and Leslie's, the silence was particularly painful, for they guessed at her need and observed Nick whenever he spoke as if his behaviour confirmed a suspicion. They feared for her – that was it – and it was a fear Alice now saw reflected in the unaccommodating stares of the passers-by. Her scale was a point of sensitivity which marked her out, their faces suggested, for lesser pleasures.

She turned to look at Nick. He was staring ahead.

'Dad's heart wasn't in it. He'd got disillusioned with variety, after the Pleasure Garden went bust. Most of his own stuff was advisory, and Bob was pencilled in for *Henry VI* and *Blake's 7*, so the agency looked as if it might finally take off. Anyway, Dad was in a rotten mood the whole of the first Minehead weekend, and when he gets to the rabbit from the hat, he's had enough. Yanks the bunny out, holds it by the scruff of its neck, sees our faces and says, "Fuck." Place goes berserk. In the back afterwards, the guy from Butlin's cancels the other gigs, I'm screaming, the rabbit's eyes are white, it's dribbling and swaying, doesn't know where it is, and Dad has to kill it with my penknife.'

'Why?'

'He didn't have one of his own.'

'Right, yes—' Alice began, and realized she hadn't been listening.

\*

The night bus was full, as usual, of gap-year students from New Zealand with friends in, or amazingly near, the birthplace of whoever they happened to find themselves sat next to. On the lower deck, a man waving a can of lager wrapped himself around the bars in front of the exit doors and whined at a small lipless woman in an anorak and dirty white bobby-socks, who swayed about, drank from the same can, and whined back. Their increasingly hopeless quest was for the origins of disagreement. 'That,' the man reiterated, 'is what I'm saying,' to which his fifteen- (or was it fifty?) year-old companion replied, 'I know *that*. I *know*. Jew fink I *don't*?'

Alice liked going home by bus. It was a sordid experience, but she liked the familiarity and the motion, the slanging matches that pre-empted conversation, the slightly rude 'what if?' of the brakes. She liked the way the windows misted up. Above all, she liked the comfort of enforced reverie which the journey gave her – now more than ever, when both origin and destination seemed obscurely threatening. Between the two there was no obligation or choice, merely a sort of serene levity. You breathed in the fumes of KFC, hung on and rafted the night away, skirting Hyde Park, Knightsbridge and Sloane Street with its gallery-style, fashionably unstocked boutiques; on to the Square, the Royal Court, and down at last to Chelsea Bridge, lit like a giant Wurlitzer.

'This is us,' said Nick as the bus leaned into Queenstown Road circus and came to a halt. Alice made no reply. Her eyes were fixed, unseeing, on a headline which read 'Earthquake in South–'.

Nick waved his hands in front of her face. Alice smiled, got up and stepped out onto the unmoving pavement. Her flat was in Winders Road, right at the other, Clapham Junction end of Battersea. Her jaw throbbed as it had not throbbed all evening. She considered the length of the road and the things on either side of it – estates, the DSS, the funeral parlour, a dubious shop selling 'old pine'.

'No, this is wrong,' she said.

'Is it?'

'Yes, I live right on the other side. Where—'

'Where what?'

'—are you?'

'Cabul Street, off Candahar.'

'Oh! The – after Afghanistan.'

'The what?'

'The campaign. You know, like Bloemfontein in Islington, after the Boer War. Victorians very keen on that.'

Nick said nothing.

'I have to memorize them.'

'Right.'

'You know I said I did walks.'

'I'd—' Nick cleared his throat. 'I remember.'

'Thank you.'

'*Thank* you?'

Nick was holding her arm, but at a slight distance, as if he was not sure of her balance, or whether he believed what he'd heard. He chuckled and frowned at the same time. 'What is there to thank me for?' He held her arm just above the elbow and shook it gently. 'You funny thing.'

'Thank you,' Alice shrugged to detract attention from her wandering voice, 'for this evening. For getting me through the play, earlier. You should have had the ASM on book. And for seeing me home.'

'What did you think I was going to do? Apologize to the audience?' He gripped her arm a little tighter and softened his voice. 'Al? Eh? Do a load of drugs with Mart, get in a cab and come back on my own?'

'No. I don't know. I'm sorry,' Alice mumbled and shrugged again, this time with a heave of her shoulders. The effect was to shake Nick off. He stepped back and out of range so that Alice could no longer smell the smoke in his coat or hair.

The mention of drugs – of Martha – had made her smart.

He was looking now not at her but straight down the street, and in his profile – forbearing, stern, with a hook-shaped vein in his temple which rose and sank – she saw impatience. The scar on his neck showed white.

Alice kept going back and forth over her words, her pleading idiocies, as they walked. She stumbled once into the road. Recovering, she sought the neutral ground of places and people they both knew, especially in the old High Street which cupped Cabul and Winders in a crescent of market trade – Notoriani's ice-cream caff, the John Hall Dining Rooms, Denny's shoe-stall; and Val, Den's wife, with her scorched-earth skin and 'naughty trotters'.

It was the sort of tactical talk Nick handled better, but Alice wanted to show willing. It had the desired effect; they slowed to a dawdle and stopped outside the inverted bay of a bath showroom. There was a plumber's merchants further on, but this was the classier point-of-sale, from which all plumbers, and any hint of effort or soil, had been excluded. In the glow of the streetlights, the rows of tubs and implements took on a menacing aspect, and Alice had a momentary vision of hell – of shower attachments come to life, with snapping coils and gargling heads, of acid bubbling on the tiled surround . . .

Nick pointed into the glass, his other hand on her shoulder.

'Do you remember what this used to be?'

Alice shuddered.

'All too well.'

For most of the 90s, Arcady Interiors had been a creperie-cum-dinner-theatre joint called, unironically, La Belle Alliance. You ate up front, watched over by photos of Bob Ladd, Felicity Kendal and assorted Radio Two DJs. Then at nine, the head waiter, Rick Pick, a high-waisted Australian, shooed you through to the matchbox-sized 'theatre', where actors destined never to leave the fringe performed a murder mystery or horror-spoof on a stage six feet wide and four deep. The shows were called things like *Night of the Nearly Dead*, or *The Hills Have Thighs*. They were often surprisingly funny. The food was inedible.

'Blimey. Rick Pick – he wrote a show a week,' Alice said wonderingly. 'I had to sit through months of them.'

'Why's that?'

'Oh, I was sent – I had, you know, friends in them. Sad to say.'

'It's all work. You weren't in any yourself?'

'No.'

Alice laughed.

A freight line crosses Battersea near Winders Road. The trains are rare, nocturnal visitors, and being long and slow they make a lot of noise. One of these rumbling giants now gave Alice a moment to think.

'But I had to go other times, too. Had to review a couple for the *Stage*.'

Nick barked at this, and the weight of his exclamation seemed to carry through the glass. Condemned to watch, as in a trance, Alice thought she saw one of the showerheads move in its chrome cradle.

'Rather you than me. What a crappy rag.' He paused. Among actors, Alice recalled, the *Stage*, with its pages of poignant thanks from cruise-ship crooners to their agents 'for a brilliant, brilliant year!', was, secretly, an index of failure. To buy it was to lower your sights. 'Y'know, if you're going to criticize something, at least do it with passion. Be a what-sisname. Be—'

'Tynan,' said Alice, because it was always him.

'Right. At least he had passion. Not like that nonce Alex Grew or Tory-boy Devereux.' Nick peered deep into the shop, as though his thoughts might just come into focus there. 'I mean, they're all so *bland*. That's what narks me. Don't get me wrong, I'm sure your – yours – were a cut above, but the standard, mostly, is just so blandly *low* and – and ordinary. Don't you think?'

Alice hummed meekly. She'd preferred the frothier conversation, about nothing in particular, with its specific undercurrent.

'Be prejudiced, be as offensive as you like, just don't be ordinary.'

'I suppose most of everything is, though, isn't it?'

'What d'you mean?'

'Well, most shows *are* ordinary. You – critics, anyone – can't help but feel ordinary about them. You can't have too much excellence, or it wouldn't be excellent, would it? Of course everyone tries their best—'

'I don't agree. It doesn't cost anything to be passionate. What's the point of doing anything if you're not passionate?'

Alice, nodding, was unconvinced, for reasons she didn't

care to inspect. Clearly, being 'passionate' could cost you dear. (She also had the fleeting impression that riding your emotions, like the early bird on top of the freight wagons, wasn't the same as getting carried away by them.) And then – a thread of pain wound its way into a coil in the corner of her left eye – then there was the simpler fear of being taken in. 'Oh, love,' Alice could still hear her father saying, when mullet-haired Gary Paddock, with the biker's jacket full of smashed crisps, went back on his word, 'it's not that he doesn't mean it. It's just he doesn't know what it means.'

Nick drew circles on the window.

'Dad nearly had someone's eye out from the *Stage*, once.' He laughed. 'That was before me, mind. Long before. When Les was big.'

Now, thought Alice. I must say something now. He's right. What *is* the point otherwise? Once we're under the bridge. Once this bus has passed.

A 337 with 'Sorry. Not In Service' on it bouldered towards them, took up the refrain of the parting train. Alice shifted her weight. Against a chorus of internal persuaders, she said out loud: 'But it's so hard!'

'What is?'

'Knowing – saying—'

'Knowing what to say?'

Gary Paddock had known, Alice thought, and wished his ghost away. They'd gone for a walk along the Kennet and Avon Canal. The date had been fixed up by friends with good intentions. Just beyond a bridge – one not unlike the bridge in front of her now – Gary had turned to her and said, ''Cos, this isn't going to work, is it? But we may as well enjoy the walk. All right with you?' In her pocket, Alice held a card with wild flowers on it she'd spent days making. Her heart was a raisin of misery. 'Oh no. No, no. That's fine.'

Nick smiled, tapping his chin.

'Knowing what to write. To say,' Alice explained, 'about a play.'

'I don't doubt it.'

Nick took one last look in the window. Then they left and walked in silence for a while. 'I'm not saying it isn't tricky,' he said eventually, less vehemently than before, 'but you know what it's like, if you're on the receiving end. You've worked for six weeks—'

'Or ten days.'

'Or whatever. You've learned your lines, rehearsed. You've got a bit in the tank after previews. You finally get to put the show on, and come the first night there's some git three rows back, refusing to clap, shaking his head and saying – next day – you don't have the presence to carry it. That you're no good.' Nick shook his head and linked arms. 'And you've been served with a repossession order. And your girlfriend isn't returning your calls. And your dog's died.'

Their footsteps were hard-edged under the bridge. Alice had felt uncomfortable earlier on, when Nick mentioned drugs, because she'd never taken or been offered any. It was humiliating to have to concede, even privately, one's ignorance. And yet she had the impression that Nick wanted to atone for this and any other error of tact by making himself appear vulnerable. He'd been cast off, too. That's what his picture of rejection – the girlfriend not returning his calls – meant. He knew what it was like.

For her part, Alice wondered if she believed in what she'd said about excellence. She thought she did. It was defensible. And that, of course, was the problem. That was where, being prepared, she came unstuck.

On the other side of the bridge, Alice couldn't hear her feet.

'It makes it difficult to go on,' Nick added. 'To maintain the illusion.'

'But lots of people think *any* review is good. My dad does. He doesn't read what you or I read. He doesn't take it as criticism. He thinks it's all great.'

'I know. And then the bastard sends you the review!'

At the staggered junction between Cabul and Winders, where one road torqued into the other, Nick slipped his arm around Alice's waist and kissed her. He drew back; pondered her face. Its dark, brown eyes and hard lashes; the simple fringe and delicate mottle of the skin, not pocked but – up close – shot through, like mother-of-pearl.

'So.'

'I don't know.'

'Whatever you want, I want.'

'All right. I – that's nice. All right, then.'

'You've got big nostrils, haven't you?'

*

There'd been an earthquake, Alice realized, with a grasping spasm of memory. That was the headline on the bus. The noise in the street. The grate.

Nick squeezed her back; held her.

There was no rush. They walked slowly around the block.

The streets were average late-Victorian terraces, but like a lot of London of that period, even the lowliest buildings had eclectic flourishes – strips of red-brick dressing, fanlights, terracotta decoration. An end-house might soar into turrets, as in Haselrigge Road. Or here, at the bottom of the steps which led to Alice's flat, there would be sentinel carvings on either side – sleeping lions – like statues meant for a gate-pier.

As they approached, Alice noted her neighbour's chimney

on the ground. It hadn't fallen. It was new and intact, awaiting the roofer, beside a pile of slates.

A particular thing might never happen, Alice reasoned, while she fought the lock, but *some*thing would. Nick stood behind her, scuffing, sniffing. The sounds he made were tender, already reminiscent of sleep. He rested his chin on her shoulder, swallowing.

'Let me have a go,' he said.

*Independent*, 17 September 1999

# Quake Strikes at Heart of London

*Jim Broudie, Home News*

The strongest earthquake to hit Britain for more than a century yesterday rattled buildings and foundations across London and the South-East of England. The quake struck at 19.34 hours GMT just south of the river in the City centre and registered 4.8 on the Richter scale, according to the British Geological Survey.

No severe injuries have been reported. But at the epicentre, in Southwark, cracks appeared in bridges, windows shattered, water mains burst and power supplies were cut, bringing traffic and rail services to a standstill.

London Bridge and Tower Bridge were immediately closed. 'We spotted small fissures in the road surface and upper pilings,' said a spokesman for the Metropolitan Police. 'The impact seems to be minor, but we're taking every precaution.' Surveyors say the bridges will remain closed at least until the end of the week.

'It was terrifying,' said Claire Vaux, a police officer already at the scene. 'The rumbling noise kept getting louder and louder, like a freight train, and windows were popping out of their frames. People were running into the road to get away from the glass. I thought "this can't be happening".'

Canary Wharf Tower and several other Docklands buildings were evacuated after the quake, which lasted between ten and fifteen seconds. A tremor of between 4.5 and 5.1 can cause considerable local damage, admits Bill Alden, a seismologist at the BGS. 'We don't build structures with earthquakes in mind, so a lot of people have had a very lucky escape.'

Unoffical estimates put the immediate cost of repairs at upwards of £500 million, but insurance claims and structural reinforcement over the next two years could swell the figure to as much as £3 billion.

The quake struck at a depth of 1.5 miles and was felt as far away as Mold in Wales and Minehead in Somerset. 'There are a number of shallow faults in the London basin, crossing the Thames, but this tremor seems to have been produced by a much deeper one in the basement rock,' Alden said. 'Britain is on a tectonic plate being squeezed by expansion of the crust in the mid-Atlantic, and the stress field that creates is quite capable of generating shocks from time to time.'

Thursday's quake was equivalent to 1,000 tonnes of TNT being set off, or the yield of a small nuclear weapon. It was the most powerful tremor in the region since 22 April 1884, when an earthquake near Colchester destroyed 400 buildings. The largest earthquake ever recorded in Britain was the North Sea quake of 1931, with a magnitude of 6.1.

London Underground Services were miraculously not affected. 'Only the media is surprised by that,' said a Northern Line spokesman. 'It just goes to show how badly we've been misrepresented *(cont. p 2, col 4)*

# Seven

THEY WERE AWAKE, but with their mouths crushed out of shape by the pillows; sounding, when they spoke, after long pauses in which either one of them might have fallen asleep, as though they had been in the desert for days without water. In this happy, between-worlds state, Nick had wondered what it would be like if people spoke to each other after sex the way actors' friends do after a bad show.

Alice watched a guillotine of streetlight scraping the down on his back while she considered the possibility.

'I thought that was *such* an interesting piece,' she croaked at last.

'And the way you handled it so confidently . . .'

'Have you been *in* much?'

Nick's squeezebox laugh turned into a coughing fit and he had to raise himself up on one elbow to breathe.

'You must be tired,' Alice added, after a pause.

'Takes it out of you,' said Nick. 'Glad I came, though.'

'Well, *you* certainly enjoyed yourself,' and so on.

Alice was not on her usual side of the bed and had nowhere to put her right arm except on the pillow above Nick's head in an attitude expressive of abandon (but actually uncomfortable, because it prevented her neck from lying flat). She took short breaths because she didn't want to make a noise or breathe too heavily, or make him aware of how awake she was.

It seemed remarkable that he was next to her, and at the same time natural. The surprise was in the naturalness, the way a plot sometimes resolves itself and you can see what it has always been perfectly possible to see. How warm it was, too! Alice winced at the memory of the extra duvet on her bed, the slightly pathetic significance of which had not struck her until Nick, with a grunt, threw it aside.

And now she didn't care anyway. Another phrase from 'Love Letters' wormed its way into her head: 'I'm not alone in the night.' Which was true, apart from the fact that it was morning, and Alice could hear the beep-beep of the delivery lorries backing down the High Street, where the stall traders and pensioners with trundle-carts would soon be gathering.

If we both disappeared now, she thought – soothed by the contemplation of a nameless disaster in which, for all its novelty, the recent tremor played no conscious part – I wouldn't mind. I wouldn't be cross at all.

The streetlight switched off, turning the room grey.

Nick's body gave a jolt and he reinflated with a shiver and stretch before settling back down. His right hand moved beneath the pillow.

''s this?'

'What's what?'

''s like—' His voice was thick and squeaky. The hand withdrew; Nick sighingly inspected a plastic mouthguard. 'Like a dental job.' He gave Alice a sly look. 'Why've you got a dental job underneath the pillow?' He squinted. 'You in the Ladies' league?'

'It's to stop me grinding my teeth.'

'You grind your teeth.'

Alice nodded and closed her eyes. She knew he was smiling.

'Why?'

'If I knew that, I wouldn't have to. I just do.'

'You grind your teeth.'

'Bruxism. I'm a bruxer.'

Pretending, she opened one eye and met his blankly comic stare.

'Breakfast and lunch, right—'

'Too early.'

'—make brunch.'

'And?'

'So brunch and sex . . . must be "brux".'

He moved closer.

\*

A while later, Alice was in the cluttered kitchen making coffee and scrambled eggs. She was aware of there being items on the small table one might not want a lover to see: unused charts from Weightwatchers, Wandsworth's final demand for council tax, one of Ray's bruising cards ('Not to worry, I've plenty on'). But the eggs were coming out just as she liked them, with flecks of white and dabs of orange, the traffic droned comfortingly a street away and the person behind her, with the blue underpants and moley back, rubbing his eyes and rearranging his testicles, was a person she could see herself – strange thought – defending. From what, exactly, Alice had no idea, though the hazily implied future romantic obstacle had the interesting effect of returning her deliciously to the present, where the sun through the dirty window was warm on her neck.

She left the stove and went to the sink; turned on the tap. There was a spoon directly beneath it which she did not see.

The water bounced up in a curved jet and onto the front of her dressing gown.

Nicholas stopped scratching, got up from his chair and caught her around the midriff, coaxing her breasts together to make one huge, comical eminence. 'I've got you now,' he said, 'haven't I?'

She turned around, to be held face to face, but Nick yelped at the clingy wetness of the silk and went to fetch a towel from the bathroom.

'I hope I've made enough,' said Alice, when he came back.

'Looks lovely. How many did you put in?'

'I don't know. How many were in the fridge?'

'Seven.'

'How many are there now?'

'None.'

'Just have to eke it out, then,' said Alice simply, angling for a laugh as she buried the toast beneath two enormous mounds of egg.

Nick didn't laugh, but ate instead with round-shouldered concentration, his forefinger guiding the top of his knife.

'This is fan*tas*tic – my favourite thing.'

He paused, while Alice sat down and pushed the table out a little.

'There's loads,' he added presently, and let his eyes wander. They lingered on the Weightwatchers' logo behind the fruit bowl and returned to the plate.

'Of course, you know who could help you with your – ' Nick waved his knife and seemed unwilling to look up – 'eating.'

At the bottom of the stairs, the post thunked onto the mat. Alice took small mouthfuls of her egg, wondering how to respond.

'With the grinding, I mean.'

She coughed. 'No. Who?'

'Dad.' Nick slurped his coffee and frowned. 'He knows hypnotherapists who specialize in that kind of thing. Did a bit of it himself in the past – went into it quite deeply, so to speak. He used to have an act – well, you know.'

'Yes, I do. I saw him. I didn't know he was a hypnotist, though.'

'Where – did you see him?'

'In Minehead. After the Jubilee.'

'We might have been there the same night.'

'I don't think so. Our rabbit didn't have myxomatosis.'

'Right, right.' Nick scratched his armpits. 'What did you think I meant?'

'About what?'

'The grinding.'

Alice flushed a little. He was being artful – putting himself beyond reproach.

'You're cross, aren't you?'

'I'm not cross.'

'Ye-es you are.' Nick clicked his tongue and charged again at the plate. 'See, if I was the sort of person who snuck insults in under the wire like that, I could understand. But I'm not. I'd never do it. It was an accident: I said "eating", I meant "grinding".' He paused. 'You shouldn't over-interpret.'

Alice was delighted by this reproof. Its willingness to voice her inner suspicions gave her unexpected confidence. She could now speak as she felt, which involved saying flatly how astonished she was that Nick had slept with her. How she had only ever gone to bed with fattish men before – well, with one man – because they – he – knew about other fat people and snoring. That's why she hadn't slept properly last night, and was probably a bit on edge. She confessed, too, to being worried about something her sister had said.

Nick put his knife and fork down, and tilted his head attentively, his arms hanging below the table, apparently cut off at the elbow.

'Look,' he interrupted, when Alice seemed on the point of losing patience with herself, 'I wouldn't be here unless I was interested. OK?' Alice nodded meekly. 'And even if I am, as Martha says, "my father's son", so what? She's right. I'm highly sexed, that's all. Actors usually are. But that's not a boast and I'm not my dad. My dad and your mum were adulterers, and I – I have a horror of adultery. I can't explain it. Secondly, I repeat, I would not be here unless I wanted to be. That's the truth, so you don't need to worry.'

This was confirmation of more than Alice had hoped for or anticipated, though she trusted herself enough not to betray her surprise. (When had the affair taken place? During her teens?) Besides, it was not the fact that Tony and Lilian had once been lovers that unsettled Alice (there had almost certainly been others); it was rather the manner in which Nick chose to declare *him*self: the way the unguardedness of the night before now assumed an air of familiarity. At least he appeared to understand the seriousness of betrayal, which impressed Alice, as she believed it would impress most women. And yet the implied solution to that possibility was a frankness of intent and desire at the outset that offered surprisingly little reassurance. Its truth was a cynic's idea of clarity, disowning complication, like clear water above soft sediment.

They washed up and got dressed. Nick had a casting at two and was meeting his father for lunch at Glass House. As they hugged, Alice breathed in the torn lining of his leather jacket, which smelled of charity shops and ink.

'Better go back and get changed,' Nick said. 'See you later.'

He took the stairs two at a time.

'You better had,' Alice called out from the kitchen. The stairwell was silent. 'Change,' she added, just before the door slammed.

*

The review didn't take long to write, probably because Alice's mind was on other things. (This was often the way; the good stuff came to you when you were half distracted. And being too poor to afford a computer helped: it meant you typed more accurately.) She planned to fax it as usual from the Spar on the corner of Falcon Road, and was about to step out of the house when, feeling in her pockets, she realized that Nick still had the keys – her only set.

She rang his mobile. No reply. She left a message; perhaps he was in the bath. They hadn't exchanged addresses, but Alice could have sworn he'd mentioned the number fourteen as they passed Cabul Road. If she went now, she'd find him in. Her hand was on the latch a second time when the phone rang.

She was out of breath as she answered, and could only manage:

'Nick . . .'

'Wrong,' said her mother. 'It's me.' Lilian was using a cordless phone, which buzzed intermittently as though she were waving a cattle prod. 'Still, I'm glad to hear you're alive and not struggling beneath a pile of rubble.'

'What are you talking about?'

'That would be awful.'

'What is it you want – I'm in a hurry.'

'If you went to classes, you wouldn't be so out of breath.'

There was no reply to this. Lilian's insults always took you by surprise. Furthermore, they dared you to expose yourself further by acknowledging the offence given. To 'come out with it'. In this respect, they were of a piece with her favourite mantra, repeated to Alice at frequent intervals and lent a special emphasis by the Separation, that *no one in the family had ever supported her*.

But the truth, as all were aware, was that Lilian's excesses had been supported for too long – and that Alice, the dependably disadvantaged daughter, was the only person who might be relied on not to point it out, because she was scared of her mother. She would only 'make noises', knowing that this was all Lilian required of her.

'Where are you, Mum?'

'Me?' Lilian sounded peevish. 'I'm still at Tanya's.' Tanya was a divorcee living in some style, just outside Bath. 'I'm so glad you're in one piece. People have been hit by falling masonry. Who's *Nick*?'

'He's in *The Tempest* with Martha. I know him through—'

'I was sorry to miss that. Of course, she doesn't ask *me* any more and I don't expect her to. I've got used to it. I don't hear from her. Not a word.' There was an injured silence. 'I just wish you could have some of her luck. That's what you need at the beginning – like I had before I met your father.' The prod buzzed angrily. 'Did it go off well?'

'I think so. Martha was really the best thing in it. I—'

'I'm sure she was.' Lilian's tone hardened. 'Much better to be in a good play than doing some crummy little comedy on television. What's it called again?'

'*Practice Makes Perfect*.'

'I don't know how the writers can let that stuff away from their pens. I suppose there aren't any good scripts any more.'

'Well, I think the way sitcoms get made is quite diff—'

'What about you? Are you still writing? The odd thing?'

Again, Alice gaped, caught between outrage and awe.

She could picture her mother now, standing in gossipy Tanya's expensive kitchen, paid for by a larcenous settlement on which Lilian probably hoped to model her own claims, smoothing her still slim hips, with one elegantly trousered leg tucked behind the other. You had to admire her nerve – and then, as quickly, feel sorry for her. She was not happy. After twenty years of motherhood, her rebirth as a performer, 'lecturing' on presentation skills to incredulous Bath businessmen, had been short-lived. It was the impetus behind her break from Ray and the confining shame she'd always felt at being a doctor-turned-piano-tuner's wife; but few companies, it turned out, needed or could afford her expertise. Like her, they preferred to make it all up as they went along. (She'd never taught before.) More significantly, with the split from her husband of thirty-two years, she had forfeited the allegiance of Martha, the favoured child – a loss Lilian lamented but was pitiably unsuspicious of having brought about by her own bad example. 'It's your life,' was what Alice could never have said out loud, whereas Martha had no qualms.

'I think you've behaved appallingly,' she said bluntly, when Lilian told them on Good Friday that she was leaving Ray. 'And being on your own is going to come as a very nasty shock.'

This had the ring of truth to it.

Lilian was horrified. What had she done to deserve such treachery?

Martha had always been her ally: the silent beneficiary of sighs and mutterings and looks askance when Ray walked into the room, vetoed a carpet or said the Somerset coast was the only place they could afford to go on holiday. Martha wouldn't remember, Lilian whispered, but when they'd had the Practice they used to go abroad. And they could have kept the Practice, too. (Ray had only ever had two fits. Epilepsy was never conclusively diagnosed.)

Then one day, when Martha was fifteen, her view of things changed. She came home from school feeling sick, opened the door with her new keys and found her mother on the half-landing being fucked by the postman.

The two adults didn't spot her at first, and when they did it was too late. Martha forgot about feeling sick. It also dawned on her that the real object of degradation in the family was not her dust-coated father, who laboured away unprofitably in his workshop and drove a turd-like Anglia, but Lilian herself; Lilian, who'd scoffed the idea of authority into oblivion; Lilian, whose liberalism ('I've given you such licence') came with so many strings attached and leading suggestions as to 'what men liked' that, even without the first-hand evidence, Martha could hardly mistake the presence of a sexual competitor.

Nor did she; Martha was pretty, not silly. What she'd seen she'd seen; and this secret, which Lilian, shaking, had begged her to keep, matured with age into a kind of determination. She resolved to play Lilian at her own game, cultivating a mystique by turns coquettish and steely, which her mother had no means of penetrating. When Martha finished at RADA and met Kwame, she began cutting her ties. To Lilian's secret fury, the sexy daughter settled down.

Alice had no such claims on her mother's sympathy – no likeness to make her loss regrettable. She was the slow thinker of the family, the one in whom size and self-consciousness had bred a bitter understanding. (Her mother once said that the sight of her in a pink costume 'put one in mind of Chipperfield's Circus'.)

The 'odd thing' was that such a formative absence of

expectation should have made their recent encounters so very nearly amicable. Mother and child spoke every week: here they were speaking again. Without any burden of obligation on either side, the door had been opened to strangers' charity. Lilian often rang up and talked away in a quietly emphatic, nothing-would-surprise-me-less monotone as though Alice were not a part of the immediate family at all, but a distant cousin of baffling origin. And Alice wondered now what her mother's response would be if she were to tell her about the play, about Nick Glass – her lover's son; the fact that she, Alice, *knew* he was her former lover's son. Lilian would be pleased, if disbelieving, about success on stage. Cool and wise and sceptical about the rest. And hurt.

Alice decided to withhold her news, partly through fear, partly in symmetrical recognition of a lifetime's stifled affection; mostly, deep down, because, after so many years, the promise of that affection, of there being a return on it some day, was still a powerful charm.

'I've just finished a piece – a review.'

'Can't you do more of that?' Lilian cajoled. 'The other's so hard.'

'I'm late, Mum. I'm walking at twelve. I can't afford—'
The prod crackled and cut her off.

'Yes, I've got to go, too,' said Lilian. 'Tanya and I are coming up today, that's why I rang. Will we see you?'

'Would you like to?'

'We can't be late back because the trains are so unreliable.'
Alice marvelled at this compression of logic.

'I'm working tonight,' she said.

'I see.'

'You have to give me a little bit of notice, Mum. I'd love—'

'It was just a thought. Bye-bye, then, darling.' Lilian hated being thwarted, particularly when making a generous gesture. 'You'd better ring Nick.'

*

Conversations with her mother were usually enough to give Alice a week-long headache, but not this morning. Today, a happy decisiveness governed her mood and there was no time to be dissatisfied. She went to Spar and faxed the review; out of habit, she sent it twice: once to *What's On*, and once to the *Independent*, with a note. They didn't use unsolicited notices, but she'd spoken to the Arts man there a year ago and he'd been blandly encouraging.

Around the corner, in Cabul Road, Alice approached No. 14. It was a typical rented property: nicotine net and russet drapes careening off the curtain rail. The front bay was peeling, the PVC frames spotted with damp. Two bins were blown with black bags and bottles. Beneath a wrenched-out battery-operated doorbell the colour of hearing-aids, the tenants' names had bleached and run.

No one answered. From the front upstairs room of the smarter, newly decorated house next door came the sound of energetic humping.

Alice smiled conspiratorially. She'd have to do the walk and spend the day in coffee shops or at Westminster Library, then maybe see a film, poke around the National Gallery and get the keys back when she went to Konditor at eleven – or, wait: a better thought occurred to her. She could find Nick at the agency. He wouldn't object, surely. She'd call at reception and wait. She didn't want to see Tony and risk looking pushy.

Alice's good humour persisted during the walk. A small group of five tourists remained meekly attentive all the way from Museum Row up through the Park to Lancaster Gate. They listened, wonderingly, outside the Science Museum, as she made topical references to London's seismic history. Her 'facts' were gleaned from the more excitable morning news-papers, which featured diagrams of where the 'inferred fault' was thought to lie beneath the city.

'It probably starts somewhere beneath Springfield Mental Hospital in Tooting, pushing deeper and running northwards to the river,' she said. 'Which is a nice coincidence because during the last great quake, of 1884, a medical student at St Bart's went mad when he saw a skeleton start to dance and had to be locked up – in Springfield. Panic ensued. People threw up on Oxford Street. The Old Bailey caught fire. Homes were destroyed.' (Who could contradict her?)

They looked for signs of more recent damage. The whole idea seemed absurd, illusory – branches and twigs that could have snapped off naturally – until they came to the half-finished Diana Princess of Wales Memorial Walk, which had several cracks in it. The raised bronze plaques that marked the new route had slid off the path and onto the grass where, more than ever, they resembled landmines.

After the walk, Alice dialled 192 at a call-box to get Glass House's number, rang it and discovered it was close by, in Orme Court. On her way there, as she passed the idlers, skaters and old couples halving their sandwiches, she had her first moment of doubt. All morning long, the ordinary accomplishment of having been held had lifted her spirits. But beside the fact of being noticed privately, the public equivalent – display, acclaim, vindication – seemed suddenly banal. And vulgar. Now that she had the chance, at last, to see an agent, albeit on a spurious personal pretext, she couldn't bring herself to take it. If only one could perform *un*noticeably! That would be the answer. Alice thought disconnectedly of *Don't Mind Me*, and of the day's big news story: the uncloaking of Melita Norwood, a great-grandmother from Brent – and KGB operative.

She shivered. The street was full of spies and disappearing acts, right down to the Latino boy by the Amex Bureau de Change, shouting out, 'R-hoom, r-hoom!' at some of the kinder faces pushing past him. He was waving a page from *Loot*. His voice pursued Alice as she hurried on down the Bayswater Road. When she couldn't hear it any more, his distress and panic became obvious. She doubled back, but it was too late. He'd gone.

*

The entrance to 9 Orme Court, through a Venetian arch, was high Queen Anne – the statelier version of Alice's terrace in Battersea, with balconies, ribbed chimney stacks, elaborate bays and that striving for a combined effect which might be thought at once comfortable and extreme, aesthetic and genteel.

A staircase rose on the right with painted white in-steps; the names of the tenants (two to a floor) were stencilled on plaques above heavy red doors: Davey & Wing Assoc.; Hudson, Grey, Sporringer; Mr G. Clopes, FRCS. A lift with a grille groaned upwards. It wobbled as it passed each floor and, finally stopping a foot short of the fourth, appeared to wait for the building to subside.

Alice stepped out. The agency was to her left, its door closed.

One of the satisfactions of growing up is that the bogey figures of childhood – mad uncle, insinuating family friend – no longer have the power to bind us. Heroes and villains contract in size to match our expanded sense of self. There are exceptions to this rule, however, and Alice's damp palms told her that Tony Glass was one of them: one of a special breed, not caricatured by their own false modesty, like Robert Ladd, but somehow empty of faith, ungraspable. While in the presence of his son, Alice had felt no anxiety, for Nicholas commanded her attention. Only now, on her own, when she least expected it, she felt uneasy – smelt Porlock and tar on the rocks; saw diesel on the harbour water. A hand moved between her and the sun.

A flustered voice buzzed her in.

On the other side of the door, affable disorder reigned. In a large room with casement windows, gluey carpets, PCs and drifts of files, books, photos, discs, Alice saw several young men and women working and walking with an air of delayed purpose. They were not of an age to remember many of the people or productions on the walls nearest the door – bills from the Pleasure Garden, a snap of Pete and Dud, Graham Chapman dressed as a carrot, a signed poster of Alan Rickman in *The Lucky Chance* (which Alice had seen at the Royal Court as a stage-struck fifteen-year-old) – but, if you passed further into the room, nodded on by the phone-bound secretary, the clients and trophies grew international, came up to date. Music and film made their entrance: here was Tony Bennett in a pub with star-struck locals, and a fur-coated Peter Sellers on the bonnet of a Rolls. Good God, there was Neville, shiny and red in a thrift-shop tux, with Jarvis Cocker, looking as usual as if he'd stepped out of a peep-show. This far end of the room was friendly, too, though one sensed the stakes were that much higher, the contracts more lucrative. (The odd man out, apart from Neville, was Leslie B, in a bar in drag. His caption read, simply, 'Barrington'.) But the string tying it all together never showed. Where was the man responsible? To whom did these people defer?

Nick and an older man came out of an office leading off to the left.

Nick wore a tense expression, Alice thought, grey under the eyes; and as he saw her without quite seeming to see her – only now, slowly, frowning – she cursed her naivety. Imagine: turning up to a new lover's place of work! Unannounced! Restraining orders had been issued for less.

It was too late to extricate herself. She'd have to brazen it out, neutralize his perplexity, and pretend to be angry.

'I'm sorry,' she said.

'You always say that.'

'I can't get in without my keys. You've got my front-door keys.'

Nick checked his pockets absently. He was expensively dressed in a pinstripe jacket, white shirt and moleskin trousers. She knew before he said it that the keys would be with his other clothes. He'd gone home to change. She should have guessed. Why hadn't she rung again? Why didn't she have a phone, like everyone else, so that he could ring her back?

'Bit of luck,' he said, fishing the keys out. 'Get some more cut, I would.'

Alice had a moment's inspiration. 'Then you can have a pair.'

'Whatever. Cool.' He turned. 'Dad, this is Alice—'

But Tony Glass was taking a call at a desk nearby.

'Al, look, I've got to go.'

'You look so nice,' she said. 'I'm sorry I came.'

'I am nice, I think,' Nick replied innocently. 'See you.'

And out he strode. The other agents waved goodbye.

\*

'The lady in question,' Tony remarked into the phone, 'is standing here, in front of me.' He looked up, mouthed the word 'Leslie' and lowered his eyes.

A voice babbled dementedly, half-corncrake, half-pixie.

'I will certainly tell her, yes. Now get some rest . . . No, I don't know. Les, I don't know yet. You leave him to me.' Tony Glass put the phone down. 'That was your friend and mine, the erstwhile spirit of music hall. He's so pleased with his review, and with *you*. It's fired him up, apparently – inspired him to finish his book.' Tony sighed. 'But let's not get excited. He's been writing it for the past twenty years. It's full of promise, I suppose. You could say that.'

They talked about Leslie. Alice was gratefully distracted to begin with, and then drawn in. It was as though she had made an appointment to have this very discussion. The fact that she could be treated so confidentially by a man of influence she had not seen for twenty years herself was flattering. It mitigated the evil of annoying his son (if Nick had been annoyed; she couldn't tell). It also reminded her that in this profession, for many different reasons, people treated chance as a deliberate force: the luck it was your job to make.

Alice could see photostats of deals from *Entertainment Weekly* on the desk nearest her. Every mention of Glass House was underlined, and the sums of money in a number of stories were eye-watering.

She wondered, by contrast, what could ever be done for a dropout like Leslie Barrington. But, as Tony reminisced, things fell into place.

'I wanted to do something for him, I suppose, that's why I sold him to Adrian on the back of – ah – Bob's involvement. And he's a friend. As well as being the most completely gifted performer I've ever met. We've known each other for forty-seven years – almost as long as I've known your father. A total liability, of course. Rude and alcoholic, but there you go. Some people only have the constitution for failure.' Tony bounced his palms against the edge of the desk. 'He used to be very well known in the circles that were thought to matter. And theatre people have good memories, because that's where their performances live. Has he – spoken about it? His act?'

'No. We've – I hardly know him.'

'Oh, you should see it before he keels over.' Tony chuckled, and pulled at the hair tufting over his collar. Alice had seen hair like that before, and recently, but couldn't remember whose. 'He does a few gay pubs still. It's an education, truly. You ask any of the old variety stars, or anyone from the sixties, and they'd tell you. Ronnie Corbett knew him. John le Mesurier. Cleese. Stanley Baxter. Of course, he was always a bit green about Stanley, all that fuss about those legs.' Another pause. 'Anyway, he wanted to give it one last go – the serious stuff, acting – before he packed it in. So I said I'd try.'

Alice began to feel that she had been wrong about Tony Glass. He was a trim, vigorous, jumpy man in his late sixties – not at all the operator of memory. His heavy-lidded eyes rarely met yours, but when they did it was with sadness, as if to say, 'Well, this is it.' The skin was dry and lined, the hair a poignant, badgered black. He looked as though he'd just taken off layers of make-up. His advocacy was touching. He evidently saw Leslie as someone who'd given himself to his art in a kind of romantic pact. It hadn't worked out, but he'd been nobly damned, and Tony respected that.

A French accent hailed him from the speaker-phone.

'Excuse me,' he said, and was silent a while.

'The answer is no,' he said at last. He spoke in a whisper

now, perched on the desk, rolling a pencil back and forth. His eyes bulged. 'All parties involved gave responsible undertakings to limit the risks. You have the money you asked for; foreign rights stay with IEM for thirty-four. You can afford his fee. I don't want to hear – Nicole, *non, je m'en fous de cette histoire. Les biens étaient distribués pour que tout le monde en partage également. Ça est tout dans le passé. Ces négoces sont bien finis, comme tu le sais bien. Alors.*'

His anger vented, Tony's eyelids dropped like blinds. He ushered Alice into his office and went to a leather-topped table piled high with papers and equipment.

'There,' he said, sitting down. 'That's better. Now we can talk.'

He was quite the actor-manager after all, Alice perceived – so reconciled to doubleness that neither the poet nor the hustler in him suspected the existence of the other. Behind glass partition walls, the room was quiet.

Tony Glass asked Alice a few questions and she answered them directly. In return, he was honest about her prospects. They discussed provisional terms and conditions. He levelled his gaze when she talked about the need to be chosen.

'That can certainly play on your mind,' he said. 'If you let it.'

# Eight: *Leslie*

I saw him from the back at first, getting off the same train as me at Windsor and Eton Riverside, so I trailed him into the Gents'. He had on a Hardy Amies check suit and expensive-looking dark brown shoes. The grey hair was clipped short and he strode along bolt upright, head and shoulders balanced, as though he were carrying a tray. I'd have put him in service, or the City, if it weren't for the Italian shoes, which made me think 'villain'. (Tony's crowd at the Gardens had a smattering of 'civic businessmen' and I'm not sure there wasn't an element of competition between them to see who could swell the most convincingly. We were all smart dressers back then – only slummers from the West End party circuit or from television wore jeans – but the villains made a point of standing out.) This one was a naff, I decided, a paintwork-starer, and as I buttoned up I consoled myself with the thought of the fruiterer from Fortnum's who'd taken to parking his van outside the stage door on Thursdays on his way back from the castle. I glanced in the bassinette mirror and shook the water from my hands. Glanced again, nearly screamed, and left the hot tap running.

No sign of the fruiterer, thank God, which meant I had half an hour alone in my dressing room to contemplate the dead.

It wasn't possible, it couldn't *be* – but, of course, the impossibility made it real. Only last week, someone in the stalls had had a heart attack and died. I'd been put off my stroke, frankly. The audience's reaction, from where I was standing (stage right), seemed unconvincing; when the ambulance team carried him out, the man's chest was still moving. Death lacked credibility, but a resurrection – now *that* I could believe in. My father, the returning soldier, a living ghost! It was already a story by Zola or Poe. (I began sketching the plot.) Seeing that his family have mourned and forgotten him, our hero shakes the Worcestershire sod from his heels, takes a new name and disappears for ever into the gloaming. Until nearly goosed by his own son in a railway lavvy . . .

I could never tell my mother. The shock would kill her, or else she'd die laughing. I suppose I suppressed the obvious truth: that he'd taken off or deserted or stayed in London after the war, and she'd fed the whole of Bewdley a lie. Rather than dwell on his guilt, however, I decided to connive in his concealment. What did he do? Where did he work? To whom, if anyone, was he attached? My costume hung sulkily on the rack, and looking at it I realized, suddenly, that he'd left me, too. For some reason, I remember smiling at the thought while at the same time wanting air. I bounded up through the theatre's damp rat-runs to the pass door and out into front-of-house.

There he was, buying a ticket. A few things about his face had changed, but I recognized the joined eyebrows from his wedding photograph. I turned, went backstage and twitched the curtains. He was sitting on his own (he was early), under the shadow-line of the circle, pouring himself a cup of tea from a tartan thermos. Then he picked up the playbill. My name was on it.

When I got back to the dressing room, Robert was half

undressed, having a shave. He knew about me, of course, and liked to tease, finding ways to prolong his semi-nakedness, forcing me into long discussions about the various things we could do to lift our scenes together, asking my advice, talking almost by way of an apology for his physical beauty.

I was usually happy to indulge.

'What ails you, Leslie?' Robert said, turning his head from the mirror so that I could see his hairy chest and belly. His nipples were large and never erect, protected by all the fuzz perhaps, though the cell we shared was always freezing. I was so lost in thought that I nearly reached out and tweaked one of them.

'He was on the train,' I mumbled. 'He can't be here *just* to see the play.'

'You're rambling,' Robert said. 'Hope you haven't got my cold.'

Robert didn't have a cold. He was the picture of health. So of course he pretended to be a hypochondriac.

'It's taken me weeks to shake it off. I still feel wretched. I *look* dreadful.'

'What's your earliest memory?' I asked.

'My mo – nanny's tits in the bath.'

Another difference between us.

*

Mine was of my dad, Ernest, waving and laughing goodbye. As a child, I liked patting the tops of milk churns huddled together on the farmer's cart. The cart stopped at the top of Cleobury Road and Dad used to walk me out to the churns. The empty ones gave a gong-like shimmer and rattle when you hit them, the full ones nothing beyond the slap of your palm. One day, as I was patting away, the cart began moving. I looked back to see Dad with his bushy eyebrows, big front teeth and cigarette, laughing at me. I liked the sensation to begin with – the grain of the road was a blur close-to, the milk sloshed like water in a cave – and then the sun went in and we speeded up. Our house got smaller as the cart drifted into the shadow of the tall hedgerows. And a few years later, of course, Dad was called up and disappeared altogether. I was five.

One of the few times my mother mentioned him afterwards was in relation to sex, though I can't imagine how we got around to talking about that. (It certainly had nothing to do with Beatrice.) She said, 'Ernest was always considerate. He let me take my teeth out first.' I never saw the yellow telegram, but she did give me a photograph, and kept the suit. A fortune-teller once told me that I was firm-hearted. It's true that I'm not sentimental. After the initial shock of seeing him again, I did not break down and weep. The impression he made on me was one of vague fallibility: something to do with his attractiveness and manliness set against the inwardness of the thermos and the tea-pouring. He'd had no reason not to like me, I decided – which was why he'd finally sought me out. Perhaps he felt that there'd been an omission of sorts, and here, now, was the opportunity to set the record straight.

I was good that night. *The Circle*, Maugham's sobering drama of impetuosity and regret across the generations (a bit like *Lady Windermere's Fan*, without the tedious wit), held more meaning than usual, and I was conscious of trying not to make my lines too pointed. I didn't look in his direction until the curtain call. But although I couldn't see clearly over the footlights, I was positive he'd gone by the end. I raced back to the dressing room, rubbed a towel over my face and caught up with him in Datchet Street.

'Excuse me,' I called out, as he approached the station

turnstile. Heads turned in the small queue forming, eyes vexed or curiously disappointed. And again, 'Excuse me,' louder and closer, to make sure of his attention.

When he looked back, from the other side, I could see he didn't know me. My father was perfectly unflustered, moved his head back with a kindly frown as who should not when accosted by an out-of-breath and slightly overweight young actor wearing too much foundation.

'Sir?'

'You're Ernest,' I spluttered.

He smiled.

'A state of being celebrated—' he began, and then stopped. 'I'm afraid my name is Frank.'

'No, it isn't.'

'I'm so sorry, young man. You've mistaken me for someone else.'

I said that I had not, and the more I studied my father's features, the more certain I became. A guard came over to wave on the last stragglers.

'By the by,' said the man who called himself Frank, 'may I congratulate you on a most convincing performance?'

He slammed shut the first door of the nearest carriage and sat facing away.

In the Officer's Watch, my resolve weakened after two pints and a couple of chasers (if a show goes down at ten fifteen, there's nothing for it but to drink quickly). I told Robert all about my encounter, secure in the knowledge that the dissimilarity of our childhood origins prevented us from empathizing too deeply. He gave me his 'I'm really listening' look – a right-between-the-eyes stare that failed to make contact by about six feet – and I tried not to imagine him interrupting me with a passionate kiss.

'He doesn't sound like a very pleasant character,' Robert

said at last. 'I should put him out of your head if I were you.'

This was like telling someone under gas to look lively, but I said nothing. One should never be surprised by a lack of interest. Besides which, none of us at Windsor, with all our combined decades of experience, would have dreamed of telling Robert Ladd to shut up. Theatrical troupes often need a favourite son and this young man was ours. In fact, he was only a year younger than me – I was thirty-five and he was thirty-four – but he looked younger. Against the purity of his skin, his hairiness seemed almost stuck-on. He wore shirts that were too big for him and moved about in a haze of goodwill. It wasn't just that he was pretty (Dirk Bogarde crossed with Peter O'Toole), a bit like Tony, only without the grey streaks and agitated manner, or that he mentioned Dirk and Peter as if they were close friends, or that his university education intimidated us. And if the rest of us had turned up to rehearsals at half-past ten, we'd have been sacked on the spot. It was something else: a simpler superstition. Some people are the embodiment of luck, or fate. Cowed by our own self-awareness, we salute them for their lack of it. (All except Tony, who back then hated Bob: they'd been up for the same part – in *The Circle*. The way Tony tells it, on the day he auditioned he fluffed every speech, whereas Bob – who'd been listening in the wings – *introduced* a stutter in order to make Teddy, his character, seem more sympathetic. And of course the false stutter won: it sounded like a *real* impediment.)

Robert Ladd came to Windsor Theatre Royal with his head full of Peter Brook and *Marat/Sade*. At the read-through for *Lear*, he treated us all to an impromptu lecture on the *Verfremdung* effect of Lear's madness and its bearing on Artaud's 'violent subjective experience'.

'I had one of those, once,' said Skip Henshaw, the director.

Poor Skip. He'd been brought up on the circuit, and spent the war in a CO camp near Trowbridge. I dare say he knew plenty about *Verfremdung*, and even more about Battenburg and where you could get two for the price of one. He was also a first-rate putter-on of shows, with hundreds of plays at his fingertips and a knack for making you feel from the off that your performance was in the can – but he, too, surrendered in the presence of the anointed.

'Robert, dear,' he pleaded one day, 'I'm so fascinated by your – approach. Yes. Do you really think the paper bag helps? We can't hear your lovely voice speaking those lovely words . . .'

'"When will you see",' came the aggrieved reply from inside a Lipton's carrier. ' "When will you SEE / When will you ever UNDERSTAND?" '

There were a number of unusual props in that production of 'terrifying images'. When, for example, Edgar brings Gloucester to the cliff edge (Act Four, Scene Five) and points out the samphire-gatherer ('dreadful trade!'), Robert argued hard for the Fool to come on as a silent choric figure, brandishing a huge quantity of the said vegetable. We pointed out that samphire was rather hard to come by these days (actually, you could get it at Covent Garden), but Robert, who didn't know what it was anyway, got very excited.

'Don't you see,' he said, with the enthusiasm of one who has only just had the idea himself, 'it doesn't have to be samphire! The image is already absurd! It could be a huge cabbage or lettuce! Or a pile of carrots!'

We managed in the end to convince him that the efficacy of an image lay in its seductive properties, and that there was a fine line between the attraction of curiosity and the creation of utter bewilderment. He settled for a small tin of creamed spinach, which I, playing Gloucester, wore as an amulet.

Robert was ever keen to get to the Truth of a Scene. In the theatre, this means simply 'please listen to me', which we did because he was so enviably innocent. Truth, anyhow, was his rallying cry. The other – a close relative – was versatility. 'Let me try it another way,' he used to say to Skip. 'I want to do it differently.' And each time the speech was identical.

I remember listening to him narrate *Peer Gynt* in the 1970s. Every syllable was an ovation. He gave an interview about Grieg and Ibsen in the *Sunday Times*, in the course of which he explained why he'd decided to give Peer a Yorkshire accent. In fact, it was a travesty of an accent, the kind a lucky star almost wills you to overlook. The audience, judging from the laughter in the bar at half time, were quite prepared to do so. They were applauding him for being a frilly old blouse with a big booming voice. Nowt wrong wi' that. The trouble is, Bob thought it was something else.

I should make it clear at this point that I'm not jealous. I'm just aware of my own limitations. If I were a painter, I'd be Rousseau: slightly inadequate, to tell the truth, but able to make of that inadequacy a recognizable tableau. The core of my act, of Mrs B, is ignorance, after all – the ignorance of habit. It's like driving, or playing an instrument. I know what I'm doing. I don't know why.

*

The other uncomfortable truth is: you know if you're good; you *don't* know if you're not. *Because no one you trust will ever tell you.* That's why the world is full of gifted amateurs and dismal so-called professionals. Well, there were plenty of the former at Tony's pub and, thank God, none of the latter.

When Tony took over the Keys to Vauxhall, it was, as they say, on the floor. We first went there on a Friday evening in high summer, and the welcome was lunar. The cigarette machine was empty, the pub trophy-cabinet bare. The lights, all two of them, with pink inverted cupcake shades, dangled from the ceiling on what looked like a couple of stripped veins. Above the 'Bar Wines' shelf, behind the solitary bottle of Cinzano, a foxed sign advertised non-existent Bell's whisky. We ordered our pints and the proprietor scowled. He had no hair apart from the ginger stuff in his ears, no teeth and a neck which sprouted six inches beneath his shoulder blades, like one of the lookers in a medieval bestiary. Apart from that he was Marlon Brando. On the inside of the toilet door, a rash of stickers suggested that we Keep Britain White.

Tony was dauntless. I could see him hatching one of his plans, nursing the thought, almost changing shape. Eyes bright, teeth bared and clenched, he whisked his way around the room with mimsy footwork alarmingly reminiscent of the MC in Cradley, and then scuttled over to the landlord. (The borrowed trait was characteristic: quite often I see Tony and fail to recognize him.) They spoke in low voices. Of course, Tony never says what he wants exactly; it's what *you* could have that interests him.

The landlord shook his head. The look of ogreish hope on his face faded into one of sad paternal indulgence. He said, 'Son, I wouldn't wish it on my worst,' and Tony school-boyishly dropped his eyes. He continued looking to one side as though his thoughts were irretrievably far away. One of his fingers happened to be pointing at the landlord's glowing cigarette. The landlord noticed, seemed struck by the fact and listened a while longer. I heard Tony say, 'If that's all right with you'; which, before too long, it was.

Amazing Ant came over with another pint. I tried to

appear enthusiastic, but my face wobbles when I'm not confident.

'Cheer up, Les,' he said. 'This place'll be the making of you. Marie Lloyd used to sing here. Can't say fairer than that.'

He'd found my weakness – the one that afflicts most cabaret acts. A single invocation of an illustrious forebear, and destiny is your friend. As I drank (the landlord had to send round to the Duke for the beer), Tony talked our dreary surroundings into a state of dazzling refurbishment.

The semicircular room in which we sat was half of an old song hall built on the site of the gates to the Vauxhall Pleasure Gardens. There were two entrances, one either side of the curved outer wall. The high black ceiling was supported by six iron pillars with griffins' feet at the base; beneath a Formica veneer, the bar was made of anciently stained oak.

'I don't see a stage,' I said.

'Behind you,' Tony whispered. 'The whole back wall is false. It won't take half an hour to come down. You see the beading three feet up from the ground?'

I saw it.

'That's not beading. It's the stage's leading edge. There's forty square feet back there full of rubbish. Nip into the lav, stand on the seat and have a look. Imagine curtains and lights, Les. I tell you, Winstone's and LaRue's will be *green*.'

'How much do I get?' I snapped, trying to sound hard-nosed.

'What do you want?' he replied – a much harder question to answer. One of his hands was doing something strange with the rim of the glass. I knew better than to look, and thought instead of Robert and the way his manner assumed success; of the way he spoke to women and then, consolingly, to me.

'We'll need a piano,' I said, 'if you want singers'; and Tony, nodding, asked if I had any idea who could play it.

\*

I had, though the man was barely of age, and I balked at the idea of being connected to him 'like that'. Tony wouldn't have minded; then again, lots of people said they didn't mind poofs, who did. Joe Orton could joke in the West End about homosexual thieves and we all knew the bogs in Peter Jones that catered, but in 1966 social gatherings were still underground.

There were hardly any pubs in London for the discerning gentleman: the only two I knew of were the Bolton in West Ken and the Cup and Ball in Percy Street, off Tottenham Court Road. Above the latter, on Sunday evenings, meetings of the Music Hall Chorus convened. These were, obviously, masked balls – coded assemblies of gay men, in which the code, or the mask, meant something in its own right. That's what I liked about the MHC. We were in love with Music Hall! And those who weren't to begin with – the shy teachers and married men; the grocers and butchers and plumbers and coalmen; the Guardsmen and bankers and dockers and cooks; even the off-duty coppers – were hooked by the end. Like all converts, in fact, they tended to be the most enthusiastic. I remember one naff at seven in the evening, all on his own, muttering in the corner about perverts being everywhere these days; how you couldn't get away from them. Now, you had to be careful with his sort. You had to decide, quickly, whether they'd come looking for men, or trouble. Not much of a choice, if you ask me. Anyway – Vera Vignette, our hostess and a former munitions inspector at the Woolwich Arsenal, patted him on the shoulder and gave him a drink; just the drink, mind you, no chat. We considered it the height of bad manners to force any attentions. And by last orders our reluctant guest thought he was Ida Barr. We had him on stage in a muffler and earrings singing, 'Oh, You Beautiful Doll'. Nice voice, too.

You could argue that we swapped one facade for another. And you'd be right, if pointlessly so. Because there's no joy to be had in stripping people bare, and no kindness either. The real person is like the real cause of unhappiness, a receding horizon, the cart that rolls away. One thing we didn't do was 'queen it'; each act, musical or comic, had substance – a shape. Granted, such things are on one's blind side, but I was never aware of self-loathing in the performances. We shared, *au contraire*, the vanity of the elect.

Concealment was reserved for the great outdoors. Coming out of the tube on the corner of Oxford Street and Tottenham Court Road, I liked to watch people on their way to the pub. Which of the streaming hundreds would turn left at Percy Street? And of those who turned, how many would turn sharp right again into a doorway with rust-red linoleum stairs? Ashamed visitors (closet cases) were conspicuous. Smoking quickly all the way from the tube, with squints and shivers inappropriate to the season and light, they would stop passers-by and ask for directions to the Blue Post, or to anywhere – real or fictitious – that wasn't their true destination. Casual shoppers declared themselves a little later on, by first walking past the pub and then pondering, three doors down, the contents of a grubby stationer's. One in ten doubled back rather too fast, like Charlie Chaplin rewound; the rest ambled on around the block, smiling at basements, drains and restaurant menus until, on their second orbit, an exasperated gravity sucked them in. Habitués were invisible, coming out or going in. We moved and lived in the blink of an eyelid.

I missed Neville to begin with. That is, I saw and ignored him. He had bad acne, a huge head with visibly unwashed pudding-basin hair – I mean, visible from the entrance to Great Russell Street, where I was loitering – and a shrunken black suit that showed his lower shins, filthy white socks and *yellow* shoes. He looked like one of H. G. Wells' tripods, only with a leg missing, so naturally I had him down as a nut from the YMCA. Then I ran into him again, this time outside the pub, where he'd stopped a proper stranger and was pointing at the sign. The stranger nodded suspiciously. Alas, the bipod belonged to us.

We were not, to begin with, very welcoming. Though our personal claims were few, we appreciated effort. But this spotty teenager had made none, and besides, he seemed too young. Vera asked him his age and was about to throw him out when an attractive short man, who looked familiar, said he'd vouch for him – that he'd come to hear him play. The spotty boy's name was Neville Clute, apparently, and he was already a Licentiate of the Royal Academy.

Well, he came in very handy as an accompanist. (Usually it was Vera or whoever else could bang out a few chords.) He knew everything, or picked it up from the tune. Between songs, he peeled and ate oranges, which he'd brought with him stuffed into a music case. He never once looked back at the room, or acknowledged our applause. Vera kept coaxing him to take a bow, but he wouldn't take the hint. He sat to one side and patted his hair.

We were still giving Vera a rousing send-off for her coloratura rendition of 'Why Am I Always the Bridesmaid?' when somebody shouted out, 'Let's hear some proper music'; and Neville, who'd just finished another orange, launched straight into 'The Lost Chord' by W. S. Gilbert. We all sang along: 'Seated one day at the organ / I was weary and ill at ease / As my fingers wandered idly / Over the ivory keys.' And as Neville neared the end ('the sound of a great Amen!'), he turned his head towards us for the first time to reveal a mouth full of orange-peel teeth. After that, he played Schubert's Impromptu in E flat – the one Françoise Rosay trills through in *Quartet*. In the first marcato section, the teeth made another appearance and Neville's short friend practically wet himself.

At the bar in the interval, I asked our prodigy where he'd got the idea – a silly question I'd never have been able to answer myself – and he said, 'What idea?'

The short friend giggled and bought some drinks.

'Thank you, Dudley,' said Neville, accepting a lemonade.

I'm afraid it's possible that I squeaked. I mouthed 'Dudley Moore' at Vera across the bar, and a few of us tried to slink him into a corner. He was already famous from *Beyond the Fringe* and his association with Peter Cook (they were about to do the first series of *Not Only But Also*) and the Establishment in Greek Street but Dud's piano skits were a separate legend in musical circles. They were in the older variety tradition of mad amateurism and mock opera. I wanted to hear *Die Flabbergast* again and said so, offering him our poky stage – a bay window, scabby upright and two dust-wrinkled aspidistras. You couldn't have done this in grander professional circumstances; no one good wants to be treated like a performing monkey. But in a club or society the atmosphere of mutual appreciation makes a request less impertinent. Sadly, he refused.

'You don't need me,' he said. 'You've got your own genius.'

They'd met a few months ago, at St Paul's.

'I was walking past one Sunday,' Dud explained, 'and I saw there was this recital on. I had a terrible hangover, so

I thought, you know, in for a penny. Can't get any worse. And it was all the Bach I used to play in college, with a load of other stuff no one really does much – Sweelinck, Daquin. The Daquin *Noëls*, Nev, d'you remember? With just that fat reed and a few mixtures. And some outrageous Max Reger – y'know, Janet's dad. Big influence.'

Vera gasped. 'Janet? Janet *Reger*? How fascinating. Does she write too?'

'Oh yeah. Yeah, well known. *Les Catalogues*. Tiny pieces, mostly . . .'

Neville frowned.

Somehow they got back to Bach, via reliable corsetry, and by the time they started on Great Pedal Solos of the Baroque, I was lost. Musicians speak a different, private language. It was like watching two kittens with a ball of string, both absorbed until the ball unravels.

Dudley left before the second half. He nudged me on the way out and said, 'For Christ's sake, give him some work.' I nearly replied, 'Well, why don't you, if you think he's so good?' Then I remembered that it's the ball the kittens are interested in, not each other.

At a stretch, the MHC might have been considered a way in to what was left of the cabaret circuit without being itself a viable source of income. We could only pay stars out of the five-bob entrance at the door and the bar, and even then they had to be doing it for love. If they weren't, things could get sticky. Kenneth Williams came along and was rude. He brayed and squawked at me as Mrs B, but was actually furious because we didn't like 'Crêpe Suzette'– a nonsense song in French which later became his talk-show party piece. (Hardly anyone found it funny. People laughed at Ken because they knew he expected them to.) I heard him on the phone downstairs afterwards: 'I've never played to such a

rotten lot of queens, Lou. It's enough to give you connip-
tions.' And very occasionally, an agent from Charing Cross
Road crept in, if Peter Rogers or Joan Littlewood was cast-
ing. My own agent at the time, Trevor Pedley of T. S. Pedley
Artistes Ltd, would bring round the casting directors for
ABC, ATV and the Beeb, who declared themselves to be
aficionados of the 'old school', but were clearly baffled by it.
I doubt if their idea of pub entertainment went much beyond
'Oom-pa-pa' from *Oliver!*. It was that, or satire, or nothing.
They took one look at Neville, winced and whispered the
word 'radio'.

Well, why not? Among pros, radio was still the place to
be. Neville was introduced to Steve Race, who was about to
present the first series of *My Music*, and got a slot for several
weeks accompanying guests on other shows – *Woman's Hour*
were very keen, I seem to recall. My BBC pitch had been
queered when I threw up over a mike in the Paris Studios,
but I was pleased for the MHC's protégé, whom we had all
begun to regard with uncomplicated affection.

Like us, he needed the money. There were no grants for
the Royal College of Organists, however impoverished the
student, and for reasons I thought too sensitive to probe,
Neville said he expected nothing of his parents.

'It's so silly,' I said to him, in what I hoped was an
obliquely sympathetic way. 'I mean, it's not as if we'd
invite them into the bedroom if we were normal. What we
do behind locked doors – what difference can it make to
them?'

'They'll get over it, I expect.'

'Ask no questions, tell no lies.'

Neville looked thoughtful.

'And you should never lock the door – in case of fire.'

Obtuse to the point of insightfulness, with an intense but

short-lived grasp of shame, Neville has always done and said what he likes. The result, if neither ambitious nor wise, is a person it is commendably difficult to disappoint.

He helped clear up after his first MHC meeting and lunged at me across the room when we were alone. I gave him a tray of soapy glasses to rinse out.

'It was worth a try,' he said.

*

Meanwhile, my agent despaired of me. I fell between two stools. The business didn't know if I was a serious professional actor or a light comedian, and the light comedians couldn't tell if Mrs B was written or 'devised'. Was she drag, in which case why didn't she flounce like Danny and tell jokes, or was she risqué and uncanny, like Barry, in which case where was the cruelty, the hook?

'Monster or Treasure, Les – how does she see herself?'

This last one was put to me by a young television producer from Cambridge called Julian. He hadn't seen my act himself, he told me (though he'd heard good things), but one of his scouts, mysteriously absent from the interview, felt that I didn't put enough distance between myself and the mask. Julian jabbered on about the Greeks for a bit, and then asked the monster/treasure question. I said that Mrs B was too tipsy to see herself as anything much, and neither did I, come to think of it – the point about masks being that they stuck. He said that it was nice to meet me and he looked forward to the Pleasure Gardens' opening. My agent, when I told him, said that it was nice knowing me, and he looked forward to £800 in back fees. His parting words were, 'Never make powerful people feel small, Leslie. If you do, they are that much less likely ever to suck your cock.'

I thought about this in relation to Robert Ladd and was

rueful. It took three hours and a sandwich in Peter Jones to cheer me up.

The next day I wrote a letter to my agent, the gist of which was 'fuck off', and another to Julian at the BBC re-extending my invitation to our first night. It was important to get the tone right. The pub variety renaissance, led by Dan Farson at the Waterman's in Poplar, had gone off the boil a bit, but, as with Farson's East End venture, nostalgia was on our side. We were reviving the Spring Gardens on one of the entrances to the original site! Tony would MC, Annie Ross was booked to sing (she topped the bill and I was her leader-in), Neville had even promised to wash his hair. Vera, something of a folklorist, made the interesting discovery that the Keys to Vauxhall was built over a ditch once known as Slut's Hole. He thought Julian should know this (hidden agenda: five years later, he seduced Julian at a BBC Light Ents do with a can of Watney's and a menacing account of 'It Ain't Necessarily So'), but I disagreed. Though the Abortion and Sexual Offences Acts had just been passed and the year's moral mood was revolutionary, we didn't want to sound coarse. Or, worse, topical.

The truth is that I was excited that summer as never before. Preparations for the opening went ahead in the spirit of a love affair. A thousand nagging doubts and complications inevitably arose – What would be the final going-in fee demanded by Tony's brewers? Would the raised gallery at the back of the tavern be ready in time? What if the publicity didn't take? Would the clubland reps and telly people consider us legit? – but even the worst of these anxieties appeared to us as minor details in a comic plot destined for resolution. I saw little of Tony, who was being kept busy negotiating with various agents. He trusted me to be good. I rehearsed diligently, and for the first – perhaps only – time in my life, I experienced what it was to be, like Robert Ladd, on a starlit path, where the streets are paved with sparkling confidence; where each day affords the stirring, inward pleasure of working in common cause.

I finished at Windsor on Saturday, September 2, and opened a week later at the Pleasure Gardens. With a certain amount of trepidation, I steeled myself to invite Bob, as I could now call him, and the cast, not sure at the time if I wanted them to be there – to see my other life in public. I even started talking it down, suggesting they had much better things to do. Then, when Saturday came around and I heard them ordering drinks, I was glad.

*

My favourite part of a performance comes near the start: beforehand, in front of the glass, when you're preparing the surprise. Maybe preparing is the wrong word. Make-up is the art of delay: you're putting off the final putting on.

Tony had fashioned an extremely small dressing room out of a cavity between the Gents' toilets and the stage. Three steps led to my door and pissed lads kept barging in shouting, 'Is this – oh, sorry, love. Scuse. Beg pardon,' and laughing as they fell back into the throng ('had it half out, I did'). The other acts came on from the other side; either they didn't need make-up or they hopped up on stage from the audience. Mrs B was – is – different. I have to have my bits around me, like a division of lead soldiers: the wig and the fur, the nose, the gum, the cream. It's difficult to say at what point she emerges. I look up and she's there, that's all. We greet each other with a wink. *I* know where she's been.

From my cubby hole, I could hear punters outside, cackling and squeaking hoarsely, calling in the rounds, spilling their beer. Before long I recognized Bob's voice, politely conspicuous among the double dees and dropped consonants. He was talking about his love for music hall, which was a bit like hearing a baronet on the subject of cold rooms and how to make ends meet.

Another man, with a deeper voice, replied. I couldn't hear him clearly. There was a break, and this second man said he'd be right back. He put his head round the door, stared at me and immediately tried to duck out. Against a spreading blush, the grey of his stubble shone silver-white, his eyebrows looming.

Bob caught the door and held it open. He gave my father's shoulder a squeeze.

'Les, this is Ernie,' he slurred. 'I want you to meet him later. Ernie's my – my accountant, wouldn't you say? Les is a star, Ern. He's a *star*. Aren't you?'

'A distant one,' I twinkled, grimly.

\* \* \*

[Music: William Tell.] Thank you, Giacomo. Ladies.
[Wait] Gentlemen. I'm sorry I'm late. Mea culpa.
[Mumble. Smile.] It's a wonder I'm here at all.
You see, I stayed up so late, last night. [Wait.] Ye-es.
Really very late. [Shakes head. Long wait.] Oh, yes.
And got home at a quite ungodly hour, I'm ashamed to say.
My husband . . . [Wait. Sway] . . . was asleep. [Wait. Smile.]
So I decided – well, I'll tell you what I did. [Pop eyes. Sigh.]
I took all my clothes off. [Eyes. Smile.] Married forty years. [Wait.]
I thought – I'll take all my clothes off downstairs and then tell my husband I've been watching the Epilogue on the television set.
[Wait. Narrow eyes.] That'll fox him. [Mumble. Smile. Wait.]
So I went upstairs. [Wait.] Up I crept. [Wait.] Not a stitch on.

[Hold.] And discovered to my surprise that I was on top of the Number 19 bus. Going the wrong way . . .

*

In the end, some loose screw of shame unmade him, like an actor recalled to himself in the middle of a speech. My father stood by the last pillar on the right, his lips apart, waistcoat undone, staring at the floor, occasionally lifting his head, staring at anything. He was lost, I think; simply amazed that his life had come to this pass. Every so often, the surrounding jollity prodded him. I heard him laugh, twice, when the time wasn't right, and that made it harder for me because I was forced, then, to notice him. I hitched up my skirts and scrutinized the dark.

I was anxious to avoid a scene afterwards. After eleven, the bar shut and we moved up to the second floor. The top of the house was where Tony now lived. (The brewers had demanded £3,000 for going-in, which Tony borrowed as part of a mortgage on the rest of the property. The idea was that if he failed to make money as a landlord, he'd have some connected freehold to fall back on.)

Bob was there, oiling the wheels, bringing Annie champagne. Watching him, I thought of our conversation in the Officer's Watch; of how blind I'd been to his casual deflections. And I found myself marvelling at his composure, the way he avoided suspicion by never suspecting himself. I'd described my father to him, told Bob his name and received off-hand advice – to which of course I listened intently, mesmerized by manner and looks. Tony's the 'real' mesmerist, but his is a declared art. There's a label on the tin. And when things go wrong for Tony – I'm thinking of Beatrice – he has regrets. I know he'd rather sing.

Bob's smoothness is much more than an art: both more and less, in fact, than actual deceit. It is a lifelong trance of self-regard. He cannot awaken from it to feel remorse, because he was never put to sleep.

He left early, crying out, 'You're shameless!' in passing. 'Leslie Barrington, you're the most shameless man I ever met!'

'What have you done with him?' I said.

His brow furrowed for a moment. He looked triumphantly mad.

'Done? Who?'

'With Ernest.'

'Oh, *Ern*. He's gone home. Sweet chap. He really is my accountant, you know.'

The party went on until two o'clock. It grew quite wild. I made a few contacts I didn't care about and Julian said he'd be in touch. Vera kissed Neville and Annie Ross reprised 'Stardust Memories'. Tony spent most of the evening doing deals in his box-room study. He reappeared towards the end and weighed in with the Kitty Lester favourite 'Love letters straight from your heart / Keep us so near', but I motioned to him to stop.

At last everyone was gone. Dawn came up over the river and it looked spent. Tony staggered down below to clear away more glasses. I opened the windows up top and tried to get some red-wine stains off the cream-glossed mantelpiece. Above the fireplace was Thomas Bewick's woodcut of the Chillingham Bull with its startled gaze and a mane that always seemed to grow out of the surrounding forest. Mum used to have a copy in her bedroom. I heard feet on the stairs.

Dad came up behind me. We were alone together. He stank.

'You have a gift,' he said without preamble, 'for what you do.' He paused. 'That will – must be such a help.'

'It doesn't matter,' I said. 'Don't worry about me. I won't say a thing.'

'It isn't always easy,' he began, and faltered. 'I should imagine it isn't always easy, when you do it – pretend, I mean – for a living.'

'Oh, I don't know. It's not as dreadful as that.'

'No, I suppose not. At least, *you* seemed – you were enjoying yourself.'

He belched and looked happier. I was relieved. We both stood at the window's edge. Over the way, a puffing water-beetle emerged from under the shadow of Vauxhall Bridge and dragged itself into the pale light.

'Have you got the time?' he remarked.

I laughed at the beginning of an old joke and at the thought of Mum removing her teeth. Then he threw himself out.

# Nine

'I DON'T UNDERSTAND,' Tanya was saying, 'why we couldn't have popped our heads round and said hello. Sneaking in and out like that, it's ridiculous.'

Lilian explained that Martha hadn't been expecting her. It would have been an unfair surprise. You had to give people a bit of notice, especially daughters.

'I'd have been proud,' said Tanya, and turned to look out of the dark vibrating window. She nodded to herself and hummed. The profile that Lilian could see had been immobilized by a small stroke years ago. One eye drooped and the yellowness of the skin seeped through the make-up.

Lilian's head lolled.

'You asleep?'

The train's rhythm broke over a set of points.

'I thought it was marvellous,' Tanya went on, not fooled. 'I reelly did. I didn't think I would, you know, because I'm not a Shakespeare fan, to be honest. I can't say why, 'xacly. Normally, if it's local, I'll go, and if it's a day out, then I'll choose something different from the usual. That's just me, reelly.'

The corners of Lilian's mouth lifted.

'There's no one like you, Tanya,' she murmured.

'Oh, you.'

'No,' Lilian swallowed, 'really.'

Tanya was pleased. When she laughed, it sounded as if someone had been thrown off a cliff, the death wail followed by the roar of phlegm hundreds of feet down. Her small ash-blonde head bobbed about on the end of a blue turtleneck.

'We aim to please, we aim to please,' she said at last, panting for breath, and adding, significantly, 'they can't say we don't.'

The guard arrived and informed them that passengers would have to 'detrain at Swindon, the next station stop', because of a points failure.

'Eddie wanted fifty–fifty,' Tanya continued, undistracted, 'and I told him no. Not after all those years. I didn't think it was fair. I told him.'

'I know.'

'You know. I'm the one who blimmin' well cleaned and cooked and looked after the kids, I said. I was the – the constant provider. I'm not saying I minded, mind. I'd do it again. Only it was all down to me in the end, and so that's what I said, what we argued, and he came round, as you know.'

Lilian listened patiently. The already long day was about to be prolonged by an unscheduled forty-mile bus journey from Swindon to Bath, and her sense of civic principle struggled to maintain interest in a familiar litany of complaint. At least she'd been spared the story of the steak knives and the blood blister.

'It's disgusting,' Lilian said, pointing at the swill of coffee and plastic stirrers on the table opposite, at which the guard was sitting. 'No one cares.' Every time the train lurched, the cold liquid trembled in a pool in one corner of the table, or dribbled over the edge. At least her new things were safe in the rack.

'I care!' Tanya cried, reaching over to clutch Lilian's hand,

and rubbing it. 'Don't you fret, my girl. You stuck it for as long as you could. I know you did. You're entitled to your share.'

The train slowed. Lilian withdrew her hand gently. She didn't think their situations, hers and Tanya's, were directly comparable, and she didn't want her fear of being pitied to betray her into unnecessary sarcasms – not that Tanya was likely to spot them. Having lavished praise on Martha in the interval, Tanya had been forced to ask if Miranda was the Temptress. No. Who was the Temptress, then? At the Bristol Royal Infirmary, where they'd trained, the doctors in X-ray used to put a call out for Nurse Mackintosh saying she was needed urgently in reception, where a Miss Marie Curie was waiting. Tanya laughed it all off.

Lilian understood. She was being asked to close with her friend in embattled sympathy, and she couldn't. It was like being asked to love someone.

'I've got to go to the loo,' Lilian said.

When she got there, she locked the door and stood in front of the mirror. For what felt like a long time she played her favourite game of trying to gaze straight at herself – to focus on both eyes at once – and found that it still couldn't be done. You had to settle for one eye at a time, or the bridge of the nose. It had driven her mad as a child. And now the train's motion was distracting. Idly, she pulled her left eye down to observe the effect and was disappointed. She cried, briefly.

Letting go of the spittoon-sized sink, Lilian awarded herself a smile of complicity, unlocked the door and pushed.

\*

'He looks a bit bloody pale,' said Jeremy Paxman. 'What's happened to make-up, can't we give him some colour? Time for a quick dab? Lisa?'

'No.' The floor manager was signalling. Everyone fell back from the set and Lisa Lee squeezed the sponge in her hand until brown juice dropped onto her trainers. Men were so vain.

'No, all right. Too bad. Thanks, Mr—'

'Bill Alden.'

'—Alden, Bill, for coming on. Christ you look awful. It's the lights. Never mind. Report's just winding up. Seen it? Good. Bags of energy. Don't frown. That's it. Here we go: Mark Edinson reporting. And I'm joined in the studio now by Dr Bill Alden, of the British Geological Survey. Dr Alden, you heard your colleague, according to him last night's tremor was "a seismic anomaly with deep-structure catastrophic implications". Sounds grim. What's he on about?'

'Well, first I think we ought to clear up some terms.' Bill raised his hands from the desk unnecessarily. 'Without wanting to be alarmist, in fact strictly speaking to be the opposite, anomaly is an unscientific way to describe what's always been a possibility – I think what he—'

'Sorry, let me get this straight, you're saying major earthquakes have always been a possibility? In SE1?'

'Well, there's a history of incidents, as Jim pointed out. The difference here is that Thursday's tremor shows signs of having been triggered along a much deeper zone of weakness than had previously been thought to exist. Or which may only now be active.'

'And that's bad news, is it?'

'Possibly, yes.'

'Possibly? It was catastrophic a minute ago.'

'Ha, yes. But geologically speaking, Jeremy, catastrophes aren't single events. The point is that, as we've seen, ninety-eight per cent of earthquakes occur along faults on or near the boundaries of the tectonic plates, often where plates collide. That still leaves us with two per cent of the, er, global seismic-energy budget, spread out over the rest of the world, which may not sound that much but can have impressive results, in North-eastern America or East Africa, for example, or—'

'Or Southwark, apparently.'

'Or Southwark. Southwark 4.8—'

'That's what it's called, is it?'

'Yes. Southwark 4.8 is what we call an intraplate event, one that takes place away from the usual centres of activity. And these events are the result of compression across a landmass caused by expansion of the crust elsewhere, where it's being formed – in the mid-Atlantic, for example.'

Bill, worried that he was being too technical, had considered leaving it there, but Paxman, who hated being called Jeremy, remained silent.

'It's a bit like referred pain – or a conveyor belt,' Bill suggested, improvising freely. 'If you have luggage coming on at one end, you're going to have a pile-up at the other.'

'And we're at the wrong end, I take it.'

'I'm afraid so. Or.' Bill's hands fell with a miked thud. 'Or we could be experiencing what geologists call post-glacial bounce, which is when—'

'That's a lot of ors,' Paxman said, brutally, 'but which is it and what can we do? Buildings are unsafe; the cost to the local authorities and taxpayers for underpinning will be staggering – what, £500 million? – before we even begin to think about architectural prevention; and the only people with smiles on their faces are structural engineers and the Institute of Chartered Surveyors.'

'I sympathize,' said Bill, who suddenly didn't. He was tired of being treated as the novelty item that had misbehaved. 'The problem with this kind of thing is precisely that it's extremely rare – just possible but not probable – and therefore taking place in an area that's not prepared. We're not in a conventionally active region, and bricks and mortar don't respond well to shaking.'

'What's the solution?'

'Well, tensile structures are best equipped to deal with earth tremors, so you could build more of those.'

'What sort of buildings?'

'Things like the Dome.'

Paxman looked at him squarely for the first time.

'You must be joking.'

'Unfortunately not.'

'Peter Mandelson, I hope you're listening. Dr Bill Alden, thanks very much. Time for a quick look at tomorrow's papers . . .'

\*

Other women thought Lilian a hard person – and moments like this gave her an insight into their jealous fear. She had been beautiful; that was part of the general resentment: a trim figure, with thick, wavy auburn hair, good teeth, amused but distant eyes; hands that tended to snatch things in fun (money, balls) as a general indication of hidden liveliness. She had also disliked, and therefore neglected, her first child. The second she found easier because, like her, Martha had been adopted, and Lilian's deep instincts favoured a child she could select, not one born with her faults, in whom the faults showed. Alice knew nothing about the adoption and was only five when Helen, the youngest – the surprise addition – died in '73. Difficult to know what she remembered of it. People spoke of numbness after loss, but the immediate trauma for Lilian and the children had been vivid – sleeplessness, resentment, play that turned nasty. It had been Ray's idea to involve Tony, temporarily, and the intervention had been a surprising success. Ray had agreed not to tell anyone else after that; not to discuss what could not be discussed. He prodded now and then, of course, saying, 'You're a dark horse,' when on a weekday afternoon Lilian returned from Henrietta Park with the girls and failed to want to describe what they'd been doing together. (Nothing.) Her face had a dazed quality, like Dusty Springfield's. (Myopia.)

Truth to tell, she couldn't wait for Alice and Martha to grow up. The playground vigil – swings, slides, grazes, ice cream, more swings, regurgitation – made her weep with frustration. Alice locking herself in the park toilet had been the high point. The other mothers made the fuss; looked at her strangely when Lilian laughed and said Alice was always up to something.

It was understanding that made affection hard. Being selfless made you miserable. People – mothers especially – understood only too well why Lilian couldn't be bothered, and didn't care to be reminded of it.

Lilian tried again, jiggled and shoved. The spring was broken. Defeated, she sat down. Shadows spread behind the window as the train emptied.

A claustrophobe would have panicked, but Lilian could feel only relief. The enforced solitude was welcome. It was Tanya, perfectly at liberty on the other side of the door, who sounded trapped.

'He's coming, pet. He's coming now. Here he is. He's here, oh . . .'

'Go away,' Lilian murmured.

'Don't you WORRY,' Tanya yelled. 'We'll have you out in two shakes. The guard's going to fetch a screwdriver and we're going to take the—'

'I'm fine, honestly.'

Lilian wanted a drink.

'You'll be fine,' Tanya echoed, lowering her voice to what she considered a confidential pitch as she spoke to the guard. 'I'm trying to keep her calm, 'cause she's had a hell of a time recently, you know. What about air?'

The guard said there was plenty of that.

'I only ask, because my former husband got stuck in a lift in Rangoon and he had heat exhaustion after twenty minutes. Former, yes. No, that's all right. No, well it was small, so less air and what not – ha, ha, ha, I s'pose they are that way over there, aren't they? Tsk, you mustn't say that these days.'

The guard said the bus to Bath would leave in ten minutes.

'But don't fret, Mrs Hutchings. Soon as we've, er, jemmied you out, I'll order a minicab for you both.' Lilian could hear Tanya squeaking. 'No, lover, no more until the morning. Best take a cab or you'll be here all night.'

'Do you have a screwdriver?' Lilian asked, without raising her voice.

'I'm just off to get one now. The operations office is locked, so it'll have to be the 7/11 by the rank. I spec they have a bar or summat behind the counter. An' I'll do the cab while I'm at it. Two birds with one stone, in't it.'

Tanya plunged off the cliff again. She left the carriage with the guard and stopped him on the platform. Lilian could see two shadow-puppets in an orange glow, chatting and pointing. Their mission didn't sound urgent, but like an old-fashioned crossed wire it compelled you to listen.

'—and such a terrible worry for her, what with no f'nancial s'curity. I told her, I said, that's it 'xacly, don't jump ship without making sure you have something to fall back on. What can you do, though? Thass it. I think it's a shame, specially after all those years. Course my case was very different. He was physical, see, and there were the little ones to think of. Threw the steak knives at me.'

'Oh, for Christ's sake,' Lilian sighed, her head falling against the window. 'They were twenty-eight years old.'

There was a lull in the platform conversation.

'What was that?'

'I dunno.'

'It's such a shame. What an end to the day.'

The guard made a polite, unhurried enquiry.

'. . . went to see a play. I wasn't fussed, personally, but her daughter's – one of them, she's got two – an actress. Yes. She's in that hospital comedy on, oh, what's it called? Thass right. Well, she's the nurse. Course, it's ridiculous. You'd never keep your job if you were that stupid. And between you and me, it was dreadful, the play. I didn't know what to say . . . and then her father, this is in the play, was the consultant – off the telly, yes. The nice one. No, on an island. Trees and like a courtyard and what have you. I couldn't make head or tail of it. You want to be supportive, though, don't you? Tell a white lie, 'xacly, where's the harm?'

'I'd best get the jemmy,' said the guard.

'No, you go. I'll stay. I'd better. Shall I? Or shall I come . . . ?'

Tanya's voice faded as she accompanied the guard to the station exit. Soon, all Lilian could hear were the shouts of men at the front of the train, a drill-like fart from the engine, the tick-tock of the carriage cooling down, the air conditioning unexpectedly flaring up. The bus beeping. The train jerking to life.

\*

Bill Alden walked out of Television Centre and into a world momentarily convinced that it was defenceless against a blind aggressor. For this fear he had to assume responsibility. Some people would treat it as fashionable paranoia, others would be upset. There might be low-level tabloid panic – the usual petrol queues, tourist desertions, insurance hikes. These things came and went. In the studio, the cameramen were laughing, staggering about; a cheery Paxman said the interview had been fine – light, but fine. The woman from make-up had watched, too, on the monitor. She stopped Bill in the corridor and asked him if he believed what he'd said. She didn't look cross any more, just tired, like someone recovering from a long sadness. He told her he hadn't meant to scare anyone. No, she said, you shouldn't do that. He got the feeling that he'd given quite a performance, the way she studied him.

Outside, beneath trails of gunsmoke cloud, TV Centre itself appeared to be falling without moving. Things had altered. The night was a statue about to come to life. The black tongue of the slip road seemed to pant.

Part of the change Bill put down to his lightness of tone. Coming so soon after the quake in Athens, the banter must have sounded strained – as if he, the expert, had a secret to hide. That made viewers suspicious.

The other part of the change was harder to put your finger on. The idea of London moving, foundering, had certainly caught the imagination. It was like God or fate – people needed their faith in the possibility of disaster, Bill decided; it made the world magical again, ungovernable in ways that didn't mock their ignorance. And the papers played up, gloating over the number of calls made to the police – 5,000 in Greater London! 500 in Kent! – as if to underline the event's essential lawlessness. (Scientists were only passively 'alerted', and never, the distancing verb implied, by their own science.) The fuss excited Bill, too, for all his professional scepticism, in ways he would have been ashamed to admit to colleagues, though he suspected that they felt the same guilty thrill. Something in the public domain at last! Calls from the press! Lucrative secondments to large-scale works! His job now, arguably, was to tame the wild sublimity of popular belief; to reassure people that when they woke to a violent shaking, it was because they'd been snoring again, and not because the ancient geology of the city had roared to life, swallowing every other certainty. But Bill Alden resisted this course of appeasement. His entire career had been spent, soberly, in search of the truly rare occurrence – and here it was. He was a catastrophist solely by definition. By nature, he was a romantic. Twenty-three million years ago, London rose from the sea, and there had been volcanoes not far from Aylesbury 270 million years before that. Mt Bicester explodes. Imagine.

Bill stepped out into Wood Lane and narrowly avoided being knocked over by a courier. The biker, no face visible, screamed abuse.

And what if it did happen? Bill looked away down the storm-drain of the A219. You wouldn't miss the buildings much, he realized with a shock. You'd miss the temporary stuff: the plastic crap which poignantly confirms daily routine: bus stops, JMB Sports, Transco barriers and Link cashpoints, triangular Give Way signs you never thought would up and take their own advice.

Visions of chaos abroad – picture-book history, Lisbon, Pompeii, 1906 – had thrilled the child who dreamt of chasms yawning beneath the milkman's feet and wanted lava flows to interrupt RE. They'd also helped to make the child a man, because the dream had lit the way to saner avenues of thought: tack-hammers and a quartz collection, Geology Soc, lab work at university, 'Deep Karst Conduits, Sinkholes and

Lessons for the Aggregates Industry' (Harrisburg/Hershey, 1998); marriage.

Bill walked faster. So far he hadn't thought about death.

He ran down the steps to catch the last Epping train, his dream of ruins all at once threatening to strip the world of its more necessary illusions. Here it comes, he thought. From Mile End, he practically sprinted to Zealand Road, past the open kebab shops and takeaways, against the wind.

On the table was a note from his wife.

*

'Pity those with ambition so small,' Lilian read aloud, 'They write their names on a toilet wall.' She'd banged on the window and shouted, without success. The facetious poet irritated her. On the whole, her sympathies were with the object of his scorn, Rod, who had nine inches but couldn't spell 'genuine'.

She wondered what had become of Tanya, the guard and the jemmy. Her friend's casual betrayals didn't bother her. Like her shrill enthusiasms for healthy food and 'vegging out', they were the expressions of need. Failure was just an annoying companion, waiting by the taxi rank while the guard made his way across the tracks and points. If anyone came it would be him, sweaty and apologetic. In the meantime, nothing.

Lilian clicked the dial-bolt from unlocked to locked and back again. With a yawn, she turned the handle and pulled the door open.

'Of course.'

She sat for a moment contemplating the many possibilities of her liberation. She had grown almost fond of her cubby hole. The sign above the loo said: 'Press to flush. Do not use while train is in station', as it had for many years in many different typefaces. The old signs were plaques, Lilian remembered. This one was a kind of green-and-cream sticker, which had begun to unpeel.

She pressed the flush.

In the carriage, Lilian was delighted to find that Tanya had not removed any of the day's spoils: her handbag, the Ghost carrier, an oversized purple sack from Liberty's with a phial of Jo Malone perfume in it, a lipstick and several pots of cream, each promising repair and recovery, stopping just short of reupholstery. After a tot from the flask in her purse, Lilian transferred the cosmetics to her handbag and filled the sack with some of the litter strewn about the carriage. On the back of a dry napkin she wrote a note, deploring the squalor, and left it on the table. Then she went back to the toilet and began scribbling on the wall, 'Dear Rod, It's a little discussed fact, but one of the main causes of urinary discomfort in women is—'

'Oh, I'll never live it down,' said a voice outside the window. 'She'll be beside herself. Is it this one?'

Lilian froze, kneeling, the toilet door open, her bags in the corridor.

'I dunno, love. Was it D or G? Anyway, we have to go in through—'

'It was further down.'

'—the front. The carriage doors're centralized, see, an' if I override it manually, it'll bugger it for the morning, 'cos they have to be reset. Openin' manually's not the problem, it's the resettin'.'

'Yoo, hoo. Lil, love, we're back.'

'It were down a bit.'

'We're back, Lil. The carvery, tsk. Cavalry's, er, down a bit more . . .'

Lilian waited until she could hear the guard clambering into the driver's cab.

The lights came on. A small voice drifted back, 'Lights are on, Don,' and Lilian, knowing they were both inside, moved quickly. If Tan and Don got into the first carriage before she was out of the toilet, they'd be able to see the length of the train and spot her making a dash for it. Thrilled at the pettiness of her subterfuge, she scuttled to the door, put her arm out of the window, reached down awkwardly, and nudged it open. The ground was four feet away at least, but it was too late to dither. She dropped the bags, turned onto her stomach and slid her legs over the painfully sharp, icy step.

'Not bad for fifty-nine. Not bloody bad.'

Two carriages to her left, Lilian could hear muffled bleatings. It was like being at school again, running away from the group, and getting the bus to the Colston Hall. People would be looking for her in all the wrong places.

She was on a siding a quarter of a mile to the west of the station, seven or eight tracks over from the main lines. Fortunately she had on her black walking shoes – not the most attractive items, but comfortable if you had bunions. She hugged the sides of the train until she reached the bow engine and then clambered out into the open, over the endless treacherous rails and greasy sleepers. In front of and slightly below her, the lights of the station formed an untidy arrow, and as she stumbled towards them the arrow moved – rose and fell as though she were a plane coming in to land.

Lilian was cold. Funnelled by semi-derelict sheds and the dead bulk of locomotives to her right, the wind found her on the bare tracks, picked at her soft jersey and mackintosh, ragged her thin trousers.

She looked back, once, to see the red eye of her engine. The moon was a searchlight trained on someone else, like those poor teachers at Bitton Grammar hunting up and down Park Street.

On she slogged, expecting every second to be hailed from behind, exerting herself to find things fascinating as a means of conquering fear. The stones of railways were hardly loose at all, she found; they were rubble that had been glued down. Occasionally a patch shifted underfoot, like a large pebble, or you blundered through knee-high strands of weed. Lilian could almost smell the sea. On the London-bound platform, the last travellers watched interestedly as a woman, dressed in a once-smart tan outfit now streaked with dirt and gripping a Ghost bag, hauled herself up the far ramp. She emerged somewhat in a spirit of contradiction beside the notice which read 'No Passengers Beyond This Point', and drifted, eyes fixed yet apparently unseeing, towards the way out.

At the taxi rank, Lilian asked to be taken home. The young man behind the urinous perspex shield wore shades. When she gave her destination, he hummed and clicked his tongue, faced with a decision.

'Are you the lady on the train?'

Lilian confirmed that she was.

'They've just gone to find you, love.'

His earlobes were hung like a curtain-rail.

'Please,' said Lilian, sweetly. 'Don't let them.'

*

A tall, heavy man in his sixties led the way to a night-blue Mercedes with stippled plastic seat covers in the back.

'Only I have to keep it clean, love.'

'I quite understand.'

'If it gets torn or dirty, I have to pay for it, see.'

'I do see.'

'Nnnerrr. Bath is it, then?'

'Bath.'

'Home town?'

'No. I'm from Bristol, actually, so not far. My par—'

'You like Bath, then?'

'Ah, ha. Of course, I've been there so long now. Thirty years. It feels . . .' Lilian realized that she couldn't say. The car swung and purred. 'And have you always been a Swindon man?'

The driver frowned into the rear-view.

'You 'avin' a laugh?'

Like Ray, he had fat cheeks but no jowls. Bulkier men aged better. Unlike Ray, his scraped-back brown-red hair bore the telltale signs of grafting.

'I lived down Somerset way for forty-odd year, on an' off. I only come back to look after my mother. She's got that Alzheimer's.'

'Oh dear, I am sorry.'

'We all got to go. An' my dad died in the war, so there's only me. An' my brother buggered off to Australia, an' good riddance to the little Lord Lucan. I know I shouldn't say it, but there it is. You can't choose . . . I an't got no time for him any road. A4 from Chipnum all right?'

Lilian had been listening, but was still taken by surprise.

'Fine. Whatever you think.'

'Only I don't reckon the M4's quicker after that, an' the A4 takes us straight in.' The driver lifted his hands an inch and bounced them twice off the wheel. 'You warm enough?'

'I'm thawing out nicely, thanks. It has got chilly, hasn't it?'

'Nnnerr. Won't be seein' July again, nor August.' He glanced back in the mirror again, ducked his head, caught Lilian's eye and looked away. 'You been up West, then? In Lunnon?'

'I have, actually. My daughter's in a play, so we went to see that. At a theatre called the Young Vic. Smallish place. She's been in a few things.'

'Which one's that, then? Which play?'

'Oh, nothing big. *The Tempest*. You might have seen her on the telly.'

'Shakespeare, innerr?' The cabbie convulsed with laughter. 'How's it go? "My hands", no, "my feet do smell of" – oh, scuse I. Our teacher at school 'ad this beard to cover up his red face, 'cos he liked a few, fair enough. And it's the only – this is the truth – the only play by Shakespeare, William Shakespeare, I've ever read, ever seen's a matter of fact.' He paused significantly. 'And the only reason I remember it – there's a wizard, innerr?'

'That's right. Prospero.'

'Thass the one. The reason it sticks in my mind is there's one bit that goes – "my feet" – wait, I'll get it.' His face stiffened and went blank. He seemed hardly aware of the road ahead. ' "I do smell all *horsepiss*." But see, Mr Darvell, that were his name, couldn't say it, cos we was too young and so he come up with "food-trough water", an' we laughed, like. We *laughed*. Me and this other vacky, my mate. An thass what I remember.'

'Your teacher was using the Bowdlerized version, I expect.'

'Dare say. Rings a bell. Anyway, we howled. An thass all. Food-trough water. Stupid I dare say.' He sniffed. 'Trivial, like.'

Lilian made an ineffectual remark about strong impressions, which the driver took seriously. His eyebrows lifted, and he grew animated.

'I 'gree. Assolutely.' They travelled on in silence. 'So what d'you reckon on 'er, then, your daughter?'

Lilian said that, as a mother, it was hard for her to judge, but the performance seemed to have gone down well.

'She the actress of the family, then?' The driver was smiling.

'Ah, yes. Well, in fact, I have two.'

'Family of performers?'

'Mmm, not quite. I used to sing a little.' She waited, but he made no enquiry. 'And my other daughter is more of an aspiring actress, I think it would be fair to say. One actual, one aspiring, if you like. Waiting.'

'Aspiring,' the cabbie harrumphed. 'I like that. You ever evacuated?'

The car turned a corner, heading into Marlborough and through the slanted market high street. Lilian leant into the soft leather of the passenger door.

'No. I'm too young. My husband was, though.' She trailed her fingers across the glass. 'He was part of the trek down to the West Country. To a little village called Porlock.' Lilian frowned, concentrating. 'Which was where he met a good friend, one of our oldest, whose son is in the cast of the play I've just seen. So there's a connection for you.'

'Arr. I was in Lynmouth thirty-odd years. Know the area well.'

He sounded unmoved by the coincidence.

'*That's* the Nick.'

'Beg pardon?'

'No. Nothing. Carry on. How extraordinary.'

'I was harbour master for a year. Couldn't make it up, could you?'

Lamely, Lilian agreed, unable to justify her apparent interest, which had no basis, as far as she was aware, in any shared experience. They accelerated out of Marlborough, under high arches, around long perimeter walls overhung with dark, threshing trees, and thrummed into the night.

'Ah, Swindon,' said the cabbie. 'Swindon, Swindon.' He shook his head. 'Don't aspire for me.'

*

The fare was sixty pounds, not forty-five as agreed in the cab office. Lilian was dully incensed; she'd forgotten to stop at the machine on their way into Bath and had barely thirty in her purse. It meant she'd have to take thirty-five from the float and pop out in the morning to replace it. She still had the keys.

There were two entrances to No. 7 Caroline Buildings. One, at street level, looked right through the shop to the garden and canal towpath. The other, down a wet well of stone steps, opened on to thin corridors between workshops, and led eventually to the main store room. There were no lights on and no sounds from the upper floors. Satisfied, Lilian crept into the store and past the pseudo-torsos of ripped-out actions, keyboards, wires, soundboards, hammers, levers and screws to the player-piano by the rear door which doubled ingeniously as a safe. The two pads of the foot-treadle hid a drawer with a lifetime's junk in it, bills and receipts not yet tabled, old address books, a few tender thank-you cards from former patients, syringes, plasters and a tin of petty cash.

'Fifty-five, sixty.' Lilian spanked the notes into the driver's hand. 'Nineteen forty-one,' she added, shaking. 'I was bloody well born in nineteen forty-one in bloody Bristol. What the hell would I know about being a vacky? I'm not the right generation. I'm only *fifty-nine*.'

'It's hard for a woman,' said the cabbie, and wound up

the window. His gears crunched as he took the bend in Pulteney Road.

Lilian stamped up the stairs, calling. Their room at the top of the house was empty, the twin beds shoved together beneath the counterpane. Downstairs, the kitchen was filthy. No one had cleaned the fridge in six months. A roux of milk and leaking tomato had formed in several compartments. On the shelves were parcels of cheese and ham in clingfilm, some tongue, a jar of low-cal mayonnaise and thirty grams of Daktacort, a prescription cream for dermatitis to which Ray seemed unwisely addicted. The hydrocortisone in it thinned the skin, and where he got rashes or fungal infections – on the elbow, in the armpit, underneath – the skin broke and took a while to mend. The dust everywhere was layers of skin, Lilian reflected. She ran her finger through the grey rime on the sills of the sitting-room bay.

It was a wretched business.

Ray had to divorce her to justify her claim on half the house, which worked out at around £200,000 in equity. The small medical pension would be split and she'd retain a nominal interest in the future of Hutchings' Tuners, if it had one. This wasn't greed; it was recompense for years of lost earnings, a windbreak against the future. She wasn't selfish – though this was what at least one daughter maintained.

But in fact she had always been perfectly willing to give up things, to make sacrifices – and the divorce itself was to be one more of them, since it meant the sacrifice of her good name and security. She wished only that the demands made on her throughout her life had not come so inopportunely, often the very split second before mental preparedness, before going on stage. It was the demands she feared, the demands that robbed her of volition.

Now everything was being prepared for her by solicitors,

in letters so costly their figures became divisions – armed figures that wrecked her sleep.

Lilian Hutchings did not have to look about her to feel the fading presence of familiar objects: the damp ceiling and dotted mirror, the gluey carpet, samplers, grey terrace and gap-toothed balustrade. People talked of moving on, and getting on, but the truth was that after a certain age your memory of what the future was supposed to represent started to fail you. With a pain in her gut, Lilian realized that she couldn't remember what it was people of her age, class, snobbery and limited experience still hoped to achieve. When she thought of Alice and Martha, whom she loved knowing that they did not love her, she could feel only a confused nostalgia for what had not yet come to pass.

The alarm tore through the house. Ray, stumbling down from the spare room, saw the light in the lounge. He looked at his wife and reached for the phone.

Lilian let go of her bleeding stomach, where the step had savaged her.

'I'm not ready,' she said.

National newspaper advertisement, April 1940

**Thank you, Foster-Parents . . . we want more like you!**

Some kindly folk have been looking after children from the cities for over six months. Extra work? Yes, they've been a handful! . . . but the foster-parents know they have done the right thing.

And think of all the people who have cause to be thanking the foster-parents. First, the children themselves. They're out of a danger-zone – where desperate peril may come at any minute. And they're healthier and happier. Perhaps they don't say it but they certainly mean 'Thank you'. Then their parents. Think what it means to them!

The Government are grateful to all the 20,000 people in Scotland and Wales and throughout the rural counties of England who are so greatly helping the country by looking after evacuated children. But many new volunteers are needed – to share in the present task and to be ready for any crisis that may come. Would you be one of them? All you need do is enrol your name with the local Authority. You will be doing a real service for the nation. You may be saving a child's life.

The Secretary of State, who has been entrusted by the Government with the conduct of evacuation, asks you urgently to join the Roll of those who are willing to receive children. Please apply to your local council.

# Ten

THE MIDDLESEX Amateur Athletic Association held its Open Road Race every year in Victoria Park, and not, as the name partly suggested, in the middle of the M11. Every year, early on the appointed day, in conditions that were always said to be ideal for running, about a hundred athletes assembled at the Hackney Harriers' clubhouse on the corner of Cadogan Terrace, and ran a 10km course certified by the race organizer and championships secretary, Mr Alan Gratton.

This was Martha Hutchings's fifth race. She'd entered her first, years ago it seemed, in a spirit of slightly sniffy *mauvaise foi*. Like a lot of fit people, she got the most out of her amateurism in the company of the unequal, and though the race was billed as a friendly event, it was in practice intensely competitive. You couldn't reasonably expect to win. There were always one or two Olympic-entry-standard runners who turned up looking prophetically distant and greased the field. What you could do was to find yourself a plausible opponent in the crowd of women, stick with her for 6km, and then sail past on the turn of the last lap. This, at least, was Martha's usual tactic. She didn't hang around long afterwards. Kwame said that she should. He played Sunday football and supported an ailing Ryman's League side in Kingston. Both were taken seriously ('You get out what you put in'). More than once he had encouraged her to stay and chat to some of the other runners, to make friends; but she wasn't keen, not seeing the point of the anti-climactic rituals, the tea and cake, sandwiches and certificates; feeling, perhaps superstitiously, that they were tinged with a contagious melancholy.

'You do not have friends,' he reflected. 'You have rivals.' Martha squeaked an unconvincing objection, but it was true. She was used to receiving affection, not giving it. For their part, the friends – other actors, mostly, and Nick, whom she had liked and distrusted for a long time – accepted that she was flirtatious but unreachable. She gave you nothing on stage, they said, which Martha took as a professional compliment. Kwame himself had made the observation while they were rehearsing their first scene together in *The Tempest*, and she had lost her temper. 'I don't have to give *you* anything,' she shouted (and Martha never liked to have to raise her voice). 'It doesn't *matter* what you think I'm giving you, as long as the audience gets it, whatever it is.'

Back home, this led to a silent row. In bed, very quietly, Kwame, who had his own problems, whispered, 'I am your audience.'

Martha shut her eyes. She had always assumed that what Kwame loved in her was precisely her brassiness; that by not gazing at each other all the time they had protected their intimacy from over-scrutiny and talk. She was wrong. What he wanted was an apology and some kindness. He'd decided to stop acting and take over his brother's building contractor's instead. Martha turned to the wall. If that was a crack and not a cobweb hanging from the cornices, he could bloody well start there.

As it turned out, the critics loved Kwame. In the *Telegraph*, Alex Grew said that his ethnicity made more sense of Prospero's discomfiture and road to enlightenment than it ever had as a 'racist marker' of Caliban's savagery. The actors had a laugh about that. Kwame was second choice for Ferdinand, and his colour incidental, though the director had taken the interpretative credit since it virtually set the seal on the transfer and a job at the National. The excellent reviews had not changed Kwame's mind, moreover, and some equally adamantine streak in Martha also refused to yield. The events of the past week had made her keen to run; to shake off career misgivings (her Miranda had been left for dead by a new woman in the *Independent*), parental melodrama and the self-doubt that had lately hung about her. But they had not disposed her to seek solace in the race, comfort or entertainment. No; what Martha required was a casual victory: the brief, brutal demonstration that at the age of nearly thirty she retained those attributes – beauty, strength, ironic calm – it had never required any sacrifice of time and effort to possess.

She was still limbering up at the start line, listening to the jovial Mr Stratton apologizing for the absence of the St John's Ambulance Brigade, when a hundred brightly attired sinewy men and women pushed past her.

Had the race begun? She'd heard a crack, but thought that was her knee.

'Come *on*,' said a woman with pink fuzz for hair, big thighs and half of what looked like a blue Tubigrip clamped over her breasts. 'Come on, come on!'

Martha sighed and sprang into action, storming out of the pack in pursuit of her tufted opponent.

She caught up with her on the first turn, by the clubhouse, where balding officials with tie-pin insignia and fluorescent safety-belts were already handing out cups of water. It was a bad idea to drink too soon; it slowed you down and the transfer of liquid from cup to mouth while running, particularly around a corner, was more complex than the pros made it appear. The woman with the pink hair, blue chest and lime-green spirit-levels in her trainers grabbed a cup and flung the contents in her face. Most of it missed, sailed over her shoulder and caught Martha instead, who put on a demoralizing spurt.

'Keep it up,' chortled a man holding a 1km sign.

Martha swore, aware that the garish woman had regained ground and was once more at her heels. She was a gasper and mutterer, and after a bare 1,500 metres already sounded like an asthmatic in a bag of flour. But to Martha's irritation, she could not be shaken off. After 3km, they were side by side, a third of the way down the field, and Martha had the chance to observe the woman's style. Her blue top proclaimed the name and logo of a respectable running club – the Mornington Chasers – but she ran as if for a bus, tripping forward flat-footedly, flapping her arms and (the bus had got away) wiping strings of drool across her chin. At several points during the middle lap, Martha plotted to overtake her. The tried and tested method of doing this was to sprint for twenty seconds, establishing a lead of five metres or so, and then to cut back, almost allowing her rival to catch up with her before she headed out again in front. This process would be repeated three times. If a fourth burst of energy was required, Martha resorted to empowering fantasy. She imagined an engine room somewhere, in the halls of a ship perhaps, with a sweaty, sexually palpitant boilerman covered in grease, throwing a series of levers. With each gear change, the ship's shadowy pistons plunged faster and harder until the screws securing the gantry on which the man stood began to chatter and unthread. Bellowed instructions would be lost in the shrieking of pressurized steam vents and demented turbines.

The last lever refused to move. For an instant, Martha considered herself to be utterly exhausted – at the very limit of physical stress and endurance. And then, as the music of crisis reached its climax, she appeared in her own dream – *ex machina* – beside the oily calendar pin-up, in her running vest (or maybe a halter-neck); grasped the lever and—

That was supposed to be the end of the strenuous part. With the last switch thrown, a beautiful, optimal efficiency usually flooded Martha's limbs. They no longer quite belonged to her. A glance down should have shown the tarmac ticking by, the pounding of her legs reduced to a mechanically contented hum. The trick was to persuade your body that it could behave automatically, without paying undue attention to will and determination and all the other mental capacities which, if dwelt on, invoked their opposites.

Instead, Martha found herself running into mean-spirited gusts of wind that spoiled her stride, catching her sideways on, making her gulp the air, tense her fists and bend her aching neck. Her legs were weak. She had a stitch. It was all she could do to maintain her pace. The woman in front of her was faring little better; her wheezing carried on the breeze like the punctured gasp of an iron lung – and yet she refused to be caught. Stylelessly, she blundered on. It was a submission to mechanical fate of a different order: the dogged kind that would not stop, and bided patiently while the age of thin, pretty people shuddered to a bone-cracking halt.

'Don't give up!' shouted Mr Stratton from the sidelines. 'You're nearly there – the others are behind you.'

Martha was walking now, accepting cups of water, listening to the cheers that weren't for her. Kwame hadn't come. He was doing trials for a South London club in the morning and reading for an insulting part in a gangland flick in the afternoon. But in the present moment of others' laughing relief, she missed him, and wondered if this feeling of strangely volunteered loss bore any resemblance to her sister's silent cravings.

'I couldn't be bothered,' she explained, at the line.

By the time she reached the clubhouse, Martha had her breath back. She felt peculiarly happy, as if her failure had rescued her from victory, and in the nick of time. Why that should feel so satisfying she could not say. She was hungry, too. In the corner of the clubhouse was a table laden with carbohydrates. It reminded her of childhood parties, Christmas teas in the school hall with its rows of crêpe-covered tables. They were, joyously, about nothing but food.

'Two doughnuts and a bacon sandwich, a milky coffee and some crisps.'

The tea-lady behind the urn smiled. 'Sugar?'

'Oh, I think so. Two please,' Martha said, still slightly overcome. 'I've been looking forward to this.'

\*

She rang Alice when she got to Clapham Junction.

Four weeks ago, they were barely speaking. Martha avoided the Fringe, where Alice could very occasionally be seen in an exciting new Canadian comedy, and she'd not been on any of the guided walks. Yet to Martha's surprise, her sister's lucky break had brought them closer together. She wished her well in her first proper affair, and privately crossed her fingers.

Martha had had Nick herself, months back. It was one of those irksome facts which threatens to gain significance by being concealed. More seriously, she knew Nicholas Glass to be – not exactly a fraudster, but certainly an experimentalist, where the affections of others were concerned. He was the sort who liked to observe the effects of desire on an awakened sensibility.

The thought had troubled Martha when she and Alice came to discussing the astonishing developments at home. The details weren't clear, but this much Ray had let slip: he and Lilian were to be reunited on the back of a terrible trip to London, which had ended with their mother in hospital and Tanya, her best friend, calling Lilian a selfish cow and dumping her clothes and belongings in the Kennet and Avon Canal. Neither Alice nor Martha was sure what to make of such a rapprochement; they agreed to keep an open mind, and Martha was touched if not wholly reassured by this pact. Alice would be in a mood to favour romantic endings. Martha was less convinced, being vaguely, guiltily aware of the temptation to wish on two ill-assorted people the kind of relationship to which she would never stoop herself. Maybe she was jealous.

Alice answered the phone.

'Oh, hi, er, Martha. Yes, do. Nicholas is just – ' and here her voice was muffled, while she made an enquiry with her hand over the receiver – 'we're just, it's a bit shameful, getting up.' More rustling. 'Can you give us half an hour? No, honestly, that's fine. I've got some news! Yes. Well, I hope so. And I want to hear about your . . . say forty minutes?'

It was a five-minute walk from Clapham Junction to Winders Road. Martha bought a paper and went and sat in one of the station arcade's new coffee bars. Boredom got the better of her after about thirty seconds and she decided to ring Kwame for a bicker. She fished the phone out of her skinny-strap back-pack and found that the line to her sister's house was still live.

The phone trembled on the bar counter, as though registering over a distance of almost half a mile the shock waves of the encounter at the other end.

Martha picked it up and listened, with her hand laid delicately on her throat, to the grunts and slaps and moans and frantic imperatives as they grew louder and more urgent; to the rhythmic knocking of a solid frame against a wall; to the smothering crackle of bedclothes over the earpiece. Fuck me. Give it to me. Fucking fuck me. I'm giving it to you. Oh, Nick. Oh yes. Oh fuck.

Martha put the phone down and watched it buzz and swivel its way into a nearby blob of froth. When the phone stopped moving, she lit a cigarette.

*

Nick was half-dressed and on his own when she reached No. 7.

'Mart, hi. She's just nipped out to the shops. Did you see her?'

'No.'

'You didn't see her?'

Martha took a deep breath.

'No, Nicholas. I'm afraid I completely failed to bump into her. How are you?'

'What?' Nick stood bare-chested on the entrance stairs, holding the door open. Martha was menaced. She could smell his armpits. Only the peculiar urge to see if she could speak the truth made her stay.

'All right, I *did* want to see Alice. She told me to drop by after my race if I felt like it, but I wasn't sure if you'd be together or not, and in view of our – our, you know – which I regret, I think, I'd probably better just go. I can see Al another time and you can make my excuses for me.'

'No, no. Don't be silly. Come up. What race?'

Nick led her into the kitchen, and Martha caught a whiff of limescale and detergent from the bathroom washing machine. Grey sheets were billowing inside it. The shelves around the cramped kitchen groaned with small plants, odd glasses, kitsch mirrors in moulded tin frames, bowls containing handfuls of ancient potpourri, and incongruous cooking ingredients – bars of creamed coconut – among the usual jars of rice and flour. The sink was piled with unwashed plates, the table covered in cups, papers and books.

As she spoke, Martha found it hard to banish the memory of her romp with the man in front of her, which had been efficient but quiet. She used to make a lot of noise during sex, or so she'd been told. These days, she reined it in.

'I'm afraid I walked the last hundred yards.'

Nick nodded. He had nothing to say about her specific failure, but was very happy to talk about running in general. He could pick up the trail of any topic and talk with authority, or even (and this was perhaps cleverer) not talk and still appear authoritative. It was part of his charm, of course; that and his legendary liberality. He was always buying rounds and offering to cook dinner. The fact that the money and food were usually not his, far from spotting his reputation as a man of generous impulses, seemed to enhance it with unworldliness.

He smoked and coughed, hacking up phlegm in his throat and swallowing it back down as he struggled into a sweat-shirt.

'You know about Dorando's marathon, don't you?'

'No. Whose?'

'Dorando Pietri? You must have, surely.'

'Must I? Means nothing to me, I'm sorry.'

'Italian runner.' Nick stubbed out his cigarette on a plate of toast-crumbs. 'Little guy. Ran this incredible race in the White City Olympics. 1908.'

He paused. The look on his face darkened. Her ignorance

gave him limited pleasure, because she attached no importance to it.

'There's a film of him in the stadium at the end, over the last two-hundred-odd yards. I can't believe you don't know it – there's only a minute or two of film, but it's really famous. Are you sure you haven't seen it?'

Martha nodded. Would it have made any difference if she had?

'Anyhow, he appears at the entrance to the track and the crowd goes berserk. There's no one else in contention; he passed this South African guy, Hefferon, a mile back; he's within grasping distance of the title – but he's in terrible trouble. He starts running the wrong way, and the guys in boaters and badges and bushy moustaches have to point him in the right direction. His legs have gone. He's drunk with exhaustion, flailing across the lanes, clutching at the air. Men are crying out from the terraces, waving him on.'

It was an impassioned commentary, and Martha was afraid of looking unmoved by it. She kept very still.

'The other athletes are behind the finishing line. And you can see one with his hand punching the air, screaming encouragement. He's enormous, twice the size of Dorando, who's tiny and pale and nothing but hollow cheeks and black hair.' Nick got to his feet. 'Ten yards from the line and it looks as if he's going to do it after all. But a second runner has entered the stadium and he's picking up speed. An American, in the final strait, with Dorando ahead, and crawling – *crawling*, with his eyes rolled up, towards the tape. The stands are like something out of *Intolerance*. Thirty thousand people in a swoon. Four yards, three yards, two. The American is close behind. And in the last yard, in the last twelve fucking inches of twenty-six miles and three-hundred and eighty-five yards, Dorando gets to his feet, reaches for the tape, and the race official with the megaphone, who can't bear to watch any more, puts an arm in the small of his back and pushes him across the line.'

Nick sat down with a heavy bump. 'And he's disqualified.'

There was a little silence, while Martha considered what to say. She finally managed a quiet 'After all that effort . . .' at which Nick heaved a sigh. He seemed to take the story very personally, as though it held a cautionary significance she was a fool for not immediately grasping.

'Of course, we know who history remembers, but that doesn't alter the fact that at the time, Dorando was fucking robbed. I mean, *fuck* posterity. Who cares what people think later on?'

Martha's gaze rested on the patch of table next to her that wasn't covered in A4 loose-leaf and printouts. A line peeped out at her from the middle of one stack. It had a familiar shape; there was an underlined word – a title, two words? – but she was at the wrong angle to make instant sense of it. She was on the point of asking Nick straight out how things were going with Alice, when all at once he ran his hands through his hair, leant on the table on one elbow and started gesturing as though they'd had a disagreement.

'You see—'

Having raised her eyes, Martha quickly lowered them again.

'—we all *run* – the great sportsmen and women *run* so much faster than the heroes of the past. We eat better, we train better; we don't have to work as hard. We've got better shoes, better tracks, better facilities. We've got – let's face it – drugs. But what would happen,' and here Nick jabbed the air with his finger, as if responding to an unfair accusation, 'if we pitted today's superstars against the stars of the

1920s and 30s. If you could make it a really equal contest, in pre-war conditions, eh? Who'd win?'

The title on the sheet of paper was *The Tempest*.

Nick was practically shouting. Again, Martha was about to tell him to calm down, when, abruptly, he seemed to read her mind and, colouring, reversed the terms of his argument. Now he was saying calmly that you'd have to bring the historical champions forward into the present day if you wanted to make a fair comparison. It wouldn't make sense, would it, to transport our contemporaries back in time, 'because you can't unknow what you know. Can you?'

He looked at her, and his crotch flinched.

'Can we?'

Martha didn't answer. She was reading, open-mouthed.

\* \* \*

Autumn had arrived, Alice's least favourite season, with its echoes of wet stockings and the rubbery sweet smell of an anorak that wouldn't do all the way up because it was too small. The confetti-leaved birch trees on Winders Road had begun to turn; and no one sat outside the pubs in the evening any more or went running past the dour red facades of Prince of Wales Drive after eight. The wheel of the seasons turned inside another greater wheel, the end of a thousand years, and that, too, appeared to fill people with anxiety. Posters on hoardings and in the papers warned of the possibility of technological collapse, which baffled Alice. If these were the last few months of innocence, why spend them worrying? She knew that momentous things were taking place in the wider world. She saw the liver-spotted hide of General Pinochet in every old face at the bus stop. And she didn't care.

She submitted willingly to her fate. Or, rather, she gave

herself over to it without any effort of will at all, the lovely thing about love being, so it seemed, how little choice one had in the matter; how it freed you from the tyranny of false priorities! There was so much in her working life to look forward to – a contract with an agent, who had the advantage of being her lover's father; the transfer of *The Tempest*; castings (already!) for the admittedly unglamorous role of a Cro-Magnon cave-wife in a pop-palaeontology special for the BBC; and a cheque for that silly review from the *Indie*, which had taken her piece and run it without changes. But all Alice really looked forward to, when she wasn't in the same room or building as him, was seeing Nick again. The rest didn't count.

She'd handed over her spare set of keys in the middle of the week, when Nick had told her of the problems he was having in Cabul Street. (The house was full of dust and he was asthmatic. His flatmates didn't pay their share of the bills on time. He didn't get on with one of them.) Alice as a result found herself in the delightful position of being able to make a selfish gesture look like a generously practical one. She did it casually – threw him the keys while he was still yawning in bed and she was putting on her silk dressing gown, as though she kept open house all the time. He thanked her soberly; caught her hand, and said:

'Are you sure? I wasn't trying to invite myself over.'

Alice fluttered with laughter.

'Oh, Christ, don't worry about it. Stay here if you need to, Nick; and if you don't, don't. Makes no odds to me. But there's no point suffering with a load of layabouts if there's an alternative, is there?'

'Well, if I do stay, it won't be all the time.'

'I wouldn't mind if it was.'

There was a difficult pause.

'It won't be, I promise. You're very kind.'

'I'm not kind. I'm . . .' but Alice didn't know what else she might be.

Nick contradicted her again, gently.

'Anyway,' Alice said, somehow making her way out of the bedroom and into the kitchen, 'you're most welcome at any time.'

'I hope you can cope with me,' was Nick's soft, sad reply.

In the Happy Shopper, as she gazed at the milk and bacon, Alice thought about this last remark. It was like being shown a cellar door and told never to open it. The confidentiality was a lure before it was a warning.

Ahead in the queue were two girls about her age also buying Sunday rations. Alice's eyes were drifting forgivingly over their hair and sweaters, the jeans they barely filled, when with the cold electric shock of delayed recognition she heard one of them mention his name.

'I've not seen much of Nicholas lately, have you?'

'No, only the other morning, on one of his commutes to the lavvy.'

They both chuckled.

'It's the second week, so he's busy. Busy and broke, so he says.'

'What happened to Jennifer?'

'Think she gave up. I mean the real interest was all on her side, but you know what Nick's like. They had a row in the middle of the street after that business with the man who delivered the fridge, and she hit him, apparently, and he told her that *she* had to do something about *her* temper.'

'Bloody hell, that's a bit rich.'

The other girl snorted.

'She was, too.'

'What?'

'Rich.'

'Why doesn't that surprise me?'

'Of course, it's all her fault.'

'Oh, of course.'

'Yes, you see – she was emotionally unavailable. She couldn't love.'

'But really, the man who delivers your fridge . . .'

'Anyway, the official version is that Nick's sad and lonely.'

'And out every night.'

'I've bought a new light bulb for the landing.'

'Poor Jennifer. She had guts, I thought. And a brain.'

'And a dying Mum. That's why she went back to Huddersfield—'

The girls paid for their milk and toilet paper and left the shop. Alice forgot her change and blundered out after them, wanting to hear more about Jennifer, the slighted Huddersfield heroine. She rounded the corner of Falcon Road and Cabul Street in time to see the two flatmates turning into a gate halfway down the terrace. At such an acute angle, Alice couldn't see which number the house was, and realized that she didn't want to know. If it wasn't fourteen, then it must be thirteen. And if it was thirteen – the tidily appointed Edwardian home with clean curtains and a noisy upstairs bedroom – why had Nick described it so misleadingly as the smoky rental property next door?

Against this tide of speculation, Alice felt the undertow of an opposing realism. There were cellar doors in every life, she reflected, and Jennifers behind them. It was a kindness to oneself not to attempt too much investigation. What could the past offer, except irrelevant comparisons and absent witnesses?

The only cure for it was the present. Alice's breathing grew more regular, and the pain in her molars subsided to a bearable throb. She felt calm again, and immediately a little sorrowful, because – looked at a different way – so much of her present happiness with Nick seemed bound up with a romantic sense of the past. His attention to her body, to her peculiar sensitivities (the underside of her breasts, the skin over the front of her hip), made Alice feel alive and part of a world of common joys. It was the sort of feeling that allowed you, the morning after, to exchange smiles with strangers in the street.

And yet sex, revelatory as it might be, was not the heart of the affair. That came afterwards, in the small hours, when dozy, thickly spoken chat fed the illusion that this was not a first encounter at all, but a reunion.

They were roughly the same age, from the same part of the country (Nick had been to school in Bristol and remembered Alice, so he said, from a Careers Day at the university). They'd bought complementary first LPs (*All Mod Cons*, *The Kick Inside*), and agreed that Virginia Wade's Wimbledon victory was a fix; that *The Magician's Nephew* was superior to anything else in the Narnia Chronicles; that the best song in *Grease*, 'There Are Worse Things I Could Do', had seemed like a tedious interlude at the time; that it was strange to think of Arthur Scargill and *Knots Landing* as belonging to the same decade. They hadn't, either of them, got all of the sex in *The Draughtsman's Contract*; and for a year at least, while cruise missiles and Greenham Common were in the news, they'd crossed their fingers when jets screamed overhead, just in case.

There were shared memories, too, of holidays on the Somerset coast, where Tony still had a cottage. Nick had never quite understood his father's obsession with the place. He'd been evacuated there, but didn't seem to enjoy it when he went back, which was almost every year during the 1970s. 'We came there a lot when Dad was with a girlfriend, or practising, or doing the show. He was never happy, whoever he was with – said it was being with abnormal people that made you treat them abnormally, and behave abnormally yourself. Then he dropped the show, signed up Bob, and immediately began saying it was the best thing he'd ever done. How much easier it was to be an agent and let someone else do the hard work. How Porlock always helped him lay down his burdens.'

Some kind of animus boiled away behind these revelations – Nick cupped his neck with a searching hand – but they held no specific accusation or resentment, and Alice could only feel that even in his father's company Nick must have spent a lot of time on his own.

He recalled different things about the cliff-top paths above Porlock Weir and the trail to Culbone, a Saxon chapel and hamlet buried in the woods – differences which made Alice's own memories touchingly complete: the anthills on the track curving up the hill to the woodland gate, the horseflies following you in a busy cloud, the raw silk of the blue sea turning grey, then blue again with the hand of the sun on your neck. Like Alice, Nick had signed the visitors' book in the church several years in succession and admitted to going back partly in order to see how his signature had changed. Culbone used to be a prison, Alice revealed. In Henry VIII's reign, it was a leper colony.

Nick found this funny. He spluttered twice: once at the timing of the observation, and then, a few seconds later, and louder, almost despairingly, at some more private resonance.

'I'm not sure where I get all this useless information,' Alice said. 'I've got a magpie brain. I – I did a school project once. Why it's stayed with me, I don't know. I used to scrub out most of my work, so that people couldn't see.'

To Alice's own ears, this last appeal for sympathy struck a hollow note.

'It's not useless,' he said. 'It's not anything – it's just . . .'

And they slept.

The next night, the third in a row they'd spent together, their wandering recollections met again in Culbone's woods. The path to the church was walled in and eerie by the early evening. If you strayed from it at the midway point, you could clamber up through the forest to a hidden palace of enchantments. Fanciful terraces and archways filled the upper reaches of those woods, and led to an overgrown courtyard enclosed by beech and oak in whose grappling canopy could be discerned two stony, tiered arcades.

'Do you remember . . . ?'

A spiral staircase in the corner of the paveless yard, choked with rampant rhododendron, corkscrewed into the trees and became yet another deer-run. They both remembered. They'd left the path together, separately, and found the old rumour of a house. Pevsner was vague on the subject, the local guidebooks mute. You had to search hard to find any mention of the spread ruin in the darkness, with no roads in or out, that once was Fernlea Combe.

'Tell me,' Nick would murmur into his pillow.

'Tell you what?'

'I don't care,' he slurred. 'Things. More things.'

\*

As Alice packed the milk into the fridge, she was unpleasantly aware of having interrupted a conversation. The others' silence cast her as the intruder in her own flat. This made her cross, though she told herself she had no right to be, and the idea of being an inconvenience filled her with dread.

'I need a new fridge,' she announced.

Nick blinked.

'Why? What's the matter with this one?'

'Well . . . it doesn't seem to get very cold, and the light never goes on, and oh, you know. I'm thirty-one – soon – and it's time I had a proper fridge.' The words drifted. 'I suppose I could get a man in to fix it.'

'You don't need a man to fix a fridge, Alice. Just get another bulb and change the setting so it's cooler.'

'Where?' Alice felt that she genuinely didn't know. 'Where can I get a bulb for this fridge?'

'What do you mean, *where*?' Nick shook his head like a wet dog. 'Morley's, John Lewis, Curry's. Anywhere.'

'Excuse me,' said Alice, and dived into the bathroom. It was as though she'd kicked something away in a moment of panic. What was she doing? She sat down and got up, washed her hands, flushed.

Outside, a moment later, she began again. 'So, Martha, how did you do?'

Martha looked preoccupied and pale.

'All right,' she offered, numbly. 'I think I was OK.'

'Personal best?'

'No. I wasn't at my best. But I was OK. I gave my best performance.'

Nick whinnied and scratched his chest.

'She dropped out. Don't be shy, Mart. Learn to love your mistakes.'

'It wasn't a mistake. Kwame doesn't play to win – well, not all the time. I didn't particularly want to carry on, that's all.'

'You mean you didn't finish the race?' Alice was stunned.

'That's right.'

'But you're usually so competitive – you normally compete so well.'

'Do I?' Martha gazed at her sister. Alice stared back, and was struck by Martha's expression. She had rings around her eyes and their skin, the skin of the sockets, had a blue membranous translucency. 'Nicholas,' Martha continued, 'has been putting my disgrace in perspective. He's been telling me about the other all-time failures on the track.'

'Dorando wasn't a failure. That's the point. He was a fucking hero. He—'

'I didn't know you knew anything about running, Nick. You never told me.'

'There are lots of things I've never told you,' Nick laughed, a little scornfully.

'I'm sure there are,' Alice conceded, with a private vision of herself being beaten to death by the idiot police. 'That would only be natural.'

It was Martha's turn to laugh.

'You two,' she said. 'Like an old married couple already.'

'We haven't argued – yet,' Alice said. 'It's early days.'

Nick yawned.

'Oh no,' Martha said. 'That's a bad sign. The arguing's the glue. If you're too proud to argue, you can't be trusted to tell each other the truth.'

It was an insight of unintended pertinence. Martha followed no such precept in her own relationships, but sensed its appeal on her sister's behalf.

'Go on, then,' Alice said, spooning coffee into a pot. 'Tell me a few.'

A lorry rumbled by in the street and rattled the windows. Five seconds later, they shook again, along with the table and chairs and storage jars with spaghetti and rice and flour in them, and the room was vibrant for some time. The flour jerked frame-by-frame against the glass.

'Nick,' Alice prompted.

She looked about the room dutifully, without feeling scared: it was still there. The tremors were disconcerting, of course; not least because, after a week of them, they could scarcely be mistaken for anything else. Amazing, how rapidly the city had become attuned to them. A lorry had more mystery – it could be a train, a falling load, an urgent delivery.

'Do you rent or own, Martha?' Nick asked.

'I own.'

Nick sucked his teeth.

'Look out for those cracks,' he advised. 'The telltale signs.'

'Of?'

'Subsidence. You might have to get your golden boy on to that.'

Martha let the sneer pass.

'And perhaps he can give Wyndham's the once over while he's at it. Any more of these,' Nick gestured airily, 'and we won't have a house to transfer to.'

Martha paused, then said:

'I think, Alice, you're about to get an answer to your request.'

'Come on,' Nick said, ruffling himself. 'It hardly takes an expert. The damage doesn't show. You go backstage in any big theatre and everything's held together with bits of carpet and gaffer tape. It's all falling apart. They've cancelled *Cats*, the *Glums*. The Coliseum's dark. Who's going to give us a licence?'

'I never thought of that,' Alice interjected, but it was a needless concession.

'There's no reason why you should have,' Martha remarked softly. 'Nick's talking rubbish.'

'Oh, am I?'

'The old buildings are the safest. Victorian mortar is made up of mud and lime, which have more flexibility than sand and cement. They've got more give. You don't live with a builder for five years without learning something.'

'I bet,' Alice sighed; then said, a little louder – 'Now you come to mention it, I think you're right. A lot of houses next to direct hits stayed up during the war, didn't they? I suppose that was because they absorbed the shock.'

Nick lifted his eyebrows in submission. It would have taken a surveyor to detect the beginnings of a sulk.

'So your fears are unfounded,' Martha concluded. 'Although if anything does happen, you'll have to get by without Mr Dankwah's assistance as I have it on good authority that he's not transferring.'

'Whose?'

'His.'

A current passed through Nick's fingers and neck.

'He's been recast?'

'No, he's learned to love his mistake.' Martha hesitated. 'He's giving up. He's got his last casting this afternoon.'

'If he's decided to give up, why even go?'

Martha thought about this. The answer was simple.

'He said he would.'

*

Alice's ascendant star was the topic of conversation for the next half-hour – the auditions, the representation and now (her latest news) the adaptation of Leslie's 'book'. Luck begets luck, was Nick's diagnosis, which Martha thought skimped somewhat on congratulation. She had none of her own to offer, however, and listened, marvelling with silent rage, to her sister's story.

Among the rest of the cast, there had been some doubt as

to whether Leslie's book actually existed, and not a little envy. Bob Ladd's memoir, *Don't Mind Me*, had been enthusiastically endorsed by a number of writer-actors who reviewed him in order to demonstrate their literary kinship – but it was not selling, Alice said, the title having proved too persuasive.

Charmed to hear of Alice's involvement in Leslie's exciting 'project', Ladd nevertheless warned her not to get her hopes up.

'Some who go dancing through bogs are lost, my dear,' he rumbled, and Alice had a momentary vision of Michael Flatley in the Grimpen Mire, looking miffed.

It was a curious thing to say. She knew the MacNeice poem – 'Elegy for Minor Poets' – Bob was quoting, as apparently did Tony Glass. At their first meeting in Orme Court, Tony had dropped the same poem into the conversation while speaking of acting and irrational hope.

Bob wanted to know: 'Who's publishing?'

Alice informed him that there was no publisher. It wasn't certain that Leslie wanted to present his work as a book, even – and indeed Tony had suggested a monologue. One-man autobiographical shows were back in fashion, he said: none more so than the life stories of minor variety stars whose affecting boast was that they had never dazzled long enough to fade.

In the bar, Alice had spoken to Leslie on several occasions, and a cautious intimacy had developed, mediated in part by Neville and talk of choirs. Leslie moved the conversation on, interpreting Alice's various courtesies as natural curiosity about life in general, and his Life in particular. He gave her two chapters – from the exercise book she had found in his dressing room. She read them, realized that Neville could not have seen them, and was intrigued.

The first passages, with their evocation of the young Antony Glass, seducing and transforming his audience, made a great impression. The romance of Beatrice and Les touched Alice, perhaps because the fact that it *was* a romance had not fully dawned on its author. Where was she now? One answer was obvious: in the clown-nosed, genteel obscenity of Mrs B; but Leslie either didn't see or couldn't face the fact. Poor Beatrice – her life had become his work.

Leslie did worry, tangentially, that certain other details of his account were too intimate for publication. All the more reason, Alice argued, to present it as a play, where the conventions were understood:

'I told him to change the names. Unless you're very disenchanted with life, you don't confuse what people say and do with who they really are.'

This was too much for Martha.

'Oh, I know, I *know*,' she said, getting up to leave. 'It's just such a shame we've nothing else to go on.'

\*

She stayed furious for the rest of the day. In the flat, seeing Alice's review, hearing the bent penny drop, she had experienced a sensation of buoyancy: like sudden success, the revelation of betrayal turned out to be a quiet thing, and the stirrings of judgement equally covert. Martha could not give a voice to her injury. She had pulled out the page from the pile and read the insults askance, while Nick talked, before slipping it back.

How sympathetic is every undeclared enmity! Alice, in her barrel of hopeless ideals, was heading for the waterfall. It would be a long, splintering drop; yet it was not in Martha's power to prevent it. There were limits to her frankness, and they had been reinforced by such phrases as 'magically inept'.

One paragraph stayed with her in its entirety: 'In her efforts to make Miranda mettlesome, Ms Challen gives her a very stale sort of chastity. This is habit and moderation as long practised in front of a mirror and then touched up for the cameras.'

On her own, and later, when Kwame came home tired and despondent, Martha grew angrier. To disabuse Alice of her sunlit dreams would be, after all, to undeceive herself.

What, in any case, could she have said? That a grand passion comes along once or twice in a lifetime and is a fantasy of possession? No one should be told that. What else? That the real thing – the art of failing to get your way and not minding – is just a better sort of contrivance? Too colourless, if true.

When, for example, Kwame returned from his last audition and revealed that the white mockney director hadn't liked him because he wasn't 'street' enough, Martha knew that a good immediate solution was a bit of sex. So they made love with *Songs of Praise* lauding their efforts in the next room. They were popularly supposed to be red-hot as a couple, but it wasn't like that. Sunday afternoons, somewhere between ski-jumping and 'Hills of the North' from Clacton, had become the acceptable routine. Even so, Martha could be reluctant.

She loved Kwame. What she resented, deep down, was her role as the compromise sexual candidate – the person who was just a little dazed and unimaginative when it came to sex. But the truth was that Martha had no one to blame for this piece of unfortunate casting but herself. For she had very early on perceived that it was important to sustain Kwame in his belief that his had been the more colourful sexual history, marked by peaks of brittle ecstasy which, crumbling, had led him to a desire for something more solid and attainable. If she felt flattened by occasional mentions of long-fled affairs with sexual athletes, it was a flattening and a comparison she had invited. She rarely named her own past conquests, or, if she did, spoke in any way so as to suggest their influence on her present behaviour. She apologized for her reluctance – her inability – to fuck as regularly as Kwame wished. She said she didn't know what the matter was; that it was a problem with her – getting close to anyone; being intimate; still. It would hurt Kwame to know, really know, that her perfunctoriness in bed, her awkwardness and deficiency, were a kind of pose. And she wondered, when she lay awake at night, if this wasn't how many people sustained their marriages and relationships – by making over the extent of their desire, experience and confidence to partners who, all unwitting, needed it more.

\* \* \*

Alice's suggestion that they try the Sunday pub quiz at the Duke was not enthusiastically received. Nick seemed disinclined to do anything much, except lounge around and drink tea. He leafed through magazines. Once, he looked up and their eyes met in a semi-serious battle of wills. Nick held her gaze until Alice felt that she should say something. As the thought formed, she noticed that the pages of the last magazine to be cast aside had not stopped turning . . . Over they went on their own, teasing and falling, one by one.

Breath control, he explained: a classic piece of 'misdirection'.

Unnerved, Alice countered by moving, rather more directly, from the settee to the bed, where Nick joined her, fully clothed.

'I like this,' he said, with his arm around her. The desert light of evening stirred the dust in the air. 'This is nice,' he added, more distantly. 'I can't get this anywhere else.'

Alice bit her lip. She was in serious pain by eight o'clock, and the temptation to rotate her jaw – to grind the aching tendons – had to be resisted.

'Will you let me try something?' Nick said.

And he brought his index finger, very slowly, to the bridge of her nose, where the tip divided and strained her eyes.

Alice could hear the room on all sides: the fizzing of a fly between blind and pane; the chime of the mattress under her right ear; Nick's breathing. The pain in her mouth resolved into a circular pulse but did not lessen.

'You have to open up,' he whispered. 'You have to trust me, or it won't work. Do you trust me, Al?'

She had never felt more awake. He tried again, without success, and at last snapped his fingers in friendly dismissal . . .

Alice made contented noises, yet at heart felt that she had failed. She was a creature of hobbled instincts, full of – he'd put his finger on it – mistrust.

'I know I have a habit of saying sorry,' she said. 'But I am, honestly.'

Nick was on the other side of the room, with his coat on. Alice looked at the bedside clock. It was midnight. The bedclothes were over by the window, the remaining sheets pungently streaked. Someone had torn down a blind and mangled the slats. Her lips had crusted over.

'Who,' Nick asked, in a cracked voice, 'is Helen?'

There was another man beside her, holding her steady. It was Tony.

'Time enough for that,' he said.

*

'Did you know . . .' Martha began, a while after they'd finished.

'Did I know what?'

Martha flicked through a book. A woman on the television was talking about her life. The uninflected tone – no doubt she would end her fable of incest, rape and industrial tribunals by thanking God – made her peculiarly unlikeable.

'Did you know,' Martha resumed, with a last look at the book, 'that the film rights to *The Naked Lunch* were originally owned by a British company?'

The woman was pointing out God's handiwork in the kitchen. Her husband worked in construction. There was a shot of him 'on site' with a hod-carrier.

'And that when the company went bust, the rights reverted to the Crown. So, when David Cronenberg wanted to make his film, he had to buy back the rights – from the Queen?'

'These people,' Kwame said, pointing at the screen. 'They call themselves architects, when they have never, not ever, built anything. Not one single thing. They are not even builders. They are *property developers*.'

'Are you listening to me?'

Kwame shook his head.

Martha waved a hand in front of her boyfriend's eyes. 'I said—'

'No.' Gently, he batted her fingers, again indicated the screen. 'You know,' he murmured, smiling, 'I never listen to a word you say.'

# Eleven: *Leslie*

IT WAS GOING so well: Victoria Palace, August 12, 1978.
Dot in the spot. Some nights you fly, and every routine is a
winner – the sailors and the bus, the late Epilogue, and – my
favourite – French caff ('*Monsieur, tu sais, je ne supporte pas
le porc*'). A good first half is always fatal, of course, and after
a few in the interval I had one of those sozzled *coups de
foudre* when, for an instant, you see yourself as others do.
It's like being disappointed in love – the same everyone-
knows humiliation. I used an obscenity in connection with a
minor royal, the band cut in and Ms Squires, who had retired
to enlarge her liver, was hauled back on for a flustered reprise
of 'Say It With Flowers'. She got the verses muddled and I
fell off the stage.

The MC, Tarby I think it was, or some other golfer,
was surprisingly sweet about it all. 'Never mind, Les, it'll
never be broadcast.' But Dot was furious. She'd sold out at
the Palladium and, this time having hired the Palace herself,
wanted to repeat her success. Forty seconds after the curtain,
she was outside my dressing room with, ominously, a nurse
in tow. In she marched and threw a huge bowl of gin-and-it
in my face. 'Les, let me tell you this,' she said. 'Nobody,
but nobody, swears on my fucking stage.' How well I recall

that lilting Llanelli accent of hers, with its gay overtones of industrial decline.

'You're finished,' she informed me. And we were.

Oh, it could all have been so different! If only I'd stayed a cub reporter on the Kiddie *Bugle*; if only I'd never listened to *Variety Bandbox* or gone to Cradley Civic; if only I'd made my career in theatre and got Bob Ladd into bed before Bob got Dad into his. If I'd never moved on to the pub-sized bottles. If, if, if.

I could have astonished the world.

Mind you, it hasn't all been bad. I played a bent Druid in *Jamaica Inn*, with Patrick McGoohan, and no less a performer than Jon Pertwee, the one in the frilly shirt, said I was a theatrical force to be reckoned with. *The Forsyte Saga*, *A Bouquet of Barbed Wire*, *How Green Was My Valley*, *The Bleedin Onedin Line* – Tony put me up for all of them, and I shat on the lot.

The trouble is, I hate telly. It may be different now, but I doubt it. I think the last time I had anything to do with the goggle-box was in the early 1980s. *Pebble Mill* was doing a post-punk feature on corrupting influences in the light of the Toxteth riots. Possessed by the urge to do exactly the wrong thing at the wrong moment, I came on streaming with fake blood, clutching a brick with which I claimed to have been hit by Michael Heseltine. My chortling co-panellists were two former presenters of *Blue Peter*, who for legal reasons I can refer to only as 'John Noakes' and 'Valerie Singleton'. They were vastly amused by my slurred banter, until the cameras stopped. Then it was like the charge of the Light Ents Brigade. Who is this wanker? Did it go out? Stick to panto, you ponce. Wait till my agent hears about this, etc., etc.

'Fucking Blue Fucking Peter,' said 'John' as he stormed off.

'Don't knock it, love,' 'Valerie' sneered. 'It got you your house in France.'

They killed that pet tortoise, you know. The paint on the shell poisoned it. Then they covered it with straw, put it in a sodding cake tin in the staff canteen, and forgot about it for six months. No holes, no air, no surprise.

But I digress.

\*

The nurse standing behind Dot, just beyond the threshold, did not leave with her. As Dot swept out, she stood to one side, and then turned to look at me. In the confusion of light her figure seemed crowned with shadow, which followed her into the room. It was not shadow, but hair, gathered into a monumental crest, like a dowager duchess or a cartoon Maria Callas. The face had changed: where her cheeks had once blushed with unspent energy and the permanent suggestion of outraged innocence, they were now dry and papery with the application of talc, the skin under the eyes tenderly dark with work.

Beatrice could never have disguised her height, of course, but the imperious bearing, which had made her seem matronly when young, was gone, and in its place a peculiar middle-aged gawkiness recalled the shy schoolgirl I had never known until that moment. The nurse's uniform was rather too short, I noticed, and yet she failed to fill it, her legs and arms poking out unevenly. She stood there twisting a handkerchief, and then collapsed into a chair. Her shelf-like chest had disappeared. The big green eyes refused to blink. One of them was clouded by what must have been a cataract.

'Tra-la, Leslie,' she said, with that half-sigh, half-laugh I'd never been able to imitate. 'I'm sorry it's taken me so long.'

'Bea,' was all I could say, and a great shame, a terrible

unnamed grief, bloomed in my heart. 'You don't catch me at my best. I can do better, I promise. How are you? What have you been doing? Did you get my invitation?'

She stared, like someone waiting for the transatlantic echo to fade.

'I heard all about it.' A little colour returned to her cheeks, and she tilted her head. I'd sent a few cards to an address Tony gave me after they separated. One of them was a ticket to a show at the Palladium, in '73, before I got stuck on the drag and cabaret circuit. That was when I really started drinking. Tony told me that he and Beatrice had split amicably: he was resigned to being a single parent (Nick's mother was a singer who'd never wanted anything to do with him); she was back looking after Uncle Mitchell in his pile in Worcestershire.

She smiled. 'I should say I read all about it. There was one review – how did it go? "She is overpoweringly and dismayingly funny. In her unrestrained modesty resides that shattering vulgarity we long to liberate from all respectable persons. She is also a fine actor." '

I've not had many like that. It was a one-off in the *Sunday Times*, when I was in summer revue at the Comedy in 1969.

'You've a good memory,' I said. 'But you'd have done better to see it.'

'Who says I didn't?' And at last she blinked.

We sat quietly while I took off my slap. As I got dressed, I made a few idle comments about my clothes, how I used to make an effort. It was painful to me to make light of something so telling I could no longer afford to care about it. It still is. I used to wear bespoke suits and Chelsea boots. But somewhere around the mid-1970s, in those last-gasp years of post-war pride and illusory prosperity, as the pound collapsed and boarded-up London came to seem more Victorian than twentieth century, I assumed a uniform for life: a cardigan to cover my shirt, a brown cord jacket with rounded collar to cover the cardigan, grey trousers and a market mac. I couldn't afford John Lewis any more.

On the rare occasion I've actually been to bed with an attractive young man, I've often felt the same way. There is a guilty horror in taking off one's clothes in full view of a perfect body, perfect in the undeniable way of youth, however ill-sorted the features. This is very good of you, I want to say, as I stumble out of things. I'd rather you weren't so good. All the stories, all the myths about the covert years, the fun and the freedom – they're none of them true. It was so frightening. I can't teach you anything. And I'm too old to learn.

'Now then,' Beatrice declared. 'We'd better be off.'

*

It was understood, without anything being said, that we would eat together, letting the relief of sharing a meal stand for all we did not know about each other and could not ask. I had no food in my bedsit on the South Lambeth Road and only a Baby Belling on which to cook, but the question of 'where' didn't, thankfully, arise. Bea said she had something she wanted to give me.

She lived at the time off King's Avenue, in Clapham, in an unlikely corner house called the Eaugate. Maybe there'd been a spring or a stream nearby in the distant past. I remember four-stack chimneys, dormer windows, odd mace-like finials atop the bay roofs and a holm oak by the front porch.

Her small ground-floor apartment had its own side entrance, and a sliver of garden behind another dark green rotting gate. The windows were sticky and I recognized the smell that greeted us when Beatrice opened the door – the reek of damp carpet, old clothes and porridge – as the smell of neglect. She apologized for the state of the place, and fed a meter criss-crossed with blue Dynotape instructions. I asked her if she went back home at all.

She stopped, her hand on the light switch. Behind her, I could just make out a spacious room with a table in the middle and a dresser at the back. There were doors off to the left and right of the end wall and a passage leading out to the garden. Her eyes glittered. I stepped back.

'Home?' she said, smiling and frowning at once. Her teeth had yellowed and, somehow, grown. Two molars were missing. She would have been in her late forties, but looked older. 'You mean Kidderminster? Why would I think of going back there?'

Falteringly, I told Bea what I knew: that she had returned to look after Maurice. I supposed that had something to do with her apparent choice of career as a nurse. She'd always been a mother hen in the *Bugle*'s offices.

Bea shrugged and turned on the lights.

'I did go back to see Maurice, but he didn't know me. He died a couple of years ago. The hot summer was too much for him, I think.'

I nodded sympathetically.

'But home – I don't know. I'm from Somerset to begin with. That's where it all began. Did I ever tell you?'

'I had no idea.'

'Ah, well.' She apologized again for the dust. 'Even the best of friends know only a very little about each other – which is probably just as well. It may be all we can afford.' Her shoulders relaxed, she leant back on the table and carried on as though I'd made a penetrating observation in reply. 'Perhaps it was wrong to go back,' she mused. 'I couldn't help it, though. I was obsessed.'

'With—?'

'He'd really saved me, you see. Picked me up. We were so young.'

I thought this was stretching it a bit where Uncle Mitch was concerned. The dapper old show-off I remembered, in his Milanese silks, must have been twice Beatrice's age at least. But if that's how she wanted to memorialize him, as a sort of arthritic knight, then it was perfectly understandable. In fact, he'd always struck me as being dependent on her. Maybe she knew this, and wanted to spare his shade the ignominy it couldn't avoid in life – the pilot turned shopkeeper.

'Anyway,' she said, breezily. 'We had our share of each other.'

She paused, and took a thick envelope out of a pocket vent in her uniform. It was folded in half, somewhat eccentrically. 'The rest is in here.' Beatrice threw the envelope on the table and it slid a few inches, leaving a bright wooden trail in the surface dust. 'Now we must eat.'

*

I was banned from the kitchen, into which Bea disappeared, shutting the door behind her. 'We can carry on talking,' she cried out. 'I'll hear you.' I asked her if I could look around, and of course there was no reply. The thick envelope teased me, but I felt the need of permission to open it.

The passage off to the left of the main room became a narrow conservatory corridor, a sort of glass lean-to, with shelves on the dry-wall side and rows of dead plants humbled by cobwebs. The kitchen was behind the inner wall; at the very end of the corridor there was glass on both sides and I could look out at the back of the house into the kitchen window. Behind it a dark presence scrubbed and scraped, holding objects up to the light.

The moving presence saw me and stopped. It rapped angrily on the pane, and I looked away, with that confused sense of having been taken for a spy when all I wished to do was make amends.

What had gone wrong? The flat was barely lived in. It was frozen in the way of lives that have survived a trauma – the war, a death, love lost. I returned to the front room and walked past the dresser and the kitchen into the bedroom on the far side. It was neat, unslept in, proud and sad. A mirrored armoire in the corner tilted slightly in its alcove. A rime-green carpet didn't meet the skirting board. The fireplace was boarded up, and the board painted a cream-white.

On two slanting bookshelves to the right of the hearth a copy of *Lorna Doone*, reminding me of *Precious Bane*, stood out. I saw maps of Somerset and Exmoor stashed between strange volumes: histories of families, of the Dyrham estate – and paperbacks, the kind you find in holiday cottages or theatrical digs, fat with damp, which belong to no one but define the place.

The armoire opened with a jiggling key. It contained a few suits, some trousers with braces attached, a couple of polyester shirts, a blue blazer with moth-eaten facings, and skirts. An awful warm breath emanated from the fabric, especially the shirts, and I shut the door.

It wouldn't close.

A fold must be caught in the hinge, I thought, but the clothes weren't anywhere near the sides of the cupboard. Stifling panic took a hold. The bodiless garments stared and seemed to twitch on their hangers, as though bones might slink from the sleeves. It was just a sock at the bottom, a tiny sock. I picked it up and my hand brushed the shirts apart. Behind them, at the back of the wardrobe on a ledge, was a series of polystyrene heads and the gubbins of heavy make-up, hidden away as if in shame – moisturizers, concealers, quality stuff.

A noise from the kitchen disturbed me.

The Eaugate had a desolate air. It was reasonably full of furniture and books, yet it felt ransacked, as though a vital element had been forcibly removed. There was nothing to soften the edges of the crockery in the dresser, or the hard pink-runnelled counterpane on the eiderdown. There were no bills or photos, no little messages, no inexplicable orna-ments, cards, private junk. The room above the news agency in Kiddie had been stuffed with knick-knacks, but this was the property box minus its properties.

It was also curiously unfeminine. With all my warped experience, I don't pretend to have many insights into women – except one, perhaps. The bigger and bolder they come, the more they prize their delicate, daily routines. Look in their handbags and bathrooms. See them unpack. The wife of a seedy Greek diplomat (don't ask) once told me she'd had Margaret Thatcher to stay in the late 1980s, and the thing that really amazed her about the Iron Lady wasn't her brass and tough-mindedness, or sleepless appetite for work, but her sheer girliness – the nighties, powders, pinks, creams and lotions impeccably laid out; arranged in front of the mirror; clucked over; dotingly applied.

The same was true of the Beatrice I knew. She paid particular and constant attention to her slides and grips, smoothed the creases in her white blouse, mumbled approv-ingly with each minuscule repair of lipstick.

Even later, during that terrible year when Tony lost the Pleasure Gardens and went back on the road, Bea was the picture of poise and elegance. Well, I saw her once – but she made an impression. It was at a student gig in Brighton.

She had Nicholas in a pram; he was crying, I think, but you couldn't really hear him above the sound of breaking glass and the hoarse, cracked laughter of girls trying to impress. Tony was in a corner of the bar, doing Chop Cup rather brilliantly, Linking Rings, the Doves, Telephone Directory, and Stuck to the Chair. A waste of his talents. One thin, stripy girl kept shouting out, 'I can do that,' 'That's easy.' Eventually, Beatrice went over to her and whispered something in her ear. There was no more noise from that quarter. She believed in Tony, you see, and the belief gave her power – circumstances didn't matter. Her pride enveloped her: she was majestic, with Julie Christie hair and a jade waxed wraparound – Julie Christie via Jean Rhys.

The woman who came out of the Eaugate kitchen with two plates on a tray looked very different, nervous and starved of company. Angry. She'd forgotten the knives and forks. The kitchen door was ajar, and I could see a pile of cutlery on the draining board, lent a dead gleam by the light.

'Don't you dare,' said a voice, as I got up to fetch the implements. A hand landed on my shoulder with uncanny force. I turned, the hand relinquished its grip and Bea merely smiled apologetically. Her hands were back by her side, worrying the handkerchief. I sat down, but found that I was breathing shallowly and had lost my appetite.

'You have to indulge me,' Bea said, when she'd laid the table to her satisfaction. 'I'm funny about the kitchen. It's a mess, but I know where everything is. I suppose—'

'You don't have to explain.'

'Oh, yes I do,' she said in a tone of pleasant though absolute contradiction.

She got up again, this time to draw the curtains. The dirt in the red velvet pleats looked like a late frost. 'I have a great deal to explain. And there's something I want you to do for me, Leslie.'

'Anything. I'd be delighted.'

'Good,' said Bea. 'You owe it to me, you know.'

I didn't know what she meant. I was feverishly uncomfortable, in need of a drink. My wrists chafed against my cuffs; the skin hurt all over. The food in front of me was a ragù of tomatoes and mushrooms, with plain spaghetti and butter and salt. It was delicious, but I could only eat it slowly. If I looked down, I knew that Beatrice was eating, too, because I could *hear* her. She made a wet, dragging, snuffling sound, hard to associate with human digestion. If I looked up, the noise stopped and she'd be sitting there, motionless, an innocent expression on her face, watching me from the other end of the table, with her chin dripping red and the front of her uniform befouled.

'This is a bit like Grandmother's Footsteps,' I said. I wanted to make a joke: to make her see that I knew things were not right, but that I made no judgement. I lost heart. 'Tell me what you want me to do.'

'What do I want?'

She breathed in deeply and looked at the envelope in the dust.

'What do I want?' she repeated.

A sad person is easily distracted by the echoes of words.

'My life has been very dramatic,' Bea said, firmly. She waved her fork and a coil of spaghetti unwound onto her fist. 'Most people complain that theirs has not been exciting enough. When an extraordinary event occurs, if someone rescues them from a fire, they say, "It was so dramatic, it was like a play." The more unusual it is, the more real they feel.'

'I know.'

'But my life isn't usual. I am unusual – all the time. No

one ever says, "That's enough, you can go now," or "Next!" There's no end to it.'

Through the curtains on my left I sensed headlights rolling and dipping to a halt. They were just bright enough to make the velvet pulse.

'Sometimes I dream that one day I'll wake up and be with you in the stalls again, Les. But it will never happen, will it? You lose the habit of doing usual things, you see – and then once people know you're unusual, you're stuck. If you sit quietly, they call it a lucid spell. And if you do things you can't quite believe yourself, things a real person couldn't get away with, well, they just happen. No one stops you, or says, "I don't believe it!" I cut Tony's son with some glass – it was an accident, I was frustrated – and there was a big scene. I had a little girl, but they said – Tony and my—'

Beatrice looked at me blankly.

'There was a little girl,' she repeated, 'but they said I couldn't keep her. I was put under observation. Drama all the way, it's most strange.'

A car drew up. People got out – people who were trying to be quiet and discreet. I could hear them giving orders, coming up the path.

'Oh, Bea,' I said.

'Don't be sorry,' she said, briskly. 'No one forces my hand.' She paused, and when she spoke again it was with a tutored deliberacy. 'You can't make someone do something they don't want to do.'

Her eyes widened at the noise outside. I went to her and tried to hold her. She leant in with her arms up against my chest, but an embrace was impossible. Her hair felt wretchedly coarse. When I put my hands through it, matted clumps dropped out. She stank of unwashed wool.

When they broke down the door, Beatrice ran to the

kitchen and barricaded herself in. I stood by the living-room window, out of the way. Her shouting, like her eating, was not a sound I recognized. I remember thinking matter-of-factly: this is unfair. This woman had an ocean of words to choose from, and not one has risen to her lips to save her.

Two bigger men, nothing to do with the ambulance crew or the man holding the jacket, forced their way into the kitchen and cried out. Beatrice smashed the window and tried to escape, but she was pulled back through and, evidently, gashed herself on the glass. I came forward, around the back of the table, in time to see the man with the needle and the other man with the jacket dragging a shrieking thing in costume, its arms and face covered in blood and spittle and sauce, off the sideboard. The kitchen buzzed, the horrid drone of electricity and infestation, and Bea appeared to flag. And then she said, quite clearly, 'That's enough. I'm all right now.'

The men set her down, and she submitted; let her arms be guided and secured. In the main room, her poise returned. She spoke quickly, efficiently, as though she were being called away to a meeting.

'Find her, would you, Les? They took her – explain everything.' Bea's eyes glanced at the envelope, as the crew bundled her towards the door. 'And don't worry. Tell her not to worry about me, but do find her. I'd be most grateful.'

I followed her to the door, where the ambulance was waiting. It was grey with small square windows, like a prison vehicle. Tony met me on the pavement and wouldn't let me back in the house. His face was white; he wanted to know what I'd seen. He told me later that a nurse on Beatrice's ward in Springfield, the psychiatric hospital in Tooting, had been overpowered, poisoned, stripped and dumped in the laundry. The perpetrators, most of them low-riskers, made no effort to escape, and by the time her body was discovered they were back upstairs watching television.

\*

Like the pain of childhood, the pain of others administers its own anaesthetic. Events crowd in to distract us and dull our sympathies.

I forgot Beatrice, or so I thought, and spent the rest of the summer with an osteopath to whom I'd been introduced by Neville.

Paul sang in a concert at St John's, Smith Square. Neville was conducting his own reconstruction of an Ireland fragment, music to Browning's 'My Last Duchess', which he sweetly dedicated to me; I wasn't there. They had a romantic dinner afterwards. Neville showed Paul his record collection, made purely medical references to his lower back (on which the strain of standing on a rostrum trying to attract attention had begun to tell) and nothing happened. Paul was much younger than us, in his mid-thirties, neat, short and solid: clean-shaven, blond-haired, serious. 'Isn't he the most wholesome thing you've ever seen?' said Neville, when the three of us got together for a drink. I wasn't sure. The sports jacket and wavy side-parting didn't fool me. He knew too much about shoes and interior decorating. Anyway, wholesome or not, Paul and I had a whale of a time the next evening, and for the rest of August, until Neville found out from someone else in his choir. He wasn't angry, or surprised. He'd not had any luck with Paul himself, and Paul was too obviously in search of a well-shod father-figure for me to qualify in anything but the short term. Still, I saw the look of defeat in Neville's face.

To make amends, I took him to see Rudolf Nureyev dance *Le Corsaire* at the Coliseum. The hazy pursuit of an

Argentinian barman in the dress circle the summer before had led me to see more of Rudi and his pound of sprouts than was perhaps strictly necessary, but I had at least caught the dancer in his prime. During the hurtling solo from the pas de deux, Nureyev leapt and seemed to sit down, midair, on the intake of breath. Time slowed, music vanished: you felt that there was room and opportunity to get up and walk round him. When he landed, it was like surfacing in a pool: the music surged back while you gasped your appreciation. That was in 1977. A year later, it was chillingly different. He ran like a skater with the ice breaking beneath him.

I applauded as enthusiastically as everyone else, and Neville transmogrified into a walking blood orange, as he does whenever he finds something to admire. He has the happy knack of having very high standards in his own field while being easily satisfied in every other. But I found myself downing huge G&Ts afterwards to calm my nerves, and muffle the thud in my ears.

I looked out into the Coliseum and realized that I was in a shell, watching the shell of a man do things badly that he had once done well. And we carried on praising him. You could be a shell and the world of form and manners and polite selfishness would treat you as it always had, out of fear. That was the sound of the ice breaking: the awful whisper that the world's attention was just another way of taking no real notice. That even the most adoring gaze was, in the end, averted. I drank more to avoid a second conclusion, and couldn't. When the people you grow up admiring, whoever they might be – actors, writers, singers, footballers, teachers – can still *do* what they do, then you can still feel that you're young. When they start to fail, that's the beginning of the end.

I laughed a lot that evening. Neville was in high spirits,

too. I wanted to get home late so that I wouldn't have to lie awake. When I finally lay down, it was almost light. I drew the curtains, had a last swig, and went through the usual one-potato, two-potato routine, ignoring a lot of noise in the stairwell outside, until I suppose I fell asleep. The police were round in the morning, saying somebody had been burgled and stabbed and had I seen anything?

One of them asked the questions; the other looked, unimpressed, at my flat. It's less frilly than some, but the feather above the mirror must have nailed me as a theatrical. They asked if I knew my neighbour. It seemed a dreadful inverted echo of the scene in the Eaugate, where I *had* known the person and nobody asked me anything.

Later the same day, I scrubbed up and caught the train to Putney with the intention of trolling along the embankment to Barn Elms Reach, where you could grope the odd cyclist or wave your cock at the men clambering over the bulk-storage containers on the other side of the river. When I got there, I discovered that the containers were gone and the whole rambling, industrial-gothic edifice of Manbré and Garton Ltd, which used to supply liquid sugar to Fuller's and Young's, was in the process of being cleared. I was bewildered and dismayed. The clearance spoke with the force of prophecy. It said what prophecies always say: I told you so. The struggling Port of London had dried up in the trade slump, and elsewhere British Leyland and the Coal Board were going bust. At the time, I found it hard to be moved by these calamities. To me, inflation in the daily round meant five pence on a pint of gold top or a pound on Bell's, though even I could see that jobs for life were a thing of the past. On the telly, the litany of claim and counterclaim, from union to management and back, had an almost pleasant, soporific effect. And the emergence of a certain breed of posh leftie actor in open collars, making the case for 'job security' in the very jobs they'd gone on stage to avoid, never failed to raise a smile. But when I looked over at Manbré Wharf that afternoon, with the tractors and dump trucks wandering about the surface of the moon, it also brought to mind the idea of hard-heartededness and what it might do to you.

Every anaesthetic wears off in the end – to reveal not pain, but its loss. And for the emptiness of that reminder there is no salve, because the pain of no longer feeling pain is beyond killing.

I saw the long skiffs beside the wharf buildings, the two chimneys next to the silos, the scaffold lettering and the smoke. Stronger than the leathery sweat of the man kneeling in front of me was the caramel stench of boiling sugar, and the sound of laughter in the Department of Half-Mourning.

*

I spent the next twenty years pissed out of my head.

Doctors told me what to expect if I didn't cut back – tremors, anxiety attacks, vomiting, diarrhoea, convulsions, hallucinations, pancreatitis, neuropathy, heart failure, dry skin. I said to them, darling, I know clubs where those are practically the house rules. And so pretty soon I decided to buy in bulk. 'You're running away from it,' said one severe young man in the Allen Clinic at Guy's. I'd gone in for a blood test, and the results were startling: about 70% proof. I said, 'On the contrary, I'm running straight back to it,' and asked if he couldn't palm me a flask of surgical to tide me over until Borough High Street.

He was shocked, but I couldn't honestly see why. If you're fed up, the argument that by drinking you're missing out on something better isn't exactly compelling. Similarly, the presumption behind a 'cure' – that you will soon find an activity you enjoy more than drinking – is false. You won't, unless of course it's preaching about how you stopped. For instructions in the latter art I humbly refer you to any memoir with 'me' or 'myself' in the title. You know the sort: *Dear Me, Don't Mind Me, Is that Me Over There?, Playing With Myself, Myself and Other Animals, Bring Me the Head of Career Restructuring*. Oh, the bathos of the soft drinks trolley in the last chapter. Scratch an addict and find a mid-ranking character actor whining about the Big Film that never came.

The cured are a garrulous minority. They seem not to know that it isn't the despair that gets you in the end. It's the hope.

My solution has been routine and repetition: a job, ironically, for life. To the world of chaos and pain and hopeful ambition, I prefer lovely old order – twice a week at the Cap and once on Saturday at the Vauxhall. Actors are obsessed with being different and taking risks, but anyone can put on a silly face. Anyone can change. Look at all those terrible films where beautiful people cover their heads in bubbly latex and pretend to be ugly. It takes courage to stick to a routine. It takes an artist to dress up and still be himself.

I tried to be different things for a while – to modernize. This was to mollify Tony, who'd stuck with me after the Victoria Palace debacle, but didn't want to be saddled with an unemployable drunk. He thought I might make some ads.

It was in the late 1980s, at the tail end of the City boom, when ad agencies were spending big money on high-concept development. In a normal film casting, you turn up, speak to a clueless assistant producer ('It's a horror film with humour and heart. The three Hs'), read a few lines and leave. Ad castings are worse. There are usually about ten of you, all trying to look like family men in front of the cornflakes or the Hovis, all wearing M&S casuals with loafers, and all gay as geese. You smirk and wink, do a breakfast scene – trying to forget your actual morning ritual, which is half an hour of retching and three stiff ones before you can even stand up straight – and, if you're lucky, go home with a 'light pencil'. You wait two days for a 'heavy pencil'. Tony then tells me how much the ad might be worth – £17,000, or three years' salary – at which point, with my availability confirmed and bags packed, the pen runs out of ink.

My big success was a Swiss-cheese commercial filmed in Wales and directed by a Spaniard for Italian TV. Or – a near miss, this – my audition for a big BMW campaign, to have been directed by Gus Key, an advertising legend of whom no one has ever heard. Mr Key interviewed me while skateboarding around a ballroom in Lancaster Gate. He fell off and broke his foot.

'Can you drive me to casualty?' screamed the legend.

'No.'

After that, I went into a decline. Tony offloaded me onto a junior for seven years, who never came to see me in anything because she was 'theatred out'. I made a little money doing some role play for Actors In Industry, and got a few print ads, including one for Stannah Stair-lifts, which was fairly relaxing. Lying there at the foot of the stairs in a studio in E5, listening to the man from Stannah on the phone arguing about ad placement and whether I could be got away from the smoked salmon and the G-strings, it occurred to me that most alcoholic hallucinations, by comparison, lacked implausibility.

Much of the rest of that smashed era is a dumpster of similar memories: the cut-price cruise, where I had berth and meals and fifty quid a week in order to appear with a one-legged woman singing 'Climb Every Mountain' (cause and effect weren't obvious: had she lost it early on, or had someone hacked it off mid-chorus?) . . . the straight man at Kennington Park Pride who said he admired me so much he was going to have a sex change in order to live his life more honestly as a lesbian . . . the semi-professional tour of *Twelfth Night* where the sweet-faced Orsino impregnated all the girls and then revealed he had syphilis.

But these are failures of an exceptional, self-dramatizing nature: the sort of thing, as Beatrice would have said, that makes a dull and safe life seem theatrical, unusual. She was the extrovert, not I. She and Dot died about a year ago.

*

'How can I help you, Leslie?' Tony asked.

'Fucking agents. Bring you to your knees, then get you to beg.'

I'd been in hospital a week, against my better judgement, and the company – bed-wetters and weeping royalists – was getting me down. The telly in the day room showed endless pictures of rubberneckers from Essex laying bunches of flowers and clearly having the time of their lives. 'She was a lovely lady,' said a lemony wisp in the next bed.

'If they had any idea how much they're despised . . .'

'It's a great loss,' Tony smarmed.

'Oh, don't start. She doesn't mean *her*, you fool. Look.' I leant over and shouted into my neighbour's lavender hearing aid. 'Who was lovely, Iris? Who was the lovely lady? What was her name?'

'Tingle-fangle.'

Iris shook her head.

'See?'

Tony breathed out. 'Why must you be so unpleasant?'

'Because,' I began, and waited for the wave to pass.

'Because I do not *like* my fellow man. And because I can't sleep.'

'It's mats tonight, until we get you billeted,' said Iris.

Tony shut his eyes.

'I can't sleep,' I reiterated. 'You could help me with that.'

When he opened them again, they looked red – and purple underneath, as they had a half-century ago. A bell sounded.

'I could sing you a lullaby,' he said. 'Quack, quack.'

Visitors came and went.

I felt a plucking at my sleeve. The giant nurse with the hair like a cartoon Maria Callas and the broken glass raining down from her torn face was leaning over me again. I was in a room full of fridges – their interiors stuffed with fungal growths, decay, the stink of solid things reduced to yellow liquid, evaporated egg, bones greenly festered and spongiform, each gruesome cabinet abandoned when the rotten matter in it left no room for fresh carcasses. For heads in wardrobes.

'Chicken or fish?' she hissed and repeated the offer several times, until another nurse, plain, petite and bored-looking, replaced her.

'What was that about heads in wardrobes?' said a concerned voice.

'He's gone again,' said Neville. 'He'll be back.'

The ward swam into focus.

'Have you only just got here?' I demanded.

'I like that. I brought you in. I've been here all the time.'

'Chicken or fish, Mr Barrington?'

'It's a rotten shame,' Iris countered. Neville and Tony and the small nurse and everyone else had milky eyes, I noticed, but Iris's were clear, and turned towards me. 'She was a lovely lady.'

*

Tony moved back to the Eaugate when Beatrice died, and at long last sold his freehold in the Keys to Vauxhall. The buyer was a young entrepreneur who, strangely enough, wanted to start a 'mixed' club night in the pub downstairs, with a cabaret act or two and 'an inclusive music policy', whatever that means. He'd heard rumours that I was still about, and would I be interested in a regular gig? Tony got me to sign a contract. That was nearly four years ago and I haven't regretted it. The closet dressing room, the sweat on the ceiling, the sugared floor, the expert musical accompaniment (when available) – they're still the same.

I tend to host rather than perform these days, and to make myself look good I book acts who are decrepit. Last week, we had Marvellous Joe Minkie. Dear Joe. He was yodelling at the Guernsey Palace of Varieties in 1929, two years before I was even born. He travels everywhere with his wife, Amy, and an oxygen cylinder, both labelled. The bar stays open for two hours after the show comes down and you can drink and chat outside with a variety of insouciant gays and straights. That's the most noticeable change, I suppose: the avowed nature of the audience, although Joe said he didn't spot anything out of the ordinary.

The club has made a name for itself, without any of the usual hype: television isn't the grail it used to be. (All those channels and nobody watching them.) It's certainly lasted longer than either the Pleasure Gardens or the Waterman's. It seems to thrive on word of mouth. And there's never any trouble. Neville fell in love with his gangly next-door neighbour there, which had a sad end, as unequal infatuation often does, but apart from that all's well. I've even had an acting job out of it, from a slick youngster who directed Tony's son in some fearfully high-minded piece about the Branch Davidians in Waco. The flatterer said he'd worked *on* cults; never *with* one.

'You know my Prospero, too, I've heard – Bob Ladd.'

We were standing under the first-floor window.

'Indeed I do,' I said. 'But not as well as some.'

\*

There was no funeral for Beatrice. Tony rang and told me she'd gone at last. We had a sombre meal, the three of us: me, Tony and Maurice's fat, worried-looking cousin – Roy or Ray, I think – the last relative, who kept talking about Bea in the present tense, and then remembering, and shaking.

I went back with Tony to the Eaugate and we began to talk.

Now I like Tony – he's a reasonable man, and one of my oldest friends – but he lives behind a screen of frosted charm and gives very little away. His kindnesses (and there have been many) can feel a touch clinical, as if he's taking notes on gratitude and its effects. Perhaps he was cut off from himself early on; someone let him down, or he did a bad thing and got away with it. You meet people like that in the theatre – people without a consistent centre. They're good about visiting you in hospital, but they can't stop smiling, either. One thing I've noticed: Tony tends to ask questions, in a slightly pained voice – 'What do you think of . . . ?' 'What can I do?' 'Is that true?' – without risking an answer or an opinion himself; if you try to force one out, the screen lowers with a whisper of injury and judgement. 'I don't have an answer to that straight away.' 'We'll see.' 'You may be right.' He's had plenty of lovers over the years, and none of them has stayed for long. Reasonableness has its pitiless aspects.

The truth is: I'm frightened of him. I'd asked him once before, after the sectioning, what had happened to the little girl and the envelope, and his surprise, then, was almost genuine – 'What letter?' Twenty years later, when I asked a second time, he was irritably amused. On both occasions, I had the impression that he simply didn't understand why I was interested.

'All you need to know,' Tony said, 'is that she is alive and cared for.'

'Adopted.'

He said nothing. I wondered if he had considered keeping her.

'Why would I do that?'

'Oh, for Heaven's sake, she was your child. She—'

Tony laughed. 'No, no, no. God, no. My child.' He broke off, still laughing, and poured himself some coffee from a flask. 'She had nothing to do with me.'

'In that case I don't see why you shouldn't tell me where she is. Beatrice asked me to find out. I gave her my word.'

'Why?'

'Because I owed it to her.'

'Why?'

I didn't have to think.

'She thought I'd taken her life. Not literally, obviously, but – what she might have become, who she might have been.'

'Mad people,' Tony said, 'take things very literally.'

'Not,' I muttered, 'that she'd have wanted to be like this, I dare say.'

Tony rolled and stretched his neck. I've often seen him do that, to relax his throat. 'You can't know what she wanted, and I can't tell you.'

'Tell me what you can.'

He pushed the flask towards me. It came out that the little girl was Uncle Mitchell's, conceived in the first full flush of Bea's return from two years with Tony, and that she'd been put into care after Beatrice turned violent again and Maurice died of a heart attack. These were the bare bones, obviously, but as Tony spoke I found myself willing him to say less, not more. The truth seemed out of kilter with the amount of experience it described. In stories you know more at the end than you do at the start, whereas in life it's the other way round.

Our discussion came to a natural close, and with the thermos so near to hand I felt thirsty. I asked Tony how he came by such a pretty flask, and he said he had an idea that Bob had left it behind. I knew I'd seen it before. It had an attractive tartan pattern, with gold edges and a genie of steam twining from the top.

'Have some,' Tony said. 'It's got your name on it.'

# Twelve

ON THE DAY OF the technical rehearsal it was discovered that the set, built for the more versatile Young Vic, did not fit the stage at Wyndham's. The arcade was too wide, so one arch on either side had to be removed; the white piano refused to drop down for the routing of the fools, and when it did it knocked over the central fountain; worst of all, from the new and lower perspective of the stalls, the fountain obscured Prospero's main entrance upstage.

'And if I stand here, Adrian,' Bob Ladd pointed out, 'or here – Adrian? – there's simply no light at all. I'm not making a fuss.'

'You're lit now, Bob.'

'Which means the people in the first five rows won't be able to see me – and they've paid the most. It's terribly unfair.'

'We'll sort it.'

'Perhaps I could just have a look at the state. If I can get under these palms . . . rather a number . . . create such a lot of shade . . .'

In the stalls, Leslie chortled to himself while Neville read.

'Can you believe anyone could be so utterly charmless?' he whispered.

Leslie seemed to be enjoying Bob's discomfiture. Since the axing of *Practice Makes Perfect* halfway through the Young

Vic run, the pressure on the star to reward his producers with a big West End opening had increased. Cracks had started to appear in Bob's smooth finish: the honeyed bass of Sunday evening radio appeals was now a rising baritone with hints of gagged soprano; he missed entrances, or came in on red; complained of tinnitus; snapped at already tearful costume designers; fumed if the director – 'less than half my age' – presumed to give him a note. Lunchtimes he spent pacing the corridor, jabbing at his mobile and occasionally yelling out, as if he needed it to be heard, 'Tell the fat idiot the part is mine and that it doesn't happen without me.'

'He hasn't changed,' Leslie said, nudging Neville. 'Underneath, he hasn't altered a bit. Isn't it astonishing? Look at him. Stop waving your arms, you great ponce, and come downstage. How does he get *away* with it?'

Neville looked up briefly, scanned the space in front of him. They were doing the log-piling scene and Nick, Kwame's replacement as Ferdinand, was having difficulty persuading Bob to stay still in the background.

'Of course, you know what the problem is, don't you?'

*. . . and for your sake / Am I this patient log-man.*

'Neville?'

'I'm listening.'

Leslie wriggled confidentially. 'Approval-seeking.'

Neville pursed his lips.

'He's a classic extrovert. Desperate for approval. And at the same time – and I suppose it's not uncommon among actors – he's absolutely incapable of love.' Leslie paused. 'Yes, that's it. I don't think Bob truly knows what it is to love another human being. Do you?'

'Think?'

'Agree? It makes sense, come on. That invisible first wife, the absurd overwritten stuff about his gropey uncle –

currying favour with the Ranks of the Abused, I suppose – the music, the art, the nobs at Covent Garden. It's all protective scaffolding.'

'I thought that was the point of this,' Neville said quickly, tapped the sheet he was holding and glanced sideways.

Leslie froze, a revolted smile on his lips.

'Go on.'

'People need their masks, or their scaffolds, if you like. There's a bit here. Where is it? "The real person is a receding horizon, the cart that rolls away." And in the last chapter, the business about knowing less at the end than you did at the start, truth being unilluminating. All that stuff.'

'Yes, yes, yes.' Leslie winced. 'But the difference is that I'm *aware* I'm telling fibs. I'm not kidding myself about anything. Whereas that berk, that fraud, hasn't even the principle to admit he's a fake. He doesn't even know it. *See.*'

'So how can it be his fault?' Neville adjusted his half-lunettes. There was a difficult silence. 'And what do your principles consist of, exactly? Making it up and having the guts to say so?'

Against the shredded beetroot of his cheeks, Leslie's eyes looked suddenly old and yellow. The plush was hard and uncomfortable.

'Too fucking right. I am who I am. I can say that at least.'

Neville put a hand to his ear. 'Sometimes I wonder,' he said.

'Wonder what?' Leslie said, but the silence rang on, punctuated by distant objections from the stage. ('Could you keep it down back there? Thanks very much.') 'Wonder *what*?' he repeated.

'I take it,' Neville said, as mildly as possible, 'that most of this is *un*true, then.' And he held up a handful of the loose-leaf typescript. 'Your memoir.'

Leslie said nothing, but the revolted smile had reappeared.

'Apart from the obvious falsehoods and traducements, I mean – like my caricature, my pass at you, the yellow socks, the – the – I must say, extraordinary and pointless allegation that I had an affair with poor Daniel next door.'

'Oh, him. That was just local colour.'

'Or with a – what was he? – a singing *osteopath* – called *Paul*?'

'You should feel honoured. For Christ's sake, I barely mention you. You're just a walk-on. Don't get ideas. I've embellished you to protect you.'

Neville's lips parted and closed. He was very still.

'I see. So how much is true?'

'It's *all* true. As true as I can make it.' A pause, then: 'It's fucking *felt*, I tell you that much. I *feel* it. Every day. Here.' Leslie thumped his chest. Spittle glistened on his chin and the hand that gripped the armrest of seat L16 had gone white. 'I suppose you want me to deny that?'

'I didn't say that.'

'Live my life in some fucking arrangement, some suburban *arrangement* to show how normal I am? Go to concerts, get my crockery from Heals and have *people* for *dinner*? Is that it? Show what a model citizen I've become?'

'I think you've moved on to a different subject.'

'The world has moved on, Neville. No one believes in you any more. Your type – the idealist. You don't exist. I don't have to apologize for what I am. At least I've still got feelings – why should I deny them?'

'No one's asking you to.'

'You pitiful man. Give me those.'

Neville held on to the pages. 'Nobody's asking you to deny your feelings.' He sounded frightened. 'It's how you act on them that matters. That's morality.'

Leslie hauled himself to his feet. His face had gone from purple to blue-black.

'Fuck off.' He leant over his cowering friend. 'Why don't you take a – give me those—' He snatched back half the pages. 'You fucking failed queer.'

*Hence, bashful cunning! / And prompt me, plain and holy innocence.*

The sound designer happened to be walking past. Neville waved him on.

'You can't publish it,' he said, wishing his voice were steadier.

'Who said anything about publishing? I'm going to per*form* it. It's going to be a one-man show, probably at the Bush. Mike Favata's giving me three weeks next spring. Alice is cutting – shaping it.'

'It doesn't make any difference.' Neville began to gather his things. 'You can't publish it and you can't perform it.'

'Why not?'

'Because,' and Neville took a deep breath. A coherent thought now might save the situation. The simple proposition often appealed to Leslie in this state, kept him off boiling point. 'It would hurt people.'

'Don't be so fucking wet.'

'It might. It could ruin a life, or lives, and you wouldn't know. The person who minded would be forced to pretend that he didn't. And who knows what might happen then? Have you thought of that?'

Leslie was staring hard at the back of the stalls.

'You've never supported me,' he said, finally.

The glasses fell from Neville's hand.

'Don't bother denying it. You know you've never lifted a finger, really. Not *really*. Or only out of some weird, martyrish impulse to avoid living your own life. I don't know what it is.' Leslie rested on the seatbacks of row K. 'Everyone's got you down as a saint, haven't they? Finally making a few bob with your choirs and score copying, whatever it is that you do. But I'm not so sure. I don't fool so easily. Oh, I *know*. You're always there. You're so endlessly, tirelessly reliable. Always ready with the judicious comment, silently plotting ways to save me from myself. Aren't you? Doing it now, aren't you?'

Neville looked away but there was no escape. He tried to conjure a judicious comment, in a spirit of appalled self-recognition, but all he could remember was the number of times he'd mopped up Leslie Barrington's vomit, wiped his arse, put him to bed and then walked back along the South Lambeth Road at three in the morning. When he got home, he sometimes rang a chatline and changed his voice, or ordered in. Escorts thought him slightly creepy. It was the music. The offbeat interest in *bands* (who the hell was James Jamerson?). The buried hint of high culture. His moist underlip.

'I'm digging myself out of a fifty-year hole dug by the man who stole my fucking career and my father,' Leslie spat, 'and all you can do is preach self-denial. Ooh. Be careful. Don't upset anyone. Mustn't piss in the punch.'

Neville had been going to mention the job in America. That it was Michael Kamen who'd come to the first night, not Michael Nyman. They were remaking *Night of the Demon* and wanted music lasting forty-three minutes and twelve seconds. A longish symphony – in tiny chunks – for a hugeish sum. He had some time for Kamen, who'd shoehorned Shostakovich into *Die Hard 2*.

'Well, let me tell you what I know about martyrs.'

Neville looked down.

'Martyrs are a bunch of cunts who'd rather die than touch

another person, fuck them or otherwise acknowledge their humanity. Sound familiar?'

There was no noise from the stage, which had emptied for lunch.

'You know what I hate? It's your caution. "Ooh no, I couldn't write a big piece – it might go wrong. I'll stick to a knitting circle of tenors from Sutton, thanks." Fifty-five years old and still got a sphincter like an asterisk, I bet.'

Inspired by his own venom, Leslie pushed Neville's face as he trampled over him to get out. It felt awful, but somehow justified and moving. Neville shook his head and Leslie, infuriated, turned and pushed it again.

'No wonder I couldn't fucking count on you.'

That didn't sound as good as he'd hoped – not sufficiently well earned. Good ideas and lines were like that. In any case, Neville's expression had not changed. You had to hand it to him. He knew how to take it.

\* \* \*

Nick and Martha were sitting in a cafe at the top of Bedfordbury which served sandwiches with made-up names, like 'le petit jambon'.

'She's better, I think,' Nick was saying. He stirred his coffee. 'We're taking a break while all this is going on. It's perfectly amicable.'

That word.

'Has it put you off?' Martha asked.

'God, no.' Nick jerked his head back to avoid a fly. 'I hope it'd take more than . . .' He saw that Martha wasn't smiling. 'Well, maybe a bit. The fit was pretty shocking. She was a different person. What can I say?'

'I don't know. What did Alice say?'

'Gibberish, mostly. But it was argumentative – two main voices, and some higher, garbled ones. It was as if she was recreating the scene. Then she clammed up – all you could hear was "mmm" after she bit her lip. I thought she might swallow her tongue, so I tried to get her mouth open and she lashed out.'

'It must have been terrifying.'

'It *was* terrifying.'

Martha pushed her plate with le petit jambon on it into the middle of the table.

'But you've no idea what brought it on?'

'Out of the blue.' Nick signalled for the bill. 'There's the tooth-grinding, I suppose. Perhaps she needs help expressing herself. Al's so pent up. As you know. It's like she lives behind a screen. I want to get to her – but I can't.'

The bill arrived.

'I'll get this,' said Nick, and began turning out his pockets for change. While he was counting, he added: 'I don't expect you remember Helen.'

'I was only a baby myself.'

'Awful for your parents.'

Martha could smell drains. In the street, the grills and stoves and Hobarts of the less exclusive cafes made the air shimmer. The sun was strangely absent, behind a gauze of its own effects.

'I remember it was hot.'

*

She remembered, in truth, considerably more – or as much, at any rate, as she had been told years ago when, in the clair-voyance of her childish inquisitiveness, she had successfully interpreted a series of silences and finally dared to ask: why did Helen go? 'You know why she died,' her mother replied.

'Because she fell in the water and couldn't get out.' The answer, evasive yet consequential, had satisfied Martha, whose one corroborating memory was of Alice on the canal bank with a bamboo fishing net in her hand. 'It was an accident,' Lilian added. 'Nobody's fault.' But this was a response to a different and unasked question, and thereafter, the image of her sister wielding the net began to take on a sinister aspect. It finished by becoming Martha's private, doll-whispered conviction that Alice, with her straight black hair and glaring reticence, was a witch. Didn't she suck Oxo cubes for dares? She also stared mutely whenever Martha cried, and screamed herself at night. The disturbance proved infectious. Martha screamed louder. Tony arrived to help them both settle. He brought sleep.

Of course it was an accident – Alice teaching baby Helen to swim, cooling her off in the canal's duckweed, losing her grip – but how the reach of grief accused the innocent! Her supervision of the 'accident' cost Alice her mother's love. It fostered silent blame. And it instructed her, Martha saw for the first time, in artifice; what people said and didn't mean. Nobody's fault.

She forgave the review, with no sense of forgiving, but increased anxiety on Alice's behalf. Everyone was worried about her. She had been ill after the attack, confused. Lilian and Ray, Leslie, Neville, whoever knew or cared, prescribed the usual rest. The first fear, naturally, was epilepsy: the voices ruled that out. Or schizotypal disorder, which sounded like the sort of thing a mad secretary might catch. Surprise prompted surmise. And yet the thing that impressed Martha most vividly about Alice's fit was how willingly the world looked past, excused, dismissed its one eye witness, almost as if the real taboo must be her sister's fitness to be loved. Nobody liked to mention Nick – not even Nick. 'Four weeks?

I don't call that a relationship,' was Lilian's worried comment. She knew better than to dwell on her own pain now; a second child in danger had cured her of it, probably. But the nature of Alice's trouble, as a result, eluded her. Something of it touched Martha, nonetheless: some glimpse of a will, a yearning to believe or to trust too long suppressed, and she was sorry. She was – sorry.

* * *

Tony met Alice after her Riverside Walk and offered his congratulations.

'What an extraordinary memory you must have, Alice. Absorbing all those facts. I loved your description of "Passage Paving". It does look like a lava-flow, doesn't it?' He chuckled and cocked his head. 'And I didn't realize so *much* of Hungerford Bridge is the original Brunel.'

'It isn't.' Alice bristled. 'The bridge supports are the only bits left. The suspension chains were reused at Clifton.'

'My mistake. *Your* performance was flawless.'

Touched, Alice muttered her thanks into a gust of wind.

'Pleasure.' Tony took her arm. 'How are you?'

'I'm fine.' She paused, gently releasing herself from his grip. 'I'm tired. And – I do appreciate your offer, but I'm really not sure it would do any good.' Her breath fought with the breeze. 'I don't think I want to go into it any more, Tony. I'm glad you were there to pick up the pieces on the night. But I'm better now, and I don't think Nick, or Mum and Dad, should have approached you.'

The agent twirled his brolly.

'As a matter of fact it wasn't Nick, or your parents. It was Bob. He's an admirer of yours, you know. He used to suffer from stage fright. I helped him, and he saw you were feeling the strain, so he called me.'

Alice wondered why it was that sympathy from the wrong quarter, and for the wrong reason, caused almost as much distress as distress itself.

'I just feel uneasy. I don't believe in picking over the past.'

They were on the Embankment now; Tony hailed a cab, and Alice winced with the sudden, uninvited insight that circumstances had played into Nick's hand: her fit, a momentary lapse of self-control, had given him the opportunity to make the break. He would never have had the strength otherwise.

'Everybody seems to know what it is I ought to be doing, and I'm not allowed to be myself. I'm sorry, Tony. I don't want to be hypnotized. To be honest, Leslie's version of events in Cradley doesn't inspire confidence.'

'Well, it wasn't like that, naturally. And you can think me devious, or you can believe me when I say I'm trying to help. All I'm offering is a relaxation technique, my dear. It's not an exorcism. What have you got to lose?'

*

It was balmy on the other side of Hyde Park, a different season altogether. Fed-up tourists sucked their ice creams and slouched towards Kensington Palace.

'Who taught you?'

'I didn't have a teacher.'

'No, but you must have learned how to – do this. You must have studied, if that's the right way of putting it.' Alice and Tony entered the Glass House office, empty now the agents had left for the day, and Tony shut the door. 'Perhaps it's just acting, which I'm not sure you can teach.' He made no reply. 'Perhaps it's sheer assertion, force of personality. Manipulation of the weak.'

'Come over here.'

'That sounds sceptical of me,' Alice apologized. The desire to cry welled up and evaporated. She hummed instead.

Tony drew down the green blinds and switched off the lights.

'Scepticism's not a bad place to start,' he said. 'It implies a kind of resistance. Extremely useful in its way.' Tony aimed a desk lamp into the far corner of the room and added under his breath, 'You might say I'm a believer in it.'

When Lilian chatted, she sounded afraid of what might be said if once she stopped. Tony's chat, by contrast, was patter – neither fearful nor intrusive, and Alice went along with it. Besides, the pain of suppressing her grief demanded a subtlety of pretence she could not always achieve by herself. Her mother and father tried to help, when they told her how well she looked, considering, though they needed too much reassurance themselves to be convincing.

Alice did not believe Tony's story about Bob. She knew what people were saying. She could hear the conversations in her head, particularly Lilian's blunt invocation of Helen. She had no wish to be turned into a case-study of 'difficult' family relations. And yet she couldn't resist: to be close to Tony was to be close to the cause of Nick; to hear echoes of her lover.

'I learnt a little from my grandmother,' Tony revealed. 'She was a traveller before she married my grandfather.'

He poured a glass of water, his eyebrows raised.

'But the person who had the greatest influence on me as a child was my foster-father – that's what he was, more or less – in Porlock.' The late, warm afternoon brightened behind the blinds. 'Where,' he added, 'I was evacuated.'

When Tony said 'Porlock', Alice thought of her pillow talk with his son, and saw the movement of Nick's throat when he spoke with his eyes closed. When Tony mentioned childhood, her mind flew to the moment Nick had said: 'I could grow old with you.' People didn't say such things unless they honestly meant them; he hadn't stopped meaning it; hundreds of lovers had survived a 'break' before; she wasn't naive to hope for more. Then she saw again the warning signs, and knew that they had always been there: Nick's mirth at withheld jokes; his silently testing references to music, clubs, drugs and clothes; his cards-on-the-table talk of sex drive and 'gratification', ostensibly as abstract concerns of living today, but implicitly, surely, as matters which afflicted him as they had never concerned her. She was thirty-one, and sweating. A black H&M shirt over a new bra from Rigby and Peller felt like pointless vanity. The more she attended to herself, to looks and parts, to so-called opportunities – like the cave-woman role in *Hominids*, for which she had auditioned in her best floaty top and straight skirt – the stronger her conviction that she was being asked to do her bit for self-deception. As if it was a project everyone was born to, but for the good of the species would never, could never discuss.

'You must have been very young,' Alice said.

'I was seven when war broke out. Very young.'

'Did the whole school go?'

'Yes, but they went to Wallingford. And I got on the train to Taunton.'

Tony talked while arranging the spread on his office chaise. He plumped a couple of cushions, invited Alice to lie down and moved his own chair closer. Behind him, on his long desk, were piles of scripts. The ones with spiral plastic spines were final drafts, probably from film companies, with Post-it notes on the front bearing the proposed actors' initials. Alice strained to see if the red letters on the top of the nearest pile were indeed N. G. It was a thick manuscript – a film series, perhaps, involving location work, travel, long periods away. The Post-it covered the first line of the title, but the second read 'the Runes'. Next to 'the Runes', Alice noted without particular interest, lay her version of the first two-thirds of Leslie's memoir, with its cuts and emendations. On the cover-page, in marker pen, the initials L. B., upside down, were visible. Her gaze wandered back to the script on top of the first pile.

What if Nick hadn't meant any of it? What if the whole world was false and nothing what it seemed?

'How,' Alice wanted to know, 'did you end up in Taunton?'

Tony took off his jacket, and rolled up his sleeves. He was wearing a dandruff-sprinkled turtleneck and some Ladd-ish loafers. The similarity between the agent and his most successful client had not impressed Alice before. It was an abstract quality of withdrawn confederacy, like judges whispering behind hands.

'By accident. The sign in front of us at the station, at Paddington, said "Stand Behind Here", so, thinking I must be on the wrong side already, I went and stood behind it and got separated from the rest of the class. And then a woman from the WVS shovelled me onto the West of England Express because it must have looked as if I was going to be left behind. And I couldn't speak up for myself.'

'You were too scared.'

'When we got to the other end, the billeting officer was very kind and said I could go back the next day or the day after . . .'

'And did you?'

'No.' Tony looked straight at Alice as though he were considering a range of options. He wrinkled his nose. 'God-awful smell of drains, isn't there?'

It was true. The autumnal drought, unbroken for the whole of September, had made the air sour with dust and diesel-motes. The warm air on the tube stank of bad eggs and rotten deodorant.

'And no birds, have you noticed?' Alice said, inventing a piece of folklore. 'That always happens when it gets hot. The birds retreat.'

'The air stops moving.'

'The air stops moving.' Alice closed her eyes, and was quiet for a moment. Then she jerked her head away from the cushion. She wanted to get up and run out of the room. Her legs refused to move. She had, she realized, no wish to move them. 'It's no good. I'm too aware of what you're trying to do.'

'Good.'

'Good? How can it be good? I'm supposed to be relaxed.'

'You're supposed to be suggestible, but that doesn't mean you have to be passive.' Tony knocked the glass by his left foot. Water dribbled onto the carpet, where the drops glistened before darkening the pile. 'Excitement on both sides is natural. You absolutely rely on adrenaline on stage, and I'm not sure that you can completely do without it off it. Probably why you can't have a laboratory study of hypnosis.'

'I don't understand.'

'Well, *my* role is to be confident and enthusiastic and charismatic, and that's hardly a model stance for a scientist, is it?'

Alice nodded, then shook her head. 'And mine?'

'Your role.' Tony leant on the desk and coughed. 'The explanation favoured by social psychologists would be that your role is to be willing – to play the part of the hypnotic subject. You want to be hypnotized, you see. And in your particular case, they'd say that any amnesia about Helen's death—'

'How can I have an "extraordinary memory", Tony, and be an amnesiac?'

'—was brought about by your desire to comply with the instruction to forget.'

'Which you gave me, when we weren't sleeping. Look, I know this is family legend, but I didn't forget about Helen. I just got over it.'

The atmosphere was oppressive. Through the glass wall, Alice fancied she could hear the hum of machines on standby.

'Indeed.' Tony got up, went to the desk drawer and pulled out a blank sheet of paper and a pencil. He gave them to Alice and sat back down. Alice was taken by surprise: it was a peculiar gesture, but not one to which she felt she could object. She could merely comment, and even then—

'Your comments, please. Whatever occurs to you, as and when.'

Tony wiped his forehead with a tissue. Alice gave an involuntary shiver.

'I haven't got any comments. I haven't forgotten *anything*.'

'It really is baking.'

'I can remember it all. But why should I? Why do you want me to?'

Alice gripped the pencil in her left hand and stabbed it into the sheet on her lap. The pencil punctured the paper and her thigh.

'I'm afraid,' Tony whispered, 'I don't have the answer to that.' He waited, and the noise of distant traffic seemed to respond. 'Straight away. Except to say that playing a role in hypnosis isn't the whole story. Because it only demonstrates – well, compliance.' He paused. 'It doesn't account for contradictions between what people can do in a trance and what they later reveal they *really felt while doing it*. It doesn't allow for our ability to do and think two different things at once—'

'I'm not sure I follow,' said Alice, reaching down for the glass of water.

'—like driving while speaking, listening and reading, talking and carrying . . . My foster-father did some work on this with a woman called Josephine Hilgard, and their findings were, shall we say, influential in *some* medical circles.'

Alice drank, and Tony Glass was distorted.

'What did he do?'

'He told his most susceptible subjects that they were insensible to pain.'

'What makes a subject susceptible?'

'Imagination. And resistance.' Tony chuckled. 'People who protest too much, but secretly want to believe. Two things at once, you see.'

The stale air had acquired a top note of phosphorus.

'Anyway, the subjects in this test group were asked to put their arms in ice-cold water and keep them there. Which they did, quite happily. But after ten minutes, he also invited them to press a buzzer with their other hand as soon as they felt any discomfort, and the majority buzzed repeatedly. My foster-father found that he could induce insensibility and sustain feeling at the same time. His conclusions were that there's a hierarchy of awareness, even with an immediate sensation like pain; and that a hypnotic response is what you get when you turn down the volume in one part of the brain and bring it up elsewhere.'

Alice's hands trembled and moved about on the paper.

'You mean, people can be distracted.'

'The hypnotically talented can be, yes.'

'But I don't need distracting.' Alice shook her head in exasperation. 'I'm not unaware. I don't have to be coaxed into saying that I remember Helen's death. Of course I do. I was there, on the bank. I opened the gate to the towpath. We went out. I got into the water.'

The room was still.

'Terrible things happen, and the explanation for them is never good enough. That's why they're terrible. And the truth is that, for all their concern, my parents don't think my acceptance of what happened is good enough. They want me to be more disturbed than I am.'

'You're assuming I blame you.'

'Not you, personally.' Tony's forgiving patience rattled her. It evoked, in a complex instant, the actor in the seaside pub, toying with unpaid-for food. 'I just have the feeling I'm being cornered.' Alice put her hand to her mouth, where a muscle spasm had numbed the edge of her tongue.

'Does that hurt?'

'Yes.' Alice nodded quickly, and the paper slipped from her lap. 'It hurts.' She took a deep breath. 'It often hurts. But that's it – it's physical. It doesn't mean something else. It's not a bloody metaphor.'

Tony picked up the sheet of paper, on which Alice had written in angry, perforated capitals the words I AM LYING, and laid it face down on the desk.

'It's like being fat,' said Alice, as the pain subsided. 'Being fat doesn't mean anything else, either. It doesn't mean you're kind and sympathetic. God, the number of people who want to confide in you about their weight or their sex lives because they think you'll *understand*. Understand what? I'm fat because my diet's rubbish and I eat too much.'

Tony caught another scrap of scribble as it slid to the floor.

'Of course you can't win,' Alice went on. 'If you turned round and said, "I don't care how much I eat, I never have, and I'm having an affair with your ex," they wouldn't believe you. They'd say you were *compensating*.'

The scribble read: I AM WAITING.

'I see.'

'Do you?'

'Tell me,' Tony continued, 'do you like being right?'

Alice was caught off guard. She felt like an insect in water, stretching and bending the surface tension. 'It can be,' she muttered fiercely, 'a source of considerable satisfaction.'

'Private satisfaction, I take it.'

'What do you mean?' She stared at him.

'Well, you wouldn't like other people to know how important it is to you, because that would make you look self-righteous. And you're not self-righteous. You're just, privately, *right*. Publicly, you'll settle for being plausible.'

'That's a horrible thing to say,' Alice said, breathlessly, privately determined that Tony should be given no proof of being right himself.

The temperature of the room had changed. Its closeness, reinforced by the glass wall and the sun behind the blinds, made the draughts – through the keyhole, from a too-small rotating fan on the third bookshelf up – coolly specific.

'Is it?' The almost uneffaceable half-smile of understanding on Tony's face melted away. 'Well, I've seen some horrible things in my time.' The sentence was bitten off while Tony chewed over its possibilities 'Perhaps,' he resumed, more cheerfully, 'I'm a horrible person. I've certainly been no good as a father. I like money and I like power, the way you seem to like personal responsibility. But I'm small-time. No one's heard of me. And perhaps I'm not as bad as you or I think. Maybe I'm only *plausibly* calculating. Maybe I just like the trappings of insincerity. Nick's the same. He rang me and said this fat bird he fancied was a really good actress, and I said I knew. That was an untypically generous thought on his part, it seemed to me. The day you came in, he was asking me for two grand to pay off – ' Tony waved, spasmodically – 'debts. He said nothing he did ever turned out right, nobody trusted him, and it was all my fault. But he looked nice, didn't he? Striped trousers, good haircut, new squeeze.'

'The trappings matter to you, do they?' Alice said, bitterly.

Tony waited an instant before replying.

'Too right they do.'

A pigeon landed on the windowsill. It was just a shape behind the canvas.

Alice sighed. 'Come on, then,' she said. 'Suggest something. I'm ready. Put me to sleep, if you must.'

'That's the spirit.' Tony said brightly, all sarcasm banished. 'But before I can do that, I'm going to have to make a quite different suggestion.'

'What's that?'

Alice's sense of the fearful and picturesque was disappointed by the bird, fidgeting and ruffling in the sun.

'I'm going to have to ask you to wake up.'

And with a dead-bolt click, the room was gone.

\* \* \*

Her mother spoke unusually softly. The grip on Alice's arm was tight, however, and when Lilian shook, as if she'd caught a bad chill, Alice shook, too. The little girl's face was covered in snot and tearstains, but she had stopped crying. They were at the bottom of the garden, near the cool basement with its smell of metal strings and sawdust, in the shade.

'I'm not angry with you, Alice. But you must tell me the truth.'

'Are we still going to see the models?'

She pronounced the word mod-*ell*, with a long second syllable. She meant the mannequins in the windows up and down Milsom Street. Lilian occasionally asked in the shops – in Jolly's and Pritchard's – to see if they were making any changes to their displays, because her oldest liked to watch the dummies being dressed. Children have odd notions of treats. Alice stood in front of the windows and shrieked with laughter at the bald women and knickerless men with cartoon teeth. People with nothing on whose arms and legs came off.

Lilian tugged on Alice's arm. Her lips were sticky; she opened her mouth before she had anything to say. It seemed to Alice that her mother was trying not to lose her temper. She could get cross quite easily.

'It is very important, Alice. That you tell me what happened.'

'But I've SAID. It wasn't me.'

The little girl began to panic. In the sunlight on the sloping lawn were the ambulancemen with her baby sister, brought down off the towpath. They were kneeling down and Ray, behind them, was holding Martha to his chest. Martha was making a fuss, screaming and pointing at Alice.

'I've said,' Alice repeated, in a sucked-in voice.

'The men need to know how long she was in the water. Did you go out onto the towpath? Listen to me. Did you take the others out?'

Alice nodded.

'But I came back – for the hat.'

'Did you,' Lilian struggled again, 'get in the water?'

Alice nodded again. She was still wet beneath the towel.

She'd got in the water when she came back to find Helen in the canal, already struggling, and Martha spreadeagled on the dusty path, pushing her further out. Martha couldn't swim, but was fascinated by the movement of the duckweed: the way it looked solid yet yielded if you put something in it, then closed over again. She'd picked up Alice's net and poked it at the others, laughing as Alice tried to dodge the stick and make it back to the bank with the baby.

'Will Helen be all right now?' Alice asked.

'Helen will be fine. She has to go to hospital, that's all.'

The men were carrying her away.

'I didn't do it.'

Her mother's face looked as if it were being wrung from the inside.

'It was *her*,' Martha screamed, before Ray disappeared indoors. Her leg kicked an instrument as they passed into the dark interior of the house and a thin chord followed them up the stairs. Outside, Alice had an idea. Helen was going to be all right, and there were still, perhaps, models to be seen that afternoon.

'It was me,' Alice confessed. 'I was teaching her to swim.'

She knew she would be believed.

The stinging blow of her mother's ringed and tanned hand did not take her completely by surprise. Through bleary eyes, she noticed the two birch trees on the right-hand side of the garden. They leaned into each other. The people who'd come to her rescue in the water were still by the gate at the top of the garden path, and one of them approached now, but Lilian headed her off.

Alice was taken upstairs and smacked. Hugged, then smacked again.

'I'll teach you to lie to me,' said her mother.

'I've said it was me,' cried Alice, ecstatic with the injustice of it all. 'Now MODELS.'

'You're never going to see the models again. D'you hear me, Alice Hutchings? Never. This is what happens when you lie.'

But Lilian was wrong. Helen died two days later and the models continued to swap limbs like crazy. Only their faces stayed the same.

\* \* \*

Tony had been expecting confusion, argument, distress – the symptomatic manifestations of an injured personality. But the Alice who emerged from a lifetime's slumber was, of course, more interesting than that: not so much a different woman or child, as a new casting from the original mould.

There was rage to begin with, naturally – though less deranged by suppression than when first (and accidentally) unleashed in the Battersea flat. Alice picked up busts and awards and hurled them at the bookshelves. She tore her Morris-print shawl and the scripts on Tony's desk in two. It was a short outburst, subsiding, soon, into articulate resignation. The angel of vengeance would not accuse or punish. It was enough for her to witness – and record.

Between the desk and the window was a dressing mirror, on a hinged stand. Alice pushed the top half with one finger and the room behind her – the shelves, the chaise longue, the signed photo of Elvis and the Colonel (signed by the Colonel) outside a motel, the shallowly breathing old man sitting in a drift of paper and smashed ornaments – swung down and away to be replaced by the ceiling rose and the green blinds.

Alice dropped the paper-knife and pushed the bottom of

the mirror. Her reflection flipped up, target-like, from the carpet.

'I've lost weight,' she said, holding out her black shirt. 'She's bought new clothes for me. That's your son's doing. She listens to him.'

'What are you going to do?'

'She loves him.'

Alice narrowed her eyes, and wiped the spit from around her mouth. 'There's nothing I can do. You'll tell her what I've just told you, and she'll be undeceived. Your wretched boy will say she's naive, and that will be the end of that little dream. No more self-deception.'

She went to the window, lifted the blinds and shuddered.

'It's only the thinnest veil,' she said, sadly. 'But it covers everything. Think what the world would look like without it . . .'

'Without what?' Tony called out.

She eyed him swiftly, and turned her face again to the rooftops, aerials, chimney stacks, clouds and trees. She saw what he could not: an unillusioned landscape; the unbearable, remotest possibility.

Alice gazed out peaceably over the city, across Bayswater Road, into Hyde Park and further east, towards Mayfair and Oxford Street, where the sky was a wash of violet. She blinked and glanced down into the red ravine of Orme Court and Bark Place, where water had begun to seethe quietly into the street from drains, from the culverted Westbourne River and its tributaries, describing minuscule deltas in uneven tarmac, like a continent seen from a plane.

'What can you see?' Tony asked in a whisper.

Alice leant her head sadly against the glass. It wouldn't do to say.

Around the corner of the narrow street the water came,

in a slingshot, breaking against wheelie-bins, cyclists and late office workers who stumbled on the kerb, caught by the surge. Alice watched as their files and suitcases, coffee cups and sandwiches flopped into the speeding stream. A woman in heels lost her balance in the cobbled gutter, and a man, mouthing 'the mains', waded across to help her when a second slingshot broke and drove them down a flight of steps.

'I can't see anything.'

In the distance, the sirens rose and a series of muffled, sub-terranean detonations thickened the air.

'What was that?' pleaded Tony. 'I heard a noise.'

The pigeon on the sill let out a cry before it flew away. Alice noticed that its head was bare, and its beak unusually protuberant, with small interior serrations just visible. Once opened, the wings shed grey-and-white feathers to reveal a veiny brown hide, and claws.

'I could have sworn I heard something,' Tony repeated, anxiously.

The bird rose swiftly on a warm evening updraught. And as it slowed, hovering high above the trees in Kensington Gardens, neither suspended nor supported, it seemed to Alice that she shared its imperturbable vision of territory and prey. She seemed to see its old haunts everywhere at once – a cave, a plain, a rocky tower, the marshlands to the east. Underground, commuters thronged the dark stairwells; lifts snapped and fell to the accompaniment of canned laughter. In the Park, trees burst into flame, their crowns shaking like pom-poms. A wave filled Oxford Street, and everything it touched, the whole honking flotsam of skidding buses, taxis, lights and signs, flared briefly white, then gold.

The vision faded.

'I can't hear anything, either,' Alice admitted, finally. 'Not a dicky bird.'

Alice left the window and together they tidied up, setting the standard lamp upright, reattaching maimed figurines to their glued-on bases.

'Tell me,' Alice asked, as they worked, 'do you tell your clients the truth? I mean, about their talent. What you really think of them.'

'God, no. It's like magic. You do your best to avoid any explanation.'

A small signed, unframed photograph of Bob Ladd had fallen off a bookshelf. Alice picked it up and laughed at the period collar, the stitching on the lapels of his jacket, the open shirt. The actor was standing in front of a corrugated tin hut with a broken sign above him that read 'age d or'.

She said, mildly: 'Look at you, then.' And didn't correct herself.

Tony sat back down very quietly.

'No,' he replied, raising a finger. 'Look at me now.'

*

'What was I saying?' Alice asked, almost as soon as she opened her eyes. She held on to her first breath, and stared at the ceiling, where layers of paint had clogged the cornices. 'Don't tell me. I could hear myself, going on about him. I talked about Nick, didn't I?'

Tony sat behind his desk. He offered her the reassurance that she had been right about the accident: all was as she remembered it. A simple tragedy for which no one bore the blame. Her mind was undisturbed; satisfied, in some way. She could probably expect fewer twinges of pain in the future. The fit was more of a mystery, but she'd been under a lot of strain, hadn't she? No job – no settled job anyway, unfulfilled ambition, tremendous appetites (as he saw it) only half acknowledged: the need, as she'd put it herself, to be chosen. Well, she had the job on *Hominids* to look forward to, and the play at the Bush. Leslie had to rewrite his last chapter, but it would be with her soon.

Alice could hardly bear to listen. The air of dutiful appeasement with which her agent rehearsed such 'strain' entangled her in an obligation of her own – to be grateful. And she was not grateful. She had been led by others to expose herself, and the recollection of how much she had divulged – of her fragile fantasies of companionship and lasting intimacy; of her extravagant but daily suppressed romantic longing; of the alternating sense of shame and elation that a grown woman of thirty-one should entertain such thoughts, when nobody else did – reinforced her present isolation. The truth had emptied her out.

'Something's gone,' Alice whispered. Her eyes roved and shut. 'I've lost a secret. I've said too much.'

'Perhaps that isn't a loss,' said Tony, impatient and exhausted. Alice's affair with his son, if he knew his son at all, couldn't be serious, but perhaps it would be a lesson to them both in the long run.

'You have so much to look forward to,' Tony added. He wanted her to go, now. 'Don't waste any more time longing for the impossible. You can spend your life longing.'

'Longing's possible, that's the point,' Alice said.

She got up and went to the door. It should have been the end of the conversation, but when her hand touched the glass she happened to see Tony reflected in it. He was yawning.

'I wish he wasn't your son,' Alice remarked softly. She hadn't planned on speaking and the words were flat, a voice without an echo.

'I can't do much about that.'

'You left my father to drown.'

There was a long silence.

'I've lost Nick to your example. I was right about you from the very start.'

'Alice.' Though he spoke her name long-sufferingly, the agent could not quite conceal his pique. 'What did I say about being right?' His voice was a hiss. 'And who do you think fetched the coastguard?'

Alice turned the handle, her heart thumping. A cold knife of self-accusation ground between her ribs.

Tony sniffed, lifted his eyebrows and said, 'For what it's worth, I think you take things too personally. You get tremendously, oh, worked up.' He ran his tongue across the front of his teeth. 'It must be a family trait.'

The hypnotist got out a plastic-packed sandwich from the top drawer of his desk. He unwrapped it and took a big mouthful with his eyes open, chewing with complete animal vacancy. After a while, he looked up.

'Still here?' he said, nicely.

*　*　*

Leslie had never visited Tony in his office before. Such representation as he enjoyed was in the manner of a gentleman's agreement, which flattered the old actor – made him think that their relationship went beyond the professional. The summons had been exactly that, however: a note left at the stage door by one of Mr Glass's underlings. And the prospect of facing Bob Ladd across a table filled Les with dread. He and Bob hardly spoke to each other in rehearsal. For obvious reasons, Bob had wanted him replaced as Caliban after the opening at the Young Vic, but it had been hard to argue with the favourable mentions in the press, and a couple of rags had even rung up to do 'My London'-style features with the rehabilitated female impersonator. Leslie knew, nevertheless, that he owed his survival in the part to Tony's influence, both with the PR-sensitive star and the producers. A summons could mean only one thing, then: Tony's influence was on the wane, and Bob wanted to have it out with him in person.

As he pulled aside the grille and knocked on the agency's door, it occurred to Leslie that he had never seen Tony and Bob together, not even in the old days at Windsor and the Gardens. It was a testament to Tony's ability to juggle people, no doubt, but the lack of precedent made him anxious.

The door was unlocked. Inside, Bob was nowhere to be seen – and if he had been, Leslie might not have noticed him. The office exerted its own fascination: machines on desks, piles of paper, heaps of publicity stills. There were framed shots, signed programmes and posters, everywhere, but Leslie saw none of them. His attention was caught by a bright young face beaming up at him from a bin. The face was unknown and unattached to a CV. It simply grinned into a plastic liner. There were thousands like it, Leslie realized. You could spill coffee on them, piss on them, tear them into shreds, and none would object.

Tony waved from his glass box.

'Come on in,' he called, his mouth full of sandwich. 'I'm sorry it's just me.'

'There's so much stuff, here,' Leslie observed, plonking himself down.

'Bob's running late with Mike at the Bush. He rang to say we could go ahead. I don't suppose it matters if he's here or not.'

'What's he doing at the Bush?'

'Well, this is what I wanted to discuss. Pardon me.' Tony wolfed down the last of his sandwich and brushed a few crumbs away from the green leather desktop. 'You see, Les, Bob would like – how can I put it? – some assurances.'

Leslie spoke calmly. 'I can give him any assurance he wants.' He swallowed. 'I can absolutely guarantee, Tony, that I'll be dry. I can't be any clearer about it. I mean, I've never *felt* so clear about it. I really feel I'm on a roll. I know that I've been given another chance, and I'm going to take it. I'm so very grateful.'

'That's good, Les.'

'You won't have cause to regret it.'

'I'm sure I won't. Look, there's no problem with *The Tempest*, as far as I can see. No, when Bob said he needed assurances, he – he and I, in fact – were looking further ahead.'

'I couldn't drink, even if I wanted to. Not now I'm on Herminevrin. Filthy stuff – makes you sick if you go near the other.'

'That's fine. I believe you.'

'I've sold quite a bit of my stuff,' Leslie said, slumping further into his chair. 'I'd forgotten you could get so much into . . . rooms.'

'Leslie, don't be so sensitive. You're not about to be sacked. Bob has a thick hide. You don't get on, and that's fine. But he's professional to his fingertips and he can perfectly well see that you give the show a kind of alternative or fringe credibility. A few insults don't bother him. Who remembers?'

Leslie had nothing to say.

'Which is why I gave him your pages to read.' Tony pointed his index finger sideways and unwound an imaginary tape. 'Well, it seemed the thing to do. Brian Cox was a hit in that monologue about the vampires in Crystal Palace, you know, and the Bush is a great venue for people like Bob to reacquire some hands-on dignity. You can't put a price on the humility and integrity you earn in places like that if you've got a good piece to perform, and the timing's right. And the timing is absolutely right, don't you think? Bob's had his fingers burnt with the sitcom, and I think he needs to show that he's more complicated than people suspect. It's a sort of paradox: he needs to go back to first principles – the grass roots – but he needs to do it with a sophisticated, metropolitan audience, where he can be seen doing it, otherwise, frankly, what's the point. So . . .' Tony opened his hands. 'Bob wants first refusal.'

Leslie didn't understand.

'He wants first refusal on the *part*,' Tony repeated. 'On you.'

'Me?'

'Oh, we might have to thrash out the particulars – name changes and so on. Although I can see a lot of mileage in keeping things just as they are, you know: having Bob playing you, but keeping the script more or less as it is, so that we get to see the spectacle of "Bob-as-Les" making a bravura song and dance about this fishy, grey figure with no scruples and no talent called Bob Ladd. It would give him absolutely limitless credibility, and it would – this is the key – completely overturn his book critics. It would be an unanswerable confession, none of this "*je m'accuse, je m'excuse*" crap you get with most showbiz diaries, because it's someone else's – if you'll forgive me – hatred and envy we're dealing with. It'd show that he can face the truth about himself, or some of it anyway. Bits would have to go, I think. The father-fucking stuff, probably. And, dare I say it, the odd paragraph about yours truly in the closing act? Not that I care, personally, you understand. It's just that other people still around could be affected. Nothing major, though. It's nothing that can't be fixed. Exciting idea, isn't it?'

Leslie nodded.

'I don't know,' he said, a moment later.

'Don't know what?' Tony said, beadily.

'I don't know if I'm happy about Robert – Bob – being cast in the role of my life. It's my life, you see. I can't just loan it out.'

'Ah, well,' Tony laughed.

'It's all I've got.'

'But *you're* an actor, Les,' Tony blazed suddenly. '*And* a writer. *You're* other people. *You* were Beatrice and Bob and me and a hundred naked coppers on a bus to Stockport. Why shouldn't one of them be *YOU*?'

'It's not the same.'

Tony was merciless. 'That is precisely what it is,' he said, and stabbed the air. 'You've said it yourself: "Anyone can be different." '

The agent picked up a sheaf of typescript and waved it in Leslie's devastated face. The upside-down initials on the front were L and B or, if turned around, B and L.

'It takes an *actor* to make different people the *same*.'

\* \* \*

The next day, Leslie got up early and paid a visit to Bermondsey antique market, off Tower Bridge Road. The dealers at the front of the market handled expensive items – silver services, gilt mirrors, spirit kettles, dog paintings – but the stallholders at the back of the car park were rag-and-bone men.

'How much could you give me for this flask?' said Leslie.

'Ken,' said a woman with plasters on her fingers. 'How much for the flask? Ken? It's a thermos, Kenny.'

A man standing with some others by a battered van fondled his chin.

'Fifty pee,' deduced the woman.

'It's a shame,' Leslie said, cheerfully, as he pocketed the four ten-pence pieces and five coppers. 'I'm having to get rid of such a lot.'

He went home, and looked at the coped ceiling in his front room. It was an attractive period feature in Guinness or Peabody Trust style, and the only thing left to be looked at, really, apart from the mattress.

# Thirteen

ALICE HAD planned it out. She'd knock, open the door, laugh self-deprecatingly (and make light of the intrusion), tell him what the present was before he opened it ('because it's so little'), wish him good luck, and then suggest a drink, say how sorry she was not to have had the chance to talk properly but they'd both been – no, *she'd* been (taking the initiative) busy. In fact, she'd come straight from filming. Yes. Oh, all right, you know. Nice food. A lot of waiting around. Blue-screen stuff. And then, perhaps when he'd settled in, they could have dinner, or do something locally. Whatever he fancied. Whichever would be easiest.

She put her hand on the cool brass handle, where it twitched once. Alice stepped back. From the other side came the sound of a chair, a shift and a scrape. Before she could advance to knock, the door opened and Nick stood in front of her. Behind him, his light room was full of flowers and cards fanning out from the mirror.

He held his fist up in mock salute.

'How long have you been out here?'

'Not long.'

'I saw the handle move. You could have knocked.'

'I was about to.'

'Aren't you supposed to be questing for fire?' He waited. 'What's the matter?'

'Nothing. I brought you this.'

Alice handed over her card and present and inspected her scarf. It was intriguing, rather than shocking, to find that she had been dismissed from someone else's thoughts as surely as that person had never left hers.

Nick turned the package upside down. He was half-dressed, in Ferdinand's twill trousers and boots.

'I'm going to tell you what it is,' Alice said, in a gabbled monotone.

'Don't tell me.'

'No, I'm going to. It isn't anything.'

'Don't *tell* . . .'

'It's jam.'

The frown on Nick's face lifted as he took a breath.

'Why,' he said, slowly, holding the breath and looking askance, 'have you bought me a pot of jam, Al?'

'Blackcurrant.'

The label, Alice thought. Look at the label.

'Blackcurrant, that's very – nice. I'm intrigued. It's a pot of jam . . .'

Dunn's Preserves were difficult to get hold of. You had to go to Fortnum's – and Alice had even told the stunned-looking woman behind the counter that she knew the heiress to the Dunn jam millions. Her name was Cressida. She was in a play with her – not Cressida's, no, *her* – boyfriend. Oh, it was a private joke.

'I just love you.'

Nick was genuinely surprised.

'And you know how dear you are to me,' he began, fatally.

'You don't have to say anything.'

'Look,' Nick said, shaking his head, 'now isn't a terrifically good time.' He stopped, winded. 'I've been worried about you.'

'It's all right.'

'No, it's not all right.'

'No, you're right. It's not all right,' Alice admitted. 'You make the sun come out for me. I don't know what I'm supposed to do. What I did wrong.'

'You haven't done anything wrong.'

Nick retreated to the card-crowned mirror, put the pot of jam on the table and his face in his hands. Another person seemed to be asking Alice's questions, and Alice was happy to let her get on with it.

'Are you seeing someone else?' she asked.

'It's not that.'

There was no more for a moment, and then Nick wiped his hands over his face and bounced the knuckles of his index finger against his chin. He stared into the glass, almost as if he expected to see there the truth of his own qualities.

'Of course,' he began cautiously, 'people have – especially our age, in this profession – affairs. They move on. You'd have to be naive to think otherwise.' His voice dwindled. 'In fact I'm not, right now. But if I see a good-looking girl, I don't see why I shouldn't.' He watched again. 'That's who I am. You have to accept people as they are.'

'I thought you'd accepted me.'

'I have. I do. But we're looking for different things.'

Alice turned decisively, and the reason for her turning evaporated with the movement. The words rose up undeniably.

'I'm not looking, Nick.' She laughed. 'If you keep looking, how can you see what you've got? How can you know when you've already found it? Or trust it? You said,' Alice shook her head, 'you had a horror of adultery.'

'I do. I have. I *do* trust you, Al. I don't trust myself, that's all. That's *why*. I can't lie to you. I'd never be certain.' He waited, before adding: 'I don't *know* what I want. I'm scared.'

It was a kind of hapless yearning for morality, this strangely male superstition that fear excused, while it predicted, misconduct. She didn't believe him, but that wasn't the point. He touched her deeply.

'It's all a risk,' Alice said finally. 'That's what putting your faith in someone means. It's nothing to be afraid of.'

Nick, who had collapsed into his chair, put his hands on his thighs and pushed himself up. He kissed Alice, who stood alone in the middle of the small room, and let her head drop against his shoulder.

'Bob wants to run through the rout and the chess scene. There's still a hitch with the rig.' He bit his lip. 'Are they making you extra-hairy?'

Nick brushed Alice's cheek, but she ignored the gesture. 'Will you think about what I've said?'

'Yes.' Nick looked down. 'I don't think . . .'

'Please.'

'Of course I will, Al. You're – fan-*tastic*. You know that.' He tried to move past her, but there wasn't enough room. 'Thanks for the jam.' He chuckled, and still she didn't move. 'I'll come up and see you some time.'

Alice was at her wits' end. She was pushing him away.

'It's "come up some time, and see me",' she said, shrinking to avoid contact.

'Is that right?'

Alice nodded.

'Well, there you go. I never knew that.'

'It's not—'

But he was gone.

*

Alice wanted to get out of the building as quickly as possible, without seeing or speaking to anyone else, but the tight backstage planning of the theatre was of no help, and with her head down, set against the wind of rejection, she ignored the exit sign, turned the wrong way and climbed to the first floor. Here were three more dressing rooms, each with its door open and slate-black mirror framed with bare bulbs. She did not have to look in any more mirrors. She could see her face from the inside. People hailed her from all three rooms as Alice passed by. She climbed again.

The door to the last room on the fly floor opened into semi-darkness. At her approach, the threshold filled with Neville Clute, who was saying goodbye to Leslie. The latter lurked inside, his rejoinders uncharacteristically wispy and high: 'All right, then. Yes. Thanks for the flowers. Have a good trip . . .'

'I must run,' Neville said, backing into the pink corridor. 'I'm late as it is.' He collided with Alice. 'Clumsy! Here we all are rushing about at the last minute. I have to catch a plane. I'm not staying.'

'Goodbye,' said Leslie. 'Thanks for the flowers.'

'It'll be a triumph,' Neville spluttered. 'The performance of your life.'

'Neville's going to Hollywood,' the darkness explained.

Alice buried a sob in congratulations.

Neville blushed. 'Not *to* Hollywood. New York, actually. But it is, you know, film work. It won't lead anywhere, I expect. But the studio *has* paid off the first chap, and they want me to see a cut. An "actioner", they call it.'

'Robots and money!' Leslie cried softly. 'You'll be late.'

'I'm going now, Les. Will you be all right?'

'Oh, I'm always all right. These things . . .' and Leslie's voice trailed away into a girlish giggle, before continuing, more sombrely, 'Perhaps, Alice, you'd like to help me finish our little game?'

It was Neville who went back into the room. Alice saw him squat beside Leslie, who sat on a stacking chair, his head bent over a chequered board.

'You've already won, darling.'

Leslie stared at the board.

After another murmured farewell, Neville strode out. He walked a little way in silence, before attempting an explanation.

'We always play the Fischer–Spassky moves. He's Fischer to my Spassky. They used the same ending in *From Russia With Love*, I believe.'

Loud bass laughter filled one of the rooms below, and seemed to produce in counterpoint a sharp high clattering from the flies. A sign on the landing read: 'Quiet. You Can Be Heard.' Behind it, the dropped tools, or props, implied the acoustic of a tall stage and empty house.

Neville's music began. In the ornate surroundings of a Victorian theatre, it sounded obviously taped, a world away from the painted panels and the portraits of Sheridan and Goldsmith. They crossed the pre-fab bridge that led to the Albery, and walked down to the shared stage door.

'I hope those cues have been reprogrammed,' Neville said. 'We had to do it from my old tape, because the computer crashed.'

At the door, he enquired hurriedly into her health. They – he and Les – had been concerned. Even more hurriedly, he said, 'And Nicholas?'; Alice said she wasn't sure if she was doing the right thing. If it was all worth it.

'Ask yourself if you could do otherwise,' he said. 'If the answer's no, then you are. And it is.' His umbrella opened to great applause. The rain thrust sparklers into the puddles. 'Give it time.'

'Neville,' said Martha, tonelessly, on her way in.

*

Alice had always had in the back of her mind the idea that, in a romantic crisis, she would prefer to suffer alone. This was pride, of course: the worldliness of her sister's, or her mother's, sympathy, and their criticism of Nick could only add to, not diminish, her distress. But it was part of a deeper, more general frustration, too. Cynical opinion, stated or withheld, blasted away possibility. What chance had love, when its profession was secretly mocked, when there was so little goodwill, and willingness to believe? The world's mistrustfulness threw you back on yourself, Alice concluded, unconsciously excusing her own.

Martha barely looked at her. She was furiously rolling up a wet *Evening Standard*, and bouncing it on the peeling veneer of reception. Outside, in St Martin's Court, a small TV crew waited, smoking, booms at half-mast.

'Anything for me, Joe?' she enquired.

'Just these,' said Joe, and handed over a bunch of irises, with a card. 'I've put the others in your room, Ms Challen.'

'Aren't they lovely?' Alice exclaimed, aware that she would have to say something to attract her sister's attention. 'I love irises. I should have got you some. Are they from Kwame?'

'No.'

'Oh.' Alice avoided Martha's angry gaze, now that she

was staring right at her. To avoid returning the look, Alice glanced over Martha's shoulder at the tall old lady in fake fur smiling beatifically at Joe the receptionist. 'Well, I expect his are already inside, waiting for you.'

She was unable to conceal the tremor in her voice. The old lady left, and the open door wafted in the paved scent, peculiar to London's passages, of mudguards and tea. The TV crew looked cold and shifty.

'They're from Mum,' Martha revealed, rotating the flowers.

'From *Mum*?'

Alice was surprised.

'It says she's in tonight. "Good luck, darling." Nothing from Dad.'

'I had no idea they were planning on coming. Did you?'

'Yes. I went down during the week.'

'I feel awful I haven't got you anything.'

'Well, I just hope they haven't been reading today's paper,' Martha sighed.

'Why, what's in it?'

'Oh, nothing. It's too pathetic.' And she stopped. 'Except.' She shook her head with her eyes closed. 'Except there's this big, crappy feature from some faceless zero about the "Nu".'

'The New?'

'*Nu*. N-U.'

'Oh, Hebrew. "Tell me what happened", isn't it? Sort of, I don't—'

'No. Nu as in Nu-metal, Nu-Power Soul.'

Alice's face was blank.

'It's the street version of the new. Look, "Nu is the *new* new". I can't even read it out, it's so cretinous.' Martha unrolled the paper and tore out a page. 'There are whole lists of things. It's mostly showbiz. Robbie's the Nu-Glam, the

*Matrix* is the Nu-Noir, Peter Snow is a Nu-Hero, because he's, listen to this, "a boffin with a streak of Indiana Jones – the kind of guy who looks cool in a plane crash".' Martha wiped a wet strand of hair away from her forehead. 'And I, apparently, am a Nu-Sloane.'

The two sisters inspected each other for a moment. Alice felt a prickly warmth beneath her eyes.

'"The Nu-Sloane",' Martha went on, '"has the old Sloane's willowy, semi-educated seductiveness, allied to a new media savvy and chic. Nu-Sloanes don't belong to a class or set, but they retain a sense of entitlement to things and people. They are comfortably off, though not necessarily wealthy; pretty, vain, flirty, ambitious, and immune to criticism. Types: young actresses, especially Martha Challen (with Kwame Dankwah)."' She stopped reading. 'My life partner. In fucking brackets.'

'It's fluff, Martha,' was Alice's immediate reply. 'It's not meant to be cruel.'

'I realize that,' Martha said, finally. 'But to show that I'm not sensitive about being called insensitive, I have to be – insensitive. Oh, anyway.' She sniffed and threw the paper into a corner bin. 'Are you coming in?'

'No,' Alice gulped. 'I don't think I should. You've only got a couple of hours. And I've just said goodbye to Nick.'

She waited for Martha to end the silence that followed, but Martha seemed slow to condole. Alice was about to give up, when her sister quietly observed that Nicholas was too wrapped up in the new part and the distractions of work for his responses to be relied on. Which was true of plenty of actors, most of the time. What had he said, anyway?

Alice was shaken. The idea that general allowances could be made for her lover's behaviour distressed her. It opened up the possibility that she was – wrong. She ran through the conversation as she remembered it.

'So.' Martha paused, and in pausing sat on the one bench in the waiting area. 'Let me get this right – you've split up on the basis that he's attracted to lots of women, which you knew, but isn't seeing anyone else?'

Alice wanted to hit her sibling. In the fuzzy grip of emotion, 'nu' suddenly sounded like an apt description – bare and cybernautical. Unfeeling.

'It isn't that simple, and you know it,' she retorted. Her glands constricted. Alice waited for the whiplash cords of pain to bind her jaw. But there were no cords of pain, no whiplash, and so, it seemed, no grounds for hesitation.

'People like YOU,' she shouted. 'It's people like you, Martha *Challen*, who don't have to try, who just have to stick out their thumbs, who fuck it up for the rest of us. You were the one who said arguments made the glue in relationships. Well, I took your advice and look where it's got me.'

'It wasn't advice.'

Alice flapped her arms. 'Nick said the same thing. He said I wasn't *natural* enough. He said I lived in my head too much. He said I should lay myself open to other people. Whatever the hell that means,' she snarled. 'But it wasn't actually me he wanted, was it?'

'You don't know that.'

'Oh, but I *do*. I was a test case. He wanted to see what someone *like* me might do who loved him – the lengths to which they'd go. Well, I've gone to them and he *despises* me for it. Because I gave him everything and kept nothing back. And now the real me has gone, too – the stiffness, the pride, even the jaw-ache, all the reserve I needed to live by – and I have *nothing left*.'

Alice gasped, the tumult of accusation and horror leaving

her momentarily breathless. Martha sat, head bowed, hands folded. Behind the desk, Joe did his best to look distracted by a clipboard and a paperback.

'I didn't—' Martha murmured.

'I know he's trouble. I'm not bloody stupid,' Alice cried. 'But nobody has any *faith* in him. It's a joke – the idea of him actually loving another person. Tony, his dad – oh well, he's not all bad, he – but he treats him like a problem case. He left him on his own when he was thirteen and pissed off on the road. And he doesn't seem to think that has anything to do with Nick's personality now. I don't know. Some people are just so obtuse, and insensitive, don't you think, Martha?' Alice twisted the knife. 'Don't you? And *cold*.'

Martha raised her face, rootled in her coat pocket for a tissue, and came up with a napkin from the cafe in Bedford-bury. Her hands were shaking.

'You win,' she said at last, almost inaudibly. 'I give up. You win.'

Alice's stomach turned. It was surely her role to concede ground.

'I don't mean to be cold, but I suppose I must be. If that's the impression I give.' Martha stopped and opened her mouth. After a moment, she added: 'Kwame's moved out.'

Alice saw the lady with the bedraggled stole come back in and wave a small parcel at the receptionist. Her eye was lazy, maybe even false, Alice noticed. She looked alarmingly like the critic from the *Stage*, years ago – the one who'd praised her Dogberry.

'He thought I was cold, too. He said it came over in everything I did. And do you know what he said proved it?'

The tall lady began a whispered conversation. She was leaving a present for someone in the cast. She wanted to hand it over personally.

Martha turned to look at her sister, who made no reply.

'A review in the *Independent*. A tiny trashing, which didn't even bother *me* that much.' Martha let her nose run freely, now. She rolled the irises in her lap back and forth. 'But that was what he said *proved* it. That I didn't care what others thought. He said the critic – what was her name? Anna? I think that was it – had me down to a tee. And she said I was "stale", "constitutionally unable to respond". Which is the first rule of acting, of course: respond. React.'

Alice's feet had grown roots.

'It's funny,' Martha went on, 'I don't expect Anna, whatever she's called, intended any real harm, but she certainly had that effect. And meanwhile there's poor Nick, fully intending to be a sod, so convinced he *will* be that he abandons someone he likes, when he hasn't done anything. It's all inside out, isn't it? That's what Mum said. What people say and what they think.'

With a final, glutinous sniff, Martha rose up and hugged her sister.

'I am,' she said, 'genuinely sad that it hasn't worked out for you and Nicholas.' It was Alice's turn to stare at the carpet. 'And I wish we were better friends, so that I could offer you some comfort, but we're not, are we? You don't like me, and I've got my own problems.' Martha laughed. 'I'm pregnant. And the future father of my child is down the football, innit.'

'It isn't true I don't . . . Martha, I had no idea.'

Martha moved towards the inner stage door.

'Make time to see Mum, Al,' were almost her last words. 'She's incredibly proud of you. She responds if you give her a chance. She does, really.'

'I'm the executive producer,' said the powdery old dowager at reception in sweetly threatening tones. 'Surely the producer is allowed backstage?'

'Bob Ladd is the producer, love.'

'Ah yes,' said the woman, who, menacingly, grew in height the more softly she spoke. 'But I'm the *executive* producer, Ms Mitchell. I'm the one with the *money*, darling. Always have been.'

The heavy fire door eased to in Martha's wake. The 'producer' caught it before it shut and followed. As she passed into the theatre's black interior, she turned her head to glance back at Alice, and the mesh in the door's window laid a grid over the solitary figure, as though she were an island.

\*

If Martha knew that Alice was Ann Hemp, she didn't need to proclaim the fact. Alice understood as much, and was dumbfounded. Her sister's forbearance lay revealed. Against it, her own actions appeared vainer, more inexcusable, by the minute. She had harboured an unreal resentment – and written it down. It had been read, and it had borne fruit. Two people were estranged who were not so formerly, and one of them was pregnant.

This was the case as it presented itself to Alice's conscience: she had *contrived* another's unhappiness – and in the fact that it was a contrivance, not a truth or a necessary evil, lay her hope of remedy. It came to her, while handing her ticket to the usher, that she would have to find Kwame. She must find him, and make him see what he stood to lose.

Alice turned around. She thrust her way out of the lobby towards the street. He was watching football, Martha said, which meant he'd be in Kingston.

At the tube entrance, amid the usual immobilized tourists,

she saw her parents, who hailed her with a jerky expansiveness. Ray looked happy but exhausted, grey of eye, and fatter than ever. His lip glistened embarrassedly: he wore a grey jacket and a tie. His wife's eyes were round and unblinking. She presented herself in profile in a questionable pink tunic, with gilt buttons.

'You're wearing a tie, Dad.'

'Oh, special occasion.' And they laughed.

Lilian laughed a little longer than either Ray or Alice. A young woman barging past dropped a cigarette butt onto the pavement, and Lilian seemed disconcerted for an instant. She touched a cheek.

'You *are* coming in, aren't you? We are sitting together?'

Alice said that she was shooting some night scenes for the programme, and to her surprise it was Ray who objected first.

'But it's your sis's big night, Al. Can't you get off early?'

'Dad. I'll try.'

'What programme?' Lilian enquired, puzzled.

'Oh, Mum. The cave-history show. I told you about it.'

Ray was sorry. 'It's a shame.'

'I *thought* that was make-up. You always had a few hairs there, didn't you, but not that many. I used to pull mine out.' Lilian opened the clasp of her handbag, poked about inside, muttered and shut it again, sliding the bag up her arm. She sighed. 'You look *so* well, darling.'

Alice was surprised. 'Do I?'

'You'd better go. Mustn't keep the cameras waiting.' Lilian caught her daughter in a clumsy embrace. 'Now, off. Scoot.'

'You look lovely, too, Mum.'

'Me?'

'Your mother always does.'

'I know.'

'Me?' Lilian repeated. 'I'm nothing these days.'

\*

On stage, Martha waited for the actors to finish their walk-through of the rout at the end of Act Four. Bob was still concerned about the descent of the piano – the right drop hadn't been programmed in and it fell jumpily, never ending up close enough to Caliban and the fools. Ariel, poised in harness above the fountain like a bandaged Eros, had developed a midair spin. Her key line, 'Hark, they roar!', which cued deafening organ music, was getting lost upstage, and the more poor Cressida Dunn shouted, the more obviously Australian her Ariel became.

'This scene is my pet noir,' yelled the jam heiress. 'You guys are beyond belief.' Then they were off, Bob badgering the tense, coke-sustained crew to fly the piano in once more with the tape and the crew explaining that there was no time, Leslie loping into the shadows.

Martha took her place in the alcove with the chessboard and the chequered decoration. Money had been spent on the West End set. The columns of porphyry and jasper were painted, not papered; there were real white and azure tiles at the base of the fountain, and the galleries had acquired filigree stucco, painstakingly worked in balsa and ply. It was as good as the real thing. As Nick joined her she noticed a further detail. On the inside of the arch, invisible to any but the lovers, and then only if one happened to look up, was an inscription in glazed ink. It read: 'Surely I am in this garden an eye filled with joy.'

They were doing the scene to run a last-minute lighting and tape check. Martha had spoken the lines many times in rehearsal and performance, but tonight, with no particular effort on her part, they sounded freshly sad. Like the inscription, they made a vow of blindness.

*Sweet lord, you play me false.*

No *my dearest love / I would not for the world.*

*Yes, for a score of kingdoms you should wrangle, / And I would call it . . .*

Her voice slipped a register, as though she had jumped two steps on a staircase by mistake. Martha thought irrationally about the production's licence; and, in a chain of nervous associations, of insurance as another kind of vow, guarding against disaster.

*. . . fair play.*

She took Nick's hand and, under her breath, let rip. She had about twenty seconds before her next line; twenty seconds in which to tell Nick exactly what she thought of him. The effort of containing her own disappointment found relief in anger on Alice's behalf. And the oath was whispered, which made it more deadly – a confession of loathing.

'Mm, not sure about hands,' Nick called to the director. 'Too much?'

Adrian thought it was too much.

'That was a bit *much*,' Nick confirmed, and squeezed back.

They trooped off stage. Martha went to her dressing room on the second floor, and put her irises in a jar. It was six thirty.

She sat silently for five minutes, and then got up and walked downstairs. From the tower came the sound of machinery clicking into starting position; on either side of her the staircase walls were green and cracked. She'd called Nick a cast-iron shit, an atrocity. Not so terrible perhaps, but insults left a bad taste, and if her instincts told her to apologize Martha thought it wise to listen to them.

'Sod it,' she said.

She reached Nick's room, knocked, heard him say 'Yes,' and walked in.

He was standing with one foot on a chair, his hands in his pockets.

Huw – the unpromoted Stephano – got up off his knees, red and wet at the mouth. He trembled, saying, 'Oh God,' several times, though Martha, so far from being shocked, felt only a sympathetic disappointment. Nick trained people in obsession, and was good at it. Poor Huw had always been a candidate. For some reason, the magic hadn't worked with her.

Now, here she was, in a quandary: unable to apologize, unable to condemn.

'Seen enough?' Nick said.

Sometimes, she wondered if she was quite human.

\*

'Will you be able to see?' Lilian asked.

Martha had reserved excellent seats for them in the middle of the stalls, six rows from the front. It was just as well, because Ray had brought only his spare bifocals, made to an imaginative prescription in a holiday emergency years ago. Ray gripped the armrests and sank his chin into his neck.

'I hope it isn't one of those productions where everyone mumbles,' he said.

They consulted their programmes, turning immediately to the actors' biographies and silently comparing entries.

'You don't get a proper article, do you, in the commercial sector,' Lilian said knowledgeably, and tapped the brochure. 'Now if this was the National, you see, you'd have someone writing, Martina Warner or someone like that, writing about the play. Oh, that's an *old* photo.'

'Odd? Why?'

'She's put on weight since then.' Lilian turned a page.

Over the gurgle in his throat, Ray manoeuvred counter-offensively. 'I thought Alice was looking slimmer.'

'Mmm. She doesn't want to lose it all too quickly.'

'I'd have liked to see *her* in this. Martha says she saved their bacon.'

'Well, you can't have everything,' Lilian reflected. 'And if she is epileptic' – the word made her feel uncomfortably responsible – 'or anything related, she'd be best to avoid, um, *live* work. For a while. Until things have settled down.'

'She's not me. It might never happen again, Lil.'

'Don't say that.'

'I said, it might *not*. Not it might.'

The people waving and mouthing greetings over the backs of their seats would be actors, Lilian thought. They sought each other out. Some would be, fleetingly, lucky; others perhaps possessed unignorable gifts. The rest hadn't a hope, and were probably the luckiest of all.

'You just never know,' she said.

\* \* \*

Alice and Nick had slept together ten days after her fit.

Nick's mood all evening was sombre. In her bedroom, he slumped in a mound of cushions, fiddling with his balls and watching *The Royle Family*. Alice stayed in the kitchen, revising notes for her South Bank Walk between visits to the bathroom to see if the swelling around her eyes and lips had gone down. She wanted to understand her boyfriend's trouble, but if he didn't talk to her, how could she? His silence aroused her to a constant effort of interpretation. At midnight, Nick came up to her and said, 'I'm tired, I don't know why.' Alice didn't know either – his slumber always appeared to her resonantly protracted – but she laid a kindly hand on the small of his back anyway.

They got into bed, where Alice submitted to being held from behind in a gesture of intimate refusal. Three hours later, Nick awoke and found her again, this time with an urgency which Alice found moving. Eyes closed, he muttered, 'You're beautiful,' and seemed to reach out to her, burying his head in her neck, holding her and stroking her until the troubling dream passed.

There was a lesson in this memory of changing moods, which Alice could not quite grasp. And why it should return to bother her now, as she stumbled along the condemned alley of Hungerford Bridge, she had no idea. On the South Bank, the wheel of the Millennium Eye was half-raised, in a halted blue blink. Above, the clouds crashed quietly. On such an evening as this she had first met Nicholas. Time then had seemed suspended yet solid, like the square span of this bridge. She'd vowed not to forget each moment. Now it flowed fast, over reflections, a currency the more precious for being spent.

\* \* \*

The train took Alice to Raynes Park and the 131 bus to Kingston Road. The upper deck was reassuringly full of overweight men and women wearing the colours of Merton Casuals: black and green strip with a red-eyed phoenix for a shield and a sponsors' logo (TLS Haulage). The kids wore hats; the men looked as if they were expecting; the women passed round zeppelins of Coke.

At the ground Alice bought a programme and a golden-goal raffle ticket. She followed the drift of supporters along a low-rise section of Merton's club offices and changing rooms towards the packed bar, where fans were buying more hats and discussing the form of the team with excited disdain: 'He'll play Packer for seventy, 'cos he's good for morale – what? It's the plates in his leg. Packer'll do seventy, then Terry'll bring on Gibbo. Yeah. Like I say, we're fucked.'

Alice was moving away, wondering how she'd find Kwame in the crowd and what she'd say if she did, when a balding man in front of her said to his taller bespectacled companion: 'Wonder what the new signing's like.'

The man with glasses and brush-like hair said: 'He played against us last season, for Frimley Green. Could be interesting. Likes to get up front.'

'What's his name?'

'Kwame Dankwah, some kind of actor.'

'Never heard of him,' said the shorter man, impassively, as they joined the stream of Casuals clicking through the turnstiles. 'Good name, though.' He paused. 'Kwame Akon produced Barbara Dickson's *Greatest Hits* last year.'

His friend guffawed.

'I love Barbara Dickson,' said the bald man seriously, before a grin cracked his face open. He caught Alice's eye and huddled into the queue for burgers. 'I don't care what anyone says. I think she's brilliant.'

Alice joined the tea-stall crocodile, bought a sausage baguette with onions, and followed the easy-listening duo around the main stand to the goal terraces. The ground speakers were playing soul and dance. When Groove Armada came on ('If everybody looked the same'), she looked at the ranks of green and black and began to suspect the DJ of a sense of humour.

In the second half, as predicted, Tim Packer, the stiff-legged Merton captain, was taken off. His replacement, the new No. 8, sprang from the bench, a good three inches taller than anyone else on the pitch and half the average weight. He dummied and swerved around the enemy's defence and, a minute before the final whistle, fired a shot between the legs of Bedfont's inert goalie.

The quietest actor Alice had ever known pointed with both hands at the sky and ran screaming towards Merton's ecstatic fans. Two yards from the barrier, he stopped and cupped an ear. The celebrations continued after full time, with Kwame playing the crowd like an Ashanti Bruce Forsyth.

'Nowhere to run, nowhere to hide,' sang Martha Reeves.

Alice was only two rows behind the goal post. She called out 'Kwame!' and the bald man and his friend turned round. Others turned, too; the eddy of attention caught the player's eye.

'It's me,' Alice mouthed, and rather pointlessly mimed applause.

Kwame beckoned and she struggled to the barrier, excusing herself. If he was surprised to see her, he didn't show it. As he hugged her, to cheers from the thinning hordes, Alice noticed the perimeter advertising. 'Dankwah Bros Construction' read one of the panels. 'For the next 1,000 years.'

A trainee mortician from Norbiton was named Man of the Match in the bar afterwards. The rest of the squad hung about in formal attire – a sort of estate-agent chic, with gold ties, blue shirts and buckled shoes. The exception was Kwame, who earned a special mention from the club chairman, Ivor Plaicette, for a goal on his first appearance. Kwame stood on the dais in a ski-jacket and wrecked jeans, with a swath of fish-print kente cloth wrapped around his neck. Behind him, a poster promised to 'Kick Racism Out of Football'. He raised a hand to acknowledge his new disciples, and stepped down.

'Now,' he whispered in Alice's ear, 'I am an important somebody.'

'You were fantastic,' Alice enthused. 'Kwame, there's something I have to discuss with you.'

'Very ex-citing.'

'I'm assuming Martha—'

She stopped, jarred by the unspoken assumption. There seemed a distance between what she was about to say, and her right to say it.

'Let me get you a drink first,' she said.

Kwame insisted on paying. Alice returned from the bar with a rum and Coke and too much change. The mix of voices, the noise from a cable sports screen, and the chirping of mobiles signalled a kind of panic. Kwame had 'moved out', Martha said. It didn't sound as if there'd been much of an argument. Perhaps he didn't even know she was pregnant. And who was Alice to mention it, anyway? Who was *she* to mount a Samaritan's defence of a partnership to which envy had always blinded her?

'Well?' Kwame bent his head.

'Kwame, this is probably none of my business.' Alice wavered. 'I know. It's a shame that you and Martha have split up—'

'You are right,' he replied. 'It is not your business.'

'A tiny bit of it is, though,' Alice persisted, while Kwame blinked. She felt silly. 'You remember that unpleasant piece in the *Independent*? The review?

The footballer frowned and nodded.

'I wrote it.'

Kwame sipped his drink politely, almost as if he hadn't heard, letting his eyes wander over the shaven heads and gazified stomachs.

'Martha told me you thought it had her down to a tee.

Well, I don't think that's right. I wrote it because I was jealous. I'm jealous of her because she's good at something she doesn't even care about.'

At the bar, the manager was berating a young girl for jamming the till.

'She's not cold,' Alice added. 'If anybody is, I am.'

Kwame considered the money in his hand.

Alice elaborated on her revelation as briefly as she could. Kwame listened inexpressively, nodding occasionally. When he spoke again, it was almost, but not quite, an interruption. His voice was formally emphatic.

'My relationship with your sister has nothing to do with you,' he said. 'Why do you want to be responsible for it?'

'Because – I feel I am. I should be responsible for my opinions.'

Welcome shook his head. 'Oh dear.'

And they were silent.

'I can agree with you,' he resumed, 'whether or not you are telling the truth. That is my decision, you see, which does not de-*pend* on your honesty.'

Welcome laid a hand on her shoulder. 'Love is not a set of opinions. I do not think anything very bad of you, Alice. Your Nicholas has foolished you, and you have lied to yourself, and that is why you are suspicious of everyone else.' He took his hand away. 'But it is not the end of the world.'

\* \* \*

The elderly couple sitting next to Bill Alden were discussing the play. They had a parental interest in the attractive, pale girl playing Miranda.

The woman said, 'She'd not have got that from me, she's too good to be mine,' and asked her husband if he thought they 'should have told her'. The husband replied that it was too late. She said: 'I wonder why we never did,' and the subject, prompted by some silent resistance, was changed.

The deformed hand in the keystone above the central arch intrigued them both. The man said it had to be part of the Moorish theme. 'Victorian fashion, wasn't it? Like the Alhambra in Leicester Square. I went there with Maurice.'

'It's very exotic,' his wife conceded, doubtfully. She kept pointing at wrappers on the floor and tutting.

The man deliberated. 'We're not talking about anything far away. The Alhambra was only a hundred yards down the road.'

'You're shouting.'

'The Combe hospital had arcades like that, Lil. And there were towers and turrets and wooded walks, you name it.'

They went off to get an ice cream and Bill thought about the keystone himself. He was interested to hear the local Alhambra mentioned, not because he'd ever visited it, but because, having worked at the university in Granada, he knew that the mutilated hand referred to the gatehouse in the original. The hand adorned the outer arch, facing downhill; on the equivalent inside arch, facing up towards the fort, was a bunch of stone keys. The two carvings were eight yards apart. It was said that when the keys fell into the hand, or the hand grabbed the keys, the Alhambra would crumble into dust. The meaning was not hard to discover. Granada was fretted with step-faults: it was an earthquake warning.

Aptly enough, the fingers had probably fallen off.

If she brought the subject up again – here they were with their tubs and spoons – he'd happily explain the reference, Bill decided. It was two weeks since his wife had left him, and he'd hardly spoken to anyone in that time. Lilian ate her ice cream in silence, and Bill tried not to feel disappointed.

The cost of the show impressed him. It was an elaborate undertaking with a full cast, a raked perspective, original music and a Prospero of reckless ebullience: brass-throated, gesticulatory, his centre of gravity about a foot in front of his belly. It was the kind of voice-led performance you simply didn't expect to see any more: the vogue had been exiled with the passing of the stentorian guard, Richardson, Gielgud, Schofield (the last not dead, just bored). And it verged, appropriately, on the embarrassing.

Prospero *was* embarrassing – a monster of vanity in whom power and bluster combined to disconcerting effect. The scale of presumption, in both character and show, was enormous. Bill didn't know whether to laugh or gasp. Robert Ladd was a relatively well-known sitcom actor, but for him to be laying claim to classical seriousness by making such a spectacle of himself was almost pitiable. Strange then, that the attempt was not without charm, and its own gentle insight. The play had to look effortful – rain screens, flying harpies, fountains – in order for you to catch the simpler note of regret behind it all, the ending of revels, the restoration that masked submission to age and fate.

When the magically suspended white piano dropped at Ariel's command, the shock was physical. Apart from the cry that went up as the instrument clipped Caliban on the shoulder, the music itself was loud enough to make Wyndham's shake. A massive vibrato chord decayed into a single, muted moan, and brought with it the sorcerer's promise of relief: *My charms I'll break, their senses I'll restore, / And they shall be themselves.*

Bill found that he preferred the bathos of Prospero's ceaseless conjuring. Mutinous winds and shaking promontories aside, the poor magician seemed unable to stop producing bunches of flowers from the shreds of his gown, or garlands for his daughter; or, in the middle of his last aria, a set of juggling balls. And most of what Mr Ladd would be earning in the wake of this huge vanity project would be a qualified disappointment, too – voice-overs, tours, the slow torture of TV carol concerts in Guildford and personal appearances.

The old couple next to him were holding hands.

Something about the decaying chord, the stifled note, bothered Bill. It wasn't going away. It was distracting the actors, too, who looked all at once as if they were trying hard not to notice it.

It was like tinnitus, a background signal – fairly ignorable until you focused on it, or traced it to its point of origin. The recent tremors across London were the same, Bill reflected. They were still going on; had, in fact, doubled in frequency, though they were now too light to be felt. They should have been short, sharp and over – like the report of a gun. Instead, they flowed increasingly into one prolonged resonance – vibrating like liquid under pressure, or the air in an organ pipe. Bill had dreams about their true meaning, in which the Thames became a crucible, the Strand a fiery ingot, and people burst into flames, but he awoke from them. He went to work. They meant nothing.

*

The taped score had run out, the piano had overshot its mark and Martha's nerves were ragged. From her position in the alcove, her view of the wings obscured by a sweating Nick Glass, she could see Leslie being mopped down and bandaged into shape for his final entrance. The piano had almost certainly fractured his shoulder. Now, the offending keyboard was being hauled back into the flies. The higher it went, the more precariously lopsided its angle seemed. Gonzalo, Alonso and the rest were trying not to corpse, and

Bob to ignore the song shadowing Neville's half-erased master tape. It was the quavering vestige of an earlier recording, impossible to identify until the refrain swayed into distant focus: 'She wrote upon it: "Return to sender. Address unknown / No such number, no such phone".'

Could the audience hear? It sounded like a terrible audition piece. The tinny accompaniment kept stopping and starting again, the singer struggling to find a key. Maybe Elvis, or the person imitating him, was being – mercifully – blanked out by the stuck note of the feedback. Well, the rest of the score had its incongruous moments; perhaps a few more didn't matter.

What did matter were Miranda's last lines as she came forward to greet the King and his courtiers – the male sex *en masse*:

> *O wonder!*
> *How many goodly creatures are there here!*
> *How beauteous mankind is! O brave new world*
> *That has such people in't!*

It was a funny speech, and Martha was concerned that Bob would overplay Prospero's response, ' 'Tis new to thee.'

She left the alcove, skirting the fountain, centre-stage right, to emerge between Alonso and Gonzalo on the apron. There she gave 'goodly creatures' directly to the audience, praying that Bob would not do the same . . . He did, of course, and the giggles cancelled themselves out like waves in a cross-current.

The silence revealed someone arguing at the back of the theatre.

Kwame shook off the usher and walked down the right aisle. He stood for a moment, about six feet from the front, calmly assessing the stalls, then sat down in a spare seat on his left.

In her cage of light, Martha recognized him by the growl of his voice and the shimmer of kente cloth. He raised a hand and she saw him smile. She uttered a cry, and the sound was alive and alien to her.

Another, lesser disturbance seemed to be taking place off-stage left. The stage manager was talking to a grey-coiffed stranger in a suit.

Telly, thought Martha. She remembered the equipment at the stage door, the gaggle of smoking techies outside.

Bob was embarked on the epilogue and the dimly lit freeze made it possible to probe the far darkness of the prompt corner. The tall old woman from reception was standing next to the man in the suit. Expanded by shadow, her high grey hair and coat appeared to have no beginning or end. They merged with the flats. She listened pacifically, but took no part in the conversation. Occasionally, her gaze drifted out to where Leslie was standing, trembling, in obvious agony. The body language of the stage manager clearly read: 'Who *is* this woman? Is she with you?' To which the suit's struggles with a microphone equally clearly replied: 'I've no idea. Don't bother me now.'

*As you from crimes would pardon'd be*
*Let your indulgence set me free.*

Blackout. Applause, enthusiastic and growing. Lights up. First bow.

As the light strengthened, Martha felt a corresponding surge in the audience's appreciation. Stepping cautiously into the full glare, Michael Aspel milked the unexpectedness of his appearance. The audience laughed and clapped, though there were groans, too: the sudden recognition, perhaps, that, for famous people, the end would always come in the guise of false acclaim.

The actors, certainly, could see that the pages in the red book were blank.

'I don't know,' said Aspel, crossing awkwardly in front of Bob Ladd and an open-mouthed Nick Glass, 'anything about the crimes you've just mentioned, my lord duke of Milan . . .'

The SM had disappeared, perhaps assuming that the woman, who seemed peaceable enough, would follow him out. She stayed, however, and examined the operations console, stroking her chin. Her finger trailed over switches; she smiled faintly. Her eye caught Leslie's, and Martha saw his mouth jut – as if punched from behind – slip to one side, sag.

'But I *do* know that your project hasn't failed. I *can* tell you that this is one ending that won't lead to despair, and that we'll be only *too delighted* to lend you the help of our good hands.'

Aspel paused; somewhere a drum began to roll. He didn't appreciate cheap, unscheduled effects. At least this one had a natural vibrancy.

'Tonight, you're freed from all faults—'

The audience roared.

The drum rolled on, louder and deeper.

'—because tonight, Robert Ludovic Fairfax Ladd, actor, writer—'

Above the assembled cast, the dangling orchestra began to sway.

'—mountaineer – this is . . . your life.'

The drum roll stopped with a bump. There was a creak, like the twisting and breaking of some vast styrofoam cup. Dust snowed from the flies.

The piano fell freely.

Huw pulled Nick to safety and Leslie, once bitten, leaned painfully out of range at the last second – but the plummeting white mass struck Bob Ladd squarely on the head, and drove him like a tent-peg through the stage.

There was a second of calm, followed by a gruesome mangled crash in the pit. In horrid mockery of applause, the suspended instruments rattled and chimed. The echo reverberated, on and on. Women and men began to gasp, 'Oh God, no.' Or, 'Oh no.' Or even, 'Goodness.'

A deep voice spoke a single word over the PA.

'Thief.'

Martha looked at the prompt corner, but the huge woman had vanished.

Aspel observed the hole in the stage and the dusty plume snaking out of it. He didn't know what to do. So he handed the microphone to Leslie, who looked at it, mystified, for several moments, before advancing onto the forestage.

He intended to address the audience. The curtain lowered behind him. A respectful silence descended on those in need of guidance.

'I'm sorry,' he began. Rows of appalled faces stared back at him. 'I'm sorry,' he repeated, quickly, and let go of the mike.

Nick rang Tony, who did not answer.

# Nothing To Be Afraid Of

## SPRINGFIELD PSYCHIATRIC HOSPITAL

Patient File: Ms B. Sadler. Ludlum Ward.
Ref: 11732/int. Ret: 04/05/78

Dearest,

If you are reading this, through the offices of my good
friend Mr Leslie Barrington, then I am free, and he, the man
I fear, is dead.

I have written to you many times, the same story, but I am
forbidden from making contact. I have no address, and the post
is checked. He collects my correspondence every week. I write
it because there is nothing else to do here. There is music
therapy, I suppose. But the piano in the studio (his donation)
has not been tuned since the crusades, and I grow tired of
listening to the others laughing and smashing drums. I could
smoke. I could watch TV, but TV reminds me that I am in an
institution and I would rather walk about. I am quite friendly
with some of the nurses. We chat and pass the time, discussing
plays and books. It must make a wonderful change from all
that pornography on the male wards. On my little forays I can
almost fancy myself free to leave – except that if I did, the
police would escort me back to hospital in a white van. So you
see, there is really nothing else to do except rehearse one's past.
Oh, there is Monopoly, but scenes occur, and you are obliged
to take an antipsychotic.

If he is dead, and you are reading this, then it will all come
out.

Maurice, your father, left most of his estate to me, and a
little to his cousin. But when I became ill (or when I was first
persuaded that this was so), the right of attorney over my
portion passed to the cousin, and he in turn arranged for a

substantial part of it – practically all – to be made over to Tony Glass.

You will want to know why he did this. He was frightened, too, of course. And the following pages will give you some idea why. When you have read them, forget them, and don't come looking for me, my love.

I would hate to disappoint you.

Your devoted mother,

Beatrice

Ref: 11732/int. / Ludlum / Sadler / 05/05/78

COMMENTS:

Patient displays usual high degree of lucidity in respect of her surroundings and status alongside persistent legatary paranoia (see retrieved corr. log; again, no sign of pages). Of greater concern, given the above, must be the brass keys found in the patient's fish-tank gravel. These keys fit the ducting entrances to the boiler room, where a set of clothes and a coat were found on May 3. There can only be two explanations for Ms Sadler obtaining these keys. Either a member of staff gave them to her having had them cut, or a member of staff gave them to a visitor to have them cut. They are part of the ward security keys. The implications are considerable.

Increase active med pending searches:
1 x 10mg Chlorpromazine x 2

Mr J. R. CLOUGH.

# Fourteen: *Beatrice*

A BILLETING OFFICER and a man from the Board of Education came round and argued with my father on the doorstep. He came back into the library with two eight-year-old boys, one chubby, smartly kitted out in his school uniform and snivelling, the other a dark-eyed, silent starveling. They didn't know each other: the small one had got on the wrong train from London, and the fat cry-baby was from Bristol. Ray Hutchings came from a reasonably well-off family in Clifton; he had labelled clothes and toffees from Quinn's toffee factory. Tony Glass was from Silvertown. He'd been sewn into his underwear and couldn't write on the card he was supposed to send home to let his parents know of his whereabouts. I coaxed the address out of him and noticed something odd about his scalp. It was dotted with spirals of red: ringworm. The first thing my father did was to shave his head and paint it with iodine. When he came back from the hospital wing, he looked like one of the patients before surgery, and that melted Dad a little. Ray couldn't sleep that night, because Tony refused to lie down. Tony said he never slept lying down. He just squatted by the bed post and hung on, resting his cheek against it. His parents and his big sister slept in the bed at home, and there wasn't room for him, too. Being flat made the blood rush to his head.

The next day, the billeting officer was back with the man from the Board, and two inspectors from the Ministry of Health. They invited themselves in and sat my father down. He gave a meek cry of disbelief, and I decided to take Ray and Tony out for a distracting walk.

I liked my lonely home and wanted the evacuees to like it, too. Fernlea Combe was a rusticated fanfare: the square villa and ornate terraces carved out of a hill, and saved only from landslip by ribs of wall, tradesmen's tunnels and the white trunks of the beech forest. The drive wound up into the hills behind the hospital wing towards the road to Allerford, but we made our way down to the gardens on the cliff edge, where two long and overgrown Venetian arcades connected by spiral staircases looked over a balustrade to the sea below. I sat on the balcony and pointed out the bathhouse built for Lord Byron's daughter, which could be reached only by a scramble along ledges and slimy ravines. Ray said the sight of the sea made him feel dizzy: if you looked between the trees all you saw was blue and the Bristol Channel soaring up to meet you. He stayed on the lawn, grizzling, while Tony and I peered down at the distant beach, with its litter of rocks and spray. 'I don't like it,' Tony said, at last. 'It's w-wet.'

We walked up through the woods to Culbone and I showed them the tiny church, with its old squire's pews and leper window. I told them about the medieval prison colony and how French prisoners used to be dumped on the shore by boat and then left to fend for themselves in the hills. Tony was more interested in the chickens running about the little churchyard. He had no idea where eggs came from, or what a pig was. Jug-eared Stan Rawle and his mother, who lived in a cottage just up from the church, came to say hello. His dad had survived Dunkirk only to be spirited away to Egypt.

When his mother left to see to the chicks, Stan said to me: 'They nutters'll aff to go, our mur says, an' your da'll aff to take a load more vackies. The man came and told.'

It was impossible to imagine the combe with lots of town children in it.

'You speak funny,' said Tony to Stan.

'You from Lunnon, then?' Stan replied, ignoring the insult and turning to me. 'Our mur says your mur wenn off with a fancy man from Lunnon and she said she would cuz she wuz a cow an' your da's a coward for not bashin' 'm an' not fightin' in the war like my da.'

'What's a cow?' said Tony.

I said it was all lies, but there was truth enough in it. The Ministry had made an inspection of Fernlea Combe and decided to let it to Barnardo's. There would be a school there as well, and the lawn would be dug for crops. The patients would be transferred to a hospital in Taunton. It had never before occurred to me that my father did not actually own the big house in which he lived and worked.

Dad was cast down by the loss of his position, but he tried not to let it show. For me, at any rate, the next two weeks, in the summer of '40, were the happiest of my life. I wasn't a popular girl at the local school. The teachers didn't like me because I was a smarty-pants, and the children mocked my size. I was eleven and already developing. But Tony and Ray were younger, and less prejudiced. They were strangers, too, after all. The house and grounds became a playground. We made dens under the attic stairs, and turned the lumber room into a galley. On the path to Porlock Weir, I introduced Tony to cows and we sat on a five-bar gate, watching the dogfights. Ray overcame his fear of heights – odd for a boy from Clifton – and we hurtled down the cliff path to Ada Byron's bath-house. On the beach, on a rocky eminence, I arrived as the

Queen of Sheba. I knew the music, because father played it on the harmonium, but I had no idea who she was. All I knew was that she'd arrived, and being a queen, she should have courtiers. Tony and Ray made offerings of seaweed and I was critical.

'I'll have them,' Tony said, sitting on the wet pile.

I remember Ray saying, 'Which of us is your king, then?'

Embarrassed, I told them that they were both princes – suitors – and Ray said knowledgeably that two were no good. I couldn't have both of them. I had to choose. 'Well, I don't want to,' I said. 'I want to be chosen. And anyway, you have to prove yourselves worthy, then we'll know.'

'You can't have a king who stutters,' said Ray, somewhat at variance with fact. 'And I don't fancy you. So who're you going to marry?'

I think I got cross. Tony said: 'I'll be the bloke what lives upstairs, if you like. But the seaweed's mine.'

We had the same argument with my father, and he smiled.

Of course, Tony was the emerging star. Ray, whose parents had given him piano lessons, ploughed away at Minuet in G on the harmonium, working the pedal-bellows with his tongue between his teeth, and I had my recitations. But Dad preferred Tony: he was natural and quick. Keen-witted. I got him to lie down at night and hummed him to sleep if it was too quiet. As for the stutter, Dad said it would disappear with time, though there were things he could try which might help. One was singing, and it turned out that Tony could sing very well. He had a hard, unquestioning boy's treble, enough to turn 'He who would valiant be' into a battle cry. And more than enough to turn an actual battle cry – 'Man in armour cruel grim! / Death follows him!' – into an ominous lament. He sang untroubled by his impediment.

'That's enough of that,' said my father, when Tony and I

had chanted our way to the end of the bloodthirsty round. 'Let's play a game.'

We were sitting by the fire, with the windows shuttered. The flames suggested an immensity of panelling, row upon row of oaken plaques ascending from the hearth to meet and map the sky. Across our high ceiling buzzed the German planes on their way to Cardiff docks, Bristol and Birmingham.

The game was called 'Stranger'.

We shut our eyes for a minute. Dad counted us down, his voice getting softer, more distant. When we opened them, everything looked the same – the glowing logs, the Georgian moulding, the grinning face with the pointed chin and empty eye sockets in the centre of the fireplace, Ray with the comics sent to him by his heroic cousin Maurice, Tony drying out his collection of seaweed.

But my father, drowsy in his chair, didn't know us any more. We had travelled many years and were strangers. Our tongue was not his tongue. He looked bemused when we spoke, as if he'd heard an echo somewhere in the room. Then he pretended to make us out in the gloom, like spectres. The library was overseas and unknown to him, to us all. It was as though we had never been.

'Are you . . . *dead*?' Tony whispered.

My father knit his brows together and hissed. '*Si. Estoy muerto.*'

Tony clapped a hand to his heart in a dramatic gesture. '*Y soy yo quién te he matado!*'

Dad gave an unpleasant shout of surprise and started up from his chair. The game was over, he announced. I was half relieved and half disappointed.

Tony asked, 'You're not really dead are you, Mr Sadler?'

'Of course not,' laughed my father. He was smiling again,

cracking his knuckles, but I could tell he was upset. The skin to either side of his nose, so dry from being indoors, moistened. 'How could I be dead if I'm speaking to you?'

The question found three awakened imaginations.

'I'm not going to die, am I?' Tony said, confidently.

And my father replied, 'Oh yes, you'll die, all right. But death is nothing. It's just . . . well, nothing.'

He was a truthful man.

Tony put his fists in his eyes and screamed.

\*

How can I explain this to you, my dear child, born in a time of peace? Only perhaps by acknowledging that peace, wherever you find it, is hardly to be taken for what it is. It is the same uncertainty of lines in a mirror and lists to be made, water to be boiled and strides to be taken from the door, as you would find in nations occupied or souls at war – with this difference: the uncertainty tends to hope and not to fear. But it is uncertainty all the same, and if the hope and fear compounded thus were not so great, oh, how could we bear life, or, as the most ordinary people sometimes will, take it? Many nights I lie awake and dream of your approach. I wonder which will be uppermost in your heart as the handle turns – the hope or the fear? You are probably not curious. Perhaps that's best. And you're long grown up anyway. I see you with a lover, your life invisibly changed if he is half kind, mercifully unaware of being happy.

\*

On the day my father left for Taunton, he explained to me that I would be staying in Culbone with Stan Rawle and his mother until he'd settled himself or the war ended, whichever was soonest. Dad gave Tony a hug and got into the back of the black bus with the rest of the patients. They had to come back for a couple of strays from the insulin ward, who'd wandered on to the terraces and fallen asleep in an alcove.

We went that night to the Rawles's cottage. The change in circumstances was striking. I'd had my own room – a room with a glazed turret, looking into the canopy of oak and walnut – at Fernlea Combe. But there was only one room downstairs at the Rawles's, and one above where we slept. As the only girl, I shared the bed with Eliza Rawle, and Stan and Tony and Ray slept on three bunk-beds borrowed, like Tony's clothes, from the WVS depot in Porlock proper. The toilet was a bucket of soil in a shed outside.

I cried that night, amazed that my father had gone, but in the morning – and for the rest of the year – we were kept busy. There were two other buildings in Culbone, a little way upstream from the church cottage. One housed a farrier and his wife; the other was home to a family of 'slow 'uns', who kept pigs and helped cultivate a stretch of land about twenty feet wide running almost the whole length of the hamlet. The harvest was beginning, and we had to dig potatoes and pick hurts (whortleberries), which Eliza sold for 5d a quart at Porlock market. School began later in September, and it was a new school for me – an overflow arrangement, because of the evacuees. This meant that I no longer had to catch a bus into Porlock, but could stay put in the Weir Hall – a corrugated-iron building with a stove in the centre which smoked when the wind blew in off the sea. Our teacher was Mr Darvell, an old schoolmaster who tried some diluted Shakespeare on us. *The Tempest* was, unsurprisingly, a success. What with the constant gales and the smoking stove, the stage effects weren't hard to imagine. Tony discovered he could act. He couldn't read particularly well, of course, but that didn't seem to matter. He just shut his eyes, counted to ten, and then leapt from the constant fog in the middle of the room shrieking 'How now? Moody?' or whatever he could remember.

Ray was shy and liked drawing. He was a bit more homesick than the rest – had been from the start. When Stan took Tony and me to see his fish traps on the rocks beneath Ada's bathhouse, Ray would stay behind and write letters home. Packages of toffee arrived for him every other week, which he shared very scrupulously.

Before the war I'd hardly spoken to Stan. I was supposed to be posh, and he often had cuts and sores. Len Rawle worked as a logger for the Dyrham estate and as a fisherman before call-up. Stan boasted about his da the whole time. His da caught fish *this* big – got a porpoise once, he did. His da chopped down more trees than the rest of the workforce put together. His da had doings with his mur when they thought he was asleep, 'but I warn't!'

'Do you miss your dad, Stan?' I asked him one afternoon.

Stan was feeding his lamb. It was his pet, oddly enough. His mother had got it for him for his birthday, and it was the only animal in Culbone not reared to be killed. Or so she'd told him. He fed it from a rancid bottle and it sucked so vigorously Stan had to hang on to the cottage door.

'Dunno,' Stan admitted, breathlessly. The lamb finished and staggered drunkenly away. 'Don't reckon it much.'

Leonard Rawle came back from Egypt the next day without his right arm – and the temperature in the cottage dropped overnight.

He ate an apple for breakfast, and threw the core at Tony. 'You gotta go.'

'Where's he to, then?' remonstrated Mrs Rawle.

Len said: 'Buggered if I care. The 'lowance from the ministry f'rim is less nor what the others pay. So off he'd a-go. Sides, I don't care f'ris eyes.' He picked up his wooden bowl and smacked it over Eliza's head. She made a small sound, reaching round to pin her bun when Len sat back down.

*

I confided in Tony: 'I wish Mr Rawle could die,' but Tony was unmoved. He didn't laugh as usual on the way to school, that was all. Both he and Stan had seen this sort of thing often enough before.

I noticed Ray writing home as soon as break came, and I could guess what was in his letter. I wrote to Dad, not telling him exactly what had happened, merely making a calculated enquiry as to when I might be sent for. He wrote back saying that we were all making sacrifices.

I suppose it takes a long time and an unusually clear perspective for any child to be able to see that their parents may not have been fair or pleasant people. At least my father was not intentionally cruel.

Matters got much worse. The billeting officer came at the end of the second week and could see that things were not right. We were being kept home from school every other day and put to work outside without proper clothing. I had chilblains by November. She took Tony away immediately, because he'd lost so much weight, and warned Mr Rawle that we would have to go, too, unless she could be persuaded that we were being adequately provided for. My heart sang, only to be disappointed: there really was no room anywhere else. The farrier and his wife had a senile grandparent to care for and were even poorer than the Rawles. The slow 'uns were unfit. And all the billets in Porlock Weir and Porlock were taken by the steady trickle of new evacuees.

I wondered why Fernlea Combe had not yet been

occupied, and Mrs Rawle said that it was being given over to lumberjills instead of vackies. Lumberjills were the landgirls working up in the plantation reaches of the forest while the men were away. The wood was needed for pit-props, telegraph poles, soldiers' coffins and so on. There would be a whole army of girls – and Tony would be lodged with them for the time being.

Len was hopping mad at being given a dressing down. He told us he'd give us what for if we went telling any more tales, and when the nice lady from the WVS returned the next week, we greeted her with smiles because we were terrified.

In fact, no one had been telling tales. When Ray left one of his letters on his school desk while he went to the toilet, I glanced at it. It was a series of nature descriptions, and requests for more toffee. And lies. 'My best friend Tony has gone away to make room for Mr Rawle.'

But of course the underlying difficulty was that Eliza Rawle had become a lumberjill herself, doing her husband's old job. And Lennie Rawle had to submit to this displacement because he could no longer fell or saw or drag or mattock or do anything very useful. I cleaned and cooked. Ray went down to the beach with Stan to empty the traps and often met Tony there. Then he and Stan came back and saw to the animals. It was difficult seeing Tony and knowing that he had the run of Fernlea Combe again. He said he'd found a book called *The Séance of Miracles: How to Work A Thousand Wonders* in a cupboard of dusty journals and that he was entertaining the ladies in the evening with card tricks.

Our evenings were less diverting. We hadn't any conscious idea, I think, how peculiar they were, although something must have made a subconscious impression because on our long morning treks down the tunnelled path to the fields over the Weir, Stan started telling us stories of all the people who'd been found in the woods.

'People with bits 'angin' off they,' he said.

I corrected him rather primly. 'You mean the lepers.'

'All mangled in the face an' all.'

'Mr Rawle's got a bit missing,' said Ray, ambiguously.

'He baint no mangler,' Stan snapped. 'He 'ad it shot off.'

Eliza came home late, after we had eaten. Len usually left her a plate of stew, which he ate half of. Then he'd sit down to oil some of the logging tools that his wife had dragged home, and his brow would darken with injured pride.

We listened to storm warnings on the radio, and Len grunted.

If he got bored, he took out his shotgun and cleaned the barrel. His idea of a game was to put an apple on my head or Ray's and throw darts at it. Stan stood on one leg by the door and told us that da used to be a darts champion 'down the Ship Inn, warn't it, Da?'

About the third time Stan said this, Len Rawle told his son to shut up.

'Puttin' me off,' he said.

'Sorry, Da.'

Len laughed. 'Sorry, he says.'

He sighed and picked up his shotgun, pointed it between Stan's legs and fired. A chunk of the door behind Stan disappeared into the wind and rain. Eliza shrieked and ran at her husband. Stan wet himself. He was a big lad for ten.

*

Mr Darvell and some volunteers put on a school concert in the Ship, across the road from the Hall. Neither Eliza nor Lennie Rawle attended. Tony sang ' 'Twas early one morning' and Ray played some carols. Then Tony did some 'tricks', one of which had us all laughing.

Dressed in a little black and red cape, with a paper top hat, his dark eyes hugely open, Tony stood behind a table with a cloth over it and said: 'Your wish is my command.' His 'voice' came from underneath the table.

People asked for better weather and an end to the war.

'I'll see what I can do,' intoned the magician.

'Can we go home now?' said a boy from London.

'I hope so,' Tony replied, vaguely.

After a bit, Ray climbed out from under the table and we clapped.

'Thank you,' said a voice from under the table.

Silence.

*

It was the beginning of December. The drone of planes began early, before it had got quite dark, and from the top of Culbone, above the spike of the church, you could see the cruciform bombers passing like a flying graveyard.

'Bristol's in for it,' Mrs Rawle said quietly.

The noise deepened. There were more bombers than on any previous occasion, their drowsy nasal din channelled and funnelled by a high wind. The weather had been getting steadily worse for weeks. Our world was mapped by sound: the near wave-crash of the treetops, the thump and hiss of breakers on the rocks, the faint report of bombs in South Wales.

We awoke to silence. The radio confirmed a raid on Bristol, with Avonmouth docks hit, and parts of Redcliff and Clifton. People weren't dismayed, the news said. It was business as usual. The wind had died and the woods were still.

Ray went to pick up his package from Quinn's, but it hadn't arrived.

Two days later, our school walk was anticipated by an ARP warden, who took Mrs Rawle and Ray aside. Mrs Rawle just stood there with one hand over her mouth and the other on her hip. The warden, visibly distressed, put his arm around Ray's shoulders. Ray was the calm centre of the tragedy, and at school he became the brave lad, playing 'Stranger' by himself. His next of kin were contacted and his cousin wired to say he'd be arriving on Saturday.

Ray walked home with Tony along the beach.

*

When I got back, there was still no sign of them, although the route across the salt marshes and the shoreline should have been quicker than the tradesmen's route through the Combe. I was worried. The wind had risen again during the day; it was bitterly cold; and in the distance I thought I detected the familiar glass-tremor of engines and airborne machinery.

I asked Stan if he'd seen them.

'I bin with Mur. You seen Da, then? He'd a-go, an' is not like 'im.'

'Perhaps he's checking his traps,' I said.

I could see the door to the toilet shed swinging on its hinges. The bucket of soil, fresh that morning, was missing. Some of it was scattered, not quite noticeably – or only if suspicion had taken hold of you – in dribbles and patches on the path leading down from the cottage to the cliff edge.

'I'll go and have a look for them,' I called out, walking into the wind.

'I'm not. It's gurt blowy,' said Stan, undecidedly. He was dithering outside the house, scratching his calf with the back of his other foot.

'You go back inside, Stan, and wait for Mrs Rawle.'

'Don't tell I what to do. Fi wan, I can do summat.'

'You go back. I'm the eldest. It's all right.'

I heard him shout and run up the hill to his mur.

There were short sideways footprints in the soft mud leading into the bracken. At the end of the churchyard began the tricky scramble down the cliff – a narrow zigzag run which forked about forty feet later, leading on the right to a gentler, shady descent towards the bathing house, and on the left to a quicker, more exposed drop, over sliced granite and scree, straight to the fish pools.

I turned left, finding handholds as I picked my way down. By the fat molar of a boulder I stopped, gaping. There in the thundering surf, like a question mark or a stone hook sticking out of the white and grey shore, was the trap.

On its inner boundary lay the body of Len Rawle. He was on his back, but he had his face in the rocks. His palm lay upward and his legs were at spasticated angles. He'd been pushed. The boys were moving quickly around and over him, like spiders binding their prey. Tony was holding a huge knife. It was a machete, filched from the store at Fernlea Combe, or smuggled from the cottage by Ray. He handed it to Ray, who hacked at the body.

After a while, Ray braved the breakers and began to haul in the net draped over the side of the fish pool. Len was going in *under* the net, untrawlably deep. Tony packed some more stones in the body's clothes and Ray seemed to be lashing a bigger rock to the ankles. Ray kicked at Mr Rawle's head.

The waves broke higher. Mr Rawle disappeared into the trap and the boys tumbled the weighted net in on top of him.

I climbed the path again. The wind boxed my ears. Between roars of salt gale, I caught a deep, not far-off groan and sputtering, and emerged from the browned and frost-shrivelled winter ferns to see a plane entering the forest canopy.

It had come down at the top of the combe, and was cutting through the tops of the trees, spraying huge branches aside. The inside of one wing struck the main trunk of a beech tree and broke away.

Voices called in the distance.

Stan and Eliza were running down their side of Culbone, waving and crying, 'He's coming.' Behind them, in unreal, silent projection, the Heinkel bomber filled the valley, sublimely out of proportion to those ornaments, fixed and moving, human and inanimate, scattered beneath its dying roll.

Its nose struck the earth of the cultivated strip and threw up a fountain of mud, twice as high as the church. Sound cut in, as though a switch had been thrown. It was as if a drawer full of plates, or a dresser, or a piano, had been dropped onto a pavement. A figure inside the cockpit hit the glass and popped out. Eliza grabbed Stan and threw him to the ground as the wing levered itself heavenwards and swept clear of the church with a choppy moan.

The plane bore down on me. In the last second its shadowy bulk was silent again, and I fell back, pulled over a knoll by hidden hands.

There was a warm gust of fuelled air – elation. The torrent of flame passed with a deafening but swiftly stoppered scream and I was in the cold bracken.

The bomber pitched steeply, striking the cliff once and gathering rubble in a landslide. Snared by gravity, the plane refused to bounce any more, but surfed the granite face in a storm of rock, down, down. Down it dragged, to the fish traps and the irretrievable surprise of Leonard Rawle.

*

The coroner recorded a verdict of accidental death. Tony and Ray had been on their way to help Leonard on the shoreline, when the plane came down. His absence was corroborated by Eliza and Stan; the boys' story, by me.

It was Tony Glass who saved my life, after all.

When Maurice Mitchell came to collect Ray, I went with him to Minehead and from Minehead caught the train to Taunton. Tony accompanied us.

He was nine years old and perfectly behaved.

'Will you come back for me?' he said, simply.

'I'll come back,' I said. 'But will *you* still be here?'

He yawned and looked out of the window. Maurice was smiling at our conversation. He seemed decent and suave, in a trilby hat and silk scarf, perhaps a shade too dandyish and sensitive (his driving seemed rather shaky for a pilot) to be the unequivocal hero. He was twenty-five, on leave. I thought he was handsome. I was in love with them both.

'I might,' said Tony, and shut his eyes very tightly, before flicking them open like Lon Chaney. 'And then again, I might not.'

I kept my promise and went back to the coast in 1948. Tony was in his last year of school at Lynton, living with his last billet 'parents', who thought the world of him. He'd grown into a handsome, sharp-featured teenager. He promised to get in touch as soon as he was working, or not long after.

I told him then that I'd witnessed the murder and had spoken to Ray. And that I understood. I had been shocked – and now I understood.

Tony sang a snatch of something, surprisingly tunelessly. 'That's as well,' he said airily. 'Because I haven't a clue what you're talking about.'

'Tell me,' I said, because I had to know, 'it wasn't your idea.'

The death filled me with horror. Its incommunicable fact.

My skin ached at strange times of the day. It wasn't the justice or injustice of the end. It was the deliberate wiping out of life, and then the wiping out of *that*.

'Look at me, Bea,' Tony replied. 'It wasn't anyone's. You even said "I wish he could die". Remember? Are *you* responsible?'

But he asked for Ray's address all the same.

'With so many tall tales going about, perhaps I should speak to him, too.' He traced a pensive circle with his foot. 'When did you see him last?'

'A month ago, on my way to Birmingham. I changed trains in Bristol.'

'I've an uncle in Brum,' Tony revealed. 'Between you and me, I don't care for him very much. What took you there?'

'I'm there quite often. Maurice and – well, Maurice lives fairly close.'

'Ah,' Tony said, slowly. 'Maurice.'

He turned and walked away; sat at a distance, looking over the bright cobbles towards the sea. I waited, and was about to go after him, when he rose and came back. He took my arm and we wound our way down to Lynmouth. We spoke of his theatrical ambitions, the money he'd need for props. I was relieved.

'I thought you didn't approve,' I said.

'No, no. I'm *very* pleased for you.' He grinned. 'You'll be – stylish.'

'You'll come and visit?'

'Some day.'

'Will you?'

The sun was in my eyes. I had to squint to see him nod.

'Will you?'

'Of course. You don't get rid of me that easily.'

And together we waited for my bus.

. . . Nick rang Tony, who did not answer . . .

# Fifteen

THE DOUBLING OF IDENTITY, in the case of Glass–Ladd, had been a 'seamless separation'. It was, the obituarists marvelled, neither destructively criminal nor obviously pathological: there was deception, it was true, but those on whom the deception had been practised – at least those who could be persuaded to comment – were unwilling to specify the harm caused by it. A few even hinted that they had been in on the scam from the start, but were soon discredited. And for a short while, the technical minutiae of division (except that it wasn't a self divided, but a self added) made the headlines.

There were separate birth certificates and separate bank accounts, separate tax codes, separate houses (Limehouse and Clapham North), separate passports, separate cars and separate driving licences; separate medical and dental records, insurance policies, pensions, businesses, VAT registration. Even more of the detail was unobservable. There was separate correspondence – and plenty of it – including cards from Tony to Bob and from Bob to Tony, about the state of their theatrical careers, commiserations, congratulations, reassurances. They never met (but of course: it was the sort of joke you made in the pub), and the experts marvelled at this feat of misdirection, made possible by the actual proximity – the understated individuality – of their professional lives. They looked alike, in their different ways.

Both houses had dressing rooms, and in the dressing rooms were cupboards. And in the cupboards were clothes. And behind the clothes were plaster heads with wigs, minor prostheses (cuts, swellings) for when Bob had a suspected abscess and Tony did not. It was that simple, that complex. Nobody missed one when the other went away, because there was no reason to. They spoke in slightly different registers, with slightly different accents.

'But they were only slightly different!'

Nick, at least, had known ('you can't fool your own'), and had assumed control of Glass House. Fortunately, he was already a director of the company, which was just as well. Because Bob had left everything to Tony and Tony had left everything to Bob and neither existed any more. There was just a body, now ashes, and the ashes bore no single name. A settlement had already been made on Bob's wife, long before he died. ('There, he wasn't *that* irresponsible!') The rest of the estate would take years to unravel, pending formal inquiries, but preliminary investigations had disclosed no financial improprieties.

If any such existed, they were well hidden.

His son continued to defend him by saying nothing. He wouldn't be drawn on what it had been like to carry his father's secret. He was discreet, avoiding print. He wouldn't talk to the press. But, as Nick wrote letters to clients and strove to convince the many occupants of Glass House that things would not materially be altered by the loss of its founder, he did find time to talk to Martha and Alice. And to them he confided the essence, as he saw it, of 'the trick'.

'You see two people who are alike, and you say "Aren't they similar? Isn't his manner of cocking his head like so-and-so's? Aren't his eyes the same colour as whatsisname's?" You don't for a minute think they *are* the same, because we all assume we're different.'

'We are all different,' Alice reminded him.

'I don't understand,' Martha said, squatting in one of Orme Court's lattice bays. Alice stood quietly, only a foot or so inside the door. 'I can see why *we* were taken in. *Our* assumptions . . .' She wheeled her hands and looked to Alice for help. 'I just don't understand why *he* did it. You're telling us about us. What about him?'

Nick reddened. He was exhausted. Alice had comforted him in the aftermath, but his confidence was shattered.

'He was afraid of being nobody,' Alice supposed. 'Perhaps he envied us. Because we none of us knew him, and that's a terrible thing. If I know someone, then they can know – and love – me back. If they lie to me, or if I lie to them, I can't. Not properly. Not really.'

They brooded on this for a moment, before Nick burst out:

'It wasn't a deception. It wasn't deceit. He shouldn't be judged in those terms. He did amazing things. It was – an *achievement*.'

Alice and Martha were silent. Nick's exertions embarrassed and troubled them. It was like watching someone trying to fit a paper lid on a cauldron. Perhaps, Alice considered, Nick was lying, too. Perhaps he, too, had been utterly duped, and could not begin to admit it, so that one pretence immediately begat another. She could see how that might be.

Martha broke first, speaking into the cold window so that her breath whirled on the pane.

'You honestly feel no rancour?'

Nick stuffed envelopes angrily.

'It wasn't a *de*ceit,' he reaffirmed. 'It wasn't *de*, it was *con*. It was *con*ceit.' His hand hit the table. 'A *pure* conceit.'

Which Alice, though she shook her head, rather agreed it was.

\*

Her own grief passed and she was glad to be rid of it. A part of her balked at being called on to behave so well, but she was made to be a friend. Nick talked about the debts he could now pay off. Martha tried out names for her child. Neville, returning from New York, took Leslie in. And Lilian changed.

When Alice went home, her mother fretted about the time ('You'll miss your train') and nothing else. Alice listened, desperately. Her fear was that she sympathized without feeling sorry. It was a decent, common fear.

The other worry was equally plain. Love had not lessened a sense of cumbersome invisibility. Her jaw was better, but that was all.

'I'm such a flat person,' Alice complained. 'I *never* change.'

She was leaning on the fishy balustrade of the Queen's Walk, outside the Festival Hall. It was the second time she'd sung 'A Passer-By' with Neville's sinfonia and the conductor, errors aside, thought the concert had gone well.

'Oh, neither do I,' Neville said, airily. 'Unless you count the continual lowering of expectations. There is always that.'

They watched a hired boat thump downstream, its windows misted, and the partygoers within condensed into a soupy squeal.

'But in others' eyes we do,' he added. 'Change, I mean – and that's what counts. When my father started looking after my mother, he racked himself with guilt about not wanting to do it. About how frustrating it was trying to din into her the names of her children, her doctor, where the keys were, the clothes pegs, anything. They had rows in the morning. He'd cry on the phone.

'It *was* hellish. But then again, he cooked and washed and put his arms round her and told her it didn't matter when she asked *me* if I'd ever met her son. And she was comforted. He turned from being a selfish man into a kind, considerate one. The fact that he wasn't aware of the change isn't the point. He didn't think he was admirable, but it wasn't up to him to decide if he was or not.' Neville smiled. 'And it isn't up to you.'

They stopped again on Hungerford Bridge. The city stretched away past 80 the Strand, the Savoy and Somerset House, like a mountainous container ship in a sky-wide dock, for ever offloading its cargo.

Hoardings for Costain-Norwest Holt, contractors for the reconstruction of the bridge, glimmered along Festival Pier.

A man on the arc-lit drilling rig in front of them looked up. He could just see a woman, gazing down, who reminded him of his ex-wife.

Bill Alden gestured stupidly. Sometimes his loneliness led him to invent a longed-for coincidence. He waved his arm again.

'That man's pointing at you,' Neville prompted, and Alice, automatically, her thoughts elsewhere, waved back.

## Acknowledgements

The author wishes to thank: the Fellows of Ledig House, the K. Blundell Trust, Priscilla and David Wilder, Fiona Gruber and Mark Williams, Ferdinand and Julia Mount, Jane and Sandy Robertson, Patricia Duncker, Holly Eley, Bridget Frost, Patrick O'Connor, Georgia Pritchett, Nigel Wrightson, Redmond O'Hanlon, Celia Robertson, Dale Rapley, Steven Rickard, Richard Fortey, Martin Smith, John and Cecily Eaves, James Greenfield, Camilla Elworthy, David Miller, Andrew Kidd, Nicholas Blake and Martin Simpson.